FIRST
POSITION

Prescott Lane

CHAPTER ONE

EMORY CLAIRE STARED at the array of bridal magazines on her fiancé Eric's dining room table, stifling an urge to throw up.

"What do you think about a winter wedding?" Molly, their wedding planner, eagerly suggested. "Colors silver and white? That could be absolutely gorgeous."

Emory wondered how Molly, an unwed thirty-something, could become the top wedding planner in Charlotte, and why she had to be so damn perky all the time, to say nothing of her big breasts. Molly was so top heavy that Emory wondered how she didn't topple over. And her voice, high-pitched and squeaky, made Emory sick, almost as much as the whole idea of a big wedding. She wished Eric hadn't hired her. Emory wished she was anywhere but here.

"That could be nice," Eric said hopefully, well aware of Emory's hesitancy.

Emory wrinkled her nose, Molly sensing her discomfort. Eric, in his mid-thirties, was a big client for her. He was on the fast track to becoming the head of pediatric cardiology at his Charlotte hospital. He'd met Emory, a child and maternity photographer, while taking photos of newborn babies in the maternity ward. Eric seemed to have an uncanny ability to know when Emory was working; more than once he just happened to cross paths with her, then persisted in asking her out. Molly planned to make sure their wedding was in the social pages, which would only boost her own career, so she surely didn't want to upset Emory in Eric's house. Still, she had no idea what Emory's problem was. She decided to switch gears.

"I have some fabulous connections in the Caribbean. Have you guys thought about a destination wedding?"

Emory flashed her eyes to Eric, signaling that may be the stupidest idea ever floated in the history of the world.

"A destination wedding might be difficult for our families and friends," he responded, tactful as always.

Emory felt her face begin to sweat. She had her late mother's soft features—alabaster skin and slender body, with rosy cheeks and lips—masking a tough core molded by her father, a high school football coach. Because of him, she could talk sports, play pool, and hold her own in a game of poker, all while looking like the angelic ballet dancer she once was. Few things rattled her. But her father hadn't prepared her for this moment. She was twenty-eight and scared. *Most women would consider Eric the perfect catch. What's wrong with me?* He was respectful and polite, not to mention a doctor who'd built his own home on a golf course in a posh gated community. His blond hair, green eyes, and lean muscular frame made him easy on the eyes and a favorite among the nurses.

"Are you OK?" Eric whispered to her.

"Yeah, I just need a drink." Emory excused herself from the dining room and walked into the kitchen, quickly looking for something to calm her nerves, but then remembered Eric didn't keep any alcohol in the house. She sadly settled for a glass of water. She'd been in Eric's kitchen many times before, but for the first time realized just how organized it was—the chrome fixtures polished to a shine, the hand towels neatly placed, the flour and sugar jars precisely filled. *How did I get here?* Everything was in order, just like Eric—safe and steady. What their relationship lacked in passion, it made up for in security.

Eric followed her into the kitchen, then touched her shoulder from behind, startling her. "What's going on?" She could feel heat rise to the surface of her skin. "Molly says we really need to pick a date in order to get the venue we want."

She took a sip of water. "I thought we agreed to have a long engagement and take our time?"

Eric looked at her curiously, a twinge of aggravation in his eyes. "We've dated for over a year, been engaged for three months, and it takes at least a year to plan a wedding. Can you give me a month even?"

She took another sip, hoping a quick stall would give her something—anything—to say, but there was nothing.

"Can you at least give me a *season?*"

Emory shrugged her shoulders. Eric was perfect; his house was perfect; and he had hired the perfect wedding planner to plan the perfect wedding. But Emory felt anything but perfect. She didn't want to hurt Eric, but knew this was not just normal wedding jitters.

"Damn it, Emory! I think I've been very patient and understanding about all your commitment issues. I'm beginning to feel like you don't want this wedding at all, or maybe it's just that you really don't want *me!*"

Emory reached for his hand. "I love you, Eric."

"Then give me something to work with here."

"All this talk of dates and venues and flowers is just so overwhelming."

"Overwhelming?" Eric threw up his hands. "This is so embarrassing. Molly is in the other room, and we need to…"

"I don't give a shit about Molly, and I don't *need* to do anything. This is the rest of our lives we're talking about."

"Didn't you think about that before agreeing to marry me?"

It was a good question. "Yes." And she had—several times. It was why she'd turned down his first two proposals, fearing that what little spark there was between them would dwindle after the honeymoon ended and the dog-days of marriage began. But Eric was nothing if not persistent, and she finally accepted his third proposal, believing that he was certain about their relationship, and she should be, too. After all, he was a smart man. Emory chalked up her nerves about getting engaged to the broken heart she suffered at the hands of her college sweetheart, Mason.

"Because you agreed to marry me," he said, trying to add some reason to the conversation, "we need a date to get married, right?"

Emory looked down at the oval cut diamond ring on her finger. "I can't give you that today," she said softly.

"Then there's no reason for us to be engaged." Eric held out his hand. "Give me the ring."

"Eric, come on."

"No, I want it back."

"Think about what you're saying."

"Oh, I'm thinking. In fact, I'm thinking real clearly now. Give me the ring!"

Emory took in his words. She believed he was thinking clearly;

he always did. She walked slowly to the sink and poured the rest of her water down the drain, setting the glass in the sink. She slipped the ring from her finger and gently placed it in Eric's hand. "I'm sorry. I'm just not ready." She walked out of the kitchen towards the front door, grabbing her purse along the way. She glanced back to Molly on her way out. "We won't be needing your help for that destination wedding—or any wedding at all."

* * *

Emory sat in her car, as the sun set over Eric's house on the gloomy Friday night. She put her hands on the steering wheel, wondering what had just happened. Rain began to fall. She looked at her left hand; it looked different without a ring. *I feel lighter.* She felt a calmness come over her, as if the rain, obscuring her view of the house, was washing away a prior life. As wonderful as Eric was, she was right to have rejected him twice before; she should've trusted her instincts a third time. She simply liked Eric more than she loved him, and that was no way to enter into a marriage.

She dialed the one person who always made her feel better, Wesley, her best friend and roommate. "Hey, girl, how's your day?"

"Awful. Eric and I just broke up."

"Holy shit! What happened?" He walked into their modest apartment, after a full day of teaching dance classes in his downstairs studio.

"I had a panic attack in front of the wedding planner," she said, putting her hand to her face. "So embarrassing."

Wesley grabbed a large water bottle from the kitchen. "She's just a big-breasted bimbo, so you shouldn't be embarrassed."

Emory sighed. "It was all just too much."

"It's just a sign you're with the wrong guy." Wesley chugged from the bottle and wiped his mouth. "And I'm gay, so I know men."

Emory laughed. Wesley was always good for a laugh. They had become fast friends in college when they were made dance partners. She always knew he was gay, though she was the first person he told. It wasn't some big surprise to her, but she pretended it was. She assumed he wouldn't have wanted her to say it was obvious—as obvious as the sun is hot. Emory helped him with the ups and downs of coming out, and even went with him to break the news to his parents, who thought he was bringing home a girlfriend. *Were they blind or just stupid?* His parents didn't take the news as well as she did and kicked them both out of their house, leaving Wesley a complete mess for months. She did her best to comfort him. Years later, he returned the favor and was there for her when Mason broke her heart, and she broke her ankle, ending her dream of a dance career. It was the darkest time of her life, and Emory still hadn't fully recovered. Her own mistakes and secrets, which only Wesley knew, continued to haunt her.

Her stomach growled. "Do you have plans tonight? I was thinking it might be a good night for take-out from Gus' Bar."

It always amazed Wesley how often Emory thought about food and how much she could eat and never gain an ounce. He always had to watch what he ate to keep his tall, slender frame—back in college and even now—but sometimes found himself giving into his own food cravings. But no matter how many buffets or combo meals Emory took in, she looked the same and never seemed to gain an ounce.

"Sounds great! Don't forget to get extra sauce."

Emory rolled her eyes. "Of course."

* * *

Emory drove along the street in front of Gus' Bar, cursing that there was no parking lot. She didn't have an umbrella. She found a parking spot a block away, then ran through the rain, side-stepping puddles along the street. She reached the front entrance, finding some relief underneath a small awning. She wrung out her long blonde hair, drenched on her shoulders and back. *This day has sucked.* But good barbecue was worth braving the elements and the embarrassment of looking like hell.

She walked inside, still wringing out her shirt. Gus greeted her at the bar. "Hey honey, you've obviously had a rough one." Gus had known Emory for years. He was one of her first clients when she moved to Charlotte after studying photography in Europe. She took pictures of his grandkids and was a repeat customer at his bar. Gus knew her mood from her order. It was a slab of ribs tonight—which meant comfort food after an awful day.

"Not the greatest, Gus." Emory frowned and flicked her wet shirt. "Could you put a little extra sauce in with that?"

"Already did, baby. It's right on top." He handed her a large sack. "Don't know where you put it."

She shrugged and smiled. *Definitely not in my bra cup.* She peeked in the sack while turning from the bar, then rammed into a hard body, the sack slamming against her chest, dumping sauce down the front of her wet shirt. The sack fell to the floor.

"Shit, I'm so sorry!" the hard body said, bending down to pick up the sack. "Didn't see you there. Are you OK?" He placed the sack on the bar while Emory grabbed some napkins from a nearby table. The hard body looked at his victim, wiping her shirt in vain. "Emory Claire?"

She stopped wiping. She knew that voice anywhere but hadn't heard it in years. She glanced up from her shirt and met familiar crystal blue eyes. "Mason?"

"Oh my God, Em, it's you!" Mason flashed the most radiant smile. He couldn't believe he was looking into her beautiful blue eyes after so many years apart.

Emory stared in shock. He looked better than she remembered, in an old t-shirt and jeans, his right arm hung in a sling. His dark brown hair was slightly longer than before, but his eyes were just the same. The guy who six years ago broke her heart and reduced her to puddles was again right in front of her. *And I look like this. Seriously, can this day get any worse?*

"Let me help you." He grabbed some more napkins. While Emory cleaned herself, he cleaned the sauce on the sack and the floor.

He started talking about something, but her brain was struggling to keep up. *What is he doing here?*

"So good to see you," Mason said, leaning in for a hug.

Emory backed away. "Oh, I don't think you want to hug me right now."

"You look great, Em, just the same." His eyes softened as he reached to push her hair back from the side of her face. His touch, just as she remembered, ignited a familiar wave of heat through her body.

She deflected the compliment. "What are you doing here?"

"I'm in town talking to the Panthers about playing here next season."

"Really?" Emory's stomach clenched at the thought of Mason living in Charlotte. She had spent the last several years trying, unsuccessfully, to forget about him. *Crap, now his face will be all over the place.*

"Yeah, I met with them today. Trying to catch on with a new team. Do you live here?"

"I do. For about three or four years now."

"Crazy that we would meet here."

"I know." Emory nodded and quickly glanced at his left hand. *No ring? Keep it together; don't come undone.* "What happened to your arm?"

"I guess you haven't been watching Monday Night Football lately." They hadn't seen or spoken to each other in years, but Mason felt disappointed that she hadn't kept up with his career. Deep down, he always thought, or at least hoped, she was watching him.

"Not really."

"I tore up my shoulder in the last game of the season in Miami." He could still remember the brutal tackle. He prided himself on having good pocket awareness but never saw or even felt it coming. He'd dropped back to pass, a routine five-step drop, and cocked his right arm to throw, his receiver sprinting down the field on a fly pattern. He released the ball just before getting hammered by a ferocious pass rush off the edge, slamming him to the ground, as the pass fell incomplete. He stayed facedown on the field, the trainers racing out to him. They slowly rolled him over—literally turning his world upside down—and plucked grass from his face mask. Mason couldn't move his right shoulder and was cut three days later when the season ended.

"Oh, I'm sorry to hear that. How is it?"

"It's doing OK. But let's hope the Panthers think so."

"Well, good luck," Emory said, feeling a sudden urge to escape, wanting her embarrassing night to end. She grabbed her sack from the bar.

Mason quickly glanced down at her ring finger. *She couldn't possibly still be single.* He had more to say—at least he thought he did—and didn't want this to be a fleeting moment between old friends. For years he regretted how things had ended; he'd wanted to talk to her, but assumed she wanted nothing more to do with him. "Would you like to catch up over dinner?" He didn't want her to go so quickly. He wanted more, and she looked fantastic, even with the rain and sauce.

His question caught her off guard, wondering why he'd ask, and why she'd ever want to sit across from a guy who dumped her. Emory held up the bag. "I've already got dinner plans tonight."

"Oh, right," Mason said, unable to hide the hint of sadness in his voice.

"Yeah, and not just that. I'm kind of a mess. But good luck with the Panthers." She walked towards the exit, hoping he hadn't noticed how affected, and conflicted, she was.

"Maybe tomorrow?" he called out.

"Maybe so." And she was gone.

CHAPTER TWO

MASON SAT ON the bed in his hotel suite, the room service tray beside him, his mind overwhelmed by seeing Emory again. He'd gone in for a drink—to unwind after meeting with the Panthers—and literally stumbled back into his past. His break-up with Emory was, without question, the biggest mistake of his life, and now he'd just seen her again. He munched on a cookie. *Does everything happen for a reason?* He wasn't sure. All he was sure about was that his mistakes with Emory had led to other mistakes, and that his world once again had been turned upside-down. He knew he had to see her again.

He pulled out his cell phone and stared at her number. It wasn't hard to find in the phonebook. It was much harder to find the nerve to call. Then suddenly his phone rang in his hand. *Could it be Em?* It was Steven, his older brother and agent, calling from his Texas law office, bombarding Mason with questions through his speaker phone.

"How was the meeting today? Any doctors present? Did they do a medical exam?" Steven was tall like Mason but had a leaner physique. He was the more sensible sibling who tried, often in vain, to steer his impulsive brother in a proper direction. Steven usually accompanied him to all team workouts and meetings to make sure Mason didn't screw things up. But he'd just finished a week long jury trial, and his wife, Olivia, was expecting their first child, so he couldn't make this trip, and re-scheduling was not an option. It was too risky. Given his injury, Mason needed to pursue any option available, at the convenience of any team, even if Mason had to do it on his own. Steven knew that was risky, too.

Mason put his hand to his head, still consumed by the sight of Emory. "Slow down, man. One at a time."

"Sorry," Steven said, taking a breath. "Just been an insane week in trial. And Liv is driving me a little crazy with the baby coming."

"Everything went fine. Coach seems cool," Mason said, taking another bite of his cookie. "Went through a quick physical with the doctors. They didn't say anything to me. Got a good vibe."

"Good," Steven said, relieved. "We have that meeting with the Seahawks tomorrow afternoon, and then we'll go from there."

Mason shook his head. *Oh, shit! I totally forgot about the Seahawks meeting.* "That's not going to work." He wasn't leaving Charlotte until he saw Emory again.

Steven switched off speaker, and picked up the phone. "What the hell did you say?"

"I need you to push back the Seattle meeting."

"What the fuck, Mason! You better get your ass on that plane!"

"Just need a few days," Mason said calmly.

"We don't have a few days! We are damn lucky we have two teams willing to look at your injured ass! Have you lost your fucking mind?" It was for times like this that Steven blamed Mason for his lack of hair. He was in his early-thirties and slightly bald, an unfortunate product, he believed, of Mason's emotional whims.

Mason took a sip of water. "Just fucking do it, OK!"

"Not without a good reason."

Mason wasn't ready to tell Steven about Emory. He wasn't sure there was anything to tell, or how his brother would react. He knew Steven had loved Emory like a little sister, and was furious with him for screwing things up. But that didn't mean Steven would understand his present situation—that Emory, for some reason, had come back into his life. At least Mason hoped she had. "Well, I just want to tour the city. Charlotte's a great town, and I want to check out the neighborhoods." Mason took another bite of the cookie. "Maybe catch a Bobcats game."

Steven knew his brother was prone to crazy ideas but couldn't believe he was acting this way now, with his career on the line. "The Bobcats suck! This is some bullshit. Now tell me the fucking truth."

Mason put down the cookie. "Look, bro, my shoulder's sore. I don't want to travel cross-country tomorrow. I need a few days."

Steven knew his brother was lying, but there was nothing he

could do. "Fine. You rest, and I will handle Seattle. By the way, there's something else I need to discuss with you."

* * *

Emory pulled up to her apartment, finding herself still shaken by seeing Mason, or perhaps it was her unexpected break-up with Eric, or maybe it was simply that she was soaking wet and covered in barbecue sauce. She couldn't decide which one it was, or if it was all of them. It had been a two-hour whirlwind. She walked towards the apartment. It was nothing fancy on the outside—or even the inside— but it was Wesley's baby. His dance studio was below the small apartment they shared, and was where he spent most of his time, teaching little ballerinas to dance. Emory helped him open it when his own dance career came to an end, and she helped out with his classes when she could, in between photography shoots.

Emory drew a deep breath and walked inside, up the flight of stairs. She found Wesley waiting for her. He looked her up and down and doubled over laughing, his strawberry-blond hair falling in his eyes. "Sweetheart, what the hell happened to you?"

She placed the dinner sack on the small dining room table. "Glad I can still make you laugh, jerk."

"It's just you said you had a bad day when you called, but I didn't expect you to look like such a hot mess." Emory stuck her tongue out at him. "Is that my dinner on your shirt?"

She walked towards her bathroom, removing her wet, stained shirt. "We'll talk in a minute." She turned on the shower, and stepped in. The smell of barbecue sauce washed away, as the water rained down on her. She closed her eyes, and Mason's blue eyes stared back at her. She shook her head to try to erase the image, rubbing her skin with the soap lather, more and more intensely, as if to cleanse her mind of the past—and now her present. But it didn't work. It never worked. *Why am I thinking about him? I should be focused on Eric.*

* * *

Mason could always tell when Steven was concerned. He rolled out his serious lawyer voice. Whatever else Steven wanted to discuss,

Mason knew it wasn't good. Steven cleared his throat. "It's your wife."

"I told you to just make the divorce happen," Mason barked. "I don't want to talk about Alexis." Alexis was a college debutante—large breasts, sweeping hair, and perfect make-up—always on the prowl for a husband. Her type had never appealed to Mason until he no longer had Emory. He often wondered why he ever married her.

"She knows teams are looking at you and wants to get her claws back into you. She and her lawyer are threatening to challenge the prenup, saying I coerced her into signing it."

"Jesus Christ!" Mason walked towards the hotel suite window, opened the curtains, and looked out over the Charlotte skyline. He remembered turning to Alexis after his break-up with Emory in his senior year, just weeks prior to the NFL draft. He was heartbroken and scared, and Alexis was ready and willing, and seemed the perfect match for a rookie quarterback. Steven never liked her and never trusted her; Alexis was everything Emory wasn't. Steven insisted Mason have a prenup and drafted it himself and ensured Alexis signed it. Far from any coercion, Alexis was thrilled she'd get $500,000 and certain other assets if they ever divorced.

"I know you want to make this quick and get her out of your life," Steven said, "but divorce doesn't work that way. I can't let her railroad you, just because you want to forget her. I wouldn't be a good brother or lawyer if I let her take everything you've worked so hard for. We need to fight her."

"I'm through fighting with her. Our whole marriage was a fight. She got what she wanted when she married me. Poisonous little so-cial climber!"

Steven felt sorry for his brother, injured and alone in a Charlotte hotel. "So much for 'in sickness and in health.'"

Steven was with Mason when doctors told him weeks ago he may never play football again. It was, at best, a 50-50 proposition. There was no guarantee his shoulder would heal well enough for him to throw, let alone endure another sack. So when his injury threatened his paycheck, Alexis made it clear she was done. Steven had heard her say so—if Mason couldn't keep up his end of the mar-riage, she couldn't keep up hers. *What exactly was her end?* Alexis married Mason to be in the spotlight, spend his money, and soak up his fame. Over his five seasons in the NFL, she cheered in the stands on Sundays—not so much for him, but for herself and the cameras. Steven wouldn't let his brother get hammered by her now.

"Do whatever it takes to get rid of her," Mason ordered.

The brothers agreed to see each other in a few days in Seattle.

* * *

Emory came out of her room wearing flannel pajamas, her garment of choice when she needed to comfort her mind and heart. Wesley already had dug into the sack, made them both plates, and set the table. When Emory sat down, he put down the rib he was gnawing on. "Spill, no pun intended." Emory recounted every detail about her fight and break-up with Eric, while the wedding planner, Molly, sat in the other room. Wesley listened intently, only occasionally interrupting to ask her to pass another rib or sauce. She didn't mention Mason. "It seems like you're OK about all this," he said.

"Marriage was never something I was after." She reached for another rib. "Didn't even mind giving the ring back."

"But it seems you lost Eric, not just the ring. Why aren't you crying like a girl in one of those chick movies you make me watch?" Emory shrugged her shoulders, unsure of the answer. She assumed it was because of Mason but didn't want to fess up. "You know, I always thought Eric was nice, polite, loyal," Wesley said, taking a drink, "but no spark there. Not like with…"

"Don't say it. Don't go there, Wesley," Emory snapped, in no mood to hear his name on the very night she ran into him.

"Geez, hit a nerve! Don't get bitchy with me."

"Don't you…"

"Be quiet and eat!" Wesley took her hand. "Look, I know you don't like to talk about that time in your life, but most of it was great. You were happy and alive and, yeah, it ended poorly, but you packed it all away—good and bad."

"Enough!" Emory licked her fingers and rose from the table and went to the kitchen. "Not tonight."

Wesley looked at her, confused. He knew everything about Emory, especially when she was hiding something. And he knew she was hiding something from him now but didn't want to push her. "Fine, let's talk about something else. How did you get barbecue sauce on you?" Emory shook her head, not wanting to discuss that either. "Did Eric throw it at you?" he teased.

Emory began to wash dishes in the sink. "I bumped into someone at the bar, and it spilled on me." *Damn, I shouldn't have given him this opening.*

Wesley noticed a slight blush on her cheeks. "So who'd you bump into?"

"Nobody." Emory scrubbed the dishes with more speed.

"Oh, come on!" Wesley cut a smile and waved his finger at her. "Don't hold back on me!"

Emory was no match for Wesley's charm—or pestering. He'd just keep asking over and over again, so she relented before he drove her crazy. "Mason," she whispered.

"Holy shit!" Wesley nearly choked on a rib.

"Yep, my thoughts exactly."

"I heard he was coming for a tryout—it was all over the papers, talking about his injury—but I never thought you'd run into him." Wesley brought his plate to the sink.

It was now obvious why Wesley had brought up Mason at dinner. "You knew he was in town, and didn't tell me?"

"Don't get so worked up, girl!" Wesley shut off the faucet and led her to the old sofa in the den. They plopped down together. "I didn't tell you," he said, patting her flannel pants, "because you always get upset when someone mentions him, and it's not like I imagined you would run into him. I mean, Charlotte is a pretty big city. What are the odds?"

Emory twirled her hair with one hand, massaging her foot with the other. "Well, you should've warned me. I looked like a total idiot, soaking wet, covered in barbecue sauce, not knowing anything about his shoulder."

Wesley leaned over and hugged her. "I bet he didn't think you looked like an idiot."

"I wouldn't take that bet."

"Fine." Wesley released her, sensing any effort to pick up her spirits was hopeless. "I'm wondering—are you more upset about seeing Mason or breaking up with Eric?"

Emory glared at him and began to rub both of her feet. "I'm not answering that."

"Damn, OK." Wesley tried to lighten the mood. "Was he wearing a ring?"

"As if I looked!" she replied abruptly. "Everything was happening so fast."

"You little liar!" He grabbed Emory's hands and began to rub her feet himself. "Of course, you looked!"

"Well, it doesn't matter anyway. Lots of men don't wear rings. I'm sure he's very happy with Alexis." The words burned her tongue. "This isn't a romance novel, Wesley."

CHAPTER THREE

ALONE IN HIS hotel suite, Mason tried to rid his mind of Alexis. He had told his brother to handle his divorce and whatever property settlement, but Steven felt the need to provide updates. It aggravated him. Mason didn't want to be burdened by the weight of details. He just wanted it over. He wanted his mistakes swept away. He pictured Emory's face from earlier in the evening; it was the perfect distraction from Alexis. She looked the same as he remembered— and she'd crossed his mind everyday for six years. He smiled remembering the first time he ever saw her.

Mason was a junior in college, making his first start at quarterback in front of the home crowd. He felt the pressure to perform. He no longer was the back-up, pacing the sidelines while wearing a backwards cap and holding a clipboard. Now he had to prove himself and lead his team. Whether it was the magnitude of the moment, or the huge defensive linemen punishing him and his offensive line throughout the game, Mason suffered a horrible debut. He completed under 50 percent of his passes and threw three interceptions, a recipe for defeat.

After the game, and the tongue-lashing in the locker room, Mason showered and walked out to nowhere in particular. He strolled aimlessly around campus, replaying the game in his head and the biting words of his coaches. "It was a mistake to offer you a scholarship" was one that kept ringing in his head. As he wandered, he heard classical music coming from an open door of the college theater. It wasn't the kind of music that interested him, but he had nothing better to do.

The theater was empty and dark, except for one light shining on the stage where a slender, tall girl in a pink leotard moved alone, her blonde hair pulled in to a bun. Mason stood at the end of the theater, unseen, transfixed by the girl's grace and strength. He knew nothing about ballet but knew good footwork when he saw it. He envied the way she moved; indeed, he could have used it a few hours earlier to escape the pass rush.

She finished her dance, as the music ended. She then replayed the music, performing the same dance again. Mason's whole body reacted to her. She extended a leg over her head, and he imagined how her flexibility could benefit him sexually. Embarrassed, he tried to compose himself. *Everybody likes a stalker in a dark theater with a hard on.* He turned to leave but bumped a folding chair in his blind spot.

The girl froze. "Who's out there?" she asked nervously and turned off the music.

"Shit, sorry," Mason said. "I just heard the music and wandered in. I didn't mean to interrupt. By the way, you're amazing."

The girl searched the darkness for who was speaking. "Are you a dance critic, or just a guy with a line?"

Mason stepped forward into the light where she could see him, and he could get a close look at her face. He had seen his share of cheerleaders and hot girls at college parties, but never pursued them, though they often threw themselves at him. Mason never took the bait; it wasn't his style. He certainly talked a good game with his teammates, but was convinced he was the lone virgin on the team. But this girl mesmerized him—her alabaster skin accented by pink cheeks and rosy lips, to say nothing of the way she moved. He just stared, at a complete loss for words.

"I guess I got my answer," she said, recognizing Mason as the quarterback. "A player, in more ways than one."

"What's that supposed to mean?" he asked playfully. This girl was more than a pretty face. She was a feisty ballerina commanding his attention.

She grabbed a towel from the stage and patted her face. "You won't be finding any action here."

Mason walked towards her. "OK, well, let's start over."

She looked down at him from the stage. "I didn't think we'd started at all."

He smiled. "It seems you know who I am, Daniel Mason, but

everyone calls me Mason. What's your name?" Mason reached the stage and stood right below her.

"Emory Claire. Do you make it a habit of spying on ballerinas at night?"

"Only after a tough game. It helps me clear my head."

She hopped down from the stage. "I'm not used to seeing football players here."

"I don't think we get many ballerinas at the games, so…"

She cut him off. "I was there today."

"You were?" Mason asked, embarrassed.

"Brutal loss." Emory shook her head. "You're fine when you're in the pocket. You fall apart when you scramble because your footwork sucks. Need to get up on your toes." She hoisted herself up on pointe.

"I just heard all that shit from my coach," he snapped. "Would rather not hear it from a girl in a leotard."

"Suit yourself. But my dad's a high school football coach, so I actually know what I'm talking about."

Mason didn't know what to say. He'd met his match, a beautiful ballerina with a football pedigree, correctly critiquing his quarterback play.

She hopped up on the stage. "Well, it was nice to meet you, Daniel Mason, but I really should get back to practicing if I'm ever going to get this right." Emory turned on her music and returned to her routine. Mason turned to leave, knowing something major had just happened, and for the first time in his life, it had nothing to do with football. He returned the following night, hoping she would be there. And she was, night after night.

* * *

Mason took one last bite of his cookie and grabbed his phone. He'd spent the better part of an hour dialing parts of Emory's number but couldn't find the nerve to complete the job. Hoping a change of scenery would do the trick, he walked down to the Atrium Bar in the lobby of his hotel. It was a slow Friday night, the heavy rain likely keeping away any crowd. He took a seat at the bar, and a couple patrons noticed him. Mason gladly signed a few autographs, as they wished him good luck with his shoulder and any contract negotiations with the Panthers.

The bartender, an elderly black man with salt-and-pepper hair, approached Mason. His name tag read Clive. "What will it be?"

"Vodka Seven to start."

Clive pulled a glass from a cabinet. He filled it with ice, poured the liquor and soda, and topped off the drink with a slice of lemon. He slid the glass to Mason, with a napkin underneath. Clive walked to the other side of the bar and grabbed a basket of peanuts, placing it in front of Mason. Clive saw his glass was already empty. "This part of your rehab, my man?"

"Yeah. I have to do at least five reps. Faster the better."

Clive laughed, refilling the glass. "What you working towards?"

"Courage." Mason slammed the second one.

"I doubled the vodka in that one," Clive said, laughing.

"Thanks." Mason massaged his forehead, feeling the buzz coming on quickly. "I guess."

"I can triple the next for you, if you'd like."

"No, man." Mason waved his hands. "Very generous, but that won't be necessary."

"What you need courage for anyway?" Clive asked, leaning over the bar. "Big time NFL quarterback like you."

"I'm not so 'big time.' Perennial back-up. Shoulder fucked-up."

Clive rolled a toothpick between his teeth. "So what you need courage for?"

"To dial a phone number."

Clive gave a sinister grin. "A woman?"

"From college—one who got away."

"Give me your phone," Clive said, eagerly extending his hand. "What?"

"Give me your damn phone. I'll dial this college woman."

"That's very nice of you, Clive, but…"

Clive raised his eyebrows. "You want to talk to the bitch or not?"

Mason put up his finger. "Yeah, but she's not a bitch."

"Relax, I meant it in a good way. Give me the damn phone."

Mason was buzzed—the double had done him in—and also a little scared of this strange bartender. He surrendered his phone and told him the number. Clive dialed, then held the phone to his ear, tapping his fingers on the bar, the toothpick between his teeth.

"Give me the phone if she answers," Mason whispered.

"No, she needs to hear from a brother first!"

Clive was out of control. His palms sweaty, Mason heard a few rings, then heard Emory answer. Clive started mumbling something, and Mason reached over the bar, wrestling the phone away from him, and quickly raised it to his ear. Clive roared a mischievous laugh.

"Uh, Em?"

Emory recognized the voice immediately. *Only one person calls me that.* "Mason?" She sat on the floor of her tiny bedroom surroun-ded by camera equipment. "What's going on? What was that strange noise?"

"Just a friend I met at the hotel," Mason answered quickly. Clive pounded his chest in approval, then moved on to another patron.

"Oh, OK." Emory rose to her feet, and began moving through her ballet preparatory positions.

"Did I catch you at a bad time?" Mason feared she may be busy, or worse, that she was with some guy. He looked in front of him, and saw Clive had refilled his glass. *Is this a triple?* He didn't care and slammed it.

"No, I'm just getting ready for a photo shoot tomorrow in Free-dom Park."

Mason exhaled. *No date on a Friday night. Good.* "So you're a photographer now?"

"I am."

"Good for you. What time will you be finished tomorrow? I'd love to see the park. I can meet you there."

Emory sat down on her bed. *Did he just ask me out on a date? No. But now I have to meet him, or I'll sound bitter.* She didn't want to give Mason any reason to believe she was unhappy or lonely. She wanted to project an image of a happy, successful woman who'd left the past behind. "Meet me at 11 by the bridge. I should be done by then."

"Great. I'll see you then." Clive looked over at Mason and pumped his fist.

"OK." Emory said awkwardly.

"Good night, Em."

"Good night." Emory collapsed down on her bed, delirious with nerves and confusion to the point she felt sick to her stomach. She stuffed her face in her pillow.

Mason stood up from the bar, beaming with pride, and slapped a high-five to Clive.

* * *

Emory tried to sleep but couldn't stop her mind from racing. *What the hell is going on?* She wondered what Mason was up to—why he would call, why he wanted to see her, what he expected in Freedom Park tomorrow, whether he was still married, whether he had feelings for her. All of this made sleep impossible. She considered waking Wesley to discuss her latest drama but decided not to bother him. He had taught for hours and deserved to sleep.

She had no answers to her many questions, other than that she still loved him, and was worried about spending time with him—that it could be a painful reminder of a love that was lost—and lost to Alexis—and she hadn't come close to finding again, certainly not with Eric. But she wondered whether this was a sign—perhaps from God—that she needed to confront her past and divulge her secrets. She tried to push that thought aside, telling herself that bumping into him in a bar was nothing more than a chance encounter. But then she thought of the Gospel of Matthew. *There is nothing covered that shall not be revealed; and hid, that shall not be known.*

The uncertainty made her stomach churn, but she couldn't control her heart fluttering with excitement, too. She'd missed Mason—his smile, confidence, and the way he made her feel. She missed sharing her life with him. She wondered whether spending time with him after so many years would feel the same as before. She was exhausted by her thoughts, but was afraid to sleep. She didn't want her memories—and her own secrets—to haunt her dreams, as they sometimes did.

She remembered their last days. *I should have seen it coming.* There were hints in their senior year, but she ignored them, choosing to believe everything was fine. It was easier that way. The NFL draft loomed in April, and Mason was under incredible pressure, with seemingly endless obligations ahead. He had to work on his flexibility and arm strength, shave precious tenths off his 40 yard dash time, deal with media questions and scrutiny, travel to the combine with countless other prospects, and hold a private work-out on campus for prospective teams.

His teammates encouraged him as he prepared for the process but ribbed him about Emory. They thought Mason should play the field—a different girl for each week of the NFL regular season. They had no idea he'd only ever had sex with Emory. She would hear some of the comments from his teammates, but never felt threatened, believing Mason was loyal and loved her, and that he wanted, in the near future, nothing more than a stable marriage. She knew Mason never considered divorce an option, having suffered through his own parents' divorce at a young age. Their plan was to marry just once.

In the midst of his preparation, and with the draft only a few months away, Emory made a trip to Texas to visit his family over New Year's. She was battling bronchitis, hopped up on antibiotics, but went along to keep family relations running smoothly. Most of all, she didn't want to disappoint his mother, Kathleen, a Texas divorcee, beautiful and imposing, with big blonde hair and a Southern drawl, who'd made it on her own as a successful interior designer. She owned every room she entered. Business was her primary focus, and she pushed her boys to do the same. It wasn't as if Kathleen looked forward to seeing Emory during the trip; she simply liked appointments kept.

Over dinner, Kathleen, Mason, and Emory discussed college life, and highlights from Mason's senior season on the field, then speculated about what round Mason might be drafted in, and by which NFL team. It could be a team in the Northeast—where they would need to get used to cold weather—or a team out in California—where they would need to learn about earthquake insurance and surfing. Or it could be some place in between. The future was unknown and exciting, Mason and Emory dreaming about the endless possibilities.

Then Kathleen put a stop to it. "Emory, have you considered *not* auditioning for that New York dance company?"

Emory stopped her dreams cold, Kathleen turning them into a nightmare. "Did you say *not* audition?"

"Yes, dear," Kathleen said.

Emory looked over at Mason, slumped in his chair. A few weeks earlier, she'd told him she was invited to audition with the American Ballet Theatre in New York, the premier dance company in the United States, if not the world, during their final semester. It had been her dream to dance professionally, and she planned to shoot for the top. Only a few applicants each year were even selected. She didn't mind that Mason told his mother but couldn't believe Kathleen would suggest she give up the opportunity. She wondered if he'd expressed some concern to his mother.

"I plan to audition," Emory said boldly. "It was quite an honor to be asked."

"Well, dear, it would just be so much easier on Mason if you were not in New York, and you moved wherever he is drafted and just danced there." Mason slumped further in his chair. "Unless, of course, a New York team drafts him, but as we all know, we can't be sure of that." Emory glared at Mason, urging him with her eyes to confront his mother. She believed he always had supported her passion for dance—that it was what first attracted him to her in the dark theater.

But Kathleen had her and her son on the defensive. She wouldn't have his NFL career jeopardized by ballet and quickly went in for the kill. "Don't you think so, Mason?"

Mason squirmed to sit up in his chair, then cleared his throat, looking down while fidgeting with his fork, with obviously no idea how to respond. The question lingered while he delayed. Emory turned to him, her eyes begging that he stick up for her, but he could only grimace under the glare of his mother. "Em, I guess that's something we can talk about?"

Hell no! But sick and in hostile territory, Emory took a deep breath and gently reminded Mason, as they'd discussed before, the career of a dancer is short—like an NFL player—and her time was now or never. She then tossed her napkin down and excused herself from the table.

Over the following weeks, Mason dropped hints that he hoped they could live together wherever he played, and that a long-distance relationship would be difficult. Emory chalked it up to an overbearing potential mother-in-law and the pressures of the draft, figuring Mason eventually would come around. Regardless, she wasn't going to let him or Kathleen get in the way of her dance career. In mid-

February, two months before the draft, she traveled alone to the American Ballet Theatre in New York. She gave a flawless audition and received encouraging feedback from the instructors but knew it was still a long shot. She was competing against the best dancers in the world.

To her surprise, after a few weeks, she received an invitation in the mail to join the company. She jumped up and down, her heart bursting out of her chest. The years and years of practice and late nights had paid off. *Is this really happening?* She needed to tell Mason for it to seem real. She tried to call him, but he didn't answer, then remembered he was lifting weights at the football training facility. She raced across campus, with the wind at her back, running faster than she'd ever run before. She didn't want to waste a second to tell him. She reached the facility and flew open the doors, rushing down the halls screaming his name. She darted up a flight of stairs and burst into the weight room, all empty except for Mason.

She ran to him, and leapt into his arms. "I did it! I did it! I got in!"

Mason placed her on the ground slowly. "Wow. That's great," he muttered.

"I know!" She hopped up and down, her face beaming brightly. "I can't believe it!"

Mason looked down at the weights resting on the floor in front of him. "What's wrong?"

"I didn't think you'd be so happy to leave me."

"What?" She reached for his hand. "I'm not excited to leave you. I'm excited I got *accepted*."

"Does that mean you have to accept?"

Emory couldn't believe what he was saying. She'd dreamed about this opportunity her whole life, and thought Mason of all people would understand. "No one turns this down." She grabbed his other hand. "It's like being drafted and refusing to play." She searched his beautiful eyes, but saw only sadness, and perhaps a touch of anger. She felt light-headed, releasing one hand from his to hold her head. She took a deep breath and sat down on an exercise bench.

"Are you OK, Em?" he asked tenderly.

"Just a little dizzy, that's all. I'll be fine."

Mason bent down to rub her back. She wasn't sure what had come over her, but assumed it was just a bad mixture of so many strong emotions at once, on the heels of her campus run. She didn't want to make a big deal of it and decided it was nothing. Mason sat down next to her on the bench, hanging his head.

"I know it's going to be hard to be apart," she said, "but there are weekends and holidays. I can travel to where your games are. We can make it work. Maybe a New York team will draft you!"

"What if I don't want you to leave me?" he asked sadly.

Why is this all about him? "I'm not leaving you, Mason! I'm following my dream!"

Mason rose from the bench and grabbed his weights from the floor. "Your dream doesn't seem to include me!" He began to curl, veins bulging in his arms.

"Aren't you proud of me? Can't you be happy for me? Support me?" Emory waved her hands wildly in the air. "Your girlfriend is one of the best ballerinas in the whole world. Do you realize that? This is the fucking Super Bowl for me!"

He dropped the weights, a loud clang echoing through the room. "Support *you?* What about me?"

Emory rose from the bench, her heart heavy and mind spinning. These were the moments they'd talked and dreamed about together. But Mason had turned it into a wrestling match over whose career was more important, and Emory didn't understand why they both couldn't have their careers and each other. She tried to compose herself but couldn't hide her anger any longer. "Is that you or your mother talking?"

"Don't bring my mother into this!" he barked.

"How about this—just defer football for a year and follow me to New York?"

Mason stared at her. "Don't be ridiculous. That's the stupidest thing I've ever heard!"

"What's stupid is you telling me *not* to go to New York. I mean, you knew I was auditioning. What did you think was going to happen?" Mason lowered his head, then she realized what she never thought possible. "Oh my God, you hoped I wouldn't get it."

He brushed her off. "I'm not discussing this anymore. It's time that you decide. Is it me or ballet?"

"Mason, that's not a choice. Either way, I am losing something I love." She took a step towards him, hoping to end this fight she didn't want. "Can we at least go celebrate tonight and deal with the details later?"

"I don't feel like celebrating you leaving me." Mason turned his back to her and walked away, returning the weights to the shelves.

"Let's just give it a few days," she said hopefully. "Nothing needs to be decided now."

Ignoring her offer, Mason grabbed his towel from the floor, and Emory began to cry. The best news of her life was leading to the loss of the man she loved. Mason walked towards her and kissed the tip of her nose and forehead. For a moment, Emory felt peace, as if he finally understood. But then he turned his back again and walked towards the exit.

"Mason, Mason," she cried out, "please don't do this! I love you! Please, please…"

When he reached the door, he turned back to her. "Bye, Em." And he was gone.

Emory sunk to the floor, tears streaming down her face, clutching her stomach, feeling she could throw up. She curled into a ball on the floor in the weight room for hours, late into the night, hoping Mason would come back to her, but he never did. Her life, her love, was gone. She pulled out her phone. "Wesley, I need you to come to the weight room right now."

CHAPTER FOUR

SHE'D HARDLY SLEPT when the alarm clock blared. Emory rolled her head under her pillow, as if that would stop the noise. She threw the pillow off her and smacked the alarm clock to shut it off. It was already morning; the night had passed quickly. She shuffled into her bathroom and looked at her puffy eyes. *I can't look like shit again.* She only had an hour to get ready for her photo shoot in Freedom Park and needed every minute of it—not only to perk up for her two little clients but also to look her best for her date later that morning. *No, not a date! An appointment! A meeting! Just two old college friends catching up.*

After a bowl of cereal, she quickly applied a dash of blush, mascara, and lip gloss, then threw on her skinny jeans, brown knee-high riding boots, and a camel colored cowl-neck sweater. She pulled her hair into a high pony tail and raced out of her room with her camera bag.

Wesley, holding his coffee mug, greeted her with a cat call. "What's the occasion?" Emory never pulled herself together for photo shoots. Her infant and child clients didn't care what she looked like, and neither did she, spending half the time on the ground taking pictures, and the other half wiping snotty noses. A t-shirt, cargo pants, and tennis shoes were her typical uniform, so Wesley knew Emory was up to something. *Shouldn't she still be upset, in flannels, looking like hell over Eric?*

"I'm meeting Mason after my shoot."

"Mason called?" Wesley sipped his coffee. "You left out that little fact last night."

"He called after you left to teach. Wants me to show him around town."

"I bet he does," Wesley teased, raising his eyebrows.

"And I thought I'd just show him what he missed out on, too."
She shook her booty at him.

This was the girl Wesley loved—sweet and spicy, rolled into a
pretty little package. "Go get you some!" He slapped her booty, as
she waltzed out the door.

* * *

Mason ordered a cab with the hotel valet and was off to Freedom
Park. He'd slept well. It was the first time in a long time his arm
didn't hurt in the morning. He had a slight hangover from Clive, but
it was well worth it, proud of himself for making the call and both
thrilled and relieved she agreed to meet him. But he still had
butterflies in his stomach, too—Emory always gave him butterflies
—like he did before a division game on Sundays. *Is this adrenaline
or nerves?* He didn't know what to expect.

He wondered whether she still had any feelings for him other
than anger, and if she would soon take the chance to unload on him.
He also wondered whether she may be in a good, committed relationship with another man, and knew he wouldn't handle that news
well. He could only imagine Emory with him. *Don't get your hopes
up.* She was still a knock-out and could have any man she wanted—
and probably did.

The cab dropped him at Freedom Park about twenty minutes
early. Mason paid the fare and made his way towards the bridge,
drenched with sunlight, as if he was walking towards a pot of gold.
As he drew closer, his pace quickened; he couldn't wait to see her
again. On a field below, he spotted Emory, laying on the ground with
camera in hand, facing two small children, her long, blonde hair
glistening in the sunlight. He leaned against a tree, far enough away
so she wouldn't spot him, watching her work—as he had so many
times before in the dark theater—and couldn't help but notice how
her jeans perfectly framed her tight, little ass. *Did she wear those on
purpose?* He adjusted his pants.

Emory at times peeked around the camera and made a funny face
at the baby. There was an elegance to her work; it was fluid and
quick, like her dance. She was happy and made the children happy.
This didn't look like work to Mason. Emory wrapped the shoot, then
held the baby on her hip, the older child holding Emory's leg. *That*

could be us. No, that could have been us. Emory chatted with the children's mother writing her a check. They left, and Emory gathered her equipment. It was game time. Mason walked towards her, his palms sweaty and legs weak, not knowing what to say first and wondering if this was a bad idea, worried this meeting was more important to him than to her. It occurred to him she wasn't very friendly at the bar or on the phone. For a moment, he thought to turn back, but his heart wouldn't let him.

Emory looked up from her bags. He gave her a slight wave with his good arm, as he came down a small hill in jeans, a t-shirt, and a dark brown leather jacket thrown over his shoulder in a sling. *Ugh, he's early. Why does he have to look so damn yummy!* She was so flustered last night at the bar she hadn't fully appreciated his body—the NFL had made him broader and harder. Her pulse quickened as he approached, but she caught herself. *He's just an old friend. An old, married friend.*

"Let me help you with all that, Em."

"You're the one with the bum shoulder," she said, zipping up the bag. "I do this all the time. It's fine."

Mason picked the camera bag off the ground. "I still have one good arm."

Emory smiled but only made brief eye contact. "Just follow me to my car while I lock this stuff up." They barely spoke on the short walk, other than for Mason to comment on the Charlotte weather and Emory to describe the layout of Freedom Park. The ease with which they once had spoken seemed lost. She could sense the tension between them and figured Mason felt it, too. Emory popped the trunk, and Mason loaded her equipment. For her own sake, she sought to put Mason in his place and make clear this wasn't going anywhere. She closed the trunk and looked directly into Mason's eyes. "Did Alexis come with you to Charlotte?"

Her direct question startled Mason, his eyes opening wide. *Why didn't I plan what to say about Alexis? I've been too busy looking at your ass!* He'd forgotten how tough and strong Emory could be, her sweet face so deceiving.

"No," he mumbled and changed the subject. "Why don't you show me around the park? Show me some of your favorite spots to take pictures."

As they walked, Emory was proud of her direct question, and that it threw Mason off his game, but regretted she learned nothing from his answer. She realized there was no need for Alexis to accompany him to Charlotte for a meeting about a potential contract with the Panthers. Emory just assumed Alexis was at home in their mansion, with their fair-haired children. Mason placed his hand at the small of her back, almost out of habit, but quickly moved it away. Emory shivered at the brief contact, praying he hadn't noticed.

They wandered around Freedom Park for almost an hour. She pointed out her favorite spots to him. The conversation flowed somewhat easier, with Emory doing the bulk of the talking, which helped to calm her nerves. She rambled on about her job, describing how she loved to shoot in natural light, during the "magic" hours, and the beautiful children with whom she worked. She talked so much about her job she feared she was boring Mason; after all, he had dumped her because she wanted a career.

But he didn't seem to be bored—at least he wasn't showing it. He smiled and nodded along as she talked. He enjoyed hearing her voice—it had been so long—and was thankful he didn't have to carry the conversation. Then her stomach suddenly growled loudly, interrupting her discussion of camera lenses that Mason was pretending to follow. He laughed at the noise. "I guess some things never change."

"My insides are bigger than my outsides."

"You know, almost every memory I have of us involves you eating," he said, though his mind also conjured up sexual images, too, Emory stiffening at his fond mention of their past. "You used to get so moody when you were hungry."

"Still do." She threatened with a smile.

"Is there some place around here to grab a bite? I don't want to see moody Emory."

She suggested a little Spanish restaurant on the outskirts of Freedom Park, a cozy place that only locals knew about, and they headed that way. Upon arrival, Mason opened the door for her, and when they were shown to a table, he pulled out her chair. Emory smiled, pleased the NFL hadn't ruined his Southern manners. A waitress approached with menus and water, informing them of the daily specials, and quickly exited. Emory fidgeted with her water and stared at her menu, finding herself hiding behind it. *This is so stupid.* After a sip of water, she dared to look up, and for a moment, their eyes met, the moment lasting a little long for her comfort, relieved when the waitress returned to take their order.

"I feel like I've done all the talking," Emory said after the waitress left. "Tell me how the NFL and Alexis have been to you." Emory didn't care so much about the NFL but wanted the scoop on Alexis, and wanted to pretend she was fine he was presumably still married to her.

"Well, considering my arm is in a sling, I would say not so well."

Why does he keep avoiding Alexis? Emory figured he was just uncomfortable talking about his wife with her, and she decided not to push it. "How's your arm?"

Mason grimaced. "Still have a ways to go." The waitress returned with their drinks.

"Well, the Panthers seem interested. Any other teams on the radar?"

"I'm going to Seattle in a few days with Steven."

Emory's face lit up. "Oh my goodness, how is Steven?"

Mason bragged about his brother's success in the courtroom and as a sports agent, and that Steven had married a few years ago and was expecting his first baby in a few months.

"Married and a baby coming, wow! That's just the best news! You must be thrilled to be an uncle?"

"Yeah, it's just great," he responded, taking a big drink of water.

"Please tell Steven congrats and hello from me. I just know he's going to be a great dad."

"Will do." *This isn't going well. She's more interested in my douche bag brother than me!*

Emory noticed a hint of sadness—or jealousy—in Mason. She was surprised how easily she could still read him. She blamed his emotional swings on his shoulder, recalling how her own injury—a broken ankle from one bad fall just weeks before graduation—had ended her professional dance career before it even started. "When I broke my ankle and couldn't dance, I thought my life was over. It gets easier over time."

The waitress brought out their food, as Mason kept his eyes fixed on Emory, listening intently, happy she was opening up. *Maybe she's not going to go off on me.* It dawned on him how similar their lives were: two driven athletes with career-threatening injuries. And worse for Emory—her career never even started.

Mason picked at his food, moving it around the plate with his fork. "Don't you like your food?" she asked.

"It's great. I was just remembering when you got hurt. Did you know I tried to visit you?" Even though Mason was already involved with Alexis, he did try to see Emory in the hospital, hoping that because her career was over, she would follow him to the NFL. *How fucking stupid. It was just as well she refused to see me.*

"I knew you came." Emory smiled. "I told Wesley to kick your ass!"

Mason nearly choked on his food, laughing. Emory told him about Wesley's studio, her part-time teaching, and their living arrangement.

"I bet the kids love you," Mason said.

"I love them."

Mason decided since Emory twice tried to pry into his personal life, he'd do the same, but didn't want to be too obvious. "Do people think it's weird that you and Wesley live together?"

"Not really."

"I mean, doesn't everyone assume you're a couple?"

"Well, since Wesley has a boyfriend, I should hope not. That would make me a very loose woman," Emory said, shooting a warning look to Mason, "which we both know I'm not." She refused to be a quick fling during his short time in Charlotte. "But I just adore Tomás. He makes Wesley happy. He's a fabulous artist, and most important to me, a great cook. They've been together about a year."

Mason's subtle approach fell flat, learning nothing except some details about Wesley's love life with some strange guy named Tomás—all of which he never wanted to think about, ever. He decided to cut to the chase. "So Wesley has a boyfriend, how about you?"

Trying to keep her face from blushing, Emory couldn't believe he'd have the balls to ask her such a personal question. She considered lying, not wanting to appear lonely, desperate, or available, but decided to be honest. She had other secrets to keep. "No."

"Ever married?" he quickly asked.

Emory pursed her lips. *What the hell? What business is it of his?* "No." She needed to seize control of the conversation, bothered he now knew her history, but hadn't come clean about his own. She had questions to ask but wasn't sure she was prepared to hear the answers. "You haven't talked much about Alexis. Do you two have kids?"

Mason took a sip of water, wishing he had one of Clive's doubles, knowing he couldn't skirt the issue any longer. "No kids, and we're getting a divorce."

Emory wasn't prepared for that answer; it hit her like an atomic bomb exploding in a quiet neighborhood. She took a drink of water, trying to hide her surprise behind the glass, then stared at her food, gripping her fork tightly, now worried he was looking for more than a tour of Freedom Park and lunch, but also a rebound to ease his broken heart. "I'm sorry to hear that. I know divorce was never an option for you."

"It's for the best. She loved the NFL player, not me. When the arm went, so did she."

Emory appreciated his honesty, and couldn't contain her emotions any longer. "She always was a bitch."

Mason smiled broadly and nodded in agreement. *There's my sassy, angel-faced girl.* Mason always loved how strong and tough Emory was.

They cleaned their plates, and the waitress returned to clear the table, leaving the check. Emory grabbed it quickly, and whipped out her credit card, wanting to leave no doubt that this had been nothing more than a meeting—an appointment. Mason began to object, but she insisted. "My city, my treat."

They left the restaurant and walked back to her car, Emory feeling a pull towards Mason she thought had long vanished. It made her shiver, and in one swift move, Mason took off his leather jacket and placed it around her, his fingers grazing her neck, as he pushed her ponytail aside. A familiar pulse of electricity shot through her body, and her mind betrayed her, thinking back to what he could do with just his fingers.

Mason eyed her with amusement, seeing she was biting her lower lip, wondering if that still meant the same thing as it did in college. *She's thinking about sex!* Hopeful, he reached over and placed his hand on her hip, pulling her towards him, an arm around her lower back and his nose to the top of her head, breathing in her scent, still fitting perfectly in his arms. *This is more like it.* Emory nestled her head in his chest and placed her arms around the middle of his back, melting into his body. Her fingers traced the outline of his muscles, and she felt a tear come into her eye, as Mason's phone then vibrated in his pocket.

She pulled away quickly like she was caught with her hand in a cookie jar. He pulled out his phone and saw it was Steven. "I'm sorry. I need to get this. It will just take a minute." He answered the phone and told his brother to hold on.

Emory felt the urge to flee, removing his jacket. "I should be going anyway. It was nice catching up. Good luck with everything."

She opened her car door, and he mouthed, "Don't go."

Mason turned and walked a few steps away to talk. "Bro, you have the worst fucking timing."

"What's up?" Steven asked, following Olivia around a baby store with an overflowing shopping cart.

The car door closed, and Mason turned back around, seeing Emory drive away. "Shit! She's gone."

"Who's gone?" Steven asked. "Mason, what are you talking about?"

Why would she just leave?

"What the hell is going on?" Steven barked, Olivia turning to her husband and placing a finger over her mouth.

"Huh?" Mason asked.

"Huh?" Steven mocked, then whispered through gritted teeth, "Did you blow off Seattle for a fucking woman? I know you haven't gotten laid in a while, but this is fucking ridiculous. Who is she?"

He watched Emory's car slip further and further away. "Em…"

Steven stopped the cart. "As in Emory Claire?"

"Yeah."

A slow smile came across Steven's face. "Now it makes sense, you staying in Charlotte."

Mason quickly brought Steven up to speed on Emory. He was happy for Mason but worried his brother's mind was too far gone to focus on getting a new contract. Steven relayed the travel plans for

Seattle, and before hanging up, gave out his last instruction. "Don't fuck this up again."

I just did.

* * *

Emory drove home with tears streaming down her cheeks, feeling she'd embarrassed herself. Everything she'd suppressed for six years had just bubbled up to the surface. *What the hell was that?* She tried to convince herself Mason would be in Seattle in a few days, so there was no point getting carried away. *You know he only wants one thing anyway.*

Emory arrived back at the apartment to find Wesley and Tomás hanging out in the kitchen. They saw her red cheeks and runny nose, and that she was shaking. They rushed to her side, unloading the camera equipment from her arms, Wesley leading Emory to the den sofa. Tomás ran to the refrigerator to fetch her a water bottle and snack, believing he could solve any problem through food.

Emory sat down and pulled her legs to her chest, sobbing. Wesley sat next to her and took off her boots, rubbing her feet. Tomás brought water and some pretzels, placing them on the coffee table, then walked a few feet away to give Emory her space. The men exchanged a worried look.

"What did that shit head do this time?" Wesley asked.

"Nothing, nothing," she cried. "I don't want to talk about him."

"OK, we don't have to right now," Wesley said, pointing to the food and water. "Are you hungry? Thirsty?"

"No, I'm just..." Emory couldn't complete the thought, lifting her hands to her face to hide her tears.

"Tell me what happened, honey."

"Nothing. Nothing happened. He's getting divorced."

Wesley raised his eyebrows. "And?" Emory shook her head, without any answers or explanations for her emotions. Tomás motioned to Wesley to offer her the food again, and Wesley gave him a snide look, then turned back to Emory.

"Why don't you go take a hot bath and lay down for a little while. You'll feel better." Emory nodded and rose slowly, walking to her room.

When the door closed, Tomás asked, "What was that all about? She probably should have eaten something."

Wesley rolled his eyes. "Will you stop with the food? Isn't it obvious? She's still in love with him."

* * *

A few hours later, Emory woke to her phone ringing but didn't answer. She saw several missed calls, all from the same number. *Eric!* Her heart sank, hoping they were from Mason, but she could only blame herself. *You left this time.*

Wesley entered her room and sat down on her bed. "Feeling any better?"

"A little," she said, "but Eric has called several times. I can't deal with him right now. I'll call him back in a few days."

"Good. Especially because tonight, we're going out."

"Where?"

"To the nightclub where Tomás has been painting that mural."

"The unveiling is tonight?"

"Yep, and you are coming to celebrate with us." Wesley smiled mischievously and gave her a wink. "Put on something hot."

CHAPTER FIVE

AN HOUR LATER, they were in a high-end, two-story nightclub welcoming Charlotte's finest art patrons, there to see the unveiling of Tomás' mural, an homage to the history of North Carolina. Tomás was a self-taught artist, having never received any formal training, but his talent and creativity were second to none, specifically chosen to paint the mural. He spent the evening receiving congratulations from one patron after another. Wesley and Emory passed the time together, drinking and laughing, though she sensed he was distracted in some way, his eyes scanning the crowd as a jazz band set up to perform.

Wesley caught the attention of someone on the second floor. "Damn, I forgot I have these special passes to the VIP section upstairs." He whipped them out of his pocket. "Want to go check it out?" Emory nodded excitedly, then walked towards the stairs together, arm in arm, flashing their passes to an attendant, and proceeded up. Emory got to the top step, and her mouth dropped. At a table on the other side of the room, in gray, pinstripe slacks and a white shirt with the top button undone, Mason sat alone.

"You're welcome," Wesley whispered.

"Wesley Charles Henderson, what did you do?" She dragged him a few steps down.

"Helping you out. You obviously still care for him."

Emory poked him in the chest. "So what's he doing here?"

"He showed up at the studio today while you were napping."

"What?" Emory asked, shocked.

"You told him we live above my dance studio, and Google did the rest."

"What did he want?"

Wesley rolled his eyes. "You, stupid! He wanted to see you, and

I told him no. I thought he might kick my ass, but he said he understood. He said he was leaving town in a few days and needed to see you before he left. So, I invited him out tonight."

"I can't believe you did that."

"You can thank me later," he said, shaking her a little. "This way, I can keep an eye on you two. Plus, he misses you."

Emory's face lit up. "He said that?" She peered from the staircase over the railway at Mason. The band began playing, and a few patrons made their way to the dance floor.

"He didn't have to. He was there looking for you. Had a cab chasing you all over town."

Emory twirled her hair. "He's getting divorced. His arm is a mess. He's just looking to feel better—or a good piece of ass."

"Good grief, keep your voice down, girl. He's like ten feet away. I don't think sex is what he's looking for, but even if it is, you're both single. Let him be your rebound from Eric. Have lots of hot sex. You be the one to use him!"

Emory punched Wesley in the shoulder. *I have thought of that, though.*

"Just stop running from him—and your past. See where it goes."

"After what I did, you know it can't go anywhere." She hung her head. "He'd never forgive me."

"Just take it slow."

"Not before the hot sex, right?" she teased.

"Hot or slow! Doesn't matter to me."

"You are impossible! I will get you back for this."

They walked back up the last few steps of the staircase, then turned towards Mason's table. He stood up, ever the gentleman, his eyes growing dark with desire as he scanned her body, making out the curve of her breasts in a backless silk halter top, her long blonde hair, loosely curled, flowing down her back. *No bra!* Her tight, black skirt showed off her killer legs accented by stiletto black boots.

A wave of heat flooded over Emory's entire body under the intensity of his stare, and she quickly reached for his hand. "Let's dance." She knew Mason hated to dance, and would be putty in her hands on the dance floor. *I'm in control here.*

"That sounds like a great idea." Wesley winked at her. "I'm going to catch up with Tomás."

Mason felt a knot in his stomach but followed along, hoping she couldn't feel the sweat on his hand. He saw only a few other couples on the dance floor. *Shit, no way to blend in, especially with this fucking sling. Clive, help!* "I think I'll need a drink first. Want anything?"

"No, I'll meet you on the dance floor."

Mason walked over to the bar, a young bartender recognizing him, and Mason autographed a napkin for him. *There isn't enough alcohol in the world to help me now.* His heart pounding in his chest, he tried to calm himself, recalling that dancing with Emory was pretty simple: everyone stared at her. He ordered a shot of whiskey and held it, leaning up against the bar, watching Emory dance alone —the grace, sexiness, power—all still the same. She knew how to draw an audience, with her long legs, flowing hair, and bare back, easily the sexiest woman in the nightclub—a fact that would escape her, but not a single man in the room, gay or straight, gawking like wolves ready to pounce.

Her eyes glistening as she swayed her hips, Mason felt himself grow hard just watching her, and adjusted his pants. *It's been a long time. Can't even use my right hand!* Mason knew what he had done to her body before and wanted it again.

The young bartender interrupted Mason's thoughts. "Damn, I'd like to tap that."

"Go fuck yourself." Mason crumpled the autographed napkin, throwing it on the ground, then walked towards the dance floor, holding his whiskey. Emory caught his eye and beckoned him to her. He slammed the shot, as their eyes locked on each other, her body moving in the most delicious way. Mason came up next to her, and the music slowed. She turned her back to him, pulling her hair to the side, and pushed her ass against his hips. Mason grabbed her left hip with his left hand, pulling her tightly to him and nuzzling her neck with his lips, breathing in her sweet smell. She felt the warmth of his breath on her neck, sending a jolt of fire between her legs. She rolled her hips side to side feeling how hard he was.

Mason saw they had attracted an audience. He was used to strangers staring at him—whether on the street, or at the grocery store, or in a football stadium. But he wasn't used to an audience for his dancing—well, at least not for any good dancing. He knew the stares on this night were not for him, but for Emory, and she was oblivious to it all.

She ran her fingers through her hair, and slowly pulled away to face him, their eyes burning into each other. She hiked her right leg up to his left hip, lifting her skirt slightly, and he caught her leg, pushing himself against her, his fingers massaging the bare skin of her upper thigh. Their faces inches apart, her fingers caressed his hair, and she smiled, pushing herself harder against him, as if daring him to take it further, but the song ended before he could.

The crowd parted, as she led Mason back upstairs to the VIP area. "Nice show," Wesley said, as they approached the table.

"I aim to please," Emory said. "Mason, this is Tomás."

"I thought you were Patrick Swayze," Tomás quipped.

"*Road House* or *Dirty Dancing?*" Mason asked.

"I haven't decided yet."

Mason laughed. "A little of both."

The foursome spent the evening drinking and talking, Mason resting his left hand on Emory's bare thigh and gently rubbing her warm skin with his fingertips, only heightening the tension and electricity between them, making it hard for Emory to concentrate on anything but Mason's fingers grazing her flesh. *Is he doing this on purpose?* Waves of heat flashed between her legs with each stroke, and she did her best to keep her breath steady, not wanting to reveal the effect he still had on her.

After an hour, Emory could take no more and felt the urge to escape again. "Sorry, boys, but I have a photo shoot in the morning. I better call it a night."

"I'll come with you," Wesley offered. "You shouldn't go alone."

"No way. You enjoy Tomás' big night. I'm fine."

Mason seized the moment. "I'll make sure she gets home."

Wesley shot Emory a concerned look, but she nodded she'd be fine. Mason helped her out of her chair, then downstairs, placing his hand on the small of her back to direct her through the crowd. Once outside, Mason hailed a cab, and they slid into the backseat. She felt him staring at her. Emory wasn't the type to just take a man to bed, even Mason. *What the hell have I started?*

"I'm not tired," Mason said. "Want to come back and have a drink at my hotel?"

She shook her head slightly. "I don't think that's such a good idea."

"Well, I guess your place it is." Mason leaned forward to give the cabbie her address, as her mouth dropped open.

I walked right into that.

The cabbie started to drive, and Mason leaned back, taking her cheek in the palm of his hand and softly kissing her lips. He then pulled away slightly, searching her eyes. Her mind had completely failed her, and Mason kissed her again, slowly at first, then placed his hand firmly on the back of her neck, pulling her closer, and parted her lips, their tongues meeting. She purred, her hands sliding to his hips, and he moaned softly, as he pushed her back onto the seat. The cabbie loudly cleared his throat, prompting Mason to stop, but not before kissing the tip of her nose and forehead. Emory blushed and tried to catch her breath.

She remembered the first time he had done that—two weeks after they met. Mason had just led his team to victory over a top-ranked college opponent, Emory attributing the win, at least in part, to Mason's lateral movement, which she'd pressed him to improve. It was a huge win for the team and for Mason, his first as a starter. She waited for him outside the locker room after the game, and when he came out, he grabbed her hand and intertwined their fingers, his other hand going into her hair. Mason leaned in and kissed her sweetly on the lips, finishing with a peck on her nose and forehead. *Our first kiss.*

Her memories with Mason were so familiar. She snapped herself back to the present, feeling Mason stroke her hand, a barrage of emotions sweeping through her. *What am I doing? I haven't seen him in six years. He dumped me. He's still married. He has no current job. And I'm making out with him like some lovesick teenager!* She felt her knees weaken, and her head spin, unable to keep up with her racing heart.

The cabbie pulled up to her apartment, and Mason paid the fare, as Emory noticed lights were on upstairs, wondering how Wesley had beaten them home. They walked inside and stopped in their tracks.

Eric sat in her den with a bouquet of flowers and her ring box on the coffee table. The men stared at each other, sizing up the competition, then looked towards her. She felt both men's eyes burning into her.

Who the hell is this guy? Mason's instinct was to pummel him, but thought better of it. He briefly left her side and extended his hand. "Daniel Mason."

Eric didn't extend his, keeping his eyes fixed squarely on Emory. "Fiancé."

Mason swallowed hard, and gave Emory a puzzled look. *Fiancé? She told me she didn't have a boyfriend, much less a fiancé.*

Emory cleared her voice and stared right back at Eric. "Ex-fiancé." Mason felt slightly better, and pulled Emory to his hip, staking his claim.

Eric walked towards her, his face turning red. "Really, Emory? After all the time you made me wait, you're going to screw the first guy who comes along!"

His body tightening, Mason stepped in front of Emory to shield her from Eric's stare. "I think it's time for you to go," Mason ordered, towering over Eric.

She grabbed Mason's arm, feeling his tense muscles. "Enough of this pissing contest." She squeezed Mason's hand to get his attention. "I need a few minutes alone with Eric. Could you please wait for me in my bedroom?" She pointed to her door.

Mason kissed Emory on the cheek. "I'll be waiting for you in the bedroom, Em," he said to Eric, then shut the door behind him.

Eric paced around the den, clearly shaken. "Are you fucking him, Emory? Is that why you wouldn't set a date?"

"What? No, no!" Emory walked towards him, touching his arm. "It's not like that. He's an old friend from college I just happened to run into. That's all."

As far as Emory could tell, Eric hadn't made the connection that Mason was an NFL quarterback. He never was much into sports; still, Emory knew this looked bad. There was no way to convince him otherwise. Eric shook his head in disbelief.

"Why are you here, Eric?"

He took her hands in his. "You haven't returned any of my calls, and I hated the way things ended yesterday. I never meant to ask for the ring back. I was just frustrated. I thought if I gave you a little nudge, you would pick a date, and things would be fine. It was stupid. We don't have to get married anytime soon. Let's just work things out. I know we can."

"How do you know?"

"Because I love you," he said sweetly.

Emory looked at the flowers and the ring, knowing any rational woman would give him a second chance. But she couldn't shake the feel of Mason's body or his lips against hers. "I shouldn't need a nudge, Eric. You deserve a woman who is excited to get married." She paused, dropping his hands. "Please give me my key back. I'll return some stuff to your house on Monday, pick up my things, and leave your key then. I'm so sorry."

That was not what Eric expected to hear. The certainty with which Emory spoke stunned him, his eyes filling with tears. Eric took the key to her apartment off his key chain and placed it on the coffee table. He then picked up the flowers and the ring, limping past Emory without saying another word, slamming the door on his way out.

CHAPTER SIX

MASON JUMPED HEARING the door slam and flew out of her room, finding Emory sitting on the sofa in tears. He sat down next to her, and she rested her head on his shoulder. He leaned back, pulling her to him as she wept, without any idea why she was crying. She didn't appear injured, so Eric hadn't hurt her. *Still can't believe she was engaged, and didn't tell me.* He wondered how long they'd dated and been engaged, and why they broke up and when. Her life seemed just as complicated as his.

Mason didn't know what to say, so he just stroked her hair as she cried. After a few minutes, she stopped, her breathing slowed and deepened. Mason looked down at her; she had drifted off to sleep. He reached for a pillow on the sofa and placed it on his knees, lowering her head onto his lap. Her chest slowly rose and fell. He gently pushed her hair back, so he could see her face as she slept.

He had seen her this way many times before in college—beautiful and vulnerable in his arms. After dating for several months, they found themselves, both virgins, on the verge of sex. Of course, they had been intimate together, using their fingers and mouths, but Emory was reluctant to take the next step. To avoid any temptation, she made a rule that they both couldn't be naked at the same time. Mason had no choice but to comply, though it was difficult; he wanted to be respectful of Emory. But all he could seem to think about was being inside her. Mason planned out, in great detail, how he wanted their first time to be. It wasn't going to be in the back seat of his car or in one of their cramped dorm rooms. He just needed Emory to be ready. And the waiting was driving him crazy.

Sometimes they went to parties with his teammates. Mason was never especially fond of these parties but felt it was his duty to go—to support his teammates and watch them make fools of themselves.

He knew Emory hated to go because the guys were crass and the girls were her total opposite. They were in college to find a husband, not a career, spending hours on their hair, makeup, and clothes, always making sure their cleavage was properly set and their skirts sufficiently high. Underwear, for those girls, was optional. One girl, Alexis, routinely seemed to shove her boobs in Mason's face, and he did his best to ignore her. Emory typically passed the time dancing alone under Mason's protective watch, until he was buzzed enough to join her.

On one particular Friday night party, the guys were having an intellectual debate—whether a girl's cup size correlated to her ability in the bedroom. Certain guys suggested that a girl with a small cup size wasn't as exciting as a girl with a large one, but others believed that a small girl had more to prove and would put out more. Leaning up against a wall, Mason kept his opinions to himself but did chuckle as the debate raged on. He knew Emory's small cup size was a sensitive topic for her, so he figured it was best to keep his mouth shut.

Emory heard the conversation and was disgusted—but pleased Mason kept quiet. She figured she had the smallest bra cup at the party—probably three times smaller than Alexis' size—and it made her self-conscious. Emory decided to prove a point, at least from her perspective, and hopefully end the debate. She held her head high and walked through the group of debaters, towards Mason with her eyes locked on his. She pressed her body against his groin and chest and threw her right leg up over his shoulder—pinning him to the wall with her leg, her foot pointing directly at the ceiling.

The debate stopped, and a hush fell over the room. She kissed Mason passionately, like a woman who knew what she wanted and aimed to get it, her fingers moving through his hair, as she wrestled with his tongue, not stopping until she was certain she'd made her point. Emory slowly pulled away, leaving Mason gasping for breath. She bit her lower lip, and he looked into her eyes. He could see something different, something that told him, in no uncertain terms, that her naked rule was now off the table. Emory took his hand. "Let's go." She smirked at the debaters as they left and gave a wink to Alexis.

They walked through the college courtyard and back to his dorm. Mason told her to wait in the lobby, running up to his room to make a quick phone call and grabbing a duffle bag from his closet he already had packed for this moment. He unzipped it quickly, looking inside to make sure he hadn't forgotten anything—her favorite toiletries, candles, bubble bath, some lounging clothes, toothbrushes, and a large box of condoms. *That should cover it.*

He raced back to the lobby and took Emory by the hand. "Where are we going?" she asked, as he led her to his car and kissed the back of her hand.

"It's a surprise." He opened her door and ran around to the driver side. He threw the duffle bag in the back seat and drove off.

After a few minutes, Emory, so excited, couldn't wait any longer. "How about a little hint?"

"No hints. I'll just say we're close. We're almost there." He put his right hand on Emory's knee and made a sweeping turn of the wheel with his left. He drove another mile, then pulled into the drive of a historic hotel on the outskirts of campus.

"Mason, you didn't!"

"I did." Mason didn't care about the expense. It drained his entire bank account, but he wanted them never to forget this moment. The hotel was the place to stay. It was where the college put up its highly-touted recruits to make a good impression, including Mason. It was where businessmen and politicians stayed when they came to town, and where fancy conventions and important meetings were held to close a deal. *I'm going to close my own deal tonight.*

They walked into the lobby, holding hands. Her mouth dropped open seeing the ornate furnishings and the crystal chandeliers, and he kissed her nose and forehead. They approached the front desk to check in. "You are staying through Sunday, Mr. Mason?"

"Yes, sir. Two nights." Emory's eyes widened, and he squeezed her hand. Mason gave his credit card to the clerk and received keys to room 302.

They rode the elevator to the third floor and walked down a narrow hallway holding hands. Mason was nervous, particularly about what to do once they got inside the room. He thought they were both ready, but a trickle of doubt remained in his mind. He wanted to make sure he did everything just right, but then reminded himself that Emory, too, had never had sex, so she wouldn't know if he messed anything up. He said a prayer that he would at least make

Emory happy, but then it occurred to him that God probably wasn't too interested in helping two college kids have pre-marital sex.

Mason placed the key in the door and led her inside. The room was small but exquisitely decorated with Victorian furniture and beautiful paintings, the stately king-size bed taking up most of the room. He set the duffle bag on a Queen Anne chair in the corner, then watched as Emory roamed around, amazed by where they were. She didn't seem nervous at all. She opened a sliding door and stepped out onto the balcony, looking out over the city, then came back inside, walking towards the bed, running her fingers across the white linens.

She placed her purse near the chair and slipped off her flats. "What's in the bag?"

"You can open it." She looked inside without saying a word, the silence making him more nervous.

"I'm sorry. We don't need to…"

She placed a finger over his lips. "I can't believe you did all this. It's so sweet."

Relieved, he wrapped his arms around her body, her face nestled against his chest. "You deserve it."

"This hotel is lovely, but you know I don't need any of this." She looked up at Mason. "I only need you."

"I know, Em. I just want everything to be perfect for your first, no, *our* first time. I love you."

"I love you, too."

"Did I forget anything?" he asked playfully. "I don't plan to leave this room until Sunday."

"One thing." Emory reached into her purse. "I've got it covered." She pulled out a packet of birth control pills.

Mason's jaw dropped. They'd never talked about her going on birth control, and Mason had just assumed that would be his responsibility. "How long have you been taking those?" he asked, thankful his first time wouldn't be with a condom.

"Years! My periods were always irregular."

"You kept that little fact a secret?"

"A woman has to have some mystery."

They looked at each other, both knowing the time for mystery was over. He ran his fingers through her hair and down her lower back, lifting her shirt a little so his hands touched her bare skin. He felt her heart beating swiftly through her shirt and realized she was just as nervous as he was. He kissed her gently, slowly parting her lips with his tongue, and found her tongue eager to meet his. She nibbled on his lower lip, and he moaned softly. He kissed along her jaw and the nape of her neck, then noticed she was biting her lower lip again.

He slowly unbuttoned her shirt, one button at a time, using only one hand, the other resting behind her head. Her breath quickened, as he removed her shirt to reveal a pure white lace bra, and she trembled slightly. *Please don't stop this time.* He kissed down her neck and onto her shoulder, and as he did, her bra strap fell down. She reached her hands down his pants, and untucked his shirt, struggling to lift it over his head. Mason pulled away to help. Emory stared directly into his eyes while she undid the button and zipper on his jeans, then lowered them, and in one sudden motion, he stepped out and grabbed her with force onto the bed. He kissed her hard and tossed her bra on the floor, trailing kisses to her breasts, then slowly sucked her nipples until she was aroused and erect. He moved down her belly, feeling her quiver beneath him. He undid her jeans and slid them off, her white lace panties matching her bra on the floor. He slid her panties down her legs and tossed them aside.

He admired her naked body before him. She was a firm package, though her white skin conveyed a sweet elegance. Emory looked at him, too—his muscles bulging through his sun-drenched body. She kissed his abs and pulled down his boxer briefs, taking him into her mouth and gliding him in and out. He moaned loudly. *I can't let her do this for long!* She slid back on the bed, and he leaned over her, bracing himself on his elbows, both realizing they were naked together for the first time. They smiled sweetly at each other and kissed slowly, Mason breathing heavily, wanting nothing more than to be inside her.

But he wanted to make sure she was ready. He kissed her belly and moved down to her inner thighs. She quivered and grabbed a pillow, as he massaged them with his hands, blowing warm air between her legs. She moaned, thrusting her hips forward, and he took her into his mouth, sucking hard. Her breathing accelerated, and he slipped a finger inside of her and felt how wet and open she was. She ran her fingers through his hair and moved her hips in a circle. She reached down, gesturing for Mason to come to her. He leaned over her and cupped her breasts. She thrust her hips up to him, rubbing herself against him. He stroked her cheek with his fingers, her skin so soft and warm.

He looked into her eyes. "Are you sure?" She nodded and widened her legs, closing her eyes, as Mason slowly pushed himself inside her. He quickly pulled out, and her eyes jumped open. "I don't want to hurt you."

"You won't." She kissed his neck. Mason slowly placed himself back inside her, savoring how tight and wet she was, contracting around him. He slid in and out. She reached again for the pillow and squeezed but knew she owned him. He slowed his pace, wanting the moment to last and for Emory to enjoy herself, too. She pushed her hips up against him and squeezed tightly.

He moaned her name sweetly. "Em." Mason pulled her hands up over her head and held them. He needed to slow down and stopped moving, keeping himself still inside her, as he kissed her breasts and sucked her nipples. Then he began to move again, slowly in and out of her, her body quivering, with the tension building. She tightened around him, moving her hips faster, encouraging him to thrust harder and deeper until she was there.

"Oh God, Mason! Yes!" Her entire body shook underneath him, as she threw the pillow over her face, and screamed. Mason continued to thrust, and finally let go, collapsing on top of her. She tightened herself a few more times, claiming every last bit of him, Mason staying inside of her, as neither uttered a word.

Mason rolled on his side, pulling her in front of him and cradling her. *Wow.* He snuck a peek at her and caught her smiling, her eyes closed. He looked forward to round two; indeed, there were multiple rounds—and positions—that weekend, as they dreamed about their future. Mason talked about the NFL, and Emory dreamed one day to dance the "Rose Adagio" from *Sleeping Beauty*, and when they got married, its music would play at their wedding.

Then Wesley and Tomás returned to the apartment, stirring Mason from the past. They saw Emory sleeping on his lap and gave him a wave before slipping quietly into Wesley's bedroom. Mason stroked her cheek. Time was short, and there was so much uncertainty between them. He had to catch a plane to Seattle in just over twenty-four hours.

CHAPTER SEVEN

EMORY WOKE UP on the sofa, the light shining through the den windows. It took her a moment to realize where she was. She raised her head from the pillow, and saw Mason asleep, his left arm draped across her chest. *I slept next to a married man. Not good.* She wiggled out from under his arm and hustled into her bathroom to shower quickly before her morning photo shoot. With no time to wash her hair, she threw it into a messy bun and quickly got dressed. She grabbed her equipment, a banana, and a bottle of water, then jotted a quick note, placing it on top of Mason's cell phone. *I shouldn't have kissed him, but it felt so good.* She touched his hair lightly and sighed before slipping out the door.

He awoke at the sound of the door, running his hands over his eyes, seeing Emory wasn't there. He peeked in her room and saw she wasn't there either. He noticed a picture of her and Eric on her dresser and cringed, massaging his arm aching from the night on the sofa. It was all quiet. He walked back to the den and saw a note on his phone. *Had to work. Need to talk. Meet at 3 in your hotel lobby. Em.*

Mason took a cab back to his hotel. Instead of going inside, he grabbed a coffee at a deli across the street. Three o'clock seemed so far away. *What does she want to talk about? Our past? Future? Eric?* He hoped Eric wouldn't be trouble. *What if she's still in love with him?* Eric obviously wanted her back. Mason knew how that felt.

He walked aimlessly around some streets, sipping his coffee, a few people staring as he wandered. He sensed they knew his face from somewhere, but couldn't place it exactly. Such was the life of a journeyman quarterback in the NFL—one who'd never fully reached his potential. He walked past a boyfriend and girlfriend holding hands, unconcerned by time or place, without a care in the world.

They stopped in the middle of the sidewalk and kissed for no apparent reason. He missed those days.

Mason turned a corner and saw a church across the street. He stopped and stared, drawn to its beauty, admiring its stately red brick facade. The heavy iron doors swung open, as the faithful filed out from Sunday morning mass. He walked closer to the church and came upon a bronze nameplate: St. Peter's Catholic Church, established 1851, currently run by the Jesuits. He looked up at the towering steeple.

It had been years since Mason saw the inside of a church, probably not since Steven's wedding. He regularly attended pre-game Sunday services, but he and Alexis never attended mass together during the off-season—not even Christmas or Easter. He regretted allowing his Catholic faith to take a backseat during his marriage. He wasn't raised that way. His life and his own choices had turned him away.

He walked through the doors, dipping his hand in holy water, and made the sign of the cross. A handful of people remained scattered throughout, kneeling in prayer after mass. His eyes scanned over the ceiling and altar, the interior of the church as majestic as the exterior, the stained glass windows illuminating a rainbow across the stone floor. An elderly, dark-skinned priest cleared the altar, while an altar boy blew out two candles nearby.

Mason slid into the last pew and got on his knees. Father Tony walked slowly down the aisle in his direction. Mason saw the altar coverings were violet, signifying it was Lent. He'd totally forgotten —he certainly hadn't given up anything this year. The only seasons he cared about, for as long as he could remember, were football season and off-season. That was how he told time. But now he was in a different place, at a different time. He closed his eyes.

God, thank you for bringing Em back into my life. Please let it be for more than these few days. I've made poor decisions, but please allow me a second chance with Em. Lately, I've prayed only for my arm to heal and another chance in the NFL, but I'll give it all up for her.

Father Tony finally made his way down the aisle and put his hand on Mason's shoulder. "We could use you," he whispered. "On

Sundays during the season, I wear a Panthers jersey under my robe. I figure it couldn't hurt."

Mason smiled then spent a few more minutes in prayer before making his way back to his hotel, where he took a short nap followed by room service for a late lunch. He showered and shaved, keeping one eye on the alarm clock in the room. It was thirty minutes until Emory. His mind continued to race, wondering what she wanted to talk about, but his thoughts were interrupted when his phone rang.

"Carolina just faxed me an offer," Steven said, looking at the document, still warm from the transmission. He sat behind his messy desk in his home office, surrounded by a laptop, paperwork, and large binders. Olivia yelled something to him from another room, which he pretended, once again, to ignore. He adored his wife and knew the son she was carrying was a great blessing, but he'd grown tired of her hormonal outbursts, louder and more frequent as her due date approached.

"Finally, some good news."

"I didn't say it was a good offer. In fact, I think it's shit. One year, $1 million. They gave us a week to decide."

Olivia continued to yell. Steven thought it was something about a food craving but couldn't be sure. It was time for business. He didn't have the energy or patience to ask what she was saying. He banged his pen against his head and closed his office door with his foot.

"That fucking blows." Mason plopped on the bed.

"We still have Seattle. Maybe they will both want you, and we can get them into a bidding war." Steven rambled on about strategy and possible incentives and whether it made sense to pro-rate any bonus he may receive or not, all while shuffling through his binders and comparing Mason's proposed salary and career statistics with those of other NFL quarterbacks.

Mason traced his fingers along the wrinkles of the hotel bed sheets, as his brother droned on. The clock was ticking, and Emory would be in the lobby soon. He wanted to get off the phone, fast.

"Am I boring you, fuck brain?"

"Very much."

"You have something more important to do?"

"Actually, yeah."

Steven slammed a binder shut. "What the hell is that?"

"I'm meeting Em in a few minutes." Mason rose up from the bed and put on some clothes.

Steven sat up straight in his chair. "Um, meeting Emory is more important that the rest of your career?"

"Yep."

"For the love of God." Steven shut another binder, as Olivia yelled to him again. He clenched his fists, shaking them to the heavens.

"I put football in front of Em once, and I'm not about to do it again." Mason took a deep breath. "You should know that. I need her back. That's most important, not football. Football would just be a bonus."

Steven leaned back in his chair and tossed his pen on his desk, knowing his brother was hopeless. "Are you going to tell her about the offer?"

"No. I'm going to wait. I don't want it getting in the way. Don't want her feeling any pressure about it."

Olivia continued to yell something. Steven cracked a smile and laughed; it was better than crying. "Look, dude, Olivia is going crazy, so I've got to go."

"That was her? I've been hearing some strange background noise. Can't believe all that was coming out of little Olivia."

"Yeah, I think it's the hormones or something. And I think she needs food." Steven stood up from his chair. "Do what you need to do. I'm your agent but also your brother. It's about time you realized life doesn't always happen on a football field."

* * *

Emory's day passed quickly. She had a shoot with a young mother pregnant with twins, then slaved in front of her computer to crop and edit her last several sessions. She hated the technical aspect of her work; her background in the arts, in dance, didn't translate to computer proficiency. It was spending time with her little clients that she enjoyed. She texted Wesley about her meeting with Mason.

She was having second thoughts, worrying about getting involved with a married man, especially one who'd left her before. She feared Mason wanted nothing more than a good time, for a short time, and she wasn't prepared to share the secrets she carried. She also knew he would be in Seattle the next day. *I need to shut this down.* But her mind was at war with itself. It felt so good to be with him again, to touch him, to feel his warm, soft lips on hers.

* * *

Mason stood in the hotel lobby, watching other guests check in at the front desk. He saw the hotel bartender, Clive, walking towards the Atrium Bar to begin his shift, and gave him a nod. Mason sat down in a chair and fidgeted with some hotel brochures to pass the time, then decided it was more appropriate to stand and wait for Emory. Mason's breath caught, as he spotted her coming through the glass turnstile doors. They smiled at each other, and he walked towards her, wrapping his good arm around her, lifting her slightly off the floor, followed by an awkward moment of silence.

Her note said she wanted to talk, but she didn't seem to have anything to say. Emory darted her eyes away from him, still embarrassed by their kiss and encounter with Eric. Mason sensed her discomfort. "Want to have a drink?"

"Sure." *Don't let him get you drunk.*

He took her hand and led her through the lobby, Emory looking at him curiously, as they walked past the Atrium Bar, continuing on to the elevator bank.

"I thought we were going to the bar for a drink?" Emory motioned back to the bar and bartender in her rear view.

"There's a bar in my room."

Emory narrowed her eyes at him. *He's not going to make this easy on me.*

Waiting for the elevator to arrive, she fidgeted with her hair, and Mason stole a glance back at Clive, who gave him a suggestive smile and thumbs-up. The bell dinged. Mason placed his arm on the small of Emory's back and followed her inside. As the door closed, Mason gave a final look to Clive, gyrating his old hips in an awkward, circular motion. *I hope Emory didn't see that.*

They rode up in silence to the top floor of the hotel. Mason led her towards his room; he couldn't help but recall walking with Emory down another hotel corridor many years ago. This walk was different, but the same excitement and nervousness came with it.

* * *

Steven emerged from his home office, massaging his temples. The Panthers were playing games; his client and brother was an unfocused mess; and his wife's pregnancy was pushing him to the limit. He pulled his thinning hair and walked into the kitchen. "Honey, are you OK?"

Olivia sat at the kitchen table, eating ice cream out of the carton with one hand, twirling the natural curls of her red hair with the other. "I'm better now," she said, digging out a huge scoop.

To everyone who saw her, Olivia had maintained her petite frame, but she thought her pregnancy had turned her into a beached whale. Steven assured her she had not—not even close—but she didn't believe him. Her hormones wouldn't allow it.

"Is there anything you need?"

"Not anymore."

Steven massaged his temples again. "Do we have any aspirin?"

"I don't know," she said, licking the spoon.

"What was all the yelling about? I was working."

She held the spoon in the air, then shrugged. "I don't remember."

Steven walked to the refrigerator and reached for a beer. It was mid-afternoon, but drinking seemed the best and only thing to do.

"Get me some whipped cream out of there!"

Steven grabbed a beer and whipped cream and walked to the table. "I just talked to Mason." Steven placed the whipped cream in front of her and sat down. He popped the top of his can and stroked her back. "He's caught back up with Emory."

Olivia put down her spoon. "Oh my God! Good for him."

"Yeah." He took a swig.

"From everything I've heard about her, she sounds terrific. I hope things work out this time." She sprayed whipped cream all over the ice cream still inside the carton. Steven watched her curiously, then took a long swig. "I'm just glad that he's done with that whore Alexis."

"Jesus, Olivia! Don't hold back."

"I never do."

* * *

Emory looked around Mason's hotel room. It was no ordinary room; it was bigger than Emory's apartment. The bedroom was separate from the main living area, with a pool table and full dining set, and also a wet bar. A massive flat screen television hung over the fireplace. The bathroom was bigger than her bedroom.

"The Panthers went all out for my visit."

Emory made her way to the balcony, looking down at the pool and surrounding gardens below, the Charlotte skyline and Bank of America Stadium in the distance. Mason watched her intently from inside, as he had done before in another hotel room, her curves just as magnificent. Emory, too, remembered the first room, closing her eyes and biting her lip. *I need to get control of myself.* She opened her eyes, startled Mason had come up beside her.

He slid his arm around her waist and leaned his forehead onto hers. "It was the best weekend of my life."

How the hell did he know what I was thinking? She took a deep breath to compose herself. "Me, too. But that was a long time ago."

Mason crouched down to look into her eyes. "We can have all that back. We can make it right."

"That's your busted arm and broken marriage talking." Emory walked back inside, and Mason followed behind.

"Is that what you think? I'm not looking for a rebound here, Em." He grabbed her arm gently, hoping she would stop and listen.

"Rebound?" Emory spun around, pushing hard on his chest with both hands. "You married your last rebound!"

Mason took a step back. *So this is what she wanted to talk about.* He braced himself, knowing full well he deserved what was coming.

Emory had waited six years for this moment. "You married her, Mason! Alexis of all people! That slut from your bullshit team parties. You married her! Do you know what that did to me? To see her gloating around campus, with her huge tits, flashing that ring. You fucking married her!"

"I'm sorry," he said softly. "It was a mistake."

"You're damn right!" She walked to the pool table and picked up the cue ball. "You wanted me to give up my dreams and follow you around the NFL like a good little wife, just smiling silently beside her man. You didn't even try to meet me half way. You just gave up and fucking walked away."

"I'm sorry," he said again.

"I heard that already. Shut the hell up!" Emory held the ball in her hand, shaking. "You were the only man I ever loved! You have no idea what I went through after you left me! You have no fucking idea!"

Mason took a step towards her. "I'm here. Tell me."

"There's no point now!" Emory slammed the cue ball on the pool table. "It's over. It's been over."

Mason came towards her, but she walked away. "Not the way I see it. You feel it, too. I'm not giving up no matter how long it takes."

She glared at him. "I will not be your rebound. I am not some easy piece of ass for you to use to ease your broken heart! I will *not* be that."

He shook his head, shocked she thought that was his intention. "Em, you know that's not…"

"Until two days ago, you hadn't even seen me or called me for years. Now you're in for the long haul?"

"I am. It's how I feel." He looked down. "I didn't think you wanted to see me again."

Emory pulled off her shirt, dropping it to the floor, exposing her red lace bra. "Oh, this isn't what you want?" She strutted towards him, unbuttoning her pants. "You don't want to fuck me right here, right now?"

Mason had never seen Emory like this. She was acting crazy. He stepped backwards until he hit the pool table behind him. *If I say no, then I'm rejecting her, and if I say yes, then she thinks this is just about sex. Shit! I can't win here.* She continued her approach, cornering him with only one good arm, hiking her right leg onto the pool table, pushing her body into his. Mason closed his eyes, wanting her, but didn't dare look at or touch her.

Emory sensed his resistance. "You don't want to?" She lowered her leg, then grabbed him, feeling he was erect.

Jesus Christ, is she trying to kill me?

"It seems your body knows exactly what you want." She rubbed him up and down.

Mason knew this wasn't right—that Emory was just trying to prove he was only after sex. "Em?" He placed his hand on her cheek.

"Of course, I want you. I want you every which way. But not like this. And it's not the only thing I want."

Emory brushed his hand aside and slowly slid off her pants, exposing her lace hip-hugger panties.

"Holy shit!" Mason scanned her half-naked body.

Emory licked her lips, her fierce eyes locked to devour him, sliding down his body until she was on her knees. His body trembled with desire. *This is a test! Stay strong!* She unbuttoned his jeans, and slowly pulled down his zipper, revealing a massive erection under his boxer briefs. She moved her hands into his jeans to pull them down, but Mason caught her hand. "Em," he said softly, tilting up her head to look into her eyes. "We can do this, and God knows, I want to. But it won't change what's between us. It won't change how I feel—how I've always felt—about you."

Her fierce eyes melted into tears. She fell back on her heels, holding her head in her hands. Mason buttoned himself up and grabbed a blanket, gently wrapping it around her, pulling her onto his lap. *We did this last night, too. I could get used to this.*

"Please let me go." She tried to wiggle away.

"No." He held her tighter. "I'm not letting you go again. I'm still paying for that mistake."

She stopped wiggling, and Mason took a deep breath. "Leaving you that day is the biggest regret of my life. I'm not sure how we have found each other again, but I'm going to make it right."

"Mason, we have so much baggage—your arm, Alexis, Eric, our own past."

Mason lowered his head, sensing his chance with Emory was slipping away. He was an imposing man, but Emory sensed how vulnerable he was—his tender, sweet soul wide open, and broken. *I'm naked, but he's exposed.* She ran her fingers gently through his hair and kissed his lips softly, a small sparkle appearing in his eyes. She saw the boy she loved. He kissed her nose and forehead.

"Don't you owe me a drink?" she asked playfully.

As Mason walked to the bar, Emory seized the opportunity to put her clothes back on. He peeked at her from behind the bar, and she blushed. "You weren't blushing a few minutes ago." He poured two glasses of wine, setting her glass on the coffee table, and took a seat on the sofa. "So tell me about Eric."

"What about him?" She took a seat next to him and grabbed her glass. "And aren't you still technically married?"

"Separated," he said quickly and took a sip of wine. "And let's not talk about that. You can imagine how that went."

"I can." She took a drink.

Mason still needed to know if Eric was going to be a problem. "So, how long were you and Eric together? What does he do?"

"We were together about a year and a half." Emory turned to face him on the sofa and crossed her legs. "We got engaged about three months ago. He's a pediatric cardiologist here in Charlotte."

"Wow." *A baby heart doctor! How the hell am I supposed to compete with that?*

"We actually broke up an hour before I ran into you at Gus' Bar."

"An hour?" *This had to be divine intervention!* "He obviously still loves you. Are you still in love with him?"

"I do love him," Emory said decisively, sinking Mason's heart. "But I love him like I love Wesley."

Mason released the breath he didn't realize he was holding. "Then why were you engaged to him?"

"Well, why did you marry Alexis?" she fired back.

Mason fidgeted at the mention of her name. "When you were screaming at me a few minutes ago, I told you that was a mistake."

She smiled, slightly embarrassed by what she'd done. "Getting engaged was a mistake, too. It was wrong to be more than friends. I convinced myself that we could base a marriage on friendship and because of that I hurt him badly."

Mason caressed her hand, and Emory drew a deep breath. "Do you still love Alexis?"

"Our relationship was *never* about love. It was about career and convenience."

"But you married her!" Emory drew her legs into her chest. "I know you were screwing her within days of our break-up."

"You don't know that!" Mason objected.

"Oh, please! Don't even bother saying shit like that."

Mason walked to the bar and refilled his glass, Emory following him with her eyes. "How could you do that? I thought you loved me. I was going through hell, and you were off screwing that bitch!"

Mason winced hearing her doubt his love. *I never stopped loving you.* He poured some extra wine in his glass. He needed her to understand why he did what he did back in college, but in hindsight, he didn't totally understand it himself. "Look, Em, after we fell apart, I was sad and on the verge of an NFL career." He walked back to the sofa. "I didn't want to do that alone. I was scared, and she was there. Things moved fast. She had no problem making my career her priority." He sat down and put his hand on her knee. "I thought that meant she loved me, and I thought that was enough."

Emory shook her head and cracked a smile. "That is so fucking dumb."

"I know. I was young and stupid." He raked his fingers through her hair. "I've made a mess of my life, but want a chance to fix it."

Emory got up from the sofa and walked to the window, staring out to the skyline, remembering she'd waited for hours for Mason to come back to her in the weight room, and even for years after. And now he had. But Emory wasn't sure about a second chance, still angry he'd left and moved on so quickly with Alexis. It still hurt, but some part of her could understand settling for someone less than perfect. *Eric.* If she got back together with Mason, she wondered whether she'd be treating Eric the same way Mason had treated her with Alexis. She didn't want to hurt Eric like she'd been hurt but knew she still loved Mason. Time, Eric, Alexis, and her own secrets hadn't changed that. *Maybe I should tell him the whole truth?*

She felt his arm slide around her waist, and his lips graze her ear. "I'm so sorry, Em. Please give me another chance. I'll do whatever it takes."

While her mind raced, there was no doubt in her heart she would give him another chance. She looked up into his eyes, waiting eagerly for her answer. "We need to take this very slowly," she cautioned.

He smiled broadly, hugging her tightly. "I can do slow. We can also go back over to the pool table. Either way is fine."

"Don't make fun of me."

"I'm kidding. Look, let's order room service and spend the night in. I don't want to let you out of my sight until I leave for the airport in the morning."

"That's not exactly taking it slow," she said. "But you know I'm always up to eat."

After room service, they spent hours together, talking and laughing about everything and nothing. It was as if their carefree college days had returned. As midnight approached, Mason whispered, "Stay."

Emory held firm. "Not tonight."

Mason pulled her onto his lap and delivered a long, deep kiss. He then put Emory in her car and asked her to text him when she arrived home safely. "I'll be back from Seattle as quick as I can."

"I'll be waiting."

* * *

Emory floated into her apartment, finding Wesley and Tomás cuddling on the sofa to an all-night action movie marathon, a bowl of popcorn on the coffee table.

"Hey, honey," Wesley said. "I was about to call the SWAT team."

Emory removed her shoes. "I could have used their help at one point."

Tomás sat up. "What? Did he hurt you?" He held out the popcorn bowl to her. "Do you need food?" Wesley smacked his arm.

"No, I nearly hurt *him*." She tossed her purse on the chair. "SWAT would have been good back-up though. I'll give you the break-down tomorrow."

"OK, dear," Wesley said, focusing his attention back to the television.

Tomás never cared for action movies, hating violence of any kind. But he watched, or rather endured, them for Wesley. It also gave him an opportunity to prepare a snack, even if it was simply popcorn.

"Oh, this is a good part!" Wesley called out.

Emory looked at the television and laughed. "Why can't you two watch musicals like normal gay guys?"

"I told him West Side Story was on," Tomás said, again offering popcorn to Emory, and she took a handful.

"You are one to talk, Emory," Wesley said. "Always crying in action movies."

Emory shrugged. "It's sad when so many people die and so brutally."

"I completely agree," Tomás said, patting the sofa cushion for her to sit beside him. "By the way, I need you to help me convince your stubborn roommate about something."

Emory raised her eyebrows. "Oh?" She took a seat next to Tomás. "This sounds intriguing."

Wesley pivoted his eyes from the television to Tomás. "Now is not the time! Don't try to get her on your side to gang up on me. I just want to watch the marathon!"

"Be quiet, Wesley. Don't talk to Tomás that way. He's my friend, too." Emory kissed Tomás on the cheek.

Wesley threw his hands in the air, paused the movie, then stuffed his mouth with popcorn.

"Go ahead, Tomás," she said.

Tomás looked at Wesley, then Emory. "Did Wesley tell you his little sister is getting married?"

Emory gave a sideways glance to Wesley. "No, he did not."

"Well, she invited Wesley and me to the wedding, but he doesn't want to go. He's being a little bitch about it."

"A little bitch? I don't want to distract from her day," Wesley said.

"She invited you, so she wants you there," Emory said. "She obviously doesn't think you'll be a distraction. I don't see what the problem is."

"I know my parents will cause a fuss, and I don't want that for her." Wesley reached for the remote. "Just drop it, both of you, and let's watch the movie."

"Put that down," Emory said. "I think it's great she invited you. It's great she's reached out to you the past few years. It's great you two have gotten closer."

Tomás nodded. "I think it's great, too."

"Nothing about my family is great," Wesley told them.

Emory took Wesley's hands in hers. "You know I love you more than anything, but Tomás is right. Your sister wants you there, and it's her day. She knows the risk she's taking and doesn't care because she loves you and is proud to have her brother there."

Wesley rolled his eyes, as Emory received a text on her phone. *Em, please let me know you got home OK. Can't sleep until you do.*

She put Wesley's hand on Tomás' hand and stood up from the

sofa. "No fighting—except in the movie. And this isn't over, Wesley. We'll talk about it more tomorrow." She walked towards her room, typing her response on the way. *Sorry, home safe. Minor gay emergency. Em.*

CHAPTER EIGHT

MASON SLEPT ONLY a few hours before catching a cab to the airport. It was early morning, but he wasn't tired, feeding off adrenaline, like before a big game. A woman so breathtakingly beautiful, once lost, had now been found. He walked briskly to the gate to head out to Seattle, wishing he could hear her voice, but a text would have to do. He was anxious to send it but thought to wait a bit, figuring she was still asleep and a ding could wake her. He waited until he boarded the plane. *Missed you all night. Taking it slow SUCKS! See you soon.*

* * *

Emory read Mason's text when she got up and smiled to herself, happy he thought about her before leaving, and that she hadn't stayed the night. She wanted to keep some mystery to their relationship; after all, they'd only seen each other for a few days. She replied to his text quickly, even though she knew he was mid-flight. She pulled herself out of bed, the unmistakable smell of a country breakfast calling her into the kitchen. She found Tomás making eggs, bacon, and biscuits.

"Wesley still mad?" she asked, twisting her hair into a messy bun.

"Yeah, still being a little bitch." He smiled and plated the eggs and bacon. "He's pretty pissed at me for telling you."

"Well, he'll just have to get over it." She sipped some juice. "You guys should go to the wedding, no doubt."

Tomás brought the plates to the table and sat down. "Maybe he's embarrassed of me."

"That's not it." She patted his arm. "He was so proud of you at the club a few days ago."

"That's different than bringing me to his family." Tomás folded a piece of bacon and took a bite.

"He's just scared, that's all." Emory devoured her eggs. "This is fantastic, by the way."

Tomás smiled and took a sip of juice. "He's just worried about his sister and his parents, too. It's not the same as your family."

Tomás was raised in a strict Catholic, working class household. His family often moved to wherever his parents could find work, always bringing with them a small stone statue of Mary displayed on their front lawn. They attended Sunday mass each week, and occasionally prayed the rosary on a weeknight. His grandmother, who lived with them, went to daily mass. They instilled in him a charitable heart, though they never had much; they always found something to give—even if it was a warm meal. In his early twenties, Tomás worried whether and when to come out to his family, concerned how they would take it, and whether they would cut off all contact with him. He gathered the courage after mass one Sunday. To his relief, his parents accepted him with open arms, and so did his grandmother.

Tomás and Emory heard footsteps and froze as Wesley came into the kitchen. "Thick as thieves." He grabbed some juice and a biscuit from the counter and took a seat next to Tomás and Emory, both looking down, slightly embarrassed to be caught talking behind his back. Wesley opened his biscuit with a knife. "So, little miss, want to fess up to what you were doing yesterday?"

"Well, it depends," she said. "Before or after, I threw my half-naked body at Mason?"

Wesley dropped the knife. "Excuse me?"

Tomás raised his eyebrows and gave her a smile. "It was just for a little while," she said playfully.

"How little?" Wesley munched on his biscuit.

"Not too long."

"How naked?"

"I told you—about half."

"Which half?"

"A little of both."

"Both breasts?"

"No. Top and bottom."

"Is that so?" Wesley took a sip of his drink, thoughtfully considering what she'd said, like he was some kind of philosopher. "Any action?"

"I tried."

"How hard?"

"Pretty hard."

"Was he?" Wesley grinned at Tomás and took another bite of his biscuit.

"Shut up," she said blushing. "We decided it was best to take things slow."

"That's too bad," Wesley said, and Tomás slapped his arm. "In all seriousness, I'm happy for you."

"Me too," Emory said, rising from the table with her and Tomás' plates.

Wesley grabbed her shoulder and whispered in her ear, "Did you tell him?" Emory shook her head walking to the sink, and Wesley shot her a disapproving look. Tomás eyed them both curiously. "He deserves to know!"

Tomás mouthed to Wesley, "Know what?" Wesley shook his head that it was none of his business.

"No lectures, Wesley." She scrubbed the plates. "Let me enjoy myself and Mason before I ruin it."

"You need to stop running," Wesley said.

"I'll stop when you stop."

Tomás had no idea what they were bickering about, but whatever it was, he knew that was a great response. Emory wiped her hands on a kitchen towel, then walked towards her bedroom, yelling back to Wesley, "That means go to your sister's wedding!"

* * *

Mason was not a high profile NFL player and never carried himself that way. He never flaunted his money, which was relatively modest by NFL standards. He was not one to drive fancy cars or buy expensive jewelry or live in a huge mansion on acres of land. Sure, he could afford some of those luxuries, and liked them, but found no pleasure in sharing those things with Alexis. When she complained, as she often did, that he was too cheap, it made him happy. As much as he could, Mason didn't want her to overly enjoy the trappings of an NFL lifestyle.

His flight to Seattle from Charlotte, while ridiculously long, was a treat. The Seahawks had put Mason in first class. He sat in an aisle seat, on the left side of the cabin, the sling holding his right arm slightly extending into the aisle. The leather seat was nice, and so were the drinks and extra room. Still, he had to contort his long muscular legs to squeeze within the confines of his area.

A young flight attendant with a cute smile and tight uniform worked the first class section, paying Mason special attention each time she brought him a drink. He was pleasant to her, but his mind was filled with visions of Emory in a red lace bra and panties on a pool table. *When will I get that chance again?* He hated she left at midnight, and that he was now flying across the country. They had so much more to catch up on after six years. He missed her already.

The plane touched down. After a few moments on the runway, the cute attendant grabbed the intercom, giving permission to the passengers to use their electronic devices. Mason reached for his phone in his pocket, and the plane jerked as it made a turn towards the gate, causing Mason to fumble his phone into the aisle. He had no chance to reach it, with his right arm in the sling. The cute attendant rushed to his aid and bent down in the aisle, holding her position to give Mason a clear view of her assets. After a moment, she came up smiling, handing the phone to him. Mason politely thanked her, and she glided back to her seat.

But Mason had no time for her. He wanted to find out quickly whether Emory had responded to his text. He pressed the power button on his phone, seeming to take an eternity to come on. The plane continued towards the gate, as his phone came to life. The plane stopped at the gate, and the seatbelt light turned off. He saw he had a message. *I recall you like slow SUCKS... Text me when you land.*

Mason unbuckled and stood up from his seat, smiling widely, then walked past the cute attendant to exit the plane. She smiled, too, but Mason ignored her, reading Emory's text over and over again. As he walked down the jetway, he typed his response. *Naughty girl. Just landed.* Mason strolled into the gate, still smiling and looking at his phone, walking right by Steven, as he hit send.

"Hey, dumb ass," Steven said, grabbing Mason's good arm to slow him down.

Mason looked up. "Sorry, didn't see you there." He gave his older brother a sideways hug, then they walked through the Seattle airport together.

"What's so interesting about your phone?"

"None of your fucking business."

"Her name wouldn't happen to be Emory, would it?"

Mason shrugged, but couldn't hold back a huge grin, giving himself away.

"This is a business trip," Steven said. "We need to get serious."

"OK." Mason chuckled, then veered into Steven's path, bumping into him.

Steven shoved his brother away. "Dude, what the hell?"

"I'm sorry, man." Mason steadied himself, then tried to walk straight.

"Have you been drinking?"

"Just a little. It was a long flight. And it's been stressful the last few days. Fun, too—don't get me wrong."

"Jesus Christ!" Steven quickened his pace. "Better straighten shit out. You've got a medical evaluation in a few hours."

"I'll be fine." Mason walked faster to try to keep up.

"I hope so. If you act like a clown and fuck things up with the doc today, we're not even going to have a chance to meet with the GM tomorrow."

* * *

Emory looked around her bedroom, sorting through her past. Thankfully, there was rather little to sort. It surprised her—she had spent years with Eric—but he'd never left much at her apartment. *Were we really together for almost two years?* Eric preferred to keep his stuff at his house, in the order and places he liked them. She saw her phone and a picture of them on her dresser. She stared at it, but couldn't remember where or when the picture was taken. She grabbed it and put it in a box. She picked up her phone, biting her lip upon reading Mason's text.

She returned to the business at hand. She picked up Eric's toothbrush and a few other toiletry items in the bathroom. She put them next to the picture in the box. She walked into the den and grabbed a wedding magazine from the bookshelf; Eric had given it to her weeks ago, but she never opened it. She rested it on top of the photo and toiletries, burying them below.

She drove to Eric's house, knowing he would be in surgery for the day. It was the perfect time to return his items and collect hers, without any more awkward conversation or fighting. She didn't have the energy for any of that. She entered Eric's house with the box under her arm, and her purse over her shoulder, placing them both on a table in the foyer. She removed his key from her keychain and put it on top of the box.

Emory looked around for anything she may have left in the house, going from room to room. There was little there, except for some pictures of them in the den. She decided she had no use for those and moved towards the master bedroom and bathroom. She had a few toiletry items to gather, and thought she may have left a shirt or two in Eric's closet. She entered the bedroom and saw a light on in the bathroom through the cracked door. *Shit! Is he here?*

"Eric?" Emory gently pushed open the bathroom door. "Oh my God!" She covered her eyes, hiding the horrible vision of Eric in the shower with some woman. She fled to the foyer and quickly grabbed her purse, but in her rush, spilled the contents on the floor—her lip-gloss, spare change, a black-and-white photo, everything.

"Damn!" Emory knelt down, hurrying to get everything back in her purse. She then reached for her keys in her pockets, but couldn't find them. She panicked, fumbling around in her purse, then hunting around on the floor for them. She saw bare feet and looked up.

Eric stared down at her, only a towel around his waist. "See anything you like?"

She stood up from the floor, his question making her sick. "I thought you had surgeries today. I told you I was coming."

"Change of plans," he said flatly.

Emory sensed this was a set-up. "Is this some attempt to make me jealous?"

"Is it working?"

"No." Emory shook her head, and laughed. "It's pathetic."

"Like you sleeping with that jerk the day after we broke up?"

Emory put her hands on her hips, expecting better of Eric, never thinking he'd try to hurt her. She figured that seeing Mason had put him over the edge, but she was in no mood to be sympathetic. "Eric, I'm not sleeping with Mason." She looked him up and down. "And I don't see anything I like. But think what you want—I don't give a shit."

Emory turned back to her purse in search of her keys and headed for the front door. She then heard a familiar high-pitched, squeaky voice. "Eric, come back to the shower."

She stopped in her tracks and twirled around, staring daggers at Eric. "Her?"

"Yeah, she's not afraid of marriage."

Emory raised her eyebrows. "You're going to marry Molly now? That was fast."

"Who knows?"

"Well, if everything works out," Emory said, with a slight laugh, "she can plan you guys a destination wedding."

Her words—the mention of marriage—stung Eric, realizing he should have just kept his surgery schedule, and none of this would have happened. His plan to shock Emory in the hopes of getting her back had gone horribly wrong. Emory again headed towards the front door, but Eric had one final effort in him. He ran between her and the door, and placed his hands on her shoulders, then lowered his hands to her arms, stroking them tenderly. "Emory, I'm so sorry. You're right. This was childish and vindictive, and..." He pulled her into his arms and kissed her forcefully, pinning her against the wall.

Emory tried to pull away, swatting at him. "Stop, stop!"

Molly entered the foyer, wearing only a towel that barely covered her large breasts, and saw Eric and Emory wiggling around together. "Well, well, well," she squeaked. "This is awkward."

Startled, Eric released her, and Emory quickly slipped out the door, slamming it behind her. He opened it, calling after her, with his voice shaking, as Emory continued to run to her car, searching her pockets for her keys as she ran and luckily finding them.

Eric closed the door and leaned his head against it, defeated. "Want to get back in the shower?" Molly asked, dropping her towel.

CHAPTER NINE

EMORY ARRIVED HOME WITH her chest pounding, knowing only one thing could settle her. She threw on a leotard and went down to Wesley's dance studio. It was dark and empty. She flicked on the lights and stood at the ballet barre, trying to calm down. *Breathe, first position.* She prepared and stretched with her eyes closed, feeling her body relax and mind lift from the day's drama. Ballet was her therapy and expression, a means for balance and control. When life failed her, the barre never did. It had been there since she was four, when her mother died and her father enrolled her in dance. *Mom, I need you.*

Emory and her mother, as they did every Friday night in the fall, drove towards the high school stadium to cheer on her father, John and his team. High school football in Georgia was serious business, as important to the faithful as Sunday service. John took pride that his little daughter often paced the sidelines with him, both before and during games. Sometimes Emory chose to stay in the stands with her mother, cheering with the crowd, enjoying the band and dance team, and stuffing her face with snacks and soda. On those nights, Emory went down to the field when the game ended to have round of catch with her dad.

One night, Emory didn't show up on the sidelines during the game. John assumed they were in the stands. But Emory was still in her car seat, her mother slumped over the steering wheel, their car twisted around a telephone pole, the work of a drunk driver who plowed into their car on a poorly-lit backroad near the stadium, killing himself and her mother instantly. Secured by her car seat, Emory didn't suffer a scratch but couldn't unhook herself, ripping at the buckles with her little hands to free herself. But as hard as she tried, she couldn't get out. She began screaming and crying for her mother to talk or move, furiously kicking her mother's seat in front of her, hoping to stir her mother to life. Emory kicked and kicked and kicked, until the game ended and help arrived. Her mother was dead at twenty-eight.

John had no idea how to care for, or console, a four-year-old girl. He was a grizzled football coach with a knack for motivating boys on and off the football field and just couldn't get through to his baby girl, who seldom spoke and seemed to have forgotten how to laugh. She preferred to cry, freely and often. He took a few weeks off from coaching—for himself and Emory—and returned for a game against a division rival. Emory sat alone on a bench on the sidelines with no interest in the game. John occasionally looked at her during the game, but she didn't respond. She missed her mother.

There was a timeout on the field, and the school band struck up the school fight song. Emory looked into the crowd, the dance team capturing her attention, swaying and stomping and moving in unison in the bleachers. Her face lit up, a huge smile crossed her lips, and she began to dance, her blonde pigtails bouncing as she did. Players surrounded her on the sidelines and danced along with her, encouraging her, as the crowd roared with delight. John turned his attention from the field, wondering what was the fuss during the timeout. He looked along the sidelines, and saw his daughter dancing and smiling —with his players and the crowd cheering her on. A tear came into his eye. The next day, he enrolled Emory in ballet, and she thrived.

A thin layer of sweat covered Emory as she danced in Wesley's studio. Ballet had rescued her when she was four, and when her relationship with Mason ended, and at other times she preferred to forget. It would now cleanse her from Eric's unwelcome touch. She was twenty-eight—on the verge of out-living her mother—and wondering where her life was going.

The studio door opened. "Emory, are you OK?" Wesley asked, knowing she only danced this intensely, and this long, when something was wrong.

Emory slowed her movement. "I'm good. Better now."

"You've been down here for hours."

"Really? I lost track."

"I've got a class soon. Is your ankle OK?"

"Fine." She grabbed a towel and patted her skin.

"What happened?" Emory told him about her encounter with Eric, during which Wesley expressed some interest in the size and shape of Eric's towel. Emory laughed, then assured Wesley she was fine, and would be even better after a shower and some dinner. She kissed his cheek and left.

* * *

Mason spent ten minutes which seemed like an hour trapped inside an MRI machine. He had to remain still, but his stomach churned. It wasn't just the alcohol from the morning flight, or that his body was slightly off from the time change, or the tight, spinning space and intermittent clicking he heard as the machine spit out pictures. He was anxious to hear from Emory. He'd texted and called several times since landing in Seattle, but no response. *Where is she? With Eric?*

A female nurse entered the room with Steven close behind. "All done," she said, pressing some buttons on a computer. Mason scooted out of the machine and reached for his phone.

"Everything go OK?" Steven asked her. Mason didn't look up, his fingers moving quickly on his phone.

"Fine," she said. "The doctor will take a look at the films this afternoon." She picked up some supplies and left the room.

"Dude, give it a rest! She's probably just banging a few guys while you're out of town."

"Fuck you," Mason said, as Steven took out his phone.

"You calling Olivia again? What's that, six times today?"

"She's pregnant, stupid. Let me just check in, and then we can head to the hotel."

* * *

After a shower and an early dinner, Emory needed to make some long overdue calls. She picked up her cell, which she'd forgotten that morning, and the battery was dead. She charged it in the den and used her land line in her room to tell several friends and family members about her break-up with Eric. They were sympathetic and sorry, but not really surprised. She decided not to mention Mason.

Emory had one last phone call to make. She put on a brave face and dialed, then paced around her room anxiously, hoping she could just leave a voicemail, not wanting to talk to her father about the break-up. Her father had been through enough in his life—she never wanted to burden him with anything else. When Mason broke up with her, she didn't talk to him for weeks because she knew he'd force the truth from her, and she didn't want him to bear it. *Let him enjoy his life without worrying about my drama.*

On the fifth ring, John picked up, startling her. "Hi, Daddy." She put a hand behind her neck, trying to calm the hairs sticking up, and sat on her bed.

"Hi, baby girl." John was alone in his office, dressed in a baggy sweatsuit, drawing plays on a chalkboard. It seemed he hadn't shaved, or left the office, in a week. He took a seat in an old chair behind his messy desk, covered with plays scribbled on napkins and an empty pizza box sitting to the side.

John still coached the same high school team in the same Georgia town, a few hours outside Atlanta. While Emory always dreamed of getting out, and college provided that, John couldn't leave and didn't want to anyway. He was a local hero, having shaped the lives of his players for decades. His former quarterback was the town sheriff; the largest defensive tackle he ever coached now sold real estate; and a speedy cornerback owned the local grocery store. John loved that his players, for the most part, remained in town to work and raise their families, and had turned out to be good and decent men. He didn't want to leave them. He also couldn't leave where his wife had died and was buried. He couldn't imagine living anywhere else, though he wished he saw his daughter more often. "You usually call after Sunday mass. I was beginning to get worried."

"How are you doing, Daddy?"

"I'm fine. Just ate some dinner. Now fiddling around with some new plays and some new schemes."

"Offense or defense?"

"Defense." He looked down at the mess in front of him and scratched his head.

"Thinking about changing to a 3-4 defense?"

His face perked up. "Well, yes I am. How'd you know we've been running a 4-3?"

"Daddy, you know I keep up with the team on the Internet."

Emory smiled, stretching out on her bed, trying to relax. "Read some stories here and there about the team."

"We've got some kids graduating, and next year I don't think we'll have the horses to stay with a 4-3. But I don't expect you called to talk about my defense."

Emory sighed. "No, I didn't."

"What is it, baby?" John sat up straight in his chair, rubbing the stubble on his face. "You can tell me anything."

"I know." She nervously twirled her hair. "It's just hard."

"Emory?" John said, the concern in his voice growing.

Emory sat up in bed and took a deep breath. "Eric and I broke off the engagement." John didn't respond, other than to let out a wry smile that Emory would never see. "Daddy, did you hear me?"

"Sure," he said, "I just wanted to make sure you were through talking."

"Daddy, now please don't worry. I'm fine. Eric just wasn't the guy for me. On paper, we seemed perfect, but my heart just didn't, well, I just didn't..." Emory stammered, her voice breaking, unable to find the words to express herself.

"Oh, honey. I'm not worried."

"You're not?"

"No. Let me ask you a question. Did you break it off?"

"Yes."

"Good for you."

"Good?"

"Absolutely," he said, proud of his daughter. "You know your name means strength. You make the decisions. And usually good ones."

* * *

Mason and Steven got out of a limo and checked into their hotel. The Seahawks, like the Panthers before them, spared no expense in rolling out the red carpet, putting the brothers in adjoining suites on a high floor overlooking the Space Needle. They quickly dropped off their bags and took the elevator back down to the lobby to decide on a place to eat, a hard rain lashing against the windows.

"It wasn't raining when we checked in," Steven observed, as

Mason stared at his phone. "I heard it rains something like 250 days a year here. That's fucking insane."

"Yeah," Mason muttered, typing another text to Emory.

"Dude, you are so pussy-whipped."

"Shut up, weatherman." Mason put his phone in his pocket.

Steven laughed, thinking Mason's dig was rather funny, and decided to give his hopeless, little brother a pass. "Where are we eating tonight?" Steven wanted to talk strategy with Mason about the Seahawks meeting the next day. He also, as instructed by Olivia, needed to get the scoop on Mason's new relationship with Emory, if it even was a relationship. Dinner, he hoped, would be a time to put down the phones, and get to talking.

But Mason again ignored his brother and just stared at the falling rain. *Where the hell is she?* A phone dinged, both brothers reaching quickly for their phones. It was another text from Olivia to Steven.

"I'm just going back up to the room," Mason said, sulking. "I'll get room service."

Steven couldn't decide who was worse company: his love-sick brother or hormone-crazed, pregnant wife. "Do what you want, bro. The weatherman is going out."

* * *

John was excited by Emory's news but would never say so. He tried not to meddle in his daughter's life, but when an opportunity presented itself, he took it. He stood up from his desk and walked to the chalkboard. "Let me tell you something, Emory." He picked up a piece of chalk and began to doodle. "I know you don't remember your mother very well, and I never wanted to bring another woman into your life, and maybe that was wrong, because you never saw growing up what true love looks like."

Emory's eyes filled with tears. "Daddy, please, you don't..." She grabbed a tissue from her nightstand and dabbed her eyes.

"No, no, baby," he said. "Your mother was the most beautiful woman I ever saw. She was the first thing I thought of in the morning and my last thought at night. Still is. She made my life so full of love. Still does. She gave me you." Emory reached for a picture of her mother on her dresser, pressing it against her heart. "Every night after you'd go to sleep, we would dance in the kitchen to that old radio. I can still remember how she smelled like lemons from the dish soap."

He continued to doodle, and Emory reached for another tissue. "I placed a rose on her pillow on our anniversary each year." John took a quick step back from the chalkboard to admire his progress, seeing it was coming together. "I still do that every year on our anniversary. Then I take the rose to your mom." He turned the chalk on its side for shading.

"Oh, Daddy," Emory said, sniffling.

John finished his work and sat back in his chair, admiring the rose he'd drawn. "My point is this. I never saw you and Eric that way. He was nice enough and would take good care of you. But I want you to have what your mother and I had. You deserve that. And you weren't going to have it with him."

She heard her phone ding in the den and plopped on her bed. "Why didn't you ever say anything?"

"You needed to figure it out for yourself. You did what you thought was best, and so did I."

"What do you mean?"

"I gave Eric permission to marry you—he's a good guy. But I didn't give him your mother's ring to give you. I didn't feel *that* good about him."

Emory laughed. "You've always been a good judge of character."

"Yes, I am. But let's not talk about me." John massaged the stubble on his weathered face. "Who's the new guy?"

Emory sat up in her bed, her heart beating out of her chest, the room spinning wildly. *How does he know?* She didn't dare tell her father. He'd loved Mason—they bonded over Emory and football—but her father had yet to forgive him for breaking her heart.

"Come on, Emory, I know there is someone new. I can hear it in your voice."

She twirled her hair feverishly. "No one *new*."

"Not good enough. Tell your old man, or I will just drag it out of Wesley."

She thought her father was joking—he probably was—but she knew Wesley would be more than happy to gossip about her love life. She couldn't take that chance. After a deep breath, she whispered, "Daniel Mason." Emory braced for her father to yell—like she had heard him so many times at referees for bad calls. But he didn't say anything. He kept quiet, snapping a piece of chalk on his desk, and shoving the empty pizza box on the floor. He squeezed a few napkins for good measure.

"Daddy?"

"Yes, I'm here."

"Well?"

"I'm reserving judgment for a later date."

With that, they talked briefly about her work and his off-season preparations. When she hung up, she heard her phone dinging frantically in the den. She hurried to her phone, seeing multiple texts and missed calls from Mason.

* * *

Mason had lost his appetite. He sat at the dining room table in his hotel suite, staring at his steak, baked potato, and chocolate chip cookie on a side dish. He kept his phone close, on the placemat, running his finger across it. *Ring, you bastard!* And it finally did. *Holy shit!* He immediately hit speaker. "Em!"

"Yep, it's me." Emory sat on the floor of her bedroom, with one hand on her phone and another massaging her left foot.

"Jesus, where have you been?"

"I just saw all your messages," she said. "It's been a long day."

"Bad?"

"I didn't say that. I got caught up in the studio, and then I had to make a lot of phone calls telling everyone about the break-up. Sorry you were worried."

"I was—all day." Mason cut into his steak, his appetite returning.

"I'm sorry. How was your day?"

"Tests, exams, and pouring rain. Sucked."

Emory didn't want to give Mason a chance to bring up Eric. "I called my dad. Told him about you."

"Really?" Mason coughed several times, nearly choking on his bite, then took a sip of water. "How is John? Does he still want to kill me?"

"I'm not sure." She switched to massaging her right foot. "I think his exact words were he was reserving judgment."

"Damn, what does that mean?" Mason recalled the way her father looked at him at graduation, after they'd broken up. It was a look as ferocious as he'd ever seen from a blitzing linebacker. *Fucking crazy eyes!*

"Just keep me happy, and he'll be happy. When are you coming back?" She hadn't lost sight of the fact that he could be moving to Seattle.

"I should be back day after tomorrow, Wednesday, late afternoon. I'll come by straight from the airport."

Emory breathed a sigh of relief. "I'm glad you're coming back to Charlotte."

"I'm going to be wherever you are," he said, adding some pepper to his baked potato and took a bite.

"Oh, really? Do I have any say in that?"

"No!" Mason joked. "Why didn't you answer any of my calls or texts today?"

"I told you I was busy. And I forgot my phone this morning, and when I got home, the battery was dead. Crazy day."

"Any craziness at Eric's place?"

Crap, he hadn't forgotten about that. "It was fine."

"You didn't answer my question," Mason said sharply, carving into his steak with a purpose. "How did things go?"

"I said things went fine."

"This is like pulling teeth. The more you resist, the worse I imagine. You don't know the terrible thoughts I've been having." He gnawed the steak on his fork. "This fucking rain isn't helping my mood either."

Emory sighed. "OK, he was there."

"Shit! I knew he'd be waiting for you."

"It wasn't exactly like that. He was with the wedding planner."

"Was he staging some kind of an intervention?"

"Not quite." Emory giggled. "He was in the shower with her." She bit her tongue to avoid giggling some more, not wanting to provoke Mason further.

"What the fuck!" Mason put down his fork and grabbed the knife. "So you saw him naked?"

"That's what you're concerned about?"

Mason calmed himself, putting the knife down. "Sorry. Had that been going on long?"

"I don't think so. I think he knew I was coming and wanted to make me jealous. That's all."

"Interesting tactic. Did it work?"

"I thought it was pathetic." Emory heard Mason exhale through the phone and felt bad for giggling. It certainly wasn't funny while she was in Eric's house, and she should've known Mason wouldn't find it funny across the country.

"So how did Eric handle your interruption?"

She hesitated, increasing Mason's blood pressure. He stood up from his chair. "Did that fucker put his hands on you?" She hesitated again, and Mason took her silence as an admission, kicking over a dining room chair.

Emory heard a loud crash. "Mason!" He grabbed the baked potato from his plate and fired it towards the garbage can near the entrance of the room, striking it hard, the potato exploding like a bomb, shattering into tiny white bits spraying across the floor.

"Fuck this, I'm coming back." He breathed heavily. "I'll be on the first flight back, and then I'm going to..."

"Mason! Stop!" Emory yelled, rising to her feet.

Her tone startled him, jolting a small amount of sanity into his mind. He paced the room trying to gather himself. "Please tell me exactly what he did."

"Only if you promise to stay in Seattle and finish your contract meetings."

"I won't promise that. If there is one mark on you, I swear to God—I'll take a football and spike it up his medical ass!" Mason kicked the garbage can across the room.

"Mason, you are making it very hard for me to tell you." Emory had forgotten how protective Mason could be. "Please sit down, and try to calm down. Then I'll tell you every detail, if you really want to know."

Mason stepped over the dining room chair and sat in front of his tray, though only the steak and cookie remained. "OK, I'm sitting down now." Emory told him about Eric and Molly and the unwanted kiss, staying calm to make sure Mason did, too. She again apologized for her dead phone battery and not calling sooner.

"Thanks for telling me. I just hate that another guy had his hands on you."

"How do you think I feel about Alexis?"

Mason gnashed his teeth. "Point taken. But Alexis is the only other woman I've been with, and not even in the same league as you."

"Really? No one else?" *He must be the only NFL player who can say that.*

"No. I was married and kept my vows to her."

"So, two women in your whole life?"

"Yes, I'm not particularly proud of that."

She laughed. "I think a low number is good."

"So, what's yours?" Mason braced himself.

"Wow! That's direct," she said, embarrassed by the question. "Can we talk about something else?"

"No."

"Mason, this is very personal. Please don't make me tell you."

Jesus, how high could it be? Teens? Twenties? Mason grabbed his phone and cookie, moved over to the sofa, and stretched out his long body. *Maybe I should just drop this, and we can talk about the rain!* "My question and your answer are personal for me, too." He munched his cookie. "I plan on having you in my bed as soon as you'll allow it, so I think I have a right to know." Mason nodded, pleased with his own logic. *Steven isn't the only smart guy in the family.*

Emory closed her eyes. *Damn, he has a good point.* "Just one," she whispered.

Mason dropped his cookie on the floor and sat up on the sofa. "Can you repeat that? I don't think I heard you right."

"There's only ever been you," she said, blushing.

"But it's been six years! And you were engaged! And traveled Europe for two years!"

"What does Europe have to do with it?" Emory laughed.

"Lots of clubs and kinky sex over there. At least that's what I heard."

"Right, tons. That's all they do over there. And you think I'm into that?"

"Well, remember that one time when we…"

"Shut up. I was so busy studying in Europe that I had no time for anything else."

"What about Eric?"

"It had nothing to do with Eric," she said, her voice cracking. "It had to do with you." Emory explained that her time with Mason was special, and that no one else could compare, and that she'd suffered a lot of grief when their relationship ended. So she guarded her heart carefully, to the point that Eric had to beg her for weeks to go out, and told him she wouldn't make love again until marriage. That was why Eric pushed so hard for a wedding date, which brought an end to their engagement.

Mason couldn't believe what he was hearing. *Dude was OK with that? Will this rule apply to us?* "I'm sorry all that happened, Em, but I'm here now, and I'm not leaving again."

"But if Alexis hadn't left you, would you be with me again? Or are you only with me by default?"

"God, is that what you think? Nothing could be further from the truth. I married her by default."

"But…"

"Em," Mason stopped her, "if I had known I had a chance to be with you again, I would have left her. But you wouldn't see me. I figured I lost you forever. I fell apart without you."

CHAPTER TEN

THE SEAHAWKS, LIKE the past several years, had fallen short of their goals and missed the playoffs. A lack of depth at the quarterback position was a central issue. The starting quarterback had sustained a concussion in the third game and was sidelined for the next six weeks. The Seahawks turned to their rookie quarterback—a late-round draft choice from a small college, with supposedly big upside, who'd shown some promise in pre-draft workouts and threw the ball fairly well in a few pre-season appearances. But nothing can prepare a rookie for the speed and ferocity of an NFL regular season game. Management's belief that he could serve as an adequate back-up turned out to be a huge mistake. The rookie was unprepared and overwhelmed, and so began the demise of another regular season.

The General Manager couldn't afford to have this happen again. His job was on the line. He needed a proven quarterback who could enter a game in a pinch and keep the team afloat if the starter went down. This type of player—the journeyman quarterback with proven ability and some fuel left in the tank—was always in short supply. Quarterbacks in the NFL typically were either very good—the starters and franchise players—or not very good at all—untrust-worthy rookies, draft busts, or over-the-hill veterans. The journey-man quarterback was in a category all his own.

When the season ended, the General Manager targeted Mason as a possible back-up. He compiled binders on Mason's career, his five-year stint in the NFL marked by occasional highs and lows. He started some games and played well, then played poorly in others. In other games, he came off the bench to rally the team to victory, but sometimes he entered a bad game and made it even worse. There seemed to be no rhyme or reason why Mason played well at times and poorly other times. But he was experienced and had the potential to carry a team for a few games, seemingly what the Seahawks needed. His arm was a concern, though. The General Manager didn't want to substitute an unproven rookie with an uncertain arm. It's why he insisted on a thorough medical examination, including an MRI.

Steven and Mason sat across a large conference room table from the General Manager and Head Coach. The General Manager held the medical assessment in his hand. It was full of uncertainty, the doctors not knowing whether the joint was healing properly and whether Mason's arm strength would ever return. It was not the news the General Manager had hoped for, but Mason perhaps could still fit in his plans, though at a reduced price.

The General Manager got straight to the point. "We have real concerns about Mason's arm." He held up the paperwork and slid it across the table to Steven, who reviewed them, then whispered something to Mason, signaling he had things under control.

"We don't," Steven replied firmly, looking the General Manager straight in the eye.

"Of course you're going to say that. All agents say that."

Steven smiled and leaned forward. "So what are we doing here?" Mason looked out the window, raining again.

"Well, we are interested in Mason, but concerned."

"Of course you're interested. You flew us out here. Nice hotel. You need a dependable quarterback. Mason fits the bill. There is no one else on the market like him."

"Right, no one in a sling." The General Manager paused, letting that sink in. "And he's been a bit up and down in the past." Mason turned his eyes from the window and locked onto him. *I left Emory in Charlotte for this shit.*

"Maybe you should draft another rookie in April?" Steven suggested. "That worked out real well for you last season."

The Head Coach rolled his eyes, having heard enough. "Mason, I don't like all this bullshit talk. You and I like football. I think you are a real good quarterback with a lot of potential. I followed you in college and in the NFL. We'd like you to be a part of the team. We wouldn't have flown you out here otherwise."

"That's nice to hear, Coach," Mason replied. "Thanks."

"That doesn't mean we don't have concerns, of course," the Head Coach said, the General Manager nodding in agreement.

"I can tell you, Coach, no one is going to work harder than me to come back from this and play well for you."

"And he will," Steven added.

"But it's not just the shoulder," the General Manager said. "We know you recently separated from your wife. Presumably going to get a divorce. That kind of instability at home can bleed over into the locker room, even onto the field."

Mason's eyes turned fire red, and he clenched his jaw. *I'd like to make you bleed, asshole!* "Like my shoulder, I'm working through that, too," he said, biting his tongue.

"You certainly have come prepared," Steven said, "and we've come prepared, too."

"I'm not surprised," the General Manager said. "I'd expect nothing less from an agent, especially one who has a brother for a client."

"The fact is that we've already received offers from two teams. Just this past week. Substantial offers over several years," Steven bluffed. "They don't share your concerns. Not at all. They are planning on Mason starting next year."

Mason had always known his brother to be a terrible liar. Steven could never get away with anything with Olivia or their mother. But Mason saw that Steven, as a lawyer and agent in a conference room, could take his lies to a different level. He was a professional liar, saving his best lies for business.

"Well, that is certainly good for you," the General Manager said to Mason, then turned to Steven. "Who are these teams?"

"You know we've been talking to the Panthers. I'm keeping the other one close to the vest. If Mason signs with that other team this week, you'll find out on the news. Or it may be the Panthers. I don't know. And I don't really care." Mason was beyond impressed now; he was stunned. Steven was a master of bullshit—a true artist—firing off world class lies. "We'll go where the money is, and where the best fit for Mason is. But if you keep dicking around, wasting our time, you're not even going to be in the game. You'll be drafting another rookie in April."

The General Manager adjusted his body in his chair, and the

Head Coach made clear he'd heard enough. "Give us a chance to talk, and we'll be in touch. OK?"

"That sounds fine," Steven replied. "We promised the other teams we'd get back to them the day after tomorrow."

* * *

Emory didn't feel like cooking dinner and also didn't feel like going out to pick up something. She thought about ordering a meat-lovers pizza for delivery, but chose instead to call Tomás, inviting him to cook dinner for Wesley, still teaching downstairs. She also wanted Tomás' help to convince Wesley to attend his sister's wedding. Tomás agreed to come over, and within thirty minutes, was at the apartment carrying a bag of ingredients to make Wesley's favorite dish, shrimp pasta. Emory greeted him with a glass of wine and took the bag to the kitchen. She boiled water and poured a cup of heavy cream. Tomás deveined two pounds of shrimp and chopped fresh garlic and shallots. When the water began bubbling, she dropped in angel hair pasta.

As they cooked, they discussed a strategy for Wesley. Tomás wondered whether he simply shouldn't attend the wedding with Wesley—perhaps Emory should go with him, which could make Wesley more comfortable in front of his family. Emory considered the idea but suggested it would do more harm than good for Wesley to pretend to be someone he's not. They talked some more, and as they finished the dish, Emory told Tomás the details of her plan, Tomás keeping the dish on very low heat.

"Damn, it smells good in here!" Wesley walked through the door. "You cooking, Emory?" He reached the kitchen and saw Tomás and Emory plating shrimp pasta, knowing exactly what they were up to. "You two think you are so sly." Wesley put his nose down to the frying pan and took in the delicious aroma of garlic and shrimp and shallots.

"Oh, come on, Wesley. Don't get all cranky," Emory said. "We made your favorite." They brought the plates to the table and sat down.

"I'm not ruining a wedding." Wesley lifted his head from the pan.

"Oh, shut up, sit down, and eat," she scolded, "before you ruin everyone's appetite."

Wesley scooted to the table. "This looks great, and I'm starving. Thanks, you guys." He pecked Tomás and Emory both on the cheek. Tomás offered a quick prayer of thanks, and they dug in. There was silence all around, except for the clang of forks against the plates, and the occasional slurp of a noodle and sip of wine. Tomás spoke first, telling them about a new project in a five star hotel, where he was tapped to create a contemporary painting for its opening in a few short weeks. Wesley offered a toast—to his new project and exquisite meal. But Tomás deflected all praise, giving his assistant full credit.

Emory told them about her long day—four photo shoots in three different locations, and one cranky baby who threw up on her. She found time to squeeze in an occasional text with Mason, who was bothered by the tone of the Seahawks meeting—he didn't like to be doubted and hated having his divorce thrown in his face. Wesley said that was good news—it was unlikely Mason would end up there—but Emory couldn't help thinking it was still a possibility. *How would that work?*

Towards the end of dinner, Emory gave a nod to Tomás that it was time to execute her plan. He agreed, but was nervous, hating even the possibility of conflict. Emory handed the phone to Wesley, who looked at her curiously, then looked over at Tomás. Emory again nodded to Tomás, urging him to proceed.

"We think it's time you call your parents," he said.

"What?" Wesley cried.

"We think it would be for the best."

"Oh, you do?" Wesley looked at both of them. "They disowned me!"

Tomás, unsure what to say next, looked to Emory for help, and Wesley saw the exchange.

"Tomás, why are you looking at her?"

"Well," Emory started softly, "remember at the club the other night when I told you I would get you back?"

"Yes."

"It's payback time now."

Wesley had no idea what was going on.

"I had a long conversation with your mom this afternoon, and…"

"You did what?" Wesley narrowed his eyes at Emory and turned to Tomás. "Did you know about this shit?"

"Not at the time," Tomás replied softly. "I just found out while we were cooking."

Wesley turned his venom back to Emory. "This is crossing the line, girl. Way over the fucking line! Obliterating the fucking line! How could you do that?"

Emory calmly placed her hand on his. "I did it because I love you, and guess what, so does your mother."

"Give me a fucking break." Wesley pulled his hand away.

"She said it."

"She loves me so much, she never calls."

"She wants to."

Emory explained that his mother felt terrible about how she and his father had treated Wesley, and desperately wanted forgiveness, but felt in no position to ask for it. Nor did she think she deserved it. She assumed after the way she behaved, Wesley never wanted to talk to her again, and so she never called. She cried the whole time on the phone, saying how much she loved and missed her son, asking that Wesley call whenever he was ready.

Wesley took a deep breath. "And my father?"

Emory shook her head and looked down at the table, again offering the phone to Wesley. "Drink a little more wine, then call her."

Wesley took a big gulp, then picked up the phone. "I'm still very pissed at you."

Emory gave Wesley a hug and left for her room. Tomás could take it from here.

* * *

Emory closed her bedroom door and checked her phone—nothing from Mason. But there were multiple texts from Eric, begging for her to call. *I guess Molly sucked in bed.* She walked to her bathroom and drew a bath, pouring in some bubbles, easing herself into the warm water, resting her head on the back of the bathtub. The warm water relaxed her muscles but could do nothing for her racing mind. *Should I bring up the possibility of Seattle? Should I move there, and give up my photography business in Charlotte? Would he dump me again if I didn't?* She dunked her head in the water, hoping it would clear her mind. She heard her phone ring and quickly jumped out of the tub, bubbles and water dripping from her body. She raced to her bedroom for her phone, praying it was Mason.

"You sound a little out of breath. What were you doing?" Mason kicked off his shoes and reclined on his hotel bed.

"I was taking a bath." Emory returned to the bathroom for a towel.

"So you're telling me you're naked and wet?"

"It seems I'm always wet with you."

"Is that so, baby?" Mason smiled broadly.

Emory flopped down on her bed. "I was talking about the rainwater and the barbecue sauce."

"You're such a tease."

Sensing his disappointment, she cupped the phone with her hand and lowered her voice. "Since you know I'm naked, why don't you join me?"

Is she serious? I'll play along. He tried to unbutton his shirt quickly, but his right shoulder made it difficult. He struggled, quietly cursing his sling and that he was right handed.

Emory heard the groans and muffled curses. "Mason, are you OK?" He didn't respond, still struggling to remove his sling. She heard straps unbuckling and realized what he was doing. "Daniel Evan Mason, don't you dare take that sling off!"

Mason froze. "Just undoing my belt buckle, baby."

"You're such a liar! You can't risk your arm for a little phone sex!"

"Well, don't answer the phone naked then!"

Emory busted out in a huge laugh, and Mason slipped his sling back on. *This is going nowhere.*

"When do you get the sling off anyway?"

"I see my surgeon on Friday and then start physical therapy. Maybe we can start the physical therapy tonight?"

"If we ever have sex again, we're going to be together. Not across the country."

If? Mason sighed. Emory rose from the bed and got a brush in the bathroom. "Want me to come with you Friday?"

"It's in Atlanta."

"So?" Emory brushed her hair.

"I know you have work."

Emory smiled. *He's thinking about my career. Maybe he has changed?* "I could move a few things around."

"That would be great."

"I suppose it comes with being your, uh…" She stopped brushing her hair, unsure of the right word. *I'm not saying girlfriend.*

"Yes?" Mason teased.

Friend isn't right either. "Your phone sex partner."

"I wish," he said, then took a risk. You don't get to be an NFL quarterback without taking some. "How about the love of my life?"

Emory dropped her brush. *Did he just say he loved me? A married man?* "Slow," she whispered, believing he'd feel differently if he knew her secret.

CHAPTER ELEVEN

"WAKE UP." WESLEY shook Emory's leg hanging off the bed. She groaned and pulled a pillow over her head, desperate for more sleep. "Wake up!" He urged more forcefully this time, moving the pillow.

She rubbed her eyes, the morning sunlight beaming through her window. "What do you want?"

Wesley sat down on the bed, his face drawn. Emory took one look at him through her sleep-deprived eyes and sensed something was wrong. She rubbed his back, and he began to cry, dropping his head in his hands, his whole body trembling. "Tomás just left me."

"Oh my God!" Emory threw her arms around him and pulled him close, gripping him tightly. "Why? What happened?"

Wesley sobbed into her shirt. "I couldn't do it, Em. I just couldn't bring myself to call her. And Tomás just didn't get it. He said he couldn't be with someone who couldn't face his own family being proud of who he was."

Emory patted his head and ran her fingers through his hair. "I can't believe Tomás said that."

Wesley looked up from her shirt, tears flowing. "He thinks I'm embarrassed by him. He said to call him when I decided to really come out." He buried his head again.

"I'm so sorry. This is all my fault. I shouldn't have called your mother. I shouldn't have put you under that pressure."

"I know you were just trying to help. But I'm just not ready," Wesley said, trying to gather himself. "Why can't Tomás just understand that?"

"He will. He loves you." Wesley shrugged his shoulders, not so sure anymore. His boyfriend left when Wesley needed him most. "What can I do to help?"

"Can you teach for me later today? I decided to go visit my sis-ter."

"Of course, I'll cover it."

"Thanks. I'm leaving now." He pointed to his suitcase on the floor by her bed. "Should be in Asheville before lunch. I'll be back for classes tomorrow afternoon."

* * *

A young teenager looked at the clock in the viewing area, bored waiting for his little sister to finish Emory's class. He stole an occasional glance at Mason, then whispered something to his mother. He did this several times, his mother offering encouragement, but he was nervous. Mason noticed the boy, hoping he would find the courage to come over.

Mason, too, looked at the clock, exhausted from the long flight and time change. The time dragged. He'd waited all day to hold Emory—to feel her soft skin, touch her flowing hair, and kiss her sweet lips. He'd missed everything about her, and now all that re-mained between him and her were a dozen little ballerinas. Mason watched her work with them. She had their full attention, demon-strating certain steps and twirling them around. It seemed she'd sur-rounded herself, surprisingly enough, with children and babies. *Had she always been so good with them?* Emory caught his gaze through the window and gave him a shy smile. He smiled back, then looked again at the clock on the wall.

The boy whispered again to his mother, seemingly more determ-ined this time. The mother pulled a pen and scrap of paper from her purse and handed them to her son. The boy swallowed hard and took a few careful steps towards Mason. "Excuse me, sir?"

Mason offered a huge smile. "Hey."

"Are you Daniel Mason?"

"Sure am."

"Could I get your autograph, please?"

"Of course." The boy handed Mason the pen and paper and looked back to his mother, his face beaming. Mason bent down on one knee to scribble his name. "Do you play football?"

"Yes, sir."

"What position?" Mason rose, handing the boy the paper and pen.

"Running back. Broke my arm last season, though. Kinda like you." He lifted his sleeve to show Mason.

"Whoa, that's a pretty big scar. Must have been an epic tackle." The boy nodded proudly. "You watching your little sister?"

"Yeah. Every week. It's so boring." His mother motioned to her son to hush. "Why are you here, Mr. Mason?"

Mason winked at the boy. "I like ballerinas."

"I know. Ms. Emory is hot!"

Mason chuckled, admiring Emory bent over. "Yes, she certainly is."

"Is she your girlfriend?"

His mother shook her head in embarrassment and mouthed "I'm sorry" to Mason.

Mason patted the boy on the shoulder. "I'm working on it, kid."

Emory ended the class and hugged her little ballerinas before they filed out of the studio to their parents. The boy's sister hugged her mother, and the family turned to leave. "Good luck with Ms. Emory," the boy said, "and the Panthers."

When her last student left, Emory locked the door and turned to face Mason, his pulse quickening. Throughout his flight, he longed to kiss and hold her again. He walked slowly towards her, then pulled down her ponytail, running his fingers through her hair. Emory felt her breath catch in anticipation of his kiss, but he didn't. Instead, his hand drifted down her face outlining her cheek, then down her neck, sending tingles down her spine. He touched her body as if he never had before. Her breath became more rapid, his fingertips grazing the contour of her breast. Mason's eyes grew dark blue, watching her nipples harden from his slightest touch. Emory locked her fingers in the belt loop of his jeans and pulled his hips towards her. Mason smiled and kissed her neck, letting his tongue linger. Emory let out a soft moan, as he placed little kisses up her neck and jaw. Her breath growing more rapid and her legs weakening in anticipation of his kiss, but he moved to the other side of her neck.

"Mason," she whispered through ragged breath. Emory needed his kiss, but Mason was in total control, knowing exactly what he was doing to her. He gently kissed her bottom lip, as her hands went to his hair, pulling herself tightly against him. He smiled as she nibbled his bottom lip, then he turned to her mouth, exploring it with his tongue, while she moaned in pleasure. They kissed passionately for several minutes, then slowly pulled apart. Mason ran his thumb across her lips, red from the intensity of his kiss. He placed a chaste kiss on her lips for comfort and smiled with a naughty glisten in his eye. "Tease," she said, gently slapping his arm. "Come upstairs. I need to change." She took his hand. "And I have something for you."

They went into the apartment, and in less than a minute, Emory emerged from her room, dressed in a cotton camisole and boxer shorts, holding a small box topped with a bow.

"What is this?" Mason's eyes brightened, so heavy from the time change and long flight.

"A surprise." Mason studied it and shook it a little. "It's nothing big. You can open it now."

He removed the bow from the box, placing it on Emory's hair, then gleefully tore it open. *What is this?* He removed a key from the box. "Wow!" Mason beamed. "Is this for the apartment?"

Emory rolled her eyes. "No, I can give you that if you want."

"Then what is it for?" he asked, confused, Emory nudging him to take a closer look. He turned over the key in his hand and saw the numbers 302. "Is this really it?" Mason couldn't believe what he was holding; it might as well have been the Lombardi Trophy.

"Yep." She bit her lip. "Special weekend."

"I can't believe you kept our key!" Emory told him she hadn't kept it. She'd read online a few years ago that the historic hotel had been sold, and the new owner was upgrading the floors and rooms. She didn't want the hotel tossing *their* key, so she called the hotel and asked if they would send her the key to Room 302, explaining it was important to her. The hotel was cordial, but must have thought she was crazy. Still, a few days later, the key arrived in her mailbox.

"I'm shocked you did that, Em."

"I never stopped thinking about you."

Mason hugged her tightly. *I don't deserve this girl.* "I'll take that key to your apartment, too."

Emory giggled and pulled away, opening the drawer of a side table. She reached inside and dangled a key in front of him, Mason grabbing it and Emory, too. With one arm, he pulled her on top of him. *My favorite position!* He ran his fingers across her cheek, with his blue eyes piercing into hers, the intensity in his eyes throwing her off balance. She tried to sit up, but Mason pulled her back, slowly kissing her neck, gently sliding his hand under her shirt onto her waist, but she pushed his hand aside.

"Hey, I was following your rules," he said, smiling. "I was going slow." Emory kissed him, then kissed him again, for several hours, keeping their hands above their clothes. Shortly before midnight, a loud growl from her stomach interrupted them, Emory covering her face in embarrassment. "I'll go make you a little snack. Be right back."

Mason kissed the tip of her nose and forehead and walked into the kitchen. Emory nestled herself into the pillows of the sofa.

Mason grabbed a bottle of water out of the refrigerator and some blueberries, then made his way back, a slow smile coming across his face seeing Emory was fast asleep. If he had full use of both arms, he'd have carried her to bed. Instead, he draped a blanket over her and settled in a nearby chair to watch her sleep.

* * *

Steven and Olivia rested in bed watching television. It was late, and they couldn't sleep, Steven worried about his brother's career and divorce, and Olivia was just too uncomfortable from the baby kicking her bladder. They hoped unfunny, late-night reruns would bring some sleep. Steven heard his fax machine downstairs. He patted Olivia's belly and walked down to his office, taking a single sheet of paper from the machine—one year, $2 million offer from the Seahawks. *Damn, still just one year. At least it's more than Carolina.*

He picked up his phone and dialed the Panthers. "Hi, it's Steven Mason... Yeah, I know it's late... I just heard from Seattle... A million more than you guys... My brother wants to be in Carolina, but you're going to have to come up, or go to two years..."

Olivia yelled down for a back massage.

"This shouldn't be so difficult... We can play hardball, too... With the extra million, my brother can buy some fancy raincoats in Seattle... If you're not going to increase the money or years, we need incentives... Base it on number of starts, snaps, games played... Be creative if you want... Let me know something soon."

He hung up and walked to the staircase, feeling his hair thinning some more. Then his phone rang, and he darted back to his office, scribbling furiously on a legal pad.

"Yes... Let me make sure I understand. One year, $1 million base salary. Another $250,000 if he starts at least four games, and another $250,000 if he plays in at least eight games... Potential total value of $1.5 million... I need to talk to him."

Olivia yelled down again, and Steven hollered back for her to be patient, needing a few minutes for business. He knew it was late, and Mason likely was with Emory. Rather than disturb them, he shot his brother a text. *Need to talk. Call me ASAP!* He made his way upstairs, and the phone rang again.

Olivia rolled across her bed, stretching for the phone on the nightstand. "How's my nephew?" Mason asked, turning the hotel key between his fingers, as Emory slept peacefully.

"Fat, or at least I am." Olivia reached back across the bed for the remote and lowered the volume on the television, hearing Steven come up the stairs.

"Oh, come on. That's not what Steven says."

"He's full of it. Anyway, he needs to stop eating all my ice cream!"

Mason let out a quiet laugh. "I'll tell him to stop."

"By the way, are you hooking up with your college girlfriend?" Olivia blurted out.

"Put Steven on the phone!" Steven walked into the bedroom and saw a devilish look on his wife's face.

Olivia massaged her belly. "Don't take that tone with a pregnant woman, Mason."

"You can't play the pregnant card with me!" Mason fired back. Olivia brought energy and excitement to any situation, and that's why Mason knew she was perfect for his brother, loosening him up —a stressed-out, hard worker who tackled any challenge, including helping raise Mason when their father left.

"Liv, are you tormenting Mason? Give me the phone." Steven pulled it from her grip. "Sorry about that. You know, Liv—as soon as she has a thought, she says it. It's part of her charm." Olivia rolled her eyes and scooted off the bed, waddling into the bathroom.

"It's fine," Mason said. "What's up?"

"I got Seattle's offer." Steven sat down on the bed. "It's better. One year, $2 million."

Mason cringed and looked at Emory sleeping. "I need to be in Charlotte," he whispered, walking to her bedroom and shutting the door.

"I figured. I just got off the phone with the Panthers, too. They are being stubborn. Added a few incentives, $500,000 worth, if you start four games and play in eight, but that's it. They won't go any further. All that's guaranteed is $1 million."

"Shit."

Olivia called out from the bathroom for toilet paper, and Steven walked to the hall closet to fetch a roll. "I'm assuming you want to discuss all this with Emory."

"Nope," Mason said quickly, "and don't you ever say anything to her either!"

"Geez, calm down." Steven tossed the roll to his wife.

"Just make the deal with the Panthers."

Steven rubbed his eyes and returned to the bed. "Mason, I really think you ought to discuss this with her. If you're serious about her, you need to tell her what's going on." Olivia sat on the bed next to her husband.

"I don't need your advice about women," Mason said.

"Oh, really?" Steven said, his voice rising, as Olivia rubbed his back. "I seem to recall telling you not to marry that bitch and telling you to beg Emory for forgiveness. Should have followed my advice then, and you wouldn't be in this fucking mess!" Olivia frowned at Steven, shaking her head that he would talk to Mason that way.

Mason clenched the phone with a fierce grip but bit his tongue. If he would have responded, he'd have been loud and disturbed Emory, and he didn't want that. Plus, he knew his brother was right. *I have made a mess of my life.*

"Sorry, man," Steven said softly. "I shouldn't have gone there."

"Don't worry about it."

"You still aren't going to talk to Emory?"

"Nope."

"If she finds out, she's going to flip."

"Then make sure she doesn't find out."

"I'll do my best, but we have to consider it might get leaked."

"You worry too much. Just wrap it up with the Panthers. And my divorce, too."

Mason hung up and ran his fingers through his hair, wondering if he should tell Emory about both offers. But he feared she'd use the Seattle offer to push him away, and he felt he couldn't ask her to give up her career for his—that wasn't such a good strategy six years ago, and they had only started back up again. It would be unfair to ask her to give up her life for football so soon. He got on his knees in front of her bed and clasped his hands together. He bowed his head. *Please, God, don't let her find out I gave up $1 million for her. She'd want me to take the better deal. And she wouldn't come with me.*

Emory opened her bedroom door, finding Mason on his knees. "Are you OK?"

"Yeah, fine." Mason quickly got up.

"What are you doing?"

"Giving thanks." *World class lie.*

"For what?"

Mason gave a huge smile to hide the guilt. "It looks like it's going to be the Panthers!"

"Really? Oh my God!" Emory ran to him, throwing her arms around his waist and squeezing tightly. Mason placed his hand in her hair and closed his eyes. "I've been so worried about you moving to Seattle!"

Mason looked at her. "Why didn't you say anything?"

"Well, you never brought it up, so I didn't either. I didn't know the status of any contract talks, so I figured you'd just let me know when you were ready. I didn't want to get in the way."

Mason sat on her bed and grabbed her hand. *But you have gotten in the way—in the most unbelievable way. And I didn't bring it up because I was staying no matter what.* "I knew things would work out this time."

"I still can't believe it!" she screeched. "I'm so happy!"

Mason was hopelessly conflicted—thrilled by her response, but riddled with guilt that he'd withheld information and lied. He tried to be happy, as Emory sat on his lap and kissed his cheek. "We should celebrate. How about I take you out on a real date tomorrow night? We'll dress up. I'll pick you up and everything."

"Perfect," she said and rolled off him into bed. "Now come to sleep. It's late." She pulled him down beside her.

"I don't think that's the best idea. We promised to go slow and with this good news, I don't think I could. I'll take the sofa." Mason didn't trust himself in bed with her and hated himself for being a liar. This wasn't the right time.

"I'll make you behave," she said sweetly.

Mason gave a weak smile. *I can't say no.* He turned off the light and crawled next to her. Emory rested her head on his chest, Mason placing his left arm around her, as she nuzzled herself into him, giving a little moan. Mason leaned over and kissed the top of her head, Emory's bare leg sliding over his. He felt himself harden. He moved his hand down, slightly pulling up her shirt, resting his hand on her bare waist. He found it hard to hold back, and ran his finger underneath the waistband of her shorts.

"Good night," she said softly. Mason removed his hand and exhaled deeply, then waited a few minutes to make sure she was in a deep sleep before making his way to the sofa.

CHAPTER TWELVE

BETWEEN HIS LIES and his shoulder, Mason didn't sleep well. He hadn't told Emory about his Seattle offer, or the seriousness of his shoulder injury, or Alexis' challenge of the prenup. He felt he had good reasons for not revealing these things, but that didn't lessen the guilt. And sleeping on the sofa wasn't helpful. He rubbed his shoulder. *Penance.* He walked to the kitchen and whipped up some eggs and bacon. It was no small feat to cook breakfast for two with one arm, then walk to her bedroom, balancing the tray of two plates and two cups of juice.

He gently pushed open the door with his knee, the squeaking door stirring Emory. Mason grimaced, regretting he woke her. "Thought we could have breakfast together."

Emory flashed him a glorious smile and pulled up her legs to make room for him and the tray on the bed. She dug into her food, savoring each bite, but noticed Mason was just moving food around with his fork. "Everything OK?"

"Fine."

She knew better but had no idea what the problem was. He had stayed over, which was great, and last night he was so happy to be a Panther. *Is he having second thoughts?* She was afraid to ask, and only one other thing occurred to her. "Are you upset about Alexis?"

There were other things rattling around in his mind, but this one certainly was taking up a lot of space. "Divorce is a huge headache." Mason pushed his plate away slightly. "I don't want to talk about her."

"OK, I understand."

Mason took her hand. "I don't want her to be a distraction to what we have, what we are starting again."

"Me neither." Emory squeezed his hand. "Just don't blindside

103

me down the road with something. You can talk to me about anything."

Mason smiled and nodded, feeling sick inside. *I can't talk to you
about my wife.* He wanted Alexis to be in the past and to build a future with Emory and hated he felt the need to lie in order to build that
future. But he saw no other way, fearing if he revealed too much,
there'd be no future to build. Indeed, Emory repeatedly cautioned
they must take things slowly, and that didn't lend itself to unloading
about the prenup or anything else about Alexis, his shoulder, or a
better contract from Seattle.

Emory scarfed down her last piece of bacon, then gave him a
quick kiss on the lips before going to shower. Mason drank his juice
in one gulp and moved the tray to the nightstand. The phone rang,
Mason seeing Eric's name appear. He seized it, debating whether or
not to answer.

"Is that my phone?" Emory called out from the bathroom. Mason
just stared at the phone ringing again—then again—until it stopped.
Emory appeared from the bathroom in only a towel. "Was that my
phone?"

"Why?" Mason tossed the phone towards the foot of the bed.
"Are you expecting a call?"

"What the hell is wrong with you?" Emory got her phone and
saw who had called. "This is nothing. He's been calling and texting
me for days. I haven't answered him. Check my phone if you want."

Mason realized he was being a jerk. "I'm sorry. I don't need to
do that." Emory kissed the top of his head and walked towards the
bathroom. "Call him back."

Emory stopped in her tracks. "What? Why?"

"He obviously has things he needs to say to you. Maybe if you
hear him out, he'll understand it's over."

"I'm not sure about that," Emory said, turning back towards the
bathroom. "Maybe later."

"Please do it now, Em," Mason begged softly, giving away his
insecurity. Emory wasn't used to seeing him lacking confidence. She
knew Mason already was upset about Alexis and didn't want to torment him further. Plus, she wondered whether Mason had a point—
perhaps a quick call would resolve things with Eric once and for all.
She closed her eyes and took a deep breath and hit Eric's number on

her phone. She took a seat on his lap, Mason running a finger under the top of her towel, whispering, "Speaker."

Eric was driving to the hospital when she called. "I'm so sorry about the other day at my house. I didn't have sex with Molly. You have to believe me."

"Eric, it doesn't matter whether you had sex with her or not." Emory rose from Mason's lap and stood with her back to him. "You knew I was coming over. You did it on purpose to hurt me." Mason grabbed her butt, and Emory swatted his hand away.

"This has gotten so out of hand, Emory. A week ago, we were planning our wedding. Can we get together tonight and just talk?"

"No," Emory said flatly.

"Please, Emory, just dinner. We can go to that little French place where I took you for your birthday. That was the first night you slept over, and we…"

Mason snatched the phone from her hand, having heard enough already. "She has plans for dinner tonight, fuck face." Emory crossed her arms, staring at Mason furiously, but he winked at her. "And after dinner, too."

"You're the guy from the other night? Give the phone back to Emory."

"Listen up, asshole," Mason barked. "Stop calling her. Stop texting her. It's fucking over."

"I don't take orders from you."

"Well, let me offer a suggestion then. Just go back to banging your wedding planner."

Eric jammed on the brakes of his car and swerved to the side of the road, putting the car in park. "She told you about that?"

"Fucking right she told me. And if you ever lay your hands on her again, I'll beat the piss out of you with a bedpan!"

Emory threw her hands in the air. As flattering as it was to have two guys fighting over her, she'd now heard enough. She grabbed Mason's arm and took the phone. "Eric, I…"

Eric cut her off. "I can't believe you told him about what happened with Molly!"

"I didn't think it was a big secret, and I was pretty shaken up about it."

"So you confide in him?" Eric put his head on the steering

wheel, cars whizzing past. "He obviously stayed the night! You must be fucking this guy!"

Mason smiled at Emory. *I wish.*

"How could you do this to us?" Eric asked.

"I swear I'm not having sex with anyone," she said, a tear falling down her cheek. "I never cheated on you, just like I'm sure you never cheated with Molly. I know you don't believe me, but that's the truth. Now, please stop calling and texting me. It's over."

Emory hung up and threw her phone on the bed, storming into the bathroom, slamming the door behind her. She dropped to the floor next to the bathtub and began to sob. *I hate hurting Eric, and Mason is infuriating.* After a few minutes, she heard a soft knock on the door. "Go away!" Mason opened the door and peeked inside. Emory fired a towel at him. "I said go away!"

He briefly thought about giving her some space but decided against it. He was unable to hide his pleasure. He walked into the bathroom and kneeled in front of her, placing his hands on her bare calves. "I don't think we have to worry about Eric calling anymore."

"Because he thinks I'm a slut." Emory kicked him with her foot, sending him flat on his ass. "Was that your plan all along?"

"I came up with it on the spot." Mason smiled, getting back on his knees. "Seemed to work out well."

"Let me tell you something," she said, pointing her finger in his face. "I know what it's like to be dumped and have your ex fuck someone two seconds later. It doesn't work out well."

Mason's lips closed into a tight line. "I'm sorry. I just wanted to get rid of him."

"Just go away!"

Mason limped to his feet and walked to the kitchen to clean up, picking up the breakfast tray along the way. He hoped that if he did some chores, he'd get back in her good graces. Then he saw Emory gathering her photography equipment in the den, seeing her nose and eyes were red.

"I have to go," she said without looking at him and made her way to the front door. "I have appointments all day."

"Em, don't leave like this." He moved cautiously towards her.

She held up a hand, freezing him a few feet from her. "I'm running late."

"Em, I'm sorry. OK?"

"You got exactly what you wanted." Emory pushed her hair behind her ears. "Just what are you so sorry for?"

Not for anything I said to Dr. Cock! Mason reached out and touched her hand. "I'm sorry I ever put a finger on Alexis. That I hurt you like I did. It makes me jealous to think of you with anyone else. I can't imagine what that must've been like for you, knowing I was off with Alexis, so soon after we broke up."

Hell. She mustered a slight smile. "I really have to go." She continued to the front door and put her hand on the knob, looking back with soft eyes to reassure Mason everything would be fine. "What time should I be ready tonight?"

* * *

Wesley finished his afternoon classes in the studio, and between the travel back to Charlotte and multiple hours of teaching, he was in no mood to cook dinner for himself. He walked upstairs and ordered a small pepperoni pizza from a local dive. There was no sense ordering a larger one; he'd be eating alone. Tomás wasn't around anymore, and he figured Emory would be with Mason.

He sat in his den, quietly waiting for dinner to arrive, the silence unsettling him. He turned on the television, flipping through several channels, but couldn't find anything to keep his attention, so he shut it off. *I don't want to be alone.* He missed Tomás—the late-night movies they watched together, the bowls of popcorn, the meals he cooked, the care he showed to everyone he met. Wesley still couldn't understand why Tomás had left. He also missed Emory's company, wondering whether she, too, would soon leave—that Mason would take her away from him. And, for the first time in a long time, he missed his parents. He hadn't thought of them, at least not in any good way, in years. It was too painful, but his visit with his sister in Asheville, and the prospect of seeing his parents and other family at her upcoming wedding, made him miss the feeling of actually being a part of a family—of being someone's son.

Wesley heard a car door close and footsteps approaching the apartment. It was too soon for the pizza delivery. *Tomás?* Wesley stood up from the sofa and walked to the top of the staircase, finding Emory coming up.

"How'd it go with your sister?" she asked, hugging him.

"She says I should talk to Mom, but I'm not sure. There's a lot to consider."

Emory patted his back. "What about Tomás?"

"Not a word."

"Do you want me to talk to him, too?" Emory teased.

Wesley gave her a disapproving look. "I think you've talked to enough people."

The doorbell rang. "I ordered pizza. It's only a small. Didn't think you'd be home. Sorry."

"It's fine. I'm going out soon with Mason."

Wesley went down to fetch the pizza, then opened the box on the kitchen table. He took a slice for himself, Emory staring longingly, as he devoured it. Wesley pulled a slice for her from the box, and with a huge smile, Emory doused her slice with parmesan cheese, folded it in half, and took a large bite.

"Guess who I saw leaving when I got home?"

"I gave him a key," she said, blushing. "I hope you don't mind."

"Of course not." He sprinkled cheese on his slice. "Have you told him yet?"

"No." Emory picked off a pepperoni and threw it inside the box.

"Do you plan on telling him?" Wesley picked up her pepperoni and ate it.

"At some point, I guess I have to."

"The longer you wait, the worse it will be." Emory reached the end of her slice and tossed the crust in the box. "You have to forgive yourself. You did what you thought was right at the time."

Emory shrugged. She wasn't so sure; she'd never been sure. "Mason will be here soon, and I need to get ready."

"That reminds me. He left something for you in your room." Emory's eyes brightened, and she dashed to her bedroom.

* * *

Mason came into the apartment, wearing navy pinstripe slacks and a cashmere sweater, his brown leather jacket hanging over his shoulder. He found Wesley eating pizza at the kitchen table, and the men exchanged an uncomfortable glance. Wesley knew Emory gave Mason a key, but found it presumptuous Mason would just walk in.

"I need a few minutes!" Emory yelled from inside her bedroom. Mason smiled slightly to himself, draping a black swing coat for Emory on a chair. It seemed he was always waiting for Emory to get ready, whether for a date or for sex, and he had no choice but to be patient.

Mason stood awkwardly, while Wesley finished his dinner, neither knowing what to say. After a few moments of odd glances and nervous smiles, Wesley cleaned up the table, and Mason took the chance to wander around the den, Wesley following him with his eyes. Mason picked up a portfolio on a bookshelf and flipped through the black and white photos of different landscapes.

"She's very talented," Wesley said, wiping down the table.

Mason looked up at him. "She always was."

"Hope you remember that this time," Wesley said, narrowing his eyes.

Mason put the book down and raised his eyes. "You have something you need to say to me?"

Wesley took a small step forward and wrung his hands together. "Yeah, I do." He knew Emory and Mason were getting close again and had some things to get off his chest, for his own sake, before they got too far.

"OK." Mason put his hand in his pocket and leaned against the bookshelf. "Go for it."

"I'm rooting for you guys," Wesley said, his voice quivering, "but I'm the one who found her in the weight room crying. I'm the one who stayed with her night after night in the hospital, wiping her tears and forcing her to eat. I was there for the nightmares."

Wesley caught himself, hoping he hadn't said too much. Mason looked at him curiously. *Nightmares?*

"So," Wesley continued, pointing a nervous finger at Mason, "you better be damn sure she's your priority this time. I may be as queer as a three dollar bill, but I'll find a way to fuck you up!"

Mason suppressed the urge to laugh, a gay ballerina issuing threats to an NFL quarterback. And Wesley's words themselves were comical, too. *Three dollar bill?* Mason knew a good threat when he heard one. He liked to throw them around himself—Eric knew that by now. But Mason would never laugh at Wesley—not at all. He absorbed what Wesley said and respected the hell out of him for saying it. *He loves my girl, too, and doesn't want anything bad to happen to her. I don't like his tone, but I respect that.* Mason reached out his hand. "I promise she's my priority, and if I screw this up, I'll kick my own ass."

Wesley shook it. "Good. That settles it. I didn't want to have to fuck you up. At least not in my own den."

"I'm relieved, too," Mason replied, pretending to wipe sweat from his brow.

"What are you guys relieved about?" Emory asked as she emerged from her bedroom, wearing a black, low-cut, v-neck halter dress, and black stilettos with red soles, all of which Mason had left for her with a note saying, "Can't wait to see you in this tonight." She looked better than he imagined, stunning, the dress hugging her hips and narrowing at her waist, plunging to the top of her breasts. Mason rarely had seen her so dolled up—his angelic ballerina transformed into a sex siren. He undressed her with his eyes, dreaming about the black thongs he'd also left for her to wear.

Mason nudged Wesley to answer, still overcome by Emory. "I just gave Mason some truth." Emory looked at them curiously, as Wesley looked her up and down. "And now I'll give you some truth. If I were straight, I'd hit it." Wesley whistled at her and took her hand.

"That's good to hear, Wesley. Thank you for that." He gave her a quick twirl in the direction of Mason, who grabbed the black swing coat and held it out, slipping it on her and leaving it unbuttoned, then leading her out of the apartment.

CHAPTER THIRTEEN

AS SOON AS the front door closed, Mason pulled Emory to him and slid his left hand around her waist, holding her close. They were alone in the hallway. Emory closed her eyes, embarrassed, and smiled slightly, his hand drifting a bit lower, her eyes flashing open. He leaned in and kissed her. Emory put a hand on his waist and another in his hair, the warmth of her body causing Mason to pull her even closer. He pushed her coat aside, kissing her neck and grazing it with his tongue, Emory moaning in pleasure. Mason suddenly pinned her against the wall and kissed her hard, his left hand gripping her butt, as he pulled her harder against him.

She gasped for breath. "Slow." Mason snapped back, placing his head on her shoulder. "Thank you for the outfit."

"I have to know." He ran his hand slowly across her bottom, kissing her neck. "Did you wear everything?"

"No." Emory moaned softly, and Mason stopped his kisses. "This dress is so tight they left slight panty lines, so I decided it was better to go without. Hope that's OK with you."

Mason knew Emory was used to not wearing panties. Ballet dancers don't wear them under their leotards—which Mason was thrilled to learn back in college—but he couldn't believe Emory would show up for their date without any panties. *Is this her idea of slow?* Mason adjusted his pants.

"Your hot body is mine. I don't want anyone else to see you in that dress. Please keep the coat on." Emory buttoned up and straightened her hair with her fingers. He led her downstairs to the parking lot. "I couldn't very well take you out on a date in a cab, so I went by the dealership earlier today." He walked her towards a dark gray Audi SUV.

"And you bought a car?" Mason opened the car with the touch of a button, and got her car door, then hurried around to the driver's side. "I can't believe you bought a car. For our date?"

"Relax, I needed a car in Charlotte, so I bought one. No big deal."

"No big deal?" *I'm not used to this.* "The contract with the Panthers must be pretty big!"

"It's good enough," he said, but went no further. Mason hadn't signed the contract yet, but the deal was effectively done. He wanted to celebrate and share the moment with Emory. He'd been through hell with Alexis, even denying himself certain luxuries despite making millions, so Alexis couldn't enjoy them. But he was a new man, with a new team, in a new city, and felt entitled to splurge on a luxury car.

"So while I was working today, you shopped for women's clothing and bought a car?"

"And planned our date. By the way, I'm sorry about this morning. I just…"

Emory cut him off. "The damage is done. Let's just move on." She placed her hand on his and gave it a little squeeze. "I'm not upset anymore. Now, where are we going?"

"It's a surprise."

Emory flashed a huge grin, recalling the short drive to the historic hotel where they spent their first night together. "I think we've had this conversation before."

Mason winked at her. "Any chance tonight can end like that night?" He pointed to their old hotel room key on his key chain, and started the engine.

* * *

Kathleen sat in the living room of Steven's home and poured herself another glass of wine. "Son, I cannot tell you how excited I am for my first grandchild."

Steven was still working on his first glass. "We're excited, too, Mom."

"Yes, this boy can't get here soon enough, as far as I'm concerned," Olivia said, her hand in a box of chocolate raisins. "I have been enjoying eating, though."

"You eat what you want, dear," Kathleen said. "I'm sure your figure will bounce back for my son without much trouble." Steven's stomach churned.

"For your *son?*" Olivia tossed a handful of chocolate raisins in her mouth for dramatic effect, Steven pleading with his eyes for her to let it go, and also motioning to his mother that her comment was inappropriate. "I'll bounce back for *me*—but Steven will benefit, I'm sure."

"Of course, that's what I meant, dear."

Steven downed his wine and poured a second glass, quickly catching up with his mother. "Mom," he said, desperate to change the subject, "Mason and I just got back from Seattle."

"Oh? How did it go?"

"It went fine. But I think Mason is picking Carolina."

"Why doesn't he tell me these things? I'm his mother, so I should know."

"Steven keeps things from me, too, sometimes," Olivia interjected. "Must be something about your boys, Kathleen."

Steven rolled his eyes. "I'm sure he was going to tell you, Mom, but I guess he's waiting for the right time." He took a sip of wine and sunk in his chair. "I don't know."

"What made him pick Carolina?"

Olivia opened her mouth to speak, and Steven shut her down. *Don't mention Emory.* She shrugged her shoulders and popped a few more raisins in her mouth. Steven quickly flashed a nervous smile to his mother. "I think he just felt a connection with the coaches and management." *Lying to teams is so much easier.* "I wasn't there for the meeting, but that's what Mason said. It's his decision anyway."

Kathleen could tell Steven was lying but decided to let it go. She would take it up with Mason directly. "I just hope he's doing what is best for him, and that you are steering him in the right direction. This may be his last contract, you know, with his shoulder and all."

* * *

Mason could no longer keep the surprise, turning towards the Blumenthal Performing Arts Center. Emory screeched, clapping her hands together, then kissed his cheek. "I can't believe you're taking me to the ballet!" The Joffrey Ballet was in Charlotte to perform *Sleeping Beauty*, which included her favorite dance the "Rose

Adagio." Emory had tried to get tickets, even using her and Wesley's dance connections, but no luck. It was sold out for months.

"I can't believe it either," Mason joked, then weaved quickly into the valet lane. "We need to hurry. The hallway was fun, but it's making us late." Mason led her towards the entrance and presented their tickets to an usher who escorted them to their box seats.

Emory squeezed his hand. "How did you get these amazing seats?" Mason just smiled back at her, as the house lights went down. Being an NFL quarterback—even a journeyman—had its perks.

Mason leaned back in his seat, while Emory leaned forward, resting her hands on the ledge, mesmerized for the next two hours. At times, she couldn't help but move her arms and hands to the music, pointing and flexing her toes for good measure. Mason, as always, enjoyed watching her move, and it helped distract him from the ballet itself, which he found ridiculous, especially the male dancers in make-up twirling around in tights. *Do these dudes call themselves ballerinas? That would be unfortunate.* It also helped distract him from the audience, young and old alike, stuck-up and overrefined, dressed in their finest black tie, silently enraptured by the absurdity unfolding on stage. He was used to a different stage—a stadium filled with 70,000 screaming fans wearing jerseys, weathering the elements along with the players, hurling cheers and insults, feasting on beer and brats.

But he tried to harness his contempt tonight. It was this contempt, he regretted, that made him cast aside Emory's dance career. So to keep himself in check, Mason kept his eyes fixed on Emory. He was proud to be with her. He was proud of himself, too—for spending two hours of his life this way. It was torture—but in a good way—and he figured he deserved it. *This is what I'm supposed to be doing with my life. Making Em happy.*

Mason occasionally glanced at the stage. There was one particularly weird scene where two guys and a girl—he had no idea who the characters were—were skipping around for some reason. His mind flashed back to the first time he met Wesley, a week or so after he began dating Emory.

He'd arrived at the college theater, unannounced as usual, to watch Emory practice, but she wasn't alone this night. A shiver went down his spine, as a young man pressed his body against hers, his hands sliding around her hips, legs, and waist, her leg draped around his body. Her leotard rose up, and his hands dropped lower and lower. "What the fuck is this?" Mason yelled, charging down the center aisle from the back of the theater, hurling himself onto the stage and tackling the man to the ground. "I'm going to kick your fucking ass!"

Emory screamed, as she pulled Mason off the man. "Jesus Christ, what the hell are you doing?"

"What am I doing?" Mason paced the stage, circling his victim as she tended to him. "What were you doing?"

"Dancing, asshole!"

"Looked like you two were dry humping! Like porn ballet or some shit!"

"For the love of God, Wesley is my dance partner!" She pushed on Mason's chest. "You're such an idiot!"

Emory helped the man from the floor. He dusted himself off, and extended his hand. "I'm Wesley. Emory's told me a lot about you." Mason glared at his hand, angry Emory hadn't told him she had a partner, and even more pissed this guy just groped his girlfriend in places he hadn't even touched. An awkward silence fell between the men and Emory, and Wesley decided to put them all out of their misery. "I'm gay."

"Oh?" Mason's heart sank, feeling like the complete idiot Emory said he was. "Well, uh, in that case, it's nice to meet you." He shook Wesley's hand, then apologized profusely.

The house lights of the Blumenthal Performing Arts Center came on, Mason thankful he'd survived all the skipping and twirling around, as Emory thanked him for a wonderful evening. He kissed her nose and forehead. "The night's not over."

* * *

An eager maitre d' in a trendy downtown restaurant approached Mason and Emory. "Good evening, sir and madame," he said with a slight bow. "Please follow me. We have everything ready." Emory, surprised by the greeting and high service, looked approvingly at Mason, then both followed the maitre d'. He ushered them to the "cheater's booth," isolated from other tables, and opened the curtains for Mason and Emory to walk inside. "I trust you'll find everything to your specifications." Mason gave a nod, and he quickly excused himself, drawing the curtains as he left.

Emory's eyes sparkled, surveying the assortment of desserts on the table. "Dessert first tonight!" he said.

She kissed him on the cheek, then removed her coat and sat down, Mason sliding across the booth next to her. "I can't believe you did this!" She grabbed her fork to dig in. "I don't know where to start."

Mason chuckled, picking up a strawberry. He dipped it in cream, and placed it softly in her mouth. She moaned, thanking him with a slow suck on his fingers. As she did, the server called out from outside the curtains, asking for permission to open them. Emory giggled, as Mason slid his fingers out of her mouth, Emory gliding her tongue along her lips, taking in all the cream. After she made her last lick, Mason granted permission to the server, who then took their drink orders and promised to return quickly, closing the curtains behind him.

"Did you enjoy the ballet?" she asked.

He took a bite of cheesecake. "It was *tremendous.*"

"Liar." She carved off a piece of key lime pie.

"Let me rephrase," he said. "It was tremendous being with you."

"I put on a pretty good show," she said suggestively. "I'm sure you remember."

Mason raised his brow and leaned in to kiss her. "Will there be a private show tonight, maybe? We could just use this booth." *No underwear.* "You could just hike up your dress a little."

Emory blushed. "I'm sure that would work out well with the server coming in and out."

"I think so. We could entertain him." Mason took a bite of chocolate cake. "It would be instead of a tip." The server returned with their drinks, and Emory granted permission this time, getting a thrill being in total control. He dropped off the drinks and left. "Seriously," Mason said, kissing the tip of her nose and forehead, "I could stay at your place tonight, and then we head off to Atlanta in the morning."

Emory waved her fork at him. "Or you could pick me up for the airport in the morning."

He kissed her neck. "Or you could come stay with me at the hotel tonight."

"We're going slow, remember?" She gently shoved him away, trying to control her own desires. "I think separate beds are better tonight."

"OK," he said, grabbing another strawberry. "I'll try another day."

"I know you will. Now pass me the bread pudding."

* * *

From his bedroom, Wesley heard the front door open and close. It was nearly midnight. He figured it was Emory, but had expected her much later, or not at all. He wondered whether Mason was with her. He shut off the television in his room, picked up his popcorn bowl, and walked into the den, finding Emory with her eyes closed, leaning against the front door, smiling broadly, her hand resting over her heart.

"Is that sex afterglow?"

"No. Just happiness, I suppose." Emory floated into the den, removing her heels along the way. She fell onto the sofa, and Wesley took a seat beside her.

"So you had a good time?"

"He took me to the ballet," she said, her head still in the clouds.

"Mason took you to the *ballet*?" Wesley cocked his head and gave her a side-eye. "He must have wanted to nap."

She delivered a gentle elbow to his stomach. "I forgot to tell you. I'm going to Atlanta in the morning with Mason to see his doctor."

"How long are you going to be gone?" he asked, with a hint of anxiety.

"Just tomorrow, Friday night." Emory patted his leg. "And I promise, you and I will spend Saturday night together."

"What about Mason?"

"Mason doesn't change what you and I have, Wesley. Just like Eric and Tomás didn't. I'll always make time for you. Mason knows that." She stood up from the sofa and pulled him up. "At least he better."

Wesley smiled mischievously. "There's a Charles Bronson marathon on. Want to watch with me?"

"Let's put Charles on in my bedroom while you help me pack."

Wesley stretched out on her bed and turned on the television, while Emory plucked various outfits from her dresser and closet. But she reached a point that stumped her. "I don't know what to do." Wesley shoved popcorn in his mouth, watching Charles destroy three bad guys at once, each with a different weapon. Emory waved her arms in front of him. "Hello? You are supposed to be helping me, remember?"

"Yeah, yeah." Wesley sat up. "This was just a really good part. What's wrong, babe?"

"I'm not sure what to pack to sleep in."

"I'm sure Mason would prefer you pack nothing."

"Maybe I should text him and see what he has planned?"

"No, that's lame. If he has any surprises, he won't want to tell you." Wesley walked to her dresser and opened two drawers, pulling out a pair of boxer shorts and a cotton shirt. "This will do." He folded them in her bag and resumed his position on the bed, extending his arm for her to snuggle.

"I love you, Wesley," she said, getting into bed and patting his chest.

"I know."

Emory heard her phone ding and reached for it on her nightstand. She read Mason's text to herself. *Thanks for a great night. I love you.*

Wesley looked at her face, as she looked at her phone, obvious to him who sent the text. "You should tell him you have another man in your bed."

"Not if you want to live."

"Probably right. Let's keep our snuggles between us."

CHAPTER FOURTEEN

THEY SAT IN the small examination room waiting for the doctor to arrive. They'd waited over an hour. Emory was tired of waiting and tired from her late night with Mason and Wesley and the early morning flight to Atlanta. Mason fidgeted with his phone and paced the small confines of the room. He took a seat on the examination table.

Emory patted him on the back. "Nervous?"

"No," he fibbed, wiping his hand on his pant leg. "More nervous about what I have planned for tonight."

"Oh, really?"

Emory leaned towards Mason and gave him a kiss, interrupted by a knock at the door. A middle-aged, pudgy-faced nurse entered with a disapproving look. She approached Mason and removed the sling from his arm. He stretched his arms in the air and flashed a huge smile. *Freedom!* The nurse didn't seem to care and advised Dr. Lewis would be in shortly. Before leaving, she told Mason to remove his shirt and extended another disapproving look for good measure.

"What was her problem?"

"I don't know. They're always real hard asses here." Mason captured Emory with both arms. "Forget about her. Now I can use both my hands. You're in so much trouble."

Emory giggled and planted a quick kiss on his lips. Mason removed his shirt, giving Emory her first real look at his scar, several inches long and discolored with purple and red blotches. Her face quickly changed, and she stopped giggling, stunned by what she saw, slowly tracing a finger along the outline of the scar, then kissing his shoulder.

"I had no idea it was this bad."

"It looks worse than it is," he said, suddenly aware he hadn't prepared Emory for what she was going to see or hear.

"How much pain have you..."

The door flew open, and Emory quickly took a seat in the corner of the room. Dr. Lewis walked in and sat in a swivel chair in front of Mason. He was an old, crusty man, with a pointy face and long delicate hands, draped in a white lab coat covering a tie and pocket protector. He lacked any kind of bedside manner, but athletes throughout the country sought him out to rehabilitate and revive their careers. They didn't give a damn about his charm or good company. Dr. Lewis was the foremost orthopedic surgeon in the Southeast.

"How are you feeling?" Dr. Lewis asked, ignoring Emory.

"Much better now that the sling is off."

He flipped through Mason's chart, then examined the scar. "Looks like it's still healing. Discoloration is normal."

"Really?" Emory asked, surprised.

It had been almost eight weeks since his injury, and in her lay opinion, it looked awful—like it happened two days ago. Dr. Lewis gave a sideways glance to Emory. He'd never seen this woman at any other appointment and wondered what she was doing in his examination room.

He moved Mason's arm into various positions, asking for a pain level. Mason said he felt no pain each time. "When can I throw a football?"

Dr. Lewis paused before answering, flipping again through Mason's chart, Emory looking at Mason with concern in her eyes. "Well, you need a few weeks of physical therapy before you try that." Mason shot Dr. Lewis an angry look, fed up being told what he could and couldn't do—by his brother, NFL teams, Alexis, and now Dr. Lewis. "Let me take a look at your latest MRI." He held up several pictures to the light, then scribbled some notes in Mason's chart, as Emory feared something was wrong. Dr. Lewis closed the chart, leaned forward, and looked directly into Mason's eyes. "Have you been following my instructions?"

"Yeah. Of course."

"My limited movement instructions?"

"Oh, those, well, I, uh, I've been doing my best with that, but I've had to travel some, so..."

Dr. Lewis put up his hand, not interested in hearing rambling excuses. "I figured as much." Mason peeked at Emory sitting in the corner, one leg crossed firmly over the other, her top foot shaking rapidly. "I know I made it clear that you had a grade 4 separation and taking it easy was part of the healing process."

"A minute ago, you said it was healing, right?"

"You'd be further along now, if you had listened."

Emory rose from her corner seat and took a step towards Dr. Lewis. "I'm playing catch up here. Has Mason done further damage to his shoulder?"

He turned to her, wrinkling his nose. "Who are you?"

"I'm Emory," she said, as if it was obvious.

"And?" Dr. Lewis pressed, expecting to receive more than a first name.

"And what?" Emory retorted, in no mood for snotty questions. She didn't like the doctor's attitude, or that of his nurse, and was pissed Mason hadn't taken care of himself. Dr. Lewis narrowed his eyes and scratched his head, at a loss for how to deal with this woman.

"I'm sorry, Dr. Lewis," Mason said, trying to avoid a stand-off between Emory and his old-school surgeon. He patted Emory's hand. "She's just concerned."

Dr. Lewis placed his hands on Mason's chart, trying to re-focus himself. "Your friend over there asked about further damage. It's really too early to tell. We won't know until you've completed PT and tried to throw a ball, and ultimately try to take a hit. This was always a 50-50 proposition."

"I'll take my chances," Mason said confidently, then Emory slipped her hand from his, retaking her seat in the corner.

"You won't have any chance at all unless you do what I say. But you do what you want. It's your career. I get paid either way."

Mason hung his head to the floor, feeling Emory's eyes burning into him.

Dr. Lewis sensed the tension between them and wasted no time wrapping up the visit. He provided Mason with physical therapy instructions and the name of a specialist to consult in Charlotte. He shook Mason's hand, ignored Emory, and left.

Emory moved from the chair and sat on the table next to Mason.

"How could you not take care of yourself? How could you not tell me how bad it is?" *Is he hiding anything else?*

"Em, I…" Mason started, then stopped, his eyes still fixed on the floor.

"A grade 4 tear, Mason? A 50-50 chance you may never play again?"

Mason knew the seriousness of it all—so did Alexis, and she left. "I didn't want to worry you," he said in the sweetest, softest voice he could muster.

But it wasn't good enough. "Maybe I should have just Googled it! I would've gotten more information that way."

"I just wanted us to be happy, and to move forward together. That's all."

The pudgy-faced nurse knocked on the door, Emory glaring at her as she entered. "Will you give us some privacy?"

"We need the room for another patient," the nurse said.

"They can damn well wait!" Emory snapped. The nurse took a deep breath, mumbling something about NFL quarterbacks and their high-maintenance women, and shut the door.

"I wasn't trying to deceive you. I just wanted to protect you from all my shitty baggage, like my shoulder."

"So you thought it was better to lie to me?"

"I didn't exactly lie."

"Mason, if this is going to go anywhere, we can't hold back. We need to talk about things—like Alexis, like your arm." She felt a twinge in her stomach, as if her own secret was attacking her body. *You are such a fucking hypocrite.*

"After all this time, can't we just be happy?"

"We can," she said. "But it can't all be surprises and new cars."

Her words struck a chord. He'd been so caught up with Emory, starting over again with her, that he'd done his best to ignore reality. If he wanted to move forward with Emory, he knew he needed to open up and face the consequences of his past. "I want more than that, Em. I do. I'll do better. Starting tonight."

* * *

The doctor's office was only a few blocks from the hotel, where they'd already dropped their bags earlier in the day. It was a crisp, clear afternoon in Atlanta that seemed more suitable for a walk back to the hotel than a short cab ride. They held hands as they walked, Mason feeling energized and free—not just that his sling was gone and that he could use both arms, but he felt he finally was putting his troubled past behind him, or at least was willing to make some effort to deal with it. Mason noticed Emory, too, walked with a spring in her step. It was as if the improvement in his arm, though still on the mend, provided her with an extra jolt. A few passersby noticed Mason on the street, and asked for an autograph, Mason delighting in teasing them about how much he hated the Falcons.

As they came upon the hotel, his phone rang. "So what did Dr. Lewis say?" Steven asked.

"It's healing—slowly. I need to do some therapy and see a specialist in Charlotte. Still can't throw."

"He's looking out for you. Being careful. You need to do what he says."

"Whatever," Mason said, opening the hotel door for Emory. "When are you and Olivia coming to Charlotte?"

"Sunday late afternoon, and leaving Monday evening after the press conference."

"Cool, that works. Looking forward to seeing Olivia, and having her meet Emory." She walked into a gift shop near the hotel entrance.

"By the way, I told Mom about the Panthers." Steven cleared his throat. "She's pretty disappointed you didn't call her yourself."

Mason looked at Emory through the gift shop window. He already had his hands full starting over with her and ending his relationship with Alexis. He couldn't deal with yet another woman. "I know I should call her," Mason said, "but all she wants to talk about is Alexis, and hoping we get back together, which is not happening. I just can't deal with that shit right now. You didn't tell her about Em, did you?"

"Of course not, but she suspects something is up."

"How?"

"I don't know. I think she just does. She was telling me the other day she hoped you took the best deal out there because it could be your last." Mason ran his fingers through his hair. "So you need to deal with Mom. I'm not getting in the middle of any more of your shit."

* * *

Emory rarely spent more than fifteen minutes getting herself ready for a night out. She didn't need to. She'd been blessed with porcelain skin and rose-colored cheeks and lips. She typically used only a dash of lip gloss and mascara, and on rare occasions, went for some eye liner. That was all she ever needed. But on this night, she took some extra time to prepare. Perhaps it was the thrill of being in a different city, or a new energy because Mason's sling was off. She wasn't entirely sure and didn't care. She was just excited to go out and wanted to make sure she looked her absolute best for whatever Mason had planned. She wondered if it was maybe another ballet, or Stone Mountain, or a dance club, or just a romantic dinner on Peachtree Street. She had no idea, which made it difficult to know what to wear, and Mason hadn't given her a single hint.

She emerged from the hotel bathroom in a gray pencil skirt with a white silk top, wearing the black stilettos he'd bought for her. She had a smokey eye and nude lip, and her blonde hair, curled loosely, cascaded down her shoulders.

Mason shut off the television and stood up, wearing a blue, buttoned-down shirt and khaki dress pants. "You look fantastic!"

"Is this OK?" she asked nervously and made a slow twirl.

"Absolutely," he said, sizing her up. *Black thong?*

"Can you tell me what we're doing now?"

Mason winked at her. "We're not leaving the hotel."

"What? Why did I get all dressed up?"

"I didn't say we were staying in the room, but we could just that, if you want."

Emory smirked at him. "Please tell me what we are doing."

"Let's go."

Emory followed Mason out of the room and down to the lobby, eyeing him curiously. *In the hotel?* Mason sensed he had Emory all confused, enjoying teasing her. They walked through the huge lobby holding hands, through various corridors branching out from the main area. Emory looked around, all turned around, unsure where they were going and what was going on. She loved Mason's surprises but didn't like to give up control—especially after a long day when she was hungry.

Mason turned a final corner towards an upscale steakhouse. "I thought we could have an early dinner."

She kissed him on the cheek. "And after dinner?"

"One thing at a time," he said cautiously, opening the door, Emory noticing his change in tone.

A young hostess politely greeted them. Mason informed her they had a reservation, then she scanned some papers on her podium. "Yes, party of three."

"That's right," Mason replied.

The hostess responded quickly. "The other guest is already here. Please follow me."

Emory stared up at Mason, confused again. "Who's the third wheel?" He didn't answer her, relishing yet another tease and also nervous the moment was upon them. He swallowed hard, as the hostess led them through the foyer, around a corner, and into a large dimly-lit room, with mahogany walls and tables and leather chairs, perfectly polished silverware and huge steak knives and candlelight on each table.

Emory saw the third wheel across the room, sitting alone at a table by a window. She walked quickly to the table, leaving the hostess and Mason behind. John Claire stood up, his daughter leaping into his arms. "Daddy!"

Mason and the hostess reached the table but stood back, giving Emory and her father some space. The hostess advised Mason their server would be with them shortly, then left.

"Oh my God, what are you doing here?" Emory stepped back to look at him, his strong body, as usual, appearing in good health. John gave a nod to Mason, still a safe distance away. "You called my dad?" Emory looked at Mason in shock.

"Yes." Mason said, gingerly approaching. He hadn't seen John in years and wasn't sure what to expect from him. But he knew if he was ever to work out his past and go forward with Emory, he had to smooth things over with John. It would take time. Dinner was only a small first step.

Emory raised her eyebrows. "That must have been an interesting phone call?"

"There were a lot of apologies from me. A bit of cursing by your dad, which I completely understood."

"I'd say so," Emory said, kissing her dad on the cheek.

Mason gave John an awkward smile, then extended his hand. John shook it, but not without returning a mildly disapproving look. John appreciated the invite but wasn't about to let Mason off easily. He had hurt his baby girl—breaking up with her and quickly getting with Alexis—to the point that Emory fled to Europe after graduation, causing John to miss out on years of his daughter's life. Mason, in truth, had missed John as well. They'd spent hours talking football, watching film, running plays in John's backyard, and dreaming about the NFL draft. He filled a significant void in Mason's life after his own father left, even accompanying Mason to a father-son awards dinner in college. Mason had missed that relationship.

Mason pulled out a chair for Emory and sat down next to her, with John on the other side of the table. Emory sensed the tension coming from her father and could feel the anxiety dripping from Mason himself. She held Mason's hand, feeling his sweaty palm, and rested it on the table. *Dad must have really threatened him.*

The server handed them menus, telling them about the dinner specials. After the server left, Emory told her father about her job and Wesley, and his recent break-up with Tomás, and John shared with her some more ideas about his new defensive scheme. Mason occasionally interjected with a short comment, but for the most part, just listened to them talk, trying to relax himself. *I need to settle into the game.* He tried to reassure himself the evening was going better than expected.

He found himself getting a bit more comfortable and stretched his arm out behind Emory, wrapping his hand around her shoulder. John stopped talking to his daughter and glared at Mason's hand, then into his eyes. Mason quickly withdrew his hand and took a drink of water, swallowing hard. Emory kicked her father under the table, eyeing him to calm down and engage Mason in polite conversation. The server returned to take their orders, spelling John for the moment. Emory ordered a cowboy ribeye, and sides of onion rings and garlic mashed potatoes for all of them to share. Her father beamed, taking pride in her aggressive order and seemingly endless appetite. The men both ordered steak as well. When the orders were finished and the server left, John decided to try to make his daughter happy.

"Mason," he said, "that was one helluva hit you took." Emory nodded her approval to her father. "How's the shoulder?"

"It's coming along." Mason appreciated John's concern, even if he was faking it. "The doctor said I can't throw just yet. Have to do some PT first. Thanks for asking."

"Well that's good to hear," John replied. "Must be nice to have your sling off, too."

"It really is. You forget how important both hands and arms are, until you lose one."

"As long as you just use your hands on the field and not on my daughter, we'll be fine." Mason responded with a nervous laugh, and Emory flashed her father a side-eye. Mason was an enormous presence—a tall, stout NFL player—but upon hearing those words, and the seriousness in John's voice, he felt like a young, pimple-faced teen showing up to take a girl to their first school dance, and being warned by her father, at threat of death, not to get into trouble or miss curfew. But Mason wasn't exactly sure whether John was serious or just jerking his chain. Mason took another drink. "Of course, I'm only kidding," John said with a crooked grin.

Mason exhaled and showed both sides of his hands. "I promise these haven't been on her." He patted Emory on the back. "We're taking things slow."

"Yes, we are," Emory assured her father. "It's only been a few days, and there's lots to sort out."

"I'd have to agree," John said, staring daggers at Mason. "If you hurt my daughter again, I'll fuck up both of your arms. And then I'll kill you slowly. I'm not kidding about that."

"Daddy? I mean, come on…"

"Did I say something wrong?" John asked.

"No, it's OK." Mason patted Emory's hand. "He told me as much on the phone, and we came to an understanding."

Mason was used to coaches becoming unhinged—he knew all coaches, deep down, were type-A crazy people, working long hours with little sleep under incredible pressure, practically living in their offices. They were prone to blow their stack. During their call a few days earlier, John screamed at Mason, like he had just thrown a pick-six in the fourth quarter of a playoff game. John had waited for that moment for six years and held nothing back when Mason called. In all his years of football, Mason had never heard such vitriol from a coach—or any human being. He could feel John's rage. Mason half-wondered if John simply had gone senile, perhaps from too little sleep, or too many hours in the Georgia sun, or too much time around snot-nosed high school students believing they knew the first thing about football. Or, maybe the intensity of coaching for so long in the deep South, where football was king, had driven John over the edge. Mason, however, knew deep down it was none of those things. John was the same as ever—a great guy and a devoted father who, rightfully so, was ultra-protective of his daughter.

"We did come to an understanding," John told his daughter. "I just wanted you to hear it, too."

"I suppose if my two favorite guys are good, then I am, too." Emory shrugged her shoulders. "I'm starving. Where's our food?"

The three large steaks that arrived, in melted butter on piping hot plates, provided a welcome diversion. So, too, did the potatoes and onion rings, making dinner more relaxed. Mason discussed in general terms his decision to play for the Panthers, and that he looked forward to the press conference Monday in Charlotte. John told many of the same stories Mason had heard years ago, several involving Emory on the sidelines under the Friday night lights, and even recalled some of the elaborate plays he and Mason designed in his backyard.

All the while, Emory worked on her ribeye. She couldn't help but eye her father's filet and Mason's porterhouse. As the men talked football, she seized the chance to swipe a bite from each of their plates, moving so carefully, like a stealth ninja, they didn't even notice. Mason and John looked at their plates, seeing their steaks looked slightly smaller, but no idea why.

Throughout dinner, John saw the attention Mason paid to Emory, the same connection they used to have—the tenderness, the thoughtfulness, the love—and wondered how it was even possible. *Emory is more forgiving than me.* John knew all about that connection; he'd seen it in his wife's eyes when she looked at him. But that was a long time ago. He missed it—a look only shared between soul mates. He was happy to see the look again, this time from his daughter. *I don't want her to lose it. She looks so much like her mother.*

Mason picked up the check, and when they left the restaurant, he gave Emory and her father some space, walking outside to have the valet pull John's car around. Mason saw Emory hug her father for a long time in the lobby.

"I love you, Daddy. Thanks for playing nice—for the most part."

"I'm doing my best. You look very happy. He better keep you that way this time."

CHAPTER FIFTEEN

MASON AND EMORY returned to the suite and plopped down on the bed fully dressed, gazing at each other, their heads resting on soft pillows. Emory played with Mason's thick, brown hair, as he closed his eyes, thankful he'd survived dinner.

"It's so nice just to relax in this great room with you," she said.

"I'm actually getting a little tired of hotels and living out of a suitcase. When we get back, I think I'm going to look at houses."

"You are? Well, good for you," she said, choosing her words carefully.

"Want to come with me?"

"Uh, I'm not sure because…" Mason put up his hand for her to stop, not wanting her to stammer or be uncomfortable, regretting he had brought it up. *No sex yet, but you bring up moving in together? Fucking idiot.* "Maybe I'll just rent a condo for a few months. Either way, I'll be close by." Emory gave an apologetic smile, and he changed the subject. "I've been wondering something. You told Eric you wanted to be married before you had sex again. Is that true for us?"

"Houses," she teased, "and now are you thinking about marrying me?"

Of course! "No, I mean, um, no, I mean, not now. I guess I should at least get divorced first."

"Probably so. Plus, it's only been a week."

Mason looked down. *I'll just be honest.* "I'm thinking about sex."

"Of course you are. I do, too, sometimes. I didn't sleep with Eric for a lot of reasons, and none of them apply to us." She paused for a moment, smiling. "You know, I like the sound of that—'us.'"

"Me too."

She grabbed his hand. "Look, I'm not having sex with you because we only just found each other again, and I want to get things right this time." *I also haven't been honest with you.* "And you're still married."

Mason leaned over her and placed his hand on her cheek. "It's over with Alexis. You know that, right?" Emory nodded. "I waited for you once before, and I'll wait again."

His phone rang. *Ring!* "Shit, it's my mother!"

"Kathleen!" Emory shivered. *Ring!* "Lots of parent issues tonight."

Ring! Mason rubbed his eyes. "I don't want to deal with this now."

"Go ahead and answer. I'll go soak in the tub." *Ring!*

Mason patted her booty, as Emory walked into the bathroom. "Hi, Mom."

"Mason, honey, I haven't heard from you." Kathleen sat on her front porch, sipping a glass of wine in the Texas heat.

"It's been pretty crazy lately," Mason said weakly and got up from the bed.

"I had to hear from Steven about the new contract."

Mason rolled his eyes. "Sorry, Mom. I should've called." His mother was not a woman to be ignored or forgotten, particularly by her boys she'd raised on her own. The least Mason could do was keep her apprised of significant events in his life. Mason took a seat on the sofa in the living room, knowing this wasn't going to be easy. He turned on the television.

"How are you, baby?" she asked, a twinge of concern in her voice.

"I'm fine, Mom." Mason flipped between channels, hoping to find something interesting to keep his attention and distract from his mother.

"You sound different," she said, taking a sip of wine.

"Maybe it's because I got my sling off today?"

"You did? Why didn't you tell me that either?"

Mason raced through more channels. "I just did." *Is anything on TV?*

"OK, dear." Kathleen twirled the wine in her glass. "Have you talked to Alexis?" She always had an affinity for Alexis, her beauty and bubbly persona, and was struck by how well Alexis and Mason photographed together and worked a room. As far as Kathleen was concerned, they were right out of central casting—a perfect fit for each other.

"No, Mom. I haven't talked to Alexis, and I don't want to." He paused his channel surfing on a nature show, where a mama bear was attempting to protect her cubs from a ferocious mountain lion. *The irony.*

"Dear, do you think there's any way for the two of you to work it out?"

"No, Mom, I don't. I've told you that so many times before." Mason loved his mother, but she had no idea what a successful marriage looked like.

"But if you don't talk to her, then how do you know?"

"Mom, the fact is—as I've told you before—I don't love her." Mason watched the eager mountain lion circling the cubs, preparing to pounce, the mama bear showing her teeth. "I never did. Not much else to say."

"Marriage isn't always about love, Son. It's a contract. You should be familiar with those. It's a deal between two people for a common goal. For some people it's children, and for others, it's a career."

He ran his fingers through his hair. "Dammit, Mom, I just…"

"Don't talk to me that way, Son."

As the mountain lion lunged at a little cub, Mason shut off the television, hurling the remote towards the edge of the sofa. "Sorry, Mom. What you are saying is just very cynical."

"Is it really? I loved your father, and that got me heartbroken." Kathleen cleared her throat. "Why do you think I never remarried?"

"Because Steven and I would've tormented any man who came near you?"

"You two were little devils. Still are," she said, chuckling, and pausing to refill her glass. "The reason is I never wanted to let someone have power over me again, and when you love someone, they have the power to hurt you."

Mason swallowed hard, knowing she was right. *I hurt the only woman I ever loved, and she paid a tremendous price. I did, too.* But he refused to concede anything to his mother, unwilling to allow her bitterness to infect his life anymore. "What about Steven and Olivia? They love each other and are very happy."

"You want love? Love your wife!"

"Too late, especially since Alexis is threatening to challenge the prenup. She's only interested in the money." Emory peeked her head out of the bathroom and yelled for Mason to bring her a pair of panties.

Kathleen set down her wine glass, and stiffened her spine. "Daniel Evan Mason, who is that woman?"

Mason darted towards the bathroom and put his finger over his mouth. "Sorry," she mouthed, "I thought you were off the phone." Emory retreated into the bathroom, and closed the door.

"Who is that, Son?"

Mason panicked, grabbing at his hair. "I think it was housekeeping."

"Asking you for underwear? I'm not stupid, Mason. What is going on?"

Mason felt an urge to be honest, but decided he didn't owe his mother a response—not tonight, not ever. He was a grown man, living his own life, and didn't need his mother's approval for what he did or didn't do. "Mom, this is really none of your business."

"You and Alexis have only been separated a few months, dear. This could look very bad in the divorce proceedings."

"I don't care. It's late. And I'm tired of how things may or may not look. I'm tired of what other people may think."

"I didn't raise you to behave this way, Son. You are still married!"

"Bye, Mom." He hung up the phone, paused for a moment to gather himself, then walked to the bedroom. He opened Emory's bag and rummaged through her clothes. He found a pair of black lace panties, and also a white cotton bra and underwear. He held both in his hands, admiring the black one, but he put it back in the bag, and walked towards the bathroom with the white. *It's only been a week, and my mother has ruined any chance tonight.* He returned to the living room and turned on the television, hoping the mama bear had protected her young cubs.

* * *

Mason slept soundly for hours, his arm draped over Emory. It was the first night they'd actually slept together in the same bed in six years, but only sleeping was in the cards tonight. *Slow.* But he couldn't control his dreams, free flowing and vivid, coming one after another. He dreamed of kissing every inch of her body, massaging her thighs while savoring the taste of her, Emory moaning and arching her back, as he caressed her with his tongue, feeling her body quiver in pleasure. "Mason!"

"Mason! Mason! Mason!" The crowd in Bank of America Stadium screamed his name, as he charged out of the tunnel to start the regular season for the Panthers. He'd earned the starting quarterback job using pictures of his mother and Alexis as throwing targets, the faces of the two women who tested and pained him most. He plastered throw after throw at them in practice, improving his accuracy, their faces exploding with each powerful spiral.

Emory's face appeared before him, sliding down his naked body and kissing his chest and abs before engulfing him in her mouth, his hands gripping the headboard behind him. Her warm tongue licking him up and down, sliding him slowly in and out of her mouth, until he could take no more. "Yes!"

"No!" Emory screamed, thrashing her arms and legs on the bed.

Mason's eyes flew open in the dark hotel room, as Emory flailed next to him. He quickly grabbed her arms to calm her. "Em, Em," he cried, his heart racing, "wake up!" But she didn't, Mason terrified with no idea what was going on. He looked around the room helplessly. *What the fuck?* He shook her. "Em!"

She finally opened her eyes, blinking several times to orient herself, her forehead and hair soaked from tears and sweat. "Mason?" she asked, looking around the room, dazed, then held her knees to her chest.

Mason reached for the lamp next to the bed and flicked on the light. "You were having one hell of a nightmare." *Didn't Wesley say something about this?* He placed his hand on her back, but she abruptly pulled away, getting out of bed and pacing around the suite, with no apparent direction. Mason rose quickly and caught her by the arm. "Baby, where are you going?"

Emory pulled away again. "I need to go dance for a little while," she said, shaking slightly. "I'll be fine."

"Dance? What?" Mason looked at her curiously and gently took her quivering cheeks in his hands. "Em, we are in Atlanta, remember? No dance studio here." He placed his arm around her, trying to lead her back to bed, but she again pulled away, then crouched down by her suitcase.

She dug through it frantically. "I have to do something. Go for a swim or walk."

Mason calmly approached from behind and hugged her tightly. "Em, baby, it's the middle of the night. You can't go out, and you have no swimsuit. Please come back to bed."

She forcefully pushed his arms away. "I can't!" she screamed, tears flowing down her face. Mason backed away, running his hands through his hair, with no idea what she needed or what he should do. He looked around the bedroom, desperately searching for something that possibly could calm her. *TV? Wine? Food? Hot bath?* He spotted his phone across the room and ran to it.

"You need to dance?" He quickly pressed some buttons, finding a classical music station, then grabbed her, holding her so tightly she couldn't resist, and swayed slowly to the music. Emory struggled to get away, her body filled with tension, but Mason maintained his strong hold, her hair, wet from tears, sticking to her face, while her night shirt, drenched with sweat, stuck against his chest. He gently rocked her side to side, careful not to step on her feet. After a few songs, Mason felt her body soften and relax, Emory resting her head on his chest, allowing him to relax his grip. He pushed her hair out of her face. "It's just a dream, Em," he whispered, still swaying.

"No," she said, her lips trembling, "it really happened."

"What?"

"Not now," she said, shaking her head. "Maybe one day."

Was it something I did? Did someone hurt her? Mason had never seen Emory, or anybody, act like this. He felt he needed to know. He felt he should know. But now was not the time to push her. He moved her back and forth to the music, until she stopped moving and yawned, closing her eyes. When she was still, Mason picked her up and carried her to bed, gently placing her down. "Sleep, baby." He kissed her forehead. "Nothing bad is going to happen."

Nearly asleep, she heard his words, but they provided little comfort. *It already happened.*

* * *

Sleep was difficult, and as night turned into day, the ringing of Mason's phone made it impossible. Someone was calling, and calling again—at least five times in five minutes. They tried to ignore it, but that was impossible, too.

"Who the fuck keeps calling me?" Mason groaned, throwing a pillow over his face.

"Good morning, baby," Emory said sweetly, stretching her arms in the air. "It's nice to wake up next to you."

Mason emerged from under the pillow and planted a kiss on her cheek. Emory smiled and reached for Mason's phone on the night stand, handing it to him. It had stopped ringing. He tossed the phone on the sheets and pounced on top of her. Emory giggled, wrapping her arms around him. *Good, I'd rather make out than talk about last night.* She ran her hands down the bulging muscles of his back. He leaned forward, kissing her slowly, and parted her lips. Their tongues met, a wave of heat rising between her legs. Mason felt it, too, as he pushed himself against her, hard. Her breath caught, Mason grabbing her thigh and pulling her leg up, grinding into her again. Emory let out a loud moan. *Ring!* Mason pulled back, his blue eyes burning into her, looking for direction.

"You better answer that." Emory pulled herself up.

Mason frowned, reaching for the phone in the sheets. "Steven! That guy has the worst timing." *Ring!*

"Do you think anything happened to the baby?" she asked, concerned.

"I can't imagine."

"The contract maybe?"

"I doubt it." *Were the details of my contract leaked?* The ringing stopped. Now worried himself, Mason suggested Emory order room service in the living room while he returned the call, not wanting her to hear any conversation with Steven involving his contract, or his divorce from Alexis, or any other unpleasant topic. There was nothing to be gained from having her present. Emory agreed to order— she was starving anyway—so long as Mason agreed to ask about the baby. Mason called his brother, immediately answering in his car.

"It's about fucking time," Steven said.

"Good morning to you, too." Mason rolled on his back, trying to recover from his sleepless night and morning arousal.

"Good morning? It's lunchtime."

Mason glanced at the clock. "I had no idea."

"You football guys live in an alternate universe."

Mason was in no mood for a lecture. "So what's up?"

"I'm driving to get donuts for Olivia. She wants donuts for lunch."

"You woke me up to tell me that."

"No. I didn't mean to wake you."

"Is everything OK with the baby?" Mason asked. "Emory was concerned."

"Yes, of course," Steven assured, swerving across two lanes of traffic into the parking lot of the donut shop.

"Well, good. So why the hell are you calling? I'm busy here."

Steven pulled into the drive-thru lane behind a handful of other cars. "I can imagine what you're busy doing."

"I wish." Mason leaned across the bed to sneak a peek at Emory on the hotel phone in the living room. She caught him spying and smiled.

Steven gripped the wheel tightly. *Why the long line?* "I thought I told you yesterday that I didn't want to be in the middle of your shit."

"What shit?"

"Mom called me about half dozen times last night and this morning, wanting to know about the new woman." Steven pulled up in the line, almost able to see the donut menu.

"I told her it was housekeeping."

"That's so fucking lame. Asking you to bring her underwear?"

"It's not her business."

Steven again pulled up, then surveyed the menu intently. "Hold on." Olivia had provided strict instructions that Steven get her an assortment of cream-filled donuts—not jelly, only cream. He ordered several different kinds, then pulled up to the window to pay. "OK, I'm done."

"Sorry I didn't give you a heads-up about my housekeeper. What did you tell Mom?"

"Nothing about Emory."

"Good, thanks."

"But she thinks I know who the new woman is."

"Why? How?"

"I don't know. She seems to always know everything. She's like a fucking wizard." Steven took the box of donuts from the cashier and placed it on the passenger seat. "And she kept going on and on about how this would look in the press, and how Alexis might use this to say you were cheating on her."

"Jesus Christ, she is ridiculous!" Mason rose from the bed and waved to Emory in the living room, watching television, then shut the bedroom door. "I'm sorry you got caught in the middle."

"You know, Mason, she's not totally wrong." Steven drove out of the parking lot, and came to a red light at a main intersection.

"What do you mean?" Mason put on a shirt and shorts.

"Alexis could make this look very bad for you," he said, fingering the box of donuts, "and for Emory." He took one for himself. "She could drag you into court and make all kinds of accusations. Ruin Emory's reputation. Fuck up your fresh start with the Panthers."

Steven examined the thick donut in his hand, cream oozing out of the side, as if the donut was begging him to bite down. *Olivia had a great idea!* He took a large bite, cream falling onto his chin. The light turned green, but before hitting the gas, he wiped his chin with his finger, licking it clean, then tossed the rest of the donut in his mouth.

"Well, just settle this with Alexis," Mason demanded, "and we can all move on."

Steven tried to speak, the thick donut occupying his mouth. "I know. I'm trying," he mumbled.

"Are you eating a fucking donut?"

"Yeah, I am. You have a problem with that?"

"Not really," Mason said, covering a laugh. "Look, I'm hungry myself. I'll deal with Mom at some point."

"You do that," Steven said firmly. "By the way, I might eat another fucking donut on the way home, if that's OK with you."

"I'll see you tomorrow." Mason collapsed on the bed, rubbing his eyes, then heard pop music coming through the television in the living room. He glanced at the messy white sheets on the bed, running his hand over them, a faint smile coming over his face. He vowed not to allow nightmares, his mother, or Steven to steal the joy he felt waking up next to Emory. He'd waited six years for that privilege, and no one was going to spoil it.

Mason opened the bedroom door to find Emory placing the room service tray on the coffee table. He paused in the doorway, leaning his head against the frame, watching Emory dance to "Summer of '69," as she lifted the lid off of each plate, taking a nibble from each and continuing on to the next. Mason stifled a laugh. Her skin glowed, and her eyes sparkled, with no evidence of any nightmare, other than tousled hair. She dipped a spoon in some yogurt, placed it in her mouth, and did a spin. Emory again caught Mason spying and removed the spoon slowly. "What are you smiling at?"

He walked towards her. "Your hair," he said, straightening it with his fingers. "It looks like we just fucked." He rubbed her waist and back.

I wish. She shook her head slightly to remove the thought, then tugged at his shirt. "I prefer you without this."

He smiled, tugging at her boxer shorts. "I prefer you without these."

"I guess we'll both have to live with disappointment." She kissed him quickly on the lips and led him to the sofa, turning off the television music.

"I love that song, by the way," Mason said, grinning. "Almost as much as 69 itself."

Emory giggled. "What are you talking about?"

"That song—it's about 69. It's called 'Summer of '69.'"

"That's not what it's about. It's about summer love. It's about when Bryan Adams got his first guitar—his 'first real six-string.'"

"Oh, right. And it just happens to be in 1969."

"You are so crazy, Mason."

"The guitar is a symbol for his dick."

"What? The song is not about sex. Bryan Adams was like 10 years old in 1969."

"I don't know how old the dude was. And I don't care really." Mason took her in his arms. "We can play the song when we're in 69, hopefully soon."

She pushed him away, blushing. "Our food is getting cold."

They scooted close to the coffee table. "Everything OK with the baby?"

"Yeah, fine." Mason removed the lids from the eggs and bacon, cheeseburger, chicken noodle soup, granola with yogurt, chicken caesar salad, and french fries. "Did you order the whole menu?"

"It all sounded so good. I got overwhelmed."

"Steven got Olivia donuts for lunch." He grabbed a piece of bacon. "Said she's very demanding about her food."

"I understand," she said, reaching for the cheeseburger.

He dunked a fry in catsup. "God help us when you're pregnant."

Emory put down the cheeseburger, and Mason offered her the fry. Faking a smile, she took it, then asked why Steven had called so many times. Mason didn't want to keep any more secrets, so he explained his mother had heard a woman's voice and was concerned how that could look in the divorce if Alexis got wind of it. And Steven thought she had a point.

But Emory was unfazed. "If any of that happens, we'll deal with it together." She took a sip of soup and added in some crackers.

"Together?" He held her hand. *I can get used to that.*

"Yes, together."

"Can we be together when we get back to Charlotte tonight?"

"I can't." She slurped up two floating crackers. "I promised Wesley I'd hang with him. He's having a hard time with Tomás and his own family."

Mason scooped up some eggs and reached for the yogurt. "I could come over late?"

She kissed him tenderly on the lips. "I have to photograph a baptism in the morning at St. Peter's downtown." She put aside the soup and picked two tiny pieces of chicken out of the salad.

"Damn, OK," he said, taking a bite of the yogurt. "You know, I think I wandered into that church a few days ago."

"It's so pretty in there. Such good lighting." She popped the chicken in her mouth.

"I was thinking I should probably start going to mass again."

"I usually go there myself. Father Tony is great."

"He encouraged me to sign with the Panthers."

"He's a big Panthers fan." She chased down the chicken with

some water. "He's like my booking agent, too. I swear he gives my business card to every pregnant couple he sees."

"Maybe we could start going to mass together? I need it."

"I'd like that," she said. "I'd like that a lot."

CHAPTER SIXTEEN

WESLEY SAT ON a swing in a playground in Freedom Park, a handful of children playing on monkey bars and slides while their parents looked on. He'd hoped some fresh Saturday morning air would provide some clarity and courage to make the call. He'd tried for an hour, alone in the confines of his apartment, but couldn't do it. He thought a change of scenery would propel him, but now, sitting on a swing surrounded by children, he thought he probably just looked like a creep.

He offered a smile to a woman, then saw she watched her child more carefully. *Maybe I shouldn't be smiling?* Wesley cleared his throat and dialed.

"Wesley?" His mother stood alone in her kitchen, grabbing the edge of the counter to brace herself. "Oh my God!"

Wesley hadn't heard his mother's voice in years—he'd lost count how many. "Yes, Mom, it's me," he said cautiously.

"I can't believe you called," she said, tears filling the crevices on her worn face.

"I'm a bit surprised, too, Mom." He looked down at the ground and kicked some dirt, his hand shaking slightly on the swing.

"I can't believe you're calling me 'Mom.'" She reached into a cabinet for a hand towel and wiped her face.

"Should I call you something else?" Wesley looked up and saw a child hanging upside from a monkey bar.

"I can think of several things," she said, with a small chuckle, looking over at a photo of her son on the kitchen counter, his strawberry-blond hair the same as hers.

"I think I've called you all those things—at least to myself."

"I expect you have," she said, sniffling, "and with good reason." She took a seat at her kitchen table, all quiet in the house. It seemed it had been quiet since Wesley left, or rather the day she and her husband had thrown him out. He was always such a vibrant, funny presence, and now all that remained was a coldness and dreariness, hanging alongside the gray walls and brown furniture, infecting her soul.

"Yeah, well, it didn't make me feel any better about myself. It didn't make me hate you, either. It just made me sad." Wesley wiped a tear from his cheek. "And I don't want to be sad anymore."

"Wesley..." Her chest heaved, as she broke down, barely able to speak. "Wesley, I... Wesley, I am so sorry. For everything."

"I know, Mom," he said, choking up himself, doing his best to keep up with his own tears. "I'm sorry, too." He noticed the parents around the playground watching him even more closely. *They think I'm a sad pervert. If they only knew what I'm dealing with here!*

"You have absolutely nothing to be sorry about, baby."

"I could have called sooner..."

"We gave you no reason to."

"...or if I wasn't gay."

She sighed. "Being gay isn't something you need to apologize for."

Wesley looked into the sky, the sun gaping through the clouds. "I've been waiting for you to say that for years, Mom." He took a deep breath and exhaled. "You have no idea."

"I was ready to say that years ago, but I was too ashamed to call you. I was afraid you wouldn't want to talk to me ever again. And I wouldn't have blamed you."

Wesley kicked some dirt. "What about Dad?"

"I am working on him, believe me. He's a stubborn old mule. He loves you but just doesn't understand. He may never understand."

"I'm happy to have you, for now."

* * *

On the flight back to Charlotte, Mason gave Emory his wallet and asked her to order a beer from the flight attendant making her way down the aisle, then excused himself to the restroom. She reached in the wallet for some cash to pay for the beer and noticed a condom stashed inside. *Is that for us? We never used those.* Her mind raced, wondering why he was carrying that around.

The attendant returned with the drinks, and a moment later, so did Mason. He opened the beer, taking a sip, as Emory pulled out the condom, dangling it in front of his face. He gagged. "Jesus Christ, Em!" He lowered her arm and took the condom. "We're on a plane." He looked around nervously to make sure no one was looking.

"Why do you have that?" she asked, her jaw set.

"I forgot it was even in there."

"But why do you even have it? You told me you'd only been with me and Alexis."

"Keep your voice down. Can we talk about this later, in private, please?"

"No, why do you have it?"

"Be quiet," Mason whispered, running his fingers through his hair. "I always used one with Alexis, OK?"

Emory loosened her seatbelt and turned to face him. "Why?"

"Later, please."

"No, now."

Mason loved Emory, but she could be stubborn when she wanted something. He knew it was hopeless to get her to back off, so he slugged the rest of the beer for patience. "I never trusted her. She said she was on birth control, but I didn't want any accidents." Emory felt her stomach clench. "So I always used one, OK?" Mason squirmed, cocking his head from side to side to try to loosen up. He explained Alexis had wanted a child, and asked several times, but Mason always refused, putting her off for various reasons—a hectic regular season or a busy offseason. The time, and the woman herself, never seemed right, so he resigned himself to wear a condom each time, never trusting she would handle the protection.

"Always?" Emory asked, leaning towards him in disbelief.

Mason closed his eyes and exhaled deeply. "Yes. Can we drop this now?"

"No!"

"Em, can you understand how difficult this is for me to discuss with you? And on a plane?"

"Not one time, never, did you ever…"

He stopped her. "No!" Emory smiled broadly and leaned back in her seat, tightening her belt. "This makes you happy?"

She bit her bottom lip. "It makes me happy to know that I'm the only woman who's ever felt you."

* * *

Wesley heard the key hit the door and stood up, dressed in black, form-fitted pants, with a lavender button-down shirt. Emory held her bag, walking into the den, as he gave her a dazzling smile. "Hot date?" Emory asked, hoping he'd reconciled with Tomás.

Wesley took her bag. "Yep, going dancing with my best girl. Get ready. The band starts in thirty minutes."

Emory needed some sleep. She also needed a shower. But apparently there was no time for either, and she wasn't about to delay Wesley's plans. It was good to see him happy, and his enthusiasm was infectious. She walked into her bedroom and slipped off her clothes. Wearing only her black lace panties and matching bra, she freshened up her make-up and hair in the bathroom.

Wesley approached, holding two pair of shoes. "Which of these works better with my shirt?" He saw her from behind. "Damn, girl, did Mason see you in those?"

Emory applied some mascara and eyed him through the mirror. "Nope. He was a perfect gentleman." She picked a pair.

"Really?" Wesley quipped. "Did the doctor put both his arms in a sling?"

Emory put on a dash of lip gloss and smacked her lips. "I told you we are taking things slow." She held up a tight red dress. "What do you think?"

"Hell yes! You look sexy in that dress!"

Emory rolled her eyes and stepped into it, Wesley zipping it up behind her. "Did you talk to Tomás when I was in Atlanta?"

"No." He stuck out his lower lip.

"Dammit." She pulled her hair up into a high ponytail. "What did you do while I was gone?"

"Well, not too much. I taught class, watched a bunch of Bond movies, and…"

"And?"

"And called my mom this morning."

"You did?" she shrieked, running to him.

"Yep." Wesley smiled. "She said she was sorry, and that she loved me."

Emory threw her arms around him. "Did you make plans to see each other?"

"Yes, at the wedding."

Emory excitedly clapped her hands. "Now let's go shake our booties."

* * *

The club was shaped like a circle with dark windows on all sides. A young, hip crowd sipped drinks at bistro tables around the dance floor, while others, as the small band played, gave their best impressions of swing and jazz dance from decades past. Wesley led Emory inside and made a beeline for the dance floor, twirling and spinning each other, laughing and smiling together. Her dress moved with her and came dangerously close now and again to swinging too high to reveal her lace panties. But Emory didn't care—not on this night. She was happy for Wesley and his mother and didn't know anyone at the club anyway. They all seemed so young, like they should still be in high school.

The band shifted to slow jazz. Slightly out of breath, Wesley and Emory went their separate ways—Wesley went to get some drinks, and Emory hustled to get the last empty table. She sat idly for a minute until a young guy in a flannel shirt and jeans, with blond bangs hanging over his eyebrows, strutted towards her and and sat down.

"You looked good out there," he said, flashing a cheesy smile and making himself comfortable. "Can I get you a drink?"

"No." Emory looked past him—he looked like a child—searching for Wesley in the crowd.

"Why not?" he pressed. "I mean, you look *hot* in here." He dragged out the word, leaving no doubt what he meant.

Emory rolled her eyes, knowing Mason would squash this boy. "The guy I came with is getting me one." She had little hope that would stop his intentions. She thought to leave the table and find Wesley, but was tired and her feet hurt. And she had grabbed the last table, and didn't want to lose it—certainly not to this idiot.

"The guy you were dancing with?"

"Yeah." Emory fanned herself with a napkin.

"My buddies and I thought he was gay." He turned and pointed to a group of guys sitting at a table across the club, laughing and drinking amongst each other and watching his pursuit.

Emory looked at them, disgusted, and turned her eyes back to him. "You and your friends were right. You all are really smart." *Where the hell is Wesley?* He turned to his friends, and with a loud chuckle, gave a thumbs-up that they got it right. Emory was in no mood for this bullshit. She'd promised Wesley a date and came out to celebrate with him, and she would be damned if some pretty boy and his loser friends were going to insult him and waste her time. He turned back to Emory in mid-chuckle, and she ambushed him. "But I still fuck him. I'll probably fuck him tonight."

The boy's face dropped, his chuckle turning to nervous laughter. "Wait, what?"

She pointed in the direction of the bar. "He's looking for a guy to bring back, too." The boy was too shocked to speak, realizing he was in way over his head. "You surprised?" The boy moved his bangs out of his eyes. "You and your buddies are so fucking smart, I thought you would have figured it out." He looked back to his friends for support and shrugged his shoulders, deeply confused and now sweating, the friends sensing something had gone very wrong. Emory was now in control. "We dance, and then we fuck. Sometimes with another guy he finds."

The boy recoiled from the table, almost falling out of his chair. "Oh my God!"

"It's a very mature relationship we have." She pointed to his group and shooed him away. "Go back to your little friends." The boy limped back to his table.

Emory renewed her search for Wesley but had no idea where he was, unable to spot him in the thick crowd. Growing concerned, she decided it was more important to find him than to keep the table. She weaved through the crowd, her tiny frame helping her squeeze her way to the bar. She spotted Wesley, with a drink in each hand, chatting up a dirty-blond haired man rubbing Wesley's arm. She sidestepped a few more people, then saw the man run his fingers through Wesley's hair. *He's getting hit on, too?* She reached the bar, and stood between Wesley and the dirty-blond flirt. "What's taking so long?" she asked, kissing him on the cheek, then rubbed off her lip gloss with her thumb, as Wesley gave her a strange look. She took one of the drinks and grabbed his hand. "Let's go dance."

Wesley gave a sympathetic smile to the flirt and offered a quick apology, Emory moving him away into the noisy crowd. "What do you think you're doing?"

"Saving you from a terrible mistake."

"How so?" he asked, raising his voice, as they dodged a couple making out in front of them, then veered around a group of young women toasting each other.

"Tomás."

"Butt out," he snapped, leading her past some preppy college students. After a few more twists and turns, they reached the edge of the crowd, near the bistro tables, and by that point, Wesley had calmed himself. He was never able to stay angry at his roommate for long. She was usually right, and just too cute. "That guy looked good though, didn't he?"

"Yes. So does Tomás."

"You ready to go?"

Emory nodded, then flashed him a devilish look. "But I've got to do one thing first. Follow me." They walked across the club towards the table with the boy in the flannel shirt, chatting up his rowdy friends, holding a beer in each hand, having seemingly recovered from the education she provided. Emory and Wesley walked close to him, holding hands, and she caught his eye, winking at him while pointing at Wesley. "It's just me and him tonight." The boy's eyes bulged from his head.

Wesley gave Emory a confused look after they'd passed the table. "Just keep moving," she said. "I'll tell you in the car."

CHAPTER SEVENTEEN

STEVEN AND OLIVIA sat in a local eatery in downtown Charlotte, sipping water at a table for four, waiting on Mason and Emory. Steven's mind raced about the Panthers press conference tomorrow; this was a business trip for him, but for Olivia, it was a chance to meet Emory and offer support for Mason.

Olivia tried to stretch herself out, flexing her feet and arching her back, the small, narrow seats on the three hour flight from Texas to Charlotte having done a number on her body. "Honey," she said, laying on her sweet Southern charm, "next time, first class please, OK?"

"What for?" Steven looked at the menu, then his watch; Mason, as usual, was late. "It's so much more money."

Olivia pouted, sticking out her lower lip. "We can afford it." She twirled her long, wavy red hair and rubbed his hand. "Plus, it would be nice to do that with you."

Steven kept his eyes fixed on the menu. "It just doesn't make sense. For like hundreds of dollars more, you get a few extra inches and a few more snacks."

"I'll take the inches," she replied, "and you can take the snacks. Deal?"

He looked up from his menu. "I don't need the snacks."

"Honey, please," she said, batting her eyes.

"What is this about?" Steven asked, irritated.

"I need the inches!" she barked, her charms vanishing.

"But it's so few…"

"I'm fat, and will take whatever few inches I can get!"

Frightened by his wife, Steven turned back to his menu to escape, hiding behind it, then heard a familiar voice. "Oh my God, Steven, what happened to your hair?" He looked up, finding Emory and Mason walking towards the table. Mason motioned for Olivia to

149

stay seated, and kissed her on the cheek. "Mason didn't tell me you were going bald!" Emory teased, giving Steven a strong hug and messing with what was left of his hair. She walked around the table to Olivia, greeting her with a hug. "I got confused and thought we were picking you guys up at the airport," Emory said, digging in her purse. "I know plane food is crap, so…"

"I hear that's true even in first class," Steven interrupted.

Olivia narrowed her eyes at him, and Steven looked away, regretting he'd opened his mouth. "You must ignore my husband, Emory. He's not a very bright man."

"I second that," Mason said with a laugh, Emory taking a seat next to him.

"Third," Emory teased, "and now balding. You poor thing, Olivia."

"It is true. I do not lead an easy life."

"Oh, because I think first class is too expensive?" Steven looked around the table for agreement, but there was none, only silence and stares.

"If your lady wants first class, you do it," Mason said.

"Absolutely!" Emory agreed. "She's carrying your child, for goodness sake."

Steven rolled his eyes, and Emory again dug in her purse. "As I was saying before I was so rudely interrupted by your husband, I thought we were getting you at the airport, so I brought a banana and water bottle for you—and the baby." Olivia's face lit up, as Emory pulled them from her purse. "But now we are in a restaurant, so I feel a bit stupid giving you food and water."

"I second that," Steven chimed in, sucking on an ice cube.

"I love you already, Emory." Olivia peeled the banana and savored a bite. "You better marry this girl, Mason." Mason liked the sound of that, raising his eyebrows at Emory.

Steven choked on the ice cube. "That's my Liv, never holds a thought back."

Liv. Emory smiled slightly to herself that Steven shortened Olivia's name, just as Mason did hers. Olivia polished off the banana, but was still hungry, motioning for a waiter to come to the table. The waiter poured water for Mason and Emory, then took all of their orders. Steven then launched into a discussion with Mason about the press conference, and the women talked pregnancy.

"I hear you are having a boy," Emory said.

"Yes, God must think the world is ready for another Mason boy. I'm not so sure myself."

"You should be concerned!" Emory laughed. "But what a thrill for you."

"Yep, there's nothing like it. At least that's what everyone says." Emory gave a polite smile, as the waiter brought their drinks. "And so far, they're right. I'm fat. I pee on myself now and again. I feel disgusting." Olivia rubbed her stomach and pulled her cheeks, but Emory shook her head in disagreement, assuring Olivia she looked great. It was her business to know. She worked with pregnant women and their children, and Olivia was one of the prettiest she'd ever seen. Olivia didn't believe Emory at all, but appreciated hearing such nice lies from someone other than Steven.

"Will you take my boy's pictures?"

"I'd love to. But what about yours?"

"My pictures? No way."

"You haven't had maternity photos taken?"

"No. I'm not one of those glowing pregnant ladies who want to see themselves."

"You don't give yourself enough credit." Olivia waved her hand in disbelief. "You are all belly. You look amazing. Trust me, I do this for a living. Let me take your photos."

Emory finally convinced Olivia, and they decided that tomorrow, while their men were off with the Panthers, they would have their own fun, with photography and maybe a visit to a spa, too. The waiter brought their appetizers—a tray of chicken wings, along with some chips and spinach dip, and refreshed their drinks. Emory reached for the wings, as Olivia dug into the dip.

"Steven, we better not wait, or there will be nothing left," Mason said, playfully swatting Emory's hand, as he took some wings for himself.

"Don't worry, I'm on my toes here," Steven said.

"I love a woman who likes to eat," Olivia said, munching on some chips.

"I sure do," Emory said, gnawing on a wing. "Always have."

"Much better than that picky bitch, Alexis," Olivia said to Mason.

"I'm glad you approve," Mason replied, then glanced at his brother, who shrugged he had no control. *Shut the hell up, woman!*

"I do," Olivia said. "I've only known Emory for, what, thirty minutes, and I love her. I'm a good judge of character that way." Emory smiled, having never met anyone like Olivia, who just said whatever she felt no matter the time or place. It seemed so liberating to Emory, but to Mason, it made Olivia dangerous. "I always hated Alexis," Olivia continued, reaching for more chips, Mason bracing himself. "We had nothing in common. She was always so concerned with her image."

"Not me," Emory said, waving a wing in the air, "I live with a gay guy in an apartment above a dance studio. I'm perfectly happy that way." The table busted out in laughter, Mason's body somewhat relaxing.

"I'm so glad you two are happy," Olivia said. "Alexis was such a drag. It just makes me sick she is challenging the prenup!"

Mason's stomach clenched, and Steven's eyes bulged, the words spewing out of her mouth before they could hush her. *You loudmouth!*

"What?" Emory looked at Mason, her eyes wide open. "Didn't think to tell me that either, huh?" She placed her napkin on the table and walked to the restroom, Mason cursing under his breath.

"Damn, Liv, that was a secret," Steven said.

"Oops, but why didn't you just tell her, Mason?"

Mason shrugged his shoulders. *Unpleasant topic? Not Emory's business? Protecting her?* Mason didn't want to argue with a pregnant woman, especially when she talked so much and seemed borderline crazy. He chose not to answer her, focusing instead on the wings before him.

Olivia turned her attention to Steven. "You think your dumb brother handled this the right way?"

"Why are you bringing me into this?" Steven asked, wishing he still had his menu to hide behind.

"Because you are handling his divorce. Because you two are joined at the hip."

"I can't control what Mason does."

"If you two knew the first thing about women, you'd know it's better to tell the truth and avoid all the drama." Olivia hoisted herself up. "I'll go fix this, boys. Save me some wings." She waddled to the restroom, and found Emory at the mirror, Olivia placing her arm on Emory's shoulder. "Men are idiots." Emory nodded in agreement, causing her to sniffle, and Olivia handed her a tissue. "Steven told me. I just assumed you knew."

"I *should* have."

"Yes, you should have, honey."

"Do you want to know what else Mason told Steven?" Emory gave a slight nod. "He told Steven to give Alexis whatever she wants."

Emory's jaw dropped. "Why?"

Olivia paused for dramatic effect. "Because all he wants is you."

"Mason said that?"

"He only wants to be able to move on with you. That's worth any price to him." Olivia touched her arm softly. "He just wanted to protect you, that's all."

Emory flashed a small smile. "Just give me a minute, and I'll be out."

Olivia slugged out of the restroom and back to the table. The men stood up for her return, unsure what to expect. Steven pulled out her chair, and she lowered herself, surveying the trays on the table. "Hell, you saved me just one lousy wing?" Each brother pointed at the other, shifting blame, as Olivia grabbed it.

"Is everything OK?" Mason asked cautiously.

"She's fine now," Olivia said, taking a bite. Steven pulled her close to him and kissed the side of her head. *I don't need this drama the day before the press conference.*

"Thank you," Mason said. "Is she coming back?"

Olivia looked towards the restroom, and the men followed suit, seeing Emory on her way back. Mason pulled out her chair and whispered as she sat, "Sorry. I just didn't want you to worry about it."

"I know," she said, patting his thigh. "We'll talk later."

* * *

Kathleen's home was her showcase. It was exquisitely designed, a blend of the old Southwest and modern decor, and she'd spared no expense furnishing it, figuring her home was her best advertisement for client development. She had a flashy website for her interior design services, but nothing could match the clients she generated merely by hosting parties in her grand Texas home. Of course, it didn't hurt to have pictures of an NFL quarterback throughout the house, either. They attracted attention, and she reaped the benefits, emotionally and financially.

But more often than not, Kathleen found herself alone. Her boys long ago had grown up and moved out, and at least Mason seemed uninterested in communicating with her anymore. She curled up in an oversized chair in her den, a glass of red wine next to her on an end table. She played with the diamond cross hanging around her neck and glanced up at the clock on her mantle, knowing Steven and Olivia would be in Charlotte by now. She also knew her sons were keeping something from her. *Who is the new woman?*

She took a sip of wine. She wasn't used to—and certainly didn't like—being kept in the dark, especially in matters involving her boys. She put the glass down and ran her hand across the leather-bound album on her lap, brushing off some dust. She opened the cover, the leather creaking, then looked through the pages, scanning the newspaper clippings and photographs of Mason in his football uniform. She'd saved every one—playground years, school newsletters, county publications, and national sports magazines. *Will there be any more?*

She closed her eyes, remembering sitting in the stadium in Miami with Alexis, seeing the crushing tackle, the force of the hit driving her son to the ground and twisting his body. It replayed in her mind, haunting her. She ran a finger over a photo of Mason in his high school jersey, her eyes filling with tears. *Why is he shutting me out?* She turned the page, then a few more, stopping on a black and white photograph of Mason after a bowl game in his junior year. Emory stood beside him, smiling broadly, without any regard for the camera, looking deeply into her son's blue eyes, alive and sparkling out of the photograph. Kathleen patted her eyes. *My baby was happy then.* She knew—indeed, she'd known for years—she was at least partially responsible for their break-up, but it rarely kept her up at night. She couldn't remember losing any sleep over it, believing the cost was worth the benefit. Her son had developed into an NFL quarterback, living out his—and her—dream, and there was no telling whether that would have happened if Mason simultaneously had to deal with a ballerina's career. He simply didn't have time for that, and neither did she.

But what had happened, she knew, was her son had become distant. *She hadn't seen the glowing smile or sparkling eyes in years. The cost was more than I thought.* She took a big gulp of wine, finishing the glass, then flipped through more pages, landing on a color picture from draft day six years ago. Mason and Alexis sat together in Radio City Music Hall, his hand on her knee, her arms wrapped around his neck. Alexis smiled brightly, but her son looked tired, a hint of sadness behind his radiant blue eyes. She hadn't noticed it before—perhaps she didn't want to—but she could see it clearly now. A fire burned inside her.

Kathleen slammed the album shut and grabbed her phone, determined not to be ignored any longer. She texted Steven first. *Find out about the new lady friend.* She then texted Mason. *Call me about "housekeeping."*

* * *

After dinner, the foursome made their way to the hotel, the same one where Mason stayed during his Panthers visit. He was still staying there until he found a place of his own, though not in the same luxurious room—this time it was on his own nickel. Steven made a reservation there, too. Before heading up to their rooms, they decided to pay a visit to the Atrium Bar, and upon entering, the brothers each received a text, about a second apart. They looked at their phones, then at each other, neither of them wanting to respond to their mother —at least not now.

They walked up to the bar, Clive greeting Mason with a big smile. Mason introduced his group, and then explained, tongue fully in cheek, how Clive was not just a bartender, but a counselor, a man of such intellect, full of solid advice about women and life itself. Indeed, his powers were so great that, with the help of some alcohol, he managed to lead Mason back to Emory. Clive flashed a sly grin, a toothpick dangling from his mouth, genuinely touched by Mason's words. He told them to order whatever they liked, Olivia ordering water and the rest getting beers. Mason dropped a fifty in the tip jar, Clive expressing his gratitude by shaking Mason's hand and gyrating their fingers together in an odd fashion and releasing with a snap. Olivia and Emory were completely smitten with the strange bartender, but Steven saw him as a bad influence, a creepy, old man no doubt looking to corrupt his impressionable brother.

Emory reached for a deck of cards on the bar. "Olivia, did Steven ever tell you he'd always lose to me?"

"No," Olivia said, raising her eyebrows at him.

"She cheats!" Steven exclaimed.

"I do not!" Emory cried, shuffling the cards. "You just stink."

"Mason, doesn't she cheat?" Steven asked, hoping his brother of all people would defend his honor.

"I don't know, man. If she does, I never caught her. I gave up trying to beat her. It was bad for my self-esteem."

Emory cut the cards into thirds and placed them on the bar. "What do you say, Steven? I'll even let you pick the game."

Steven rubbed his hands together. "It's so on, little girl. Straight-up poker, one hand, five cards."

"Fine. Olivia can watch to make sure I don't cheat."

"And Mason will watch, too." Steven patted his brother on the back and took a long swig of beer.

"When I win, which I will, you fly Olivia home first class."

"Oh, I so love this game" Olivia said, a twinkle in her eye. "Cheat if you must, Emory. And Mason, you can help." Mason winked at her, Olivia seeing a confidence, a smoothness, in him she'd never seen before. She'd only ever known Mason with Alexis —tense, hesitant, and dreary. Steven had told her about how Mason used to be, but she'd never seen it for herself, until now.

Steven took the three stacks of cards and made one pile, placing it in front of Mason. "You shuffle. I don't trust Emory at all." Mason took the cards, as Steven looked at Emory. "By the way, when I win, you admit you're a cheater and tell me how you do it."

"Deal the cards, baby."

Mason dealt, and Steven put on his game face, again rubbing his hands together, but now also cupping them together and blowing on them. Emory watched all of Steven's tells with amusement and flashed a look that she knew something he didn't. She asked for one card.

Steven eyed his brother. "Don't you dare help her cheat."

Mason threw his hands up. "I wouldn't dream of it." He slid a card to Emory, who peeked at it, her face revealing nothing. Steven looked at his hand and asked for two cards, twisting his wedding ring on his finger and again blowing on his hands. Mason gave him the cards, Steven flipping them around in his hand, licking his lips. Olivia tried to sneak a peek at what he was holding, but he shielded his hand.

Clive came back over. "What you white people doing?"

"High drama here," Olivia said. Steven looked again at his cards, licking his lips again and giving his ring one final twist for good measure. He suddenly flew out of his seat, unable to contain himself any longer, and slammed four aces on the bar. "Take that, ballerina! We're flying coach!" He slapped Clive and Mason a high-five, as Olivia gave him a disapproving look.

Emory looked at the aces and tilted her head to the side. "Damn, that's really good, bald man." She rested her hands on her face-down cards. "I didn't think all that weird shit you were doing—blowing yourself, licking your face, twisting your ring—would work."

Steven beamed, so happy with himself. "Just a few tricks that I've picked up over the years."

"Well, like I said, that was all a bunch of shit." Emory suppressed a laugh, and Steven looked at her, confused, realizing she hadn't yet played her hand. Emory flipped her cards revealing a straight flush to the king. "Enjoy first class, sweetie!" she shrieked, hugging Olivia tightly.

Steven slumped in his chair, his ego shattered. "What the hell?" Mason burst into a huge laugh.

Clive raised his hand to Emory, and she slapped it. "Little white woman beat yo' ass, bro!"

"This is impossible! There is absolutely no way." Steven scratched his head. "Let me see the deck." Mason passed the cards to him, and Steven inspected them, like a detective dissecting a crime scene. *They look normal.* He got up from the bar stool and exited the bar with what little pride he had left, giving a parting shot on the way out. "This isn't over!" Olivia yelled back that he had only a few weeks to learn some sportsmanship for the sake of their son, as Clive nodded in agreement.

"Looks like it's my turn to go perk someone up," Mason said.

"You do that," Olivia said. "We need some girl time anyway. Clive will keep an eye on us, too."

"Damn right I will," Clive said. Mason asked for two longnecks before calling after his brother.

"Can't believe they ditched you two fine white women," Clive said, refilling their drinks. "I'd never let you two out of my sight!"

"Hard to believe, isn't it, Olivia?"

"Yeah, I think they went out to lick on each other," Olivia said, realizing that didn't sound quite right, holding her belly to control her laughter. "I mean, lick on their wounds."

"That's some messed-up shit you just said," Clive replied, "and you ain't even been drinking."

Clive excused himself, and Olivia took a sip of her water. "Steven told me you two were very close." Olivia liked the friendly relationship her husband had with Emory, watching them tease each other, particularly enjoying that Emory seemed always to have the upper hand on her stressed-out husband. It was an unusual sight.

"Yeah, I'm an only child, and Steven was always like a brother to me. You really get to know someone sitting together in a football stadium in freezing weather, pouring rain, or scorching heat."

"I suppose so."

"Do you know Steven never missed one of Mason's games in college, even though he was in law school?"

"I didn't know that. Steven doesn't talk about himself much. Half the time, he's talking about Mason."

* * *

Mason found Steven sitting alone in the lobby, his head in his hands. Mason handed him a beer. "Dude, did you fucking help her cheat?" Steven took a long sip of his beer.

"Of course not. Are you done pouting like a little girl?"

"Yeah, I'm done. I just needed some air."

Mason took a seat next to his brother. He knew he needed to talk to Steven about Olivia's big mouth, hoping his brother could reign her in at least a little bit, but he wasn't optimistic his brother, or anyone else in the whole world, could contain her mouth. It was just out of control. He needed to find out exactly what Olivia knew. "I can't have Olivia bringing up Alexis, and talking about the prenup to Em. That's not helpful."

"I know." Steven took a long drink. "You can blame me for some of that."

"I sure as hell can. What the fuck happened to attorney-client privilege?" Mason flicked Steven's ear with his finger. "Does Olivia know about the Seattle offer? I don't want her blurting out something to Emory."

Steven assured him Olivia didn't know any details about the Seattle offer, but urged him to just come clean like Olivia had suggested. It would avoid any problems. The last thing Steven wanted was a huge fight before the press conference, and he wasn't sure how long he could keep the details of the contract offers from being leaked.

"I'll think about telling her," Mason said, standing up. "Let's go back inside."

Steven took out his phone. "You mean you don't want to check back with Mom first?"

* * *

"What have you two been talking about?" Mason asked, concerned.

"I was just promising Olivia I would teach the next Mason boy how to play cards and dance, since you two can't do either." Emory and Olivia giggled together.

"Wow, maybe we should've just stayed in the lobby?" Mason wondered.

Clive gave a wide smile. "I wish you would have." He handed the men another longneck, and Mason dropped a twenty in the tip jar.

Olivia jumped in the fun. "While you guys were outside doing whatever, Emory told me about the real gems that Steven brought to Mason's games. And by gems, I don't mean Emory."

A twinkle came into Mason's eyes. "I may have heard about them before," he said, then turned to Steven. "But I need to be reminded."

Steven threw his arms up in surrender. He couldn't understand how he'd turned into the laughing-stock of the evening. *A sanction for violating attorney-client privilege?* But whatever the reason, it didn't matter. His wife was having a good time, and he hadn't seen his brother this happy, this eager, this carefree, in a long time. He saw Emory was different, too. He'd seen her only once—at college graduation—since Mason stupidly broke up with her, remembering how she looked that day, a shell of the once happy-go-lucky girl, beyond thin, with her skin no longer shiny, hobbling around with her foot in a boot. But the old Emory was now back. She and his wife could tease him all night, and it would be fine with him.

"Apparently there was a real dorky girl who read her contracts law textbook for the whole game," Olivia said.

"Such a nerd!" Emory said. "Didn't say a word the whole game. Weirdo."

"Hey, she was a very nice girl." Steven retorted, but couldn't help laughing. "Very studious."

"And there was the one who dressed all in black to protest the brutality of the sport," Olivia said, piling on.

Mason looked at Steven. "Why did you bring her?"

"I don't know. It was a long time ago," Steven said, shrinking on his stool. "She looked really good in black, maybe?"

"She was a troll!" Emory blurted out.

Olivia elbowed her husband. "I sure hope you think you've up-graded."

"I have, baby." Steven kissed her cheek and rubbed her belly. "First class now."

Mason looked at the three of them, his three favorite people in the world, laughing and enjoying themselves. Miraculously, and with the help of Clive, he now found himself with all of them in a hotel bar in downtown Charlotte. For so many different reasons, this was unthinkable just a few weeks ago.

* * *

Tomás stood in front of a blank canvas in his art studio, surrounded by half-painted ones littered on the floor. He looked over the myriad color choices at his disposal, but none seemed right. In fact, nothing seemed right. He held a paintbrush in his hand. He'd tried to force various ideas, hoping that the mere act of beginning would stir some direction, but it hadn't. It only stirred more frustration and failure.

The hotel had forwarded him a significant advance for the painting, having made the request on short notice. But the nice advance didn't ease Tomás' trouble—it was beyond a mere deadline. He was without ideas or imagination, his creative energy eroded. He saw the wreckage on the floor around him and wondered whether Wesley had suffered, as he had. He was surprised Wesley hadn't called, but figured that he, too, wouldn't reach out to a person who'd broken his heart.

As a matter of course, he'd always invite Wesley to review a painting or sculpture or other work before presenting the finished product to a client. Wesley each time provided constructive criticism —a different color here, or a different emphasis there. Wesley made the art better, just as he made Tomás better. But he couldn't call Wesley now about the hotel painting, or any other lingering work. It would be selfish and beyond awkward, and Wesley was not without pride. He simply had no incentive to help anymore. Tomás put down his paintbrush and worried about his deadlines—and his own pride.

He walked into the small kitchen adjoining his studio, hoping that food would help spur some creativity. He opened the refrigerator door and grabbed a hard boiled egg, placing it on a paper plate. He cracked the egg and peeled the shell, staring at the pieces scattered on the plate, then the canvases on his floor. *What a broken mess.* He looked at a picture hanging on his wall, a picture of him and Wesley visiting Sea Island last summer.

Tomás shook salt and pepper on the egg, and took a tiny, unsatisfying bite, tossing the remainder in the trash. He walked to a chair and turned on the television, flipping around until he found an action movie. He curled up his legs and leaned his head against the back of the chair. There was gunfire and blood. He knew Wesley would love it, and wondered if he was watching.

* * *

Emory sat barefoot on the sofa in Mason's hotel room, her legs tucked underneath her. She twirled her hair with her left hand and watched as Mason turned on the fireplace. She closed her eyes, still unsure if the whirlwind that had become her life was real. She felt

Mason sit beside her and saw him holding two glasses of wine, handing one to her. She placed her glass on the coffee table. "I think I've had enough tonight." Mason frowned and took a sip from his glass. "Before you get even more drunk, tell me about Alexis."

Mason shook his head, leaning in for a kiss, but she pushed away, smiling. "OK, if we have to," he said, "it might help if I drink some more."

"We do have to." She took his glass and placed it on the table. "I felt left out at dinner. Everyone knew about the prenup but me."

"I'm sorry you felt that way."

"And I don't even give a shit about the prenup. Give her all your money, or don't—I don't care."

"If you don't care, then why do we need to talk about this?"

"Because, Mason, that's what people in relationships do. They share things with each other."

"I just don't want our relationship to become about Alexis or Eric or anything else other than us."

Emory took a deep breath. "I understand that. But if you really love me like you say you do," she said, her voice cracking, "then I should be the first to know things, not the last."

He closed his eyes and lowered his head, hoping his sullen demeanor would make her stop. "It's just a fucked-up mess."

But Emory didn't stop. She lifted his head and stroked his cheek. "You can't keep things like that from me, OK? I can handle it."

Mason was tired and frustrated, and a little drunk, too, in no mood to fight or see her cry, but she was pushing him. "Before I agree, how about you tell me about your nightmare?"

She removed her hand from his face. "That's not the same. That's in the past, and Alexis is happening right now."

"Bullshit, it was like two nights ago."

Trembling slightly, Emory knew he was right. *Just tell him.* Mason leaned close to her. "I'm worried. Just tell me, did someone hurt you?"

"Oh God, it's nothing like that. The only person who hurt me was me."

Mason didn't know what that meant, but it had been a good night, and he didn't want to ruin it. He also didn't want her to come back at him with more Alexis questions. *Some things are better left unsaid.* He threw his arms around Emory and flipped her over his shoulder. "I'm taking you to bed." He walked towards the bedroom door, kicking it open with his foot, Emory giggling and slapping him on the back.

"Mason, you neanderthal, put me down!"

He plopped her down on the bed, and leaned over her, his blue eyes filled with desire. "Stay with me tonight."

It was getting harder and harder for Emory to resist, but she stuck to her guns. "I can't because I don't have my equipment for my shoot with Olivia tomorrow." Mason hung his head, and Emory couldn't bear it. "Why don't you sleep at my place?"

"Sounds good to me. Location is not important."

"I said *sleep*," Emory emphasized.

"I know, I know. I'll be good," he said, tickling her.

Emory wiggled around the bed, laughing and pleading for him to stop, his hands all over her body. She couldn't remember laughing so hard in years. Overcome with happiness, she blurted out, "I love you," then quickly covered her mouth with her hand, completely em-barrassed, her face turning bright red. She hadn't expected to say that. She had certainly thought it but never intended to say so out loud this soon. *So much for slow.* The alcohol, she knew, forced the words out of her mouth—they just couldn't be denied, or taken back, like her love for Mason.

He looked down at her, stunned. He'd said the same thing on the phone a few days earlier, and she hadn't responded, which worried him. But now she'd said it, too—the very words he longed to hear again. There was no going back now. "I know we have things to work through," Mason said, holding her face in his hands. "But I promise you, Em, this time I will be worthy of your love."

CHAPTER EIGHTEEN

EMORY SAT BETWEEN Olivia and Wesley, as three nail technicians worked on their feet. "This is the best idea you've had in a while, girl," Wesley said, wiggling his toes in the water. "Thanks for inviting me."

Emory pointed to Olivia giving her credit. "She told me about Tomás, and honey, there's nothing better for a broken heart than hitting the spa."

"Thank you, Olivia, I'm feeling better already." Wesley leaned his head back, easing his mind. "We're not just doing feet, huh?"

"We're doing it all!" Emory said, giggling. "Manis, pedis, facials, massages, and Olivia, you're getting your hair and makeup done for our shoot."

"We deserve it all," Olivia said, "for all the shit we put up with from our men." Wesley and Emory nodded in agreement, but then Olivia turned serious. "But what I really need is a wax. Must be a damn forest down there by now!" Wesley and Emory, along with the technicians, erupted in laughter. "Was that inappropriate?"

"No way," he said. "I come here once a month to take care of that area. They have this hard wax they use. Hurts less."

Olivia appreciated the tip. "I might try that."

"Too much information, Wesley," Emory said.

"Whatever, it's not like I said she should vajazzle herself."

Emory hid her face, mortified, regretting she'd allowed Wesley to come, but Olivia was intrigued. "Is that popular in Charlotte? It seems all the Texas housewives are doing it."

Wesley quickly asked, "Emory?"

"I wouldn't know," she said, then apologized to the technicians for her friends.

"Oh, come on," he said, "we ballerinas are all bare down there. You can't have more than a landing strip."

"I prefer Brazilian," Olivia volunteered.

Emory turned bright red. "Someone help me!"

"Nothing to be embarrassed about," Wesley assured her, leaning forward and winking at Olivia. Emory knew she needed to get control of her company fast. She needed something to distract them, like waving a bone in front of a puppy. "The press conference should be on any minute." The spa manager turned on the television, and after flipping through some channels, landed on Mason, wearing his new Panthers jersey, #11, on stage next to Panthers management, dozens of microphones before them. The room was overflowing with reporters and fans, but Olivia and Emory could still make out Steven in a folding chair in the back corner of the room, the bright lights shining off the top of his head.

Mason fielded questions with ease—it was a good situation for him; he had moments where he'd wondered if he'd ever play again, but no longer; his recovery was going well, and doctors were optimistic; he didn't know whether he'd be the starting quarterback, but would work hard to be; he looked forward to digging into the playbook and learning the offensive system; he couldn't wait to meet his teammates. And on and on it went. He looked the part of an NFL quarterback and spoke with confidence, Emory watching him with pride. "Doesn't he look handsome?" she whispered to herself. The Panthers management gave some concluding remarks, and then it was over. Steven had worried, as usual, for nothing.

Relieved it was over, Emory leaned back in her chair, and Olivia nudged her. "Looks like someone will be celebrating tonight while I'm flying home first class."

"I do have a little something planned. Steven is helping me with it."

"Oh," Olivia said, "he didn't tell me anything about it."

"He'll probably fill you in on the plane."

"I'm sure Mason would prefer a congratulatory fuck," Wesley chimed in, "instead of whatever lame shit you and Steven have cooked up."

* * *

In the cold outside their hotel, Mason and Emory waved goodbye to Steven and Olivia. When they'd left, Mason wrapped both his arms around her, then made a move towards the lobby door, but Emory stopped him, waving to the valet. "I have other plans for us tonight." Her car appeared, and she excitedly pulled Mason towards it. Mason asked where they were going, but Emory didn't say a word. She quickly turned on the heater and pulled out of the hotel, stopping at a red light to reach into her glove compartment for a bandana. "Put this over your eyes. I don't want you to know where we're going until we get there."

Mason smiled mischievously. "I remember doing this with you when..."

"Shut up, and put it on." She slapped his arm. "And no peeking." Mason tied the bandana around his eyes, Emory making sure it was tight. After driving a few more minutes, he felt the car slow down, and Emory turned off the ignition, telling Mason she'd be right back. He heard the car door open and shut, then Emory talking to someone, but he couldn't make out what was said. Suddenly, he felt a rush of cold air, as Emory opened his door and took his hand. "No peeking."

Emory led him a few feet, then through a door, slamming hard behind them, causing Mason to jump. They walked through a seemingly endless dark hallway towards an elevator, and rose slowly. Mason heard a ding, Emory gripping his hand tightly. She led him out of the elevator, then a few more feet, and dropped his hand. Mason felt her hands on his cheeks, removing the bandana. It was pitch black and cold. He squeezed his eyes shut, and blinked several times, trying to adjust to the darkness. *Where the hell are we?*

Then he heard it—an unmistakable sound—and he knew. "How did you...?" Mason's jaw dropped, his eyes open wide, hundreds of beaming lights popping on at once, standing on the first row of the owner's suite at midfield of Bank of America Stadium, looking down at the field and surrounded by 70,000 empty seats.

"Steven helped me. He's very persuasive with management."

"You make my surprises look amateur." Mason pulled her to his side, kissing her nose and forehead.

"I plan on being in the stands for all of your games," she said, taking his hand and walking up a few steps into the suite, then removing her coat, revealing a Panthers jersey, #11, with his name on the back.

"I like the way that looks." *It would look better on the floor!*

Emory gave him a smile over her shoulder and pointed to a chilling bottle of champagne. "I thought we should toast your new start." She removed the bottle from the ice. "And our new start together." Mason took the bottle and placed it back in the ice, holding her tightly in his arms, as she melted into his warm body.

Mason thanked her, then pulled back slightly, looking into her eyes. "Not just for all this, which is unbelievably great, but for giving me another chance."

"We both are getting another chance," she said, Mason looking at her, confused. "I wasn't there when you got drafted, so this is my chance to show how proud I am of you."

"I wanted you there so badly that day."

"It didn't look that way on TV?"

"You watched?" Mason ran his fingers through his hair, remembering when his name was called, his family had erupted in cheers, and Alexis kissed him, playing it up perfectly for the cameras. *I subjected Em to that.*

Emory pouted her lips and nodded. "We had dreamed about that moment for so long. I had to be there for you, even if I was alone in my bedroom."

"God, Em, I'm so sorry." *And she wants a second chance? I don't deserve her.*

"You don't need to keep apologizing for the past." She shook her head. "I forgive you."

Mason had hoped so, though she'd never told him before, but was prepared to apologize for the rest of his life if he had to. "Enough about all that, we don't have much time." Emory grabbed the champagne and popped the top, pouring them each a glass.

"What should we toast to?"

"I'll toast to you," he said, "since I don't need anything else."

Mason knew exactly how he wanted to celebrate and wanted to be completely sober. He kissed her softly, and she moaned, pulling him firmly to her. Their lips parted, and he gently stroked her tongue with his, Emory feeling a familiar spark radiating through her body. Mason felt it, too, as he slid his hand under her shirt and unhooked

her bra, caressing her tenderly while they kissed. His other hand slid
to her bottom, and Emory wrapped her leg around his waist, pulling
him closer to her, feeling how aroused he was. Wesley's words
flashed in her mind. *Congratulatory fuck!*

Emory pulled back. "Probably not a good idea to have sex in the
owner's suite." She smoothed her shirt down and hooked her bra.

"At least not on the first day," he said. *But when?* The lights of
the stadium went dark.

"Steven promised we wouldn't stay too long, so I guess our time
is up."

"Our time is just beginning."

* * *

Mason rented a condo on a three-month lease, while waiting for
Emory to be ready for more. She found herself sleeping with Mason
at the condo most nights, though that's all they did, despite Mason's
best efforts. But over the next few weeks, they found there was little
time for the glitz and glitter of new romance. Mason was busy with
press conferences and appearances and continuing his physical
therapy, but made it a point to keep in touch with Emory's father, all
while doing his best to avoid his own mother. Emory spent the
majority of her days teaching dance and taking photographs, making
sure to reach out to Olivia about her pregnancy on an almost daily
basis. Overall, Mason and Emory settled into a nice routine,
spending their free time together, including Sunday morning mass,
and even invited Wesley out with them on occasion to distract him
from missing Tomás. Emory adjusted well to the attention Mason
received from fans when they were at church, or dinner and a movie,
or just walking down the street. She realized, as he did, the attention
was fleeting and came with the job.

CHAPTER NINETEEN

EMORY WALKED INTO the kitchen of her apartment and found Wesley making her favorite breakfast, French toast. He usually made it only on her birthday, which wasn't today, so she sensed something was up. She prodded Wesley for information as he plated the French toast, but he insisted she eat first. They sat awkwardly at the kitchen table, Emory refusing to eat until he spilled, though sad her breakfast was growing cold. After much back and forth, Wesley pulled out The Charlotte Observer from a kitchen drawer.

"Bad photo of me in there?" Emory found herself in the newspaper every other week. The public, or at least the reporters, seemed fascinated with Mason's girlfriend—who she was, what clothes she wore, where she went. It usually was nothing more than a blurb or two in the Style section. She learned to live with it, but preferred to be behind the camera.

"Nothing about you," Wesley said, and motioned to her plate. "I worked hard on that."

"Something about Mason in there?"

Wesley shuffled the paper, finding the front page of the Sports section, and set it in front of her.

QB Mason Accepted Less Money from Panthers

As she read the details of Mason's contract, her face turned from pink to red to crimson, the local reporter wondering why a quarterback, still recovering from shoulder surgery, would accept $1 million less to sign with the Panthers in what could be his final contract. The reporter acknowledged there was an additional $500,000 in incentives with the Panthers, but he saw no way those would ever be reached: it was doubtful Mason would start four games, or ever play in eight. So Mason had turned down a better offer from Seattle to play in Carolina. At this stage of Mason's career, the reporter could find no good reason for doing so, but speculated it might be the new girlfriend.

"You didn't know, did you?" Wesley asked, as Emory rose from the table, taking the paper with her, along with her keys and purse. "There's probably more to the story that you don't know."

"And I'm going to damn well find out."

* * *

Emory parked illegally at the hospital. She got out of her car, with the paper in hand, and slammed the door. She quickly walked inside and up a flight of stairs into the physical therapy center, blowing past the receptionist who called after her. She entered the exercise room and saw a young female therapist stretching out Mason's shoulder. He smiled at Emory, happy and surprised to see her, but she didn't respond, other than to glare at him as she approached, like a tiger stalking her prey.

"What's wrong?" Mason asked, the therapist releasing his arm.

Emory threw the paper at him. "What the hell is this?"

Mason picked it up and read the headline. He hadn't seen the morning paper and didn't know the story broke. *Why hadn't Steven warned me?* He skimmed the article. *Shit, it's pretty much accurate.* The therapist excused herself, having no therapy to offer here.

"Why are you so mad?" he asked. *Should I just start apologizing now?*

"Why am I mad? Are you fucking serious?"

"Yeah, I didn't want to be in Seattle. Raining all the time. I don't even own an umbrella. I wanted to be in Charlotte with you," he said, reaching for her hand.

Emory held up hers, ordering him to stop. "Oh, don't even try it. Don't even try to get all sweet with me. Again, this is something you never even mentioned to me, and decided without me."

Mason wiped his hands with his towel and hung it around his neck. "Em, we had just started seeing each other and things were, well, delicate between us. No amount of money was going to make me leave you."

"Did you ever consider that I would have gone with you?"

Mason raised his eyebrows. "You would have moved to Seattle?"

"I guess we'll never know, because you didn't fucking tell me I had a choice."

"I knew if I told you, you would've made me go to Seattle. Am I wrong?"

Emory knew he was right: she wouldn't have wanted him to stay in Charlotte for her and less money. But she was a stubborn woman, taught to be relentless from her father, and wasn't about to concede anything. "You should've told me."

"Em." He again reached for her hand, but she swatted it away.

"Don't! I'm pissed." Mason smiled at her, trying not to, but just couldn't help himself. "What's so fucking funny?"

"It's just weird to have an angel yell at me."

She threw her arms up in the air and stormed out in a huff, making her way back to her car, quickening her pace, as she recalled parking illegally. *The last thing I need is a ticket to cap off this awful morning.*

A man in a white lab coat rushed after her. "Emory!" he called, then grabbed her arm.

She stopped in her tracks and turned around. *A parking ticket is preferable to this.* "Hi, Eric."

"Are you OK?" he asked, sizing her up. "You look flustered, walking so quickly."

"Just a weird morning."

"Something happen here at the hospital?"

"No, not here," she lied. Emory didn't want to get into any details. She wasn't in any mood and owed Eric nothing.

"I've seen you in the paper a few times lately."

"I'm not thrilled about that," she said, rolling her eyes and walking again towards her car.

Eric followed her like a puppy. "Maybe I should get your autograph? Or his?"

She glared at him, unimpressed by his lame attempt at humor, and put her hand on her car door. She didn't have the energy to deal with Eric and frankly didn't care anymore. Over the past few weeks, she'd moved on with Mason, even if he seemed intent on infuriating her, and needed to save her energy to whip Mason into shape. Eric again put his hand on her arm. "I've got to go," she said, wiggling her arm out of his hand.

"Can we just talk?"

"I have nothing to say." She opened the door, and Eric gently pushed it closed.

"I miss you," he said sadly, a tenderness in his voice.

Emory knew she wasn't going to get away easily. She turned towards Eric and exhaled deeply, trying to regroup and shift her attention from one difficult man to another. "You have two minutes. Talk!"

Eric apologized again for his behavior with Molly, and then kept on and on about it, irritating Emory who looked at her watch, having heard all that before. He promised if Emory gave him another chance, he'd be willing to wait until she was ready to marry him. But Emory shook her head, and then he lowered his head onto her shoulder, whispering again about how much he missed her, and hoping at the very least they could be friends down the road.

Emory knew Mason wouldn't be pleased if she had a friendship with Eric—or any man other than Wesley, really—and wasn't sure she'd want one anyway. She pushed Eric's head up from her shoulder, and he looked into her eyes. "You love him, don't you?"

Stunned he'd ask, Emory didn't know how to respond. She loved Mason—she always had—but didn't want to tell her ex-fiancé that. Regardless, it was none of his business, so she let her silence say everything.

"You couldn't set a date because you still loved him?"

She closed her eyes to hold in her tears, feeling guilty for hurting Eric so badly—and leading him on and agreeing to marry him—when she still was in love with Mason. "I'm really sorry, Eric." Eric appreciated her words and pulled her into a hug, another man's arms making her very uncomfortable. She patted him on the back awkwardly and gently pushed him away, then opened her car door.

Mason exited the hospital and saw their embrace. "What the fuck is this?" he yelled, walking quickly towards them.

"Maybe I can get that autograph now," Eric whispered to her.

"Suggest you shut up," Emory said, then called out to Mason, "Eric was just apologizing for his behavior."

"Looked like more than an apology," Mason said, drawing closer.

Emory grimaced. *Shit, he saw the hug.* Mason reached them and glared down at Eric. "I thought I made myself clear on the phone that you're not ever to put your hands on her."

Eric, an esteemed doctor, thought it best to ignore Mason, not wanting to get in a shouting match or worse with the new Panthers quarterback outside of his hospital. "Bye, Emory. I'll see you around. I'll buy you lunch in the cafeteria sometime."

Mason flashed Emory a warning look. "The hell you will!" he said, then turned to Eric, walking back inside. "You touch her, and I'll get your scalpel and slice your balls off! You won't be fucking Molly then, my man!" Eric disappeared into the hospital.

"Good God, Mason!" Emory slammed her car door. "You are out of control!"

"What? I come chasing after you and find you in another guy's arms! *That's* out of control."

"Oh, don't try to turn this around on me," she said, poking his chest. "I just bumped into Eric. I didn't want to talk to him. I didn't want to hug him, either. I pushed him away. Didn't you see that?"

"Yeah, I saw that," Mason said, trying to calm down. "But what did he mean he'll be seeing you?"

Emory drew a deep breath to settle herself, then explained she sometimes does photography shoots in the maternity ward at the hospital, and that she'd actually met Eric while working there, so she was bound to run into him on occasion. Mason stood still, contemplating what she'd said. His phone rang, but before he answered, he ordered, "OK, but no lunches with that cock! And you have to tell me every time you run into him!"

Emory looked at him, disgusted. She had no intention of ever having lunch with Eric but wasn't about to let Mason tell her what to do, and there was no way she was going to tell him every time she caught a glimpse of Eric. Bumping into Eric from time to time wouldn't be a big deal, and if she were to tell Mason, it would just cause a big fight. She didn't want that and wouldn't be controlled. Emory opened her door and got in her car.

Then Mason banged on her window. "That was Steven! Olivia is in early labor!"

* * *

The airplane reached cruising altitude, and Emory powered on her phone, activating the wi-fi connection and e-mailing clients to reschedule appointments interrupted by their urgent trip to Texas. She tried to concentrate but was nervous about Olivia and still aggravated with Mason. She even found herself feeling a bit sorry for Eric. *No man's balls should be threatened with a scalpel!* After tending to her work schedule, she decided some music could help ease her mind.

She put in her left ear bud and attempted to put in her right, but Mason grabbed her hand before she could. "Can we talk about us, please?"

"I don't feel like it. I'm only interested in the baby."

"Steven said things are going well," Mason assured her. "The labor is fine. And we'll be there soon."

But Emory didn't like his calm tone. He had no idea about pregnancy, especially early delivery. She tried a second time to insert her right ear bud, but he grabbed her hand again, rubbing her knuckles.

"Carolina was a better fit for me."

Emory pulled her hand away. "Now is not the time, Mason. Your deceit will have to wait."

"Deceit?" Mason shook his head. "You know, most women would be flattered if a guy gave up a million bucks for them."

"Flattered?" Emory took out her left ear bud. "That you think I'm so fragile or stupid that you have to make decisions without me?"

"Em, just hear me out."

"No, it's the same old bullshit as in college."

Mason raised his eyebrows. "What's that supposed to mean?"

"You decided what you wanted and didn't try to work things out with me."

Mason sighed. "This isn't the same thing."

"It is," she said, putting in both ear buds. "If there is any chance for us to make this work, you better get your shit together, and stop keeping things from me."

Mason sat back in his chair, knowing there was no reasoning with her when she got this way. All that was important, as he saw it, was being in Charlotte with her, but she seemed intent on punishing him for it. *Can't she just see my good intentions, and leave it at that?* Left with nothing else to do, Mason called for the flight attendant and ordered a scotch.

* * *

The waiting room of the maternity ward was large with a sufficient number of chairs for several families to gather. But it was now largely empty, the only sound coming from a television in the corner of the room repeating an afternoon newscast. Olivia's parents, sitting near the entrance in a tired daze, had seen it at least seven times, while waiting for hours to hear news about their daughter.

Mason and Emory rushed inside, and her parents greeted them with a huge smile, so happy to finally have some family to talk to and also a welcome distraction from the newscast. They congratulated Mason on his deal with the Panthers and quickly were smitten with Emory, an obviously good-natured woman with a good head on her shoulders—a welcome contrast from Mason's soon-to-be ex-wife.

But what Mason and Emory most wanted was an update on Olivia. Her father, Noah, summed it up quickly—Olivia seemed fine but was just taking her sweet time to deliver; they hadn't seen Steven in several hours; and they wished there was a way to change the channel. Mason and Emory walked towards the television to try to figure it out, in the direction of a polished, older woman entering the room from the opposite side, the three of them stopping in their tracks, a mere ten yards apart. Mason hadn't prepared for this moment; he'd been too distracted with Emory's blow-up and Eric's appearance, then rushing back to Texas, to think about it. He also hadn't considered he'd have to deal with this in the presence of Emory. It was now happening too quickly, and he had no idea what to do.

His mother looked Emory up and down. *I'll be damned, "housekeeping" is her!*

Mason instinctively walked toward his mother, his heart pounding and palms sweaty, and nudged Emory to take a seat. She refused, in no mood to be controlled or cast aside, but tried to harness her anger and worry to present a united front. She took Mason's hand, and they walked the few remaining yards together. Mason hugged his mother. "Mom, you remember Emory?"

"Nice to see you again, dear," Kathleen said, as if she were speaking to a child, Emory politely smiling in return. "Looks like I have to get you into a maternity ward to talk to you, Son."

"Mom, let's please not..."

"And once I do have your attention, we can't even talk alone."

Emory bit her tongue, as Mason glanced across the waiting room at Olivia's parents, hoping they weren't watching his personal drama unfold. But of course they were; there was nothing else to do. "Mom, please, we can talk alone later," he said, forcing a hopeful smile. "This is not the place."

"Honey, I don't trust you'll make time for me. We have time now, at least until the baby comes."

"I'll make time later, Mom. And keep your voice down. I'm not even sure what you want to talk about."

"What do I want to talk about?" she asked, her voice rising. "I want to talk about your marriage and, well, your adultery." Emory's mouth fell open.

"Jesus Christ, Mom!" Mason cried, waving his hands for her to lower her voice.

"Don't add blasphemy to your sins, Son."

Mason turned and gave a polite smile to Olivia's parents, trying to assure them that everything was fine, then turned back to his mother. "Mom," he whispered sternly, "there is no adultery going on here. I frankly wish there was, but there's not, so you don't have to worry about that. And as for my marriage, it's been over for a long time."

"But you're not divorced, Son," Kathleen said calmly. "You're asking for problems, personally and publicly with *her.*"

Emory had heard enough and took a step forward. "I'm right here if you have something to say to me."

Kathleen was more than happy to unload on Emory and looked her directly in the eye. "You're not good for my boy."

"I'm the best thing that's ever happened to *your boy*, Kathleen." Mason rolled his eyes and tried to get her to hush, but she wouldn't be contained. Noah turned off the television, so he could hear the soap opera more clearly, his wife opening a bag of chips, as if she were watching a movie. "Ever since he left me, his personal life has been shit. For some reason, you don't seem to care. But you should —more than his career." Kathleen waved her arms dismissively, a fire burning inside. "As for me," Emory continued, "you are entitled to your opinion, but you should rethink it."

"How dare you tell me what to do!" Kathleen barked, as Olivia's mother fired chips into her mouth, Noah dropping his jaw and snagging a chip for himself.

"Mom, please…"

"I'm telling you how it is, Kathleen. Mason is too scared to talk to you."

"Em, come on…" Mason begged, throwing up his hands in defeat.

"No, she never respected me or my career or our relationship either," Emory snapped, then composed herself. "But I don't give a damn about any of that. Not anymore."

"You should care what I think!" Kathleen threatened. *I can get rid of you again.*

"Why? Your thoughts are mean and self-serving. I care about your son—very much. More than you—you encouraged him to marry a woman he didn't love! What kind of mother does that?"

Mason stepped between them. "OK, Mom, Em, let's walk outside. I'm sure Olivia's parents don't care to hear all this."

Olivia's parents frowned and sadly put away their chips, as Mason led the women towards the door. Emory quickened her pace, her anger mounting, and separated herself slightly from Mason and Kathleen. When they reached the door, Steven blew through it. "Noah Daniel Mason is here!"

CHAPTER TWENTY

MASON HUGGED HIS brother tightly, and Emory kissed him on the cheek, joking whether the baby had more or less hair than Steven did. Steven then hugged his mother and embraced Olivia's parents. He informed everyone that the labor was relatively painless, but long, and Olivia was doing great. Mason suggested the new grandparents visit Olivia and the baby first, which everyone agreed made sense, allowing him an opportunity to talk privately with Emory and ease the tension between them, before seeing his nephew for the first time.

Steven led his mother and Olivia's parents out of the room, and Mason and Emory took a seat in the chairs, alone in the waiting room, in silence. Emory folded her arms and stared straight ahead, looking at the rows and rows of empty chairs. *It's the same thing as in college. Maybe I was wrong, and he hasn't changed. Why did I even come?*

Mason hung his head, staring at the carpet, excitement for his brother and nephew overshadowed by despair and embarrassment for Emory and his mother. *What the hell just happened?* "I need peace, Em," Mason said.

"And I need honesty and support. You could stick up for me in front of your mother, you know? That would be something new and different."

"It was just so awkward, with Olivia's parents in here and…"

"Tell me about it. How do you think I felt?"

Mason ran his fingers through his hair. "Let's talk about the first thing you said. Honesty. I can give you that."

She turned to face him. "Then why didn't you tell me about the Seattle offer?"

"The only offer that mattered to me was yours—that you would give me another chance. I knew as soon as I saw you at Gus' Bar that I was staying in Charlotte—contract or not."

Emory paused for a moment, considering his words, wondering if she'd heard them right. She replayed what he said in her mind, the stubborn guy who wouldn't compromise six years ago now willing to give up his football career just for a chance to be with her again. "Mason, I would never expect you to do that. You love football. I could never be responsible for you losing that."

"I know, that's why I didn't tell you," he said, smiling slightly. "Understand? You would've made me go. And the Seattle offer came in less than one week after we ran into each other. There was no way I was going to ask you to move across the country for me, especially so soon."

Emory closed her eyes, again letting his words sink in. This was a different man than the one who left her in the college weight room. Mason was making her a priority. Still, she didn't like being left out of important decisions and was fed up with his secrets—the shoulder, the prenup, and the contract—even though she was keeping her own. But she could understand his logic; he was acting out of fear. *So am I.* She opened her eyes and looked at him. "Are you keeping anything else from me? Now is the time to come clean. I won't tolerate anymore lies from you."

"No. You know everything now."

"Don't lie to me anymore." Mason nodded his head. "OK, now let's talk about your mother." She flashed a wry smile.

Mason sighed. "I don't know what to do about that."

"First of all, if we are going to work, you need to support me. You need to tell your mother about us—where we are, where we're going. You can't let her talk to me the way she just did—the way you let her in college, too."

"I didn't want to create a scene."

"It was your mother creating a scene—at my expense. I mean, I waited for over a minute for you to say something to her, to stick up for me. You never did. So, I handled things myself."

He wiped a tear from her cheek, kissing her nose and forehead. Mason loved his mother but knew it was time to put her in her place. He just wasn't sure how to do it. "I won't allow her to talk to you that way again. I promise."

Olivia's parents and Kathleen returned to the waiting room and saw Mason and Emory holding each other, Mason wiping another tear falling down her face. Emory quickly tried to compose herself, as Mason looked up at Olivia's parents and his mother. "We're both just so happy about the baby!"

* * *

Mason lightly knocked on the door to Olivia's room, and Emory pushed it open slightly, peeking inside, holding a bag in her hand. Steven sat on the bed next to Olivia with baby Noah in her arms. Steven rose from the bed, and Emory hugged him tightly. He shook Mason's hand, thanking them both for flying in on such short notice. Emory put down her things, crept over to the bed, and kissed Olivia on the cheek, Olivia pulling back the blanket, so Emory could get a good look at Noah. Mason came up behind her, placing his arms on Emory's shoulders.

Emory glanced up at Mason. "He's beautiful!"

"Don't confuse my nephew," Mason replied, squeezing her shoulders. "Shouldn't we say he's handsome?"

Emory elbowed him and ran her finger across Noah's cheek. "How did everything go, Olivia?"

Olivia recounted her labor and delivery, which unexpectedly came a month early. Her water broke while resting in bed next to Steven, sound asleep with his mouth open. She nudged him several times to wake up, a dreadful snore coming from his nose, but to no avail, and then yelled and shook him violently. He jumped from his sleep, rolling towards her, coming dangerously close to landing in a sea of amniotic fluid on the sheets. After the laughter in the room died down, Olivia then discussed, in great detail, the dilation of her cervix and size of her placenta, Mason cringing and pleading that Steven make her stop.

"We heard there were some fireworks in the waiting room," Steven said.

"It was embarrassing more than anything," Mason said, then turned to Emory. "We're working through it."

"What is this all about?" Olivia asked.

"Nothing," Mason said to her, hoping to change the subject. "When do you get to go home?"

Steven wasn't about to let it go. "I wish I had been there," he said, sighing. "Olivia's dad said it was tremendous. Really great. Really helped them pass the time."

"Glad we could help," Mason said.

Steven turned to Emory. "If Olivia's dad was telling me right, some of the things you said to my mom, wow!"

"What did you say, girl?" Olivia asked.

"Nothing very nice," Emory said, smiling, "but everything was true. I don't want to re-live it now and spoil this happy time."

"Exactly," Mason agreed, handing Emory her bag and trying again to change the subject.

"I brought you a little something, Olivia," Emory said.

Olivia's eyes lit up. Emory waited until Steven took Noah, then handed her the bag. Olivia peeked inside and took out a package, quickly tearing it open like a child on Christmas morning. "Steven, look at this," she said excitedly, holding a leather bound album. Steven handed Noah to Mason, as Olivia turned page after page of her maternity photos, her hand over her mouth, stunned. Mason couldn't recall ever holding a baby before, worried he somehow might fumble him with one false move, and decided it was best to take a seat in a nearby chair to brace himself and protect his nephew.

Steven and Olivia flipped through the album. "Emory, these are incredible," Steven said. "You are truly an artist."

"It helps to have a beautiful subject." Emory looked over at Mason sitting in the chair, not realizing he had been holding Noah. Her chest swelled, feeling she could faint, and grabbed the bed railing for support.

"Em, are you OK?" Mason asked.

Olivia looked up from the album. "Are you feeling weak?" Steven reached for a small carton of apple juice near the bed.

"Oh, I'm fine," Emory said, trying to pull herself together.

Olivia nodded. "It does something to a girl to see her man holding a baby." Emory grabbed the trash can, raced for the door, and vomited. Olivia began to clap excitedly. "She's pregnant! This is so exciting!"

"No, she's not." Mason handed Noah to his brother and went out to the hallway, finding Emory kneeling on the floor over the trash can. Mason bent down beside her and held her hair back. "Em, baby, what's going on?"

"Must have eaten something bad on the plane."

Mason rubbed her back, as a nurse approached with a towel and water. "Let's go to the hotel. It's been a long day." He helped her to her feet.

"No, you stay. Be with your family. I'll be fine by myself."

"I've actually had enough family time today. We'll come back tomorrow before flying out. I have something else I need to take care of, too."

* * *

In the hurry to get to Texas, Mason had left Charlotte without booking a hotel. He wanted Emory to rest as soon as possible, so he settled for a cheap hotel next to the hospital. The first thing Emory did was take a shower in the room, hoping that would calm and refresh her, but instead it left her shivering on the bed, her hair wet from the shower. Mason sat behind her, rubbing her hair with a towel, occasionally feeding her small sips of chicken noodle soup he had delivered to the room.

"You don't need to dry my hair. It's fine."

"I'm sorry about this shitty hotel. I can't believe there's no blow dryer."

"The hotel is fine," she said, taking the towel and rubbing her own hair.

"Maybe you have a fever?" Mason rose from the bed and rummaged through their bags. "I must have some aspirin in here somewhere."

She watched Mason's mad search, opening every zipper of their bags and rifling through their toiletry items. *He's so good. I'm a fucking liar.* Her stomach began to churn, knowing no medicine could cure what ailed her, and she doubled over.

"Jesus, not again!" Mason left the bags and rushed to her side, rubbing her back. "Maybe the soup was a bad idea?"

Emory took a few deep breaths and slowly rose her head. "No, I'm OK. I'm not going to get sick again."

Mason picked her up and moved her to the top of the bed, wrapping the covers around her, all the way up to her neck. "Try to go to sleep. I bet you'll feel better in the morning." Emory nodded but knew there'd be no sleep tonight, only nightmares, and she didn't want to expose him to that again. "I'll join you," he said. "Just let me do one thing first." Mason got his phone and leaned back next to Emory, allowing her to see the text he was sending his mother. *Date tom. am., just me and you. Meet in the hospital chapel at 9. House-keeper busy. Love, Mason*

He turned out the light and draped his arms around Emory, closing his eyes and releasing a deep breath. He thought about the day, waking up in Charlotte, fighting with Emory and his mother and Eric, adding a new member to his family, Emory getting sick, and now trying to unwind in a barebones Texas hotel room. But more than all of that, what stuck out most, surprisingly enough, was something Olivia had said—that Emory was pregnant. At the time Olivia said it, he thought it was obnoxious, like most of the things coming out of her mouth, but now the words warmed his heart. Of course, he knew she wasn't carrying his child and quickly dismissed the faint notion that another man, or Eric, got her pregnant. *Impossible.* But he thought about her one day pregnant, hopefully soon, after they got married, though none of that was going to happen until Alexis was out of his life, so he needed his brother to hurry up with the divorce. He glanced at her sweet face on the pillow, shrouded in the darkness, relieved he had no more secrets and anxious to begin the life he should have had. He nuzzled his head into her hair and drifted off to sleep.

Emory remained awake, her eyes wide open, listening to Mason breathe softly, peacefully, beside her. His warm body provided some comfort to her body, but she couldn't escape her mind, memories seeped into her veins, leaving her to surrender to the sadness of her past. She saw Wesley's face, rushing into the weight room and picking her up from the floor. She saw him cooking for her, completing at least half of her homework, and reminding her to shower. What saved her—the only thing that ever saved her—was dancing. *First position.*

Their dance showcase was in less than a month, and she and Wesley practiced long hours to be ready. After a particularly grueling rehearsal, they returned to her room with Mexican food. Emory's appetite had suffered with the break-up, losing weight she couldn't afford to lose. Wesley hoped some guacamole dip would help, but instead, after a few chips, she rushed into her bathroom and threw up. She reached under her sink for a towel, saw amongst the clutter an unopened box of tampons. *When did I buy these?* It wasn't unusual for her to have short, light periods, but she couldn't remember her last one. She counted the days in her head and grabbed her birth control packet off the counter, checking to make sure she hadn't missed a pill. And she hadn't. She counted and checked again to make sure, reaching the same results, then sunk to the floor, sick to her stomach, holding the tampon box.

Wesley peered his head through the bathroom door. "Everything OK?"

Emory looked up, white as a ghost and with tears in her eyes. "I think I'm pregnant."

After picking his jaw up off the floor, Wesley took her to a doctor, who confirmed she was pregnant. He stayed in the examination room, as she shivered on the cold, steel table, covered only by a paper sheet, staring at the white ceiling in disbelief. *My dance career is finished before it ever began.* The doctor turned out the lights and patted her knee. "Let's see how far along you are." As Wesley ran his hand over her forehead, the doctor placed cold gel on her belly, then the ultrasound probe, a loud swoosh filling the room. "That's the heartbeat," the doctor said.

Emory closed her eyes. *I wish Mason was here.*

"It seems you're already about twelve weeks along." He pushed a few buttons on the machine. "I'll print you a picture." He removed the probe and gave her some tissues to wipe herself, then handed a black and white picture to Emory.

"She's on the pill. Never missed one," Wesley said. "How could this happen?"

Emory slowly leaned her head down on the table and stared at the clock, looking at each hand move, all so very slowly. Three months already. *Due in early Fall, when Mason's starting his first NFL season.* Wesley touched her arm, Emory not realizing the doctor had been talking to her. "Sorry, what?" she looked up, confused.

"Wesley was asking how this could've happened on the pill. A lot of new fathers ask me that, actually," the doctor said, smiling at

Wesley, who bit his tongue. "It's not foolproof. Have you taken anything that could counteract it?"

"Like what?"

"Like antibiotics?"

Emory placed her hand on her forehead. "Over New Year's, I
was sick, and the school doctor gave me something."

"New Year's," the doctor said, stroking his chin. "That fits with
the timeline."

Emory leaned up on her elbows. "But I know I've had a period
since then." She looked at Wesley for confirmation, but he had no
clue. *Mason would know.*

"Sometimes women have their period the first few months of
pregnancy." The doctor patted her foot. "It's not uncommon. Or perhaps you simply mistook spotting for your period. That's very common as well."

Emory looked back at the clock, convinced she'd entered some
parallel universe. *Pregnant, young, alone.*

"You are still early enough in the pregnancy that you have options. We do have a counselor on staff who can assist you. If you are
going to continue the pregnancy, you need to gain some weight and
take prenatal vitamins." The doctor handed some pills to Wesley.

"Can I still dance?" Emory asked softly.

"I don't see why not, but everything in moderation. Don't overdo
it."

On their way out of the office, Emory swore Wesley to secrecy,
but she needed more than that. She needed a plan.

Mason had been asleep for hours. It was well past midnight. He
flopped his heavy arm across her flat stomach, stirring her from her
past. She knew she needed another plan.

CHAPTER TWENTY-ONE

WESLEY NEEDED A jolt before his morning class began. It was his least favorite class of the week—a group of twelve-year-old boys who'd rather be playing video games, but whose parents made them attend, either to lose weight or improve their footwork for some "real sport." In fact, Wesley was certain one of the boys was attending his class for some sort of punishment. None of them wanted to be there for the hour, and Wesley didn't either. He typically got a charge out of teaching his classes, but only because his students reflected his own enthusiasm. This class gave back aggravation and hatred. It annoyed Wesley, but he never turned a paying student away. He needed to pay the rent.

An hour before the class, Wesley rolled out of bed and walked to a coffee shop down the street, hoping some caffeine would energize him. He ordered a cappuccino and bran muffin. He dropped some sugar and cream into his cup and took a seat at a table near the counter. He picked at his muffin, waiting for the cappuccino to cool. He looked around at other customers in the shop—a man in a suit racing off to an executive-level job, a woman in scrubs grabbing a black coffee before heading into surgery, a young father with kids on their way to soccer. Wesley wondered about his own place in the shop: a single, gay man living with his college friend and teaching dance below their simple apartment. *How long can this last? Have I done the right thing with my life?* He took a sip of his coffee and stared into the cup, taking comfort in the belief his relationship with his family was on a better track and that he had made the best choices he could, as life came at him. Then something really did come at him.

Tomás walked into the shop, well-dressed as usual, even at this early morning hour. He noticed Wesley immediately, wearing clothes he knew Wesley had slept in. Wesley looked up briefly from his cup and saw Tomás, then averted his eyes back to the cup, pretending not to see him. Tomás himself didn't know what to do: he couldn't turn around and leave, which would be too obvious, but he had to walk past Wesley to get to the counter and didn't know what to say. Tomás noticed a newspaper carousel by the door and pretended to read the day's headlines while formulating a plan.

Wesley could tell Tomás was stalling, churning inside. He took a long drink in satisfaction and decided to take the upper hand. "Tomás," he called out.

His heart sinking, Tomás put back the newspaper and slowly turned around. "Wesley, is that you?" he asked, squinting his eyes to see across the small room.

"Yep." Wesley motioned him to come over. "Have a seat."

Tomás gathered some courage and slowly walked towards the table. "How have you been?" he asked, taking a seat.

"Pretty good," Wesley said. "Can I buy you a drink?"

"No, I just came in to get a paper."

"Oh, I thought you had the paper delivered to your house." Wesley took another sip, delighting in tweaking Tomás, now squirming in his chair.

"I discontinued it a few weeks ago," he lied.

Wesley picked at his muffin. "It's been awhile since we've seen each other."

"It has."

"Would you like some of my muffin?" Wesley offered.

"No, I'm good. Like I said, I just came in for the paper."

"Right. I forgot," Wesley said, grinning. "How's your art?"

Tomás cocked his head to the side. "Been hard to put ideas on canvas lately. A bit of a struggle."

Wesley offered no sympathy. "We all have our struggles," he said flatly, then enjoyed the silence that fell over the table, clearly making Tomás uncomfortable. Wesley took another long sip of his drink, as if to congratulate himself for his zinger.

"How was your sister's wedding?" Tomás asked, reaching for something to say.

"It's not until June." Wesley paused to pick at his muffin. "I decided to go."

"That's great! Why didn't you call me?"

"I didn't know I was supposed to."

"I had asked you to call if you patched things up with your family."

Wesley stirred his cappuccino. "I guess I forgot that, too," he said, then looked directly into Tomás' eyes. "Just like you apparently forgot to take care of me when I needed you most."

"That's not what happened," Tomás said, stiffening his spine. "I wanted you to be true to yourself."

Wesley smiled. "That's the funny thing, Tomás. I was."

"No, you weren't. You…"

Wesley cut him off. "I was, Tomás. I was being true to myself. I'm a gay man—a scared, gay man—just doing my best to get by," Wesley said firmly, without any regard for the eager ears of the other customers. "That's me. That's how I am at home, at work, and with my family. Take it or leave it, and you left it."

Tomás sat back in his chair, surprised by Wesley's honesty, hitting him like a freight train. Wesley ordinarily was so full of jokes and clownish ideas, that he rarely, if ever, ventured into any direct discussion like this. Tomás had always assumed that Wesley's reluctance to deal with his family was from a lack of pride, never considering it was from a lack of confidence. He reached across the table for Wesley's hand, but Wesley pulled away.

"I'm good. I don't need that."

"Please, I…"

"I've got to get to my class." Wesley stood up and looked down at Tomás. "But you think about what I said. You treat strangers better than you treated me. When you get a handle on yourself, you call me."

* * *

Mason thought about having breakfast with his mother in the hospital cafeteria, or just visiting with her in the waiting room of the maternity ward. But he wasn't hungry, and the waiting room didn't have real good memories from the day before. He finally decided on the hospital chapel because his conversation demanded privacy, not wanting to worry about the tone of his mother's voice around other people, or whether they could hear a sensitive talk between a mother and son. He also figured it wouldn't hurt to have some divine intervention. Mason needed to set things right. As far as he was concerned, the time for ignoring and bickering and public fighting was over.

He sat alone in a pew in the small, quiet chapel, skimming through a prayer card containing a list of the Ten Commandments. He hadn't seen them since Sunday School twenty years ago, now reading them carefully, pausing at the fourth one. *Damn, that one is tricky.*

"Thanks for inviting me, Son," Kathleen said, walking through the chapel entrance. "I can't remember the last time we had a date." She took a seat next to him.

"Me neither. I thought the chapel would be a fun spot."

"I'm glad you think about places like this. Shows I raised you right."

She reached up to straighten his hair, but Mason swatted her away, smiling. "You did a good job, Mom. I know it wasn't always easy doing it alone. Steven and I never made your life easy."

"Still don't. But you're right. I just did the best I could under the circumstances."

"I know."

"And now I have an NFL player and lawyer to show for it. And, of course, a beautiful new grandson."

"He's beautiful, isn't he? Don't know how someone as ugly as Steven could create that."

Kathleen laughed. "Your brother's not ugly."

Mason smiled, then paused, needing to get down to business, as time was short. "You know how you said you did the best you could under the circumstances? That's what I'm doing, too, Mom."

Kathleen knew where this was going and patted his hand. "It's not that I don't like her, Son. I do, but you lose all reason when it comes to her."

Mason rolled his eyes. "Mom, you know I'm not a rational person. That's you and Steven."

"But you just don't think straight around her."

"Of course I don't, Mom." He took her hand and looked in her eyes. "That's because I love her."

"But you passed on a better contract because of her."

"She didn't even know about it."

"It could be your last contract!"

"I don't care, Mom. I love her. I've loved her my whole life."

Kathleen exhaled, twirling the diamond cross on her necklace. "I just don't know. When you were with Alexis, you could focus on your career, and..."

"Mom, please!" He could feel his blood pressure rising, the tiny hairs on the back of his neck standing up. "Alexis and I are done. My career is going to last, what, maybe another five years if I'm lucky. Then what? I want to be happy beyond that."

She patted his hand. "Son, I want you to be happy," she said sweetly. "That's all I've ever wanted."

"I know, Mom, but my version of happiness is different than yours. And remember, I tried your version, and it didn't work out too well for me," Mason said, his voice shaking. "So if you want me happy, you need to let go a little bit." A tear fell from his eyes, and he wiped it away.

She couldn't bear it—her huge son, an NFL quarterback, crying in a small hospital chapel. She threw her arms around him and squeezed him tightly, Mason putting his head on her shoulder. "I need your help, Mom," he said, sniffling. *Honor thy father and mother.* "I really do."

Holding her son, Kathleen found peace in his words. *My boy needs me.* She couldn't remember the last time her sons needed her. It meant everything. "Whatever you need."

* * *

Emory held Noah in her arms, humming softly and rocking him slowly in the corner of the hospital room. Olivia rested on the bed, with Stephen beside her, feeding her an early lunch of roast chicken and mashed potatoes from the hospital kitchen.

"So, Stephen, what did you get Olivia?" Emory asked, tickling Noah's nose.

He stabbed a piece of chicken with his fork. "For what?"

"For bearing your child!" Emory winked at Olivia. "It's called a push present."

"A what?" He fed her the piece of chicken. "Is this some rule I'm supposed to know about?"

"Not a rule," Olivia teased, with her mouth full, "just common courtesy."

Stephen scratched his head, then gripped the stubble on his face for support. "I've got more chicken," he said, laughing.

"Better make sure Mason knows about the push present rule, Emory?" Olivia winked at Steven, who then narrowed his eyes, urging her to mind her own business. Emory looked up at them both, confused. "Oh, come on," Olivia said, "feeling faint and puking. We think it's great."

"I don't know what you're talking about." Emory then suddenly realized Olivia, and perhaps even Steven, truly thought she was pregnant, and had even discussed it. Little did they know, she and Mason hadn't even had sex this time around. "I'm not pregnant. Just a little food poisoning."

"Sure, OK, whatever," Olivia said. "Mason said the same thing."

Emory's eyes widened. "You told Mason you thought I was pregnant?"

"You mean you haven't told him?" Olivia replied.

Emory looked to Steven for help. "There's *nothing* to tell."

Steven picked up a piece of chicken. "I guess we were wrong," he said, shrugging, then shoved another bite of chicken into Olivia's mouth.

Mason barged into the room with his mother, holding her hand. "Where's my nephew?"

"And my grandson?" Kathleen countered, nudging her son in the stomach. Olivia pointed to Emory quietly rocking Noah in the corner, Mason's chest swelling at the sight. Kathleen walked eagerly towards her, and Emory noticed a bounce in her step and a brightness in her face, as if some weight had been lifted. "He looks beautiful in your arms," Kathleen said. Emory gave a quick look to Mason, still standing in the doorway, and he nodded, indicating progress had been made. "Mind if I have some grandma time?"

"Of course." Emory gently passed Noah to her and rose from the chair, offering it to Kathleen, who got lost in him immediately.

Mason teased Steven that he now had more hair on his face than on his head, then swiped a piece of the hospital chicken, offering his sympathies to Olivia. Emory quietly retrieved her camera from her bag and snapped a picture of Kathleen holding Noah. "Oh goodness,

please don't do that, dear," Kathleen said, primping her hair. "I'm
due to have my roots done."

Emory pushed some buttons so that the image appeared on the
camera screen and knelt down next to Kathleen. "Look how beautiful
you two look together. I imagine you looked the same thirty years
ago holding Steven."

"Thank you, dear." She squeezed Emory's hand.

Mason walked to them and eyed the image over their shoulders.
He kissed his mother on top of her head and winked at Emory.
"Noah's better looking than Steven already." Steven tossed a piece
of chicken at his brother, striking him in the temple, then falling to
the floor by Emory.

"I agree with you, Mason," Olivia said.

"You want me to fire some at you, too?" Steven teased. "You're
not all delicate and pregnant anymore." Emory picked up the chicken
and threw it back at him.

"Good for you, dear," Kathleen said. "You can see how I had my
hands full raising both of them."

"I have a hard enough time with one." Emory smiled up at Mason.

Kathleen saw the sweetness and love between her son and
Emory—it was obvious from the way they looked at each other.
She'd seen the same thing in the old post-game photo she kept in her
album. "You're doing a good job, dear. I've always thought that."
Emory hadn't heard such loving words from a maternal figure in
over twenty-five years. For all the kindness and love her father had
shown her, she'd missed out for so long on the kindness and love of
a mother. Emory leaned over the chair arm and wrapped her arms
around Kathleen's neck, careful not to disturb Noah whose eyes had
just closed, Kathleen looking sweetly at her son during the embrace.

"I'll make sure to send you a copy of the picture when we get
back to Charlotte," Emory said and stood up. "Who's next for a picture?" Steven launched another piece of chicken in her direction.

CHAPTER TWENTY-TWO

WHEN EMORY RETURNED to Charlotte, so did her nightmares—as bad as they'd ever been. She found herself afraid to sleep in the same bed as Mason, fearing she'd scare him and he'd then question her again about them. He hadn't brought up her bad dreams in a while, and she wanted to keep it that way, but she wondered if it was time to come clean. *Maybe that's the only way out.*

She stood alone at the ballet barre below her apartment, the lights dim, staring at herself in the mirror. She felt weak and tired, dark circles under her eyes, and put her hands on her cheeks, stretching them downward. She hadn't recovered from seeing Mason holding Noah. The moment had brought everything back, making it all more vivid and real. She couldn't suppress it any longer. The temporary high she felt taking pictures of Kathleen and the family in the hospital room and throwing food at Steven, had long since passed. It seemed like years ago. She slowly brought her hand to her chest, massaging her heart, never thinking the hole inside could get any worse. But just over the past few days, the hole in her heart indeed had grown deeper and wider, all of her worry and pain spilling out like a volcano, bubbling to the surface and affecting her body and mind.

A slow, somber melody played, and she began to stretch. *First position.* She placed her leg on the barre and bent to the side, continuing to stretch until her body felt limber. She started to dance, slowly at first, and rose up on her toes. As the music grew faster, so did the intensity of her movement. She shifted gears, gaining strength and power, then made a series of jumps across the floor, landing in front of the mirror. Her body felt tired, but Emory had a new resolve within. *I will tell him tonight.*

Mason pulled up in front of the dance studio. He'd been consumed with physical therapy and team commitments since coming back from Texas. He hadn't spent the time he wanted with Emory and knew his days were only going to get busier with performance drills starting the next day. And he was nervous about that, having not thrown in months and unsure whether he even could. He figured a night with Emory would calm his nerves, and a surprise visit would be a good start. He carried a bouquet of pink tulips towards the door, expecting to go upstairs to her apartment, but spotted her at the barre, cooling down.

Emory wasn't in her usual leotard, but a see-through, pink ballet sweater with a black bra and a skimpy black shorts. He saw her flat stomach, and the curve of her waist, her blonde hair cascading down her back. Mason stood in the shadows of the viewing area, admiring her. "Any chance I can get a private dance?"

Emory jumped. "You scared me!" She took a deep breath to compose herself. "What are you doing here?"

"I've missed you the last few days." Mason said, walking towards her and pulling the bouquet from behind his back. She smiled and thanked him, as he kissed her cheek. She held them to her nose, breathing in the sweet smell of spring. Mason took the bouquet and dropped it to the floor, then wrapped his arms around her waist. "So, how about a private dance?" He began to kiss her neck.

Emory moaned softly. "This is a pretty public place for a private dance."

"You've never been shy before." Mason untied the front of her sweater, opening it, and placed his hands on her warm, bare waist, pulling her close. He'd missed holding her, touching her, everything about her. He made his way around her body, kissing her lips, neck, and shoulders, her sweater falling to the floor.

She felt a twinge between her legs. *Maybe I should do this before I come clean and ruin everything?* She untucked his shirt and began to undo the buttons. He picked her up, Emory wrapping her legs around him. Breathing heavily, she removed his shirt quickly, watching herself in the mirror, and threw his shirt to the floor. Mason began to move quickly, holding her with one hand and undoing her black bra with the other. Emory pulled back slightly, causing Mason to stop, but then she removed her bra and flung it on the floor, biting her bottom lip. Mason's eyes took her in. She kissed him hard on the lips and pushed herself into him, the warmth of her breasts covering his hard chest.

"Holy shit!" Wesley screamed, as he walked into the studio, quickly covering his eyes.

"What the fuck!" Mason yelled. *Is this some kind of fucking punishment?* He shielded her from Wesley's view, as she quickly grabbed her bra and sweater.

"I'm so sorry, guys," Wesley said nervously, looking the other way. "I have a private lesson tonight."

Emory threw Mason his shirt. "It's OK, Wesley, we're all covered up now." She grabbed the bouquet from the floor, and Wesley turned around, careful to avoid looking at either of them. Emory led Mason out of the studio, Mason glaring down at Wesley along the way, and then she offered Wesley an apologetic smile. "I was giving a private lesson, too."

Mason slapped her backside, as they walked upstairs. "That was embarrassing," she said, walking into the kitchen.

"I was really enjoying myself, too," he said. "I liked the mirrors."

Emory blushed, getting a vase for the bouquet. "Me too."

"Do you think he looked at my butt?"

"Don't be ridiculous." Emory grinned, filling the vase with water. "It's mine anyway." She carefully arranged the tulips in the vase, then drew a deep breath. *Tell him now.* "Mason, I need to talk to you about something."

"What's up?" he said, kissing her neck. "But before I forget, are you free tomorrow after my performance drills? I have a little something planned."

Emory pulled away. "That's tomorrow?" *Can't tell him now. Shit!*

"I know, it snuck up on me, too. I'm a little nervous." He pulled her close again. "So I need you to distract me, to keep me nice and loose."

"Don't you think you should conserve your energy?" she teased.

"Probably so. What did you want to talk about?"

"Nothing that can't wait," she said and bit her bottom lip, pulling him closer and unbuttoning his shirt. *Thank God men are so easy to distract!*

Mason picked her up and placed her on the kitchen counter. In a matter of seconds, their shirts were on the floor, Mason trailing kisses to her breasts. His tongue outlined her aroused nipple, and she moaned. Mason cupped one breast with his hand, while slowly sucking on the other, the warmth between her legs turning into a blazing fire. He ran his hand down her shorts, and his eyes flashed open. *Thongs!* Emory gave him a knowing smile, as she undid the zipper and button on his jeans, stroking him up and down. His phone rang loudly, vibrating on the kitchen counter.

"Fuck!" Mason leaned his head on hers in defeat. "I swear I'm being punished."

"Just ignore it," she whispered.

Ring!

"If that's Steven, I will kill him, I swear."

Ring!

"I'm just going to hit decline," Emory said, reaching for the phone, as Mason kissed her neck. She saw the caller ID on the screen, and her body turned stiff and cold.

"What?" he asked.

Ring!

"It's not Steven."

She turned the phone, so Mason could see the screen. *Why the fuck is Alexis calling me?* The ringing stopped, an uncomfortable silence fell between them.

"Why is she calling you?" Emory asked, wondering when Mason last spoke with Alexis. She figured the lawyers were handling everything, and that husband and wife were not speaking. *Have they been talking behind my back? Does she want Mason back?*

"I have no idea," Mason said, handing her the sweater and bra and putting back on his shirt. "I haven't spoken to her since I got hurt, I promise." He knew how awkward this was for Emory, and it was just another reminder how difficult it was to move on with Emory, sexually or otherwise, while still married. There would be no sex, again, tonight.

Ring!

"Jesus!" Mason yelled, looking at his phone. "It's her again!"

Emory hopped down from the countertop. "Put her on speaker." Mason did, then answered.

"I was wondering how many times it would take for you to pick up." Alexis said, strolling through the shoe section of a high-end boutique.

"What do you want?"

"Well, right now, I'm looking at the most fabulous pair of Christian Louboutin shoes that would just do wonders for my calves." She held the shoe up, wanting the salesman to bring them to her, then continued to look around.

Emory rolled her eyes. "You called to talk about shoes?" Mason asked.

"No, you never did understand my need for designer shoes." Alexis snapped her fingers that she needed a few more pair. "I'm calling because I wanted to congratulate you on the Panthers contract."

"Who told you about that?"

"A little thing called Google." Alexis sat down and slipped off her shoes, waiting impatiently for the salesman to return. "I wish you had accepted the larger Seahawks contract, but whatever."

"What do you want?"

"I'm glad you asked." The salesman returned with several boxes and knelt down in front of Alexis. "I'm thinking a little piece of that contract should be mine, since I'm still legally your wife."

"We'll see what Steven thinks about that."

"Yes, please ask him," she said, wiggling her toes. "And when you talk to him, ask him how he feels about adultery?" The salesman raised his brow.

So did Emory. *Maybe I shouldn't have asked for speaker.*

Mason looked at Emory, warning her with his eyes to stay quiet. "What are you talking about? I never cheated on you."

The salesman slipped a pair of red heels on her feet, and Alexis stood to admire herself in a mirror. "Emory Claire? Did you not think I would find out? Google works for that, too!"

Mom saw this coming. Mason slammed his fist on the counter. "Leave her out of this, Alexis!"

"Now why would I do that?" she said, sitting down to try on another pair. "Our whole marriage was about her. You started dating me to get back at her. You fucked me to try to forget about her. You proposed to me because she wouldn't see you anymore." The salesman stared at the boxes to harness his fear of the woman before him.

Alexis had just spewed a mouthful, and Emory tried to process her words as quickly as she could. *They never loved each other.* Mason had told her that his marriage was about career and convenience, but she found that hard to believe. Now Alexis confirmed Mason was telling the truth. *How very sad.* Emory wondered if everything Alexis said could've been avoided if she'd just been honest about her pregnancy. *If I had spoken up, it would have spared everyone a lot of pain and angst, including myself.*

Mason clenched his fist. "I'll ask again. Why are you calling?"

"To personally tell you I want everything, plus 50% of your future earnings." Alexis motioned she would take all the shoes.

"That's bullshit, and you know it!" Mason barked, Emory massaging his shoulders.

Alexis cackled. "I could always withdraw my divorce petition, and we could continue our happy marriage. Me spending money and traveling around, and you thinking about Emory all the time. We got along so well that way."

"You're such a fucking bitch!" *I can't believe Emory is hearing all this. Will she stick it out with me?*

"You mean, you don't want to get back together?" Alexis walked to the register to check out. "Then give me what I want, or I will tell everyone how my shitty, cheating husband left me for some washed-up dancer. I'm sure the Panthers would like that storyline in the paper so soon after you signed."

Mason threw his hands up in disbelief. "You left *me*, Alexis." Emory stepped away, knowing there was nothing she could do to soothe him.

"If you want to take that risk with sweet Emory's reputation, that's fine. I'm sure all the pictures in the paper of the two of you together would prove my case. You took less money to be close to your mistress who wrecked our marriage." The salesman looked at her—part confused, part terrified.

Mason took a deep breath. "Emory and I have done nothing wrong. And I was more than fair in the prenup…"

"Fair?" she interrupted. "You want to talk about fair. Let's talk about how fair it is to be married to a man in love with another woman." The salesman quickly processed her purchase, hoping she'd leave before he was subjected to any more craziness.

"Alexis, we both used each other," Mason said calmly. "Let's just move on."

"Seems like you're more anxious to move on than I am. I have nothing better to do." The salesman placed her shoe boxes into several bags and handed her a receipt. "I will drag this out until I get what I want. And I will drag little Emory with me if I have to."

"Fuck you!" Mason hung up, and paced around the kitchen, taking several deep breaths to gather himself. He then walked to Emory, pulling her into a hug, and she buried her head in his shirt. "I'm sorry you heard all that. I'll talk to Steven. It will be fine," he said, hoping to convince himself, too.

* * *

They left the apartment and headed to Mason's condo for the night, where they could avoid seeing Wesley again and hopefully attempt to relax before the morning drills. But before relaxing, Mason needed to clear his head. He walked out to the balcony of his condo, and called Steven to unload—about Alexis' threats and new demands, begging him, once again, to finalize the settlement and divorce. Gripping the balcony ledge, he didn't know how much more he—or Emory—could take. "I have to protect, Em."

Steven sat quietly on the steps of his back porch, Olivia and Noah napping inside on the sofa. He listened attentively to Mason, but felt helpless to resolve the situation. He didn't have a magic wand. "Maybe we have to pay her what she wants, or she's just going to keep demanding more."

"Then do it. I've been saying that for months."

Steven paused. "There has to be another way." He looked up into the sky, hoping for direction from some higher power. Divorce law was never his specialty, and handling a family member's divorce, he knew now, was clearly a mistake. He was much more comfortable negotiating with, and lying to, NFL teams to secure contracts for his brother. Management was easier to handle than his brother's wife.

Mason glanced at Emory in his kitchen, picking kung pao chicken out of a carton with her fingers, so happy with this simple pleasure. "It doesn't matter. I'm starting over with Em. Please just do it."

"OK, but there's just one more problem." Steven rose from the porch step and took a few steps onto his lawn, kicking a stick towards the fence. "She wants to see you before she signs anything."

"Why?"

"Her lawyer called me today. She's refusing to sign anything until you talk to her face to face."

Mason sunk to the ground. "Can this get any worse?"

Steven walked up the steps of his back porch and saw his wife and new baby sleeping peacefully. At times, he envied his brother's NFL career, and the excitement and opportunities that came along with it, while he, the dutiful agent, stayed in the background. *Not now.* Mason was in pain, in deep emotional turmoil, with performance drills a mere twelve hours away. Steven needed to focus his brother, or there wouldn't be a future NFL career, reminding Mason how to approach the drills, and to take it easy at the outset.

Mason tried his best to listen, but his mind was elsewhere. "How am I going to tell Em I have to meet Alexis?"

"Dude, your mind is fucked!" Steven walked into his backyard and hurled another stick at his fence. "Is Emory there?"

"Yes, why?"

"Put her on the phone."

"She's eating right now. I'm not sure I should interrupt her."

"Just put her on the phone, Mason!"

"Don't you think this should come from me?"

"Put her on the damn phone!" Steven took a seat at his patio table and braced his head with his hand.

Mason walked back inside, and Emory peeked up from the carton, able to tell from his drawn face something was wrong. "What's the matter?" she asked, licking her fingers.

"Steven wants to tell you himself."

"About Olivia and the baby?"

Mason shook his head and handed her the phone. Steven recounted the history of the divorce and Alexis' demands, and new demands, most of which Emory already knew. But Steven wanted to make sure she knew every detail. Emory took a deep breath when he was finally through. "Well, buy the bitch a plane ticket, and make sure it's coach."

Emory hung up and slipped the phone into Mason's pocket. She walked Mason to the den, pushing him down on a leather chair and straddling herself on top of him. "Get Alexis out of your head."

"I know, I know," he said somberly.

"Don't let her take any more time from us—or from your career."

"I know, I know," he replied again, more convincing this second time.

"She had six years with you that should've been mine. *Ours*. I'm not about to waste one more second worrying about Alexis. You shouldn't either. Let her say whatever the hell she wants."

Mason looked into her steel eyes—Emory was one tough woman. He knew most women wouldn't put up with all his bullshit, but she seemed unfazed by it. As long as he was honest with her, she seemingly took things in stride. "I told Steven my priority is to protect you from this mess, and I will."

Emory smiled and kissed his lips. "How are you feeling about tomorrow?"

"Nervous, but my arm is feeling good."

"You're going to do great. I'm going to pray for you tomorrow."

"Thank you, babe." He ran his hands through her hair. "I really need to sleep well, and I sleep better with you next to me. Will you stay?"

Emory knew she couldn't say no. She just hoped her nightmares wouldn't return. The last thing she wanted was to embarrass herself and keep Mason from a restful night. She hoped sleeping beside him would bring some semblance of peace.

CHAPTER TWENTY-THREE

EMORY BELIEVED IN the power of dance and also the power of prayer. Prayer, like dance, sustained her through good times and bad. When she worried about herself, she usually found herself at the ballet barre. When others were involved, she usually found herself on her knees. And she now found herself before an array of prayer candles, holding her rosary beads, in the rear of St. Peter's. She lit a candle, thanking God for shielding her from nightmares last night and for bringing Mason back into her life. She prayed for his health and success. She looked up at a statue of Mary holding Jesus in her arms, thinking of her own mother and baby, both lost to her, and put her head down, releasing tears like a river escaping a dam. *God, please give me strength. I need a sign.*

Father Tony touched her shoulder from behind. "Looks like you are struggling, my child."

"Yes, Father," Emory said, startled, wiping her face. "My past."

"You've come to the right place," he assured her. "In Philippians, God tells us to forget what lies behind and strain forward to what lies ahead."

Is this my sign?

Emory thanked him for the encouragement, and he left without another word. She reached for a devotional card near the candles and recited a few more prayers until her phone dinged, echoing through the empty church. She rummaged quickly in her purse to mute it and saw a text from Mason. *Killed it. Meet me at Myers Park.*

* * *

Mason stood near a side street in the historic Myers Park neighborhood. He looked at his watch; he was a few minutes early. His shoulder was sore, but the excitement he felt from throwing for the first time since his injury—and finishing the drills—was well worth it. Performing well made his shoulder feel better, too. He completed short throws and long out-routes, crossing routes and post-patterns, shaking off the rust and hitting receiver after receiver in stride. It felt good to be on the field again. It felt good to begin to develop a rapport with his receivers—to learn their talents, to see how they made their cuts, and to adjust the velocity of his passes to their speed. It was only the first day, but an important one, and he'd passed his first test. His coaches were impressed, and management was relieved. Leaving the field, he offered a quick prayer of thanks for stubborn, old Dr. Lewis and his grouchy nurse.

Waiting for Emory, his excitement shifted to nervousness. *This could go either way.* Mason always acted on impulse, rarely thinking things through, but what he'd done this time was more than impulsive—it was brazen and rash, beyond anything he'd ever done before. To pass the time and calm himself, he texted his mother and brother about his successful morning, and both quickly responded with congratulations.

Emory drove into Myers Park and saw Mason, finding it odd to see him standing alone. She pulled up next to him and rolled down her window. "Good job this morning." He flashed a mischievous grin. "Why are you standing there? Where's your car?"

"A few blocks away."

"Did you have car trouble or something?"

"No. I'm good."

She looked at him, squinting her eyes. "Then what are we doing here?"

"Park your car, and I'll show you." Emory drove a few feet and parked at the curb. Mason took her hand. "It's such a beautiful day. I thought we could just take a stroll."

"OK," she said cautiously, with a sideways glance, a slight breeze blowing through her hair.

They held hands walking down a cobblestone sidewalk underneath large, sprawling oak trees, with sunlight glistening from moss dangling above them. The trees surrounded large houses, each with a different style of architecture from a day gone by. They walked a few blocks, Mason recounting his completions and Emory recounting the power of prayer. He then stopped abruptly, pulling her into a kiss, then turned her around to face a white Acadian house across the street, with large, white columns and a huge wrap-around porch with a swing. It was gated with bricks and ironwork, the driveway a paved flagstone. The house itself was large, but not overwhelming, not even close to the stately mansions nearby.

He led her across the street to a keypad at the front of the property. "Punch in the code," he said, as Emory looked at him curiously. "It's 302, by the way."

Her jaw dropped. *Our hotel room.*

Mason dangled a key in front of her. "Welcome home."

She stared at the key, then Mason, then the house. Her mind spinning, she couldn't believe what he just said. She gazed at the front of the house, seeing a garage on the far side, with Mason's Audi SUV parked in front. Her mouth moved as if trying to say something, but nothing came out.

Mason took her hand, nervously. "You don't like it?"

"I…" Emory started. "We…" She drew a deep breath. "It's lovely and charming and…"

"Ours." Mason rubbed her hand, then punched the code. Emory was frozen, speechless, watching a huge wrought iron gate open before her, as if it was some theme park ride. He pulled her hand to follow him, but she couldn't move, her feet planted firmly on the sidewalk.

Mason looked back at her. "Come on." She shook her head slightly. *Shit, she's not ready.* He could hear his heart pounding. "Em?"

She looked into his piercing blue eyes and could see his fear. "What about Alexis and the prenup? What if she wants the house?"

Mason put his hands on her waist. "We agreed not to give her any more of our time, right?"

"Right." Emory nodded to convince herself. "But the house, it's got to be so much?"

"Don't be silly," Mason said, waving her off. "It's not that much. Plus, you haven't seen the inside. It's a fixer-upper."

Emory smiled. "I suppose I'm used to that."

"I'm about all fixed up now. As for the house, I thought we'd fix it up together. Maybe start a family one day?"

Her breath caught. *Family?* "Don't we have to have sex first?"

"Ready when you are!" Mason led her towards the front door. "Now, the house won't be ready for a couple of months—I'm sure we'll have sex by then," he said, winking, "and you don't have to move in until you're ready, of course." He opened the front door, but she hesitated again, staying on the porch. "Let's leave all our baggage out here. It's time to start fresh." Mason held his breath, waiting to see if she'd take a step—not just inside the house, but into their future.

Philippians? Another sign? Emory decided to leave her secret buried in the past and jumped ahead into his arms. "I love you, Mason! I can't believe you bought us a house!" He twirled her around. "You're so damn crazy! I absolutely love it!"

CHAPTER TWENTY-FOUR

OVER THE NEXT week, Emory and Mason planned their new home, while Steven haggled mercilessly with Alexis and her lawyer. Mason, through Steven, repeatedly made offers to her, but each time they were met with counteroffers bordering on absurd. Alexis refused to budge off of her demands, even though her lawyer, though not particularly bright, seemed a fairly reasonable, plain-spoken man.

Mason insisted the fighting and haggling stop, and they each resolve simply to end his six-year mistake. But the over-arching problem was that Alexis didn't see it as a mistake; she got what she wanted—fame and fortune. It seemed to him she had some sick pleasure in dragging out the process, as if she never wanted to let Mason go or perhaps just didn't want him to move on. She preferred to keep some contact with Mason—even if through contentious negotiations—than to bring finality to their relationship.

A turning point was Steven's threat to file for divorce in Charlotte, where Mason had just bought a house and was a welcome addition to the community, participating in charity and other public events as much as possible. Mason would have the upper hand there. Alexis' lawyer, of course, had pursued litigation in Texas, which already was expensive, and the thought of adding another forum—Mason's home turf—was risky and cost-prohibitive. But Alexis was unfazed by Steven's threat. It presented an opportunity to tarnish Mason's reputation in Charlotte before he'd even taken a snap for the Panthers, and to drag Emory through the mud, too.

Her lawyer reminded Alexis that litigating in multiple courts undoubtedly would delay any resolution, leaving her with inadequate financial means potentially for years. She certainly didn't want to have to get a job. Moreover, the lawyer told her Steven wasn't afraid to present Mason's case in a Charlotte—or even a Texas—

courtroom, where his story of overcoming a horrific shoulder injury, and a season later potentially quarterbacking the Panthers on opening day, was a compelling one that would garner sympathy, particularly when coupled with Alexis' abrupt departure. The lawyer didn't like the odds: he thought the prenup would be enforced in Charlotte, and likely in Texas, too. Plus, he wanted this over, and more importantly, wanted his fee.

After days of effort, her lawyer finally convinced Alexis that Mason's latest offer was too good to pass up. He sold her on the deal —all property rights, a $5 million lump sum payment, and 35% of Mason's future earnings—and she'd get her wish to see Mason before she signed anything. Her lawyer didn't know why Alexis wanted to see Mason, or what she planned to do, but figured it was just for closure. Steven expected there was some sinister motive, or perhaps not—Alexis was a loose cannon whose moves couldn't be predicted. Still, he knew putting Alexis and Mason in the same room likely would lead to disaster, and potentially jeopardize his months and months of work. Indeed, if Alexis mentioned Emory and threatened her to Mason, Steven was sure it would blow everything up.

But Mason wanted it over, and Alexis wanted to see him. Steven's hands were tied; there seemed no other way to finalize. They all agreed to meet and sign the paperwork the following day at her lawyer's office in Texas. Mason hopped on a red eye flight, and Emory tagged along to photograph Olivia and Noah.

* * *

Steven sat in his home office, as heavy rain thrashed against his window. He reviewed the final draft of the settlement agreement, just needing signatures at this point. The terms of the agreement would strap Mason, especially given the car and house he'd just bought. Steven could understand the car purchase but had advised Mason not to buy the house until the dust had cleared with Alexis, but he didn't listen. Mason, as usual, did whatever he wanted.

Steven pulled open a cabinet and took out a file folder with the prenup agreement he'd drafted years ago. He stared at Alexis' signature on the document, allowing her a lump sum payment of $500,000 and property rights in the event of divorce. The terms were clear as day. But now Alexis had negotiated, or threatened, her way to ten times that amount, plus a significant cut of Mason's future earnings. Steven was disgusted with Alexis—and himself—feeling he'd failed his brother. He placed the final settlement agreement and the file folder in his briefcase, slamming it shut and lowering his head on top of it.

Olivia stood in the doorway, cradling Noah. "Honey, what's wrong?"

"Just work stuff."

Olivia walked over to him and sat on his lap. They looked down at Noah together, and he squeezed her waist, resting his forehead on her shoulder. "Is this about Mason? You don't get upset about work otherwise." Steven nodded. "Everything is getting settled tomorrow, right?" He nodded again. "Can we add a term that I get to rip that bitch's hair from her head?" she blurted out, then covered her mouth for cursing in front of the baby.

Steven gave a weak smile and gently urged her to get off his lap. He stood up, walking to the window with his hands in his pockets, watching the rain fall from the tree leaves into puddles below. "I really can't wait to see Emory again," Olivia said, rocking Noah slightly. "I'm glad she decided to come. I know this must be awkward for her, but I'll make sure she has a great time. She's going to take some pictures."

Olivia continued to talk, but Steven didn't attempt to listen. His client was his brother, making irrational decisions at an emotional time, without the benefit of a seasoned divorce lawyer to guide him. He shouldn't ever have represented Mason. *Could I have fucked this up any more?*

Olivia walked over to Steven and turned his face towards her. "Stop beating yourself up. When you finish this tomorrow, you'll have helped him get what he's wanted for years—a life with Emory."

* * *

Steven had never been to the lawyer's office. They'd only ever spoken by phone. He knew the lawyer's reputation was that of an ambulance chaser whose clients ranged from two-bit criminals to uninjured plaintiffs claiming damages in auto accidents or slip-and-falls. Steven had considerable difficulty even finding the lawyer's office, located in a sketchy part of town, adjacent to a gas station and slightly hidden by a run-down grocery store. It was not in an area he and Olivia ever frequented, and certainly not with Noah.

Mason sat next to Steven on one side of a rickety table in a small, disheveled conference room, yellow legal pads tossed about, and overflowing banker boxes cluttering the floor and table. It felt more like an unorganized closet, with a musty smell, than a conference room. As Steven picked at a hole in the seat cushion of his chair, the brothers whispered amongst themselves, agreeing they were in hell, waiting for Alexis and her lawyer to appear. The receptionist offered them something to drink, but both men declined. Mason was too nervous, and Steven couldn't rule out that Alexis might poison him.

Mason expected Alexis would've hired a prominent lawyer in a fancy suit to litigate her case, and that they'd now be sitting in some grand boardroom in a large downtown firm located on a high floor. But Steven was not surprised by where they sat: it made perfect sense to him. Alexis didn't want to pay for any high-priced legal services, considering herself more than able to conduct the negotiations herself, and she had. She didn't need some well-to-do lawyer calling the shots. She also knew that her methods of threats and smears, of character assassination of an injured NFL quarterback, may not be palatable to square lawyers trained in more conservative methods. She needed a lawyer only as a formality—one who could be her puppet, and who wasn't afraid to cut a few corners if necessary. And she certainly didn't want to pay the exorbitant hourly rates of downtown firms or concede any portion of her settlement to a high contingency fee. No lawyer was going to take her money, at least not much of it. She'd obviously retained this lawyer on the cheap. It pained Steven the lawyer had bested him or, worse, that Alexis had.

As Steven placed his briefcase on the table and took out the settlement agreement, the door to the conference room flew open, Alexis strolling in with her lawyer lagging behind. Her hair and make-up were flawless, and her low-cut, black dress fit perfectly, Mason noticing her red stiletto heels. Her lawyer provided a sharp contrast—a tall, slender man in his mid-fifties, with slick, black hair combed straight back. His black suit a size too large, he left the top button of his dress shirt unbuttoned, and kept his thin, brown tie loose at the neck. He hadn't shaved in at least two days, and looked like he could fill-in at the nearby gas station.

The brothers didn't stand to greet them. Alexis and her lawyer walked to their side of the table, Alexis smiling directly at Mason along the way. He looked different to her in some way. Of course, she hadn't seen him since his shoulder had healed, but it was more than that. She eyed him seductively, trying to figure out what was different. He looked refreshed but also nervous. Mason scanned her, too, an attractive woman by any standard, but her presence disgusted him, especially dressing as if she were going to a cocktail party. Steven could feel the tension radiating off of Mason and gave him a slight kick under the table. He needed his brother calm and cool to finalize the deal.

The lawyer stepped over a banker box and pulled out her chair. As she sat, her dress moved slightly, exposing her lace bra strap. Her lawyer motioned to her it was showing, but she waved him off. "I like the way it looks." Her lawyer sat next to her, shuffling some papers, as Alexis turned to Mason. "You look well." Mason looked away, avoiding eye contact, not wanting to get sucked in. Steven had warned him not to—and, most importantly, to keep his mouth shut. Alexis turned her attention to Steven. "How are Olivia and the baby?"

"They're fine," Steven said dismissively, pushing the agreement across the table to her lawyer. "I'm sure you'll find everything in order. Let's get this done." Before the lawyer could take the agreement, Alexis snatched it with her left hand, flashing her wedding ring, Mason squirming in his chair. Steven noticed the exchange. *What the hell is she doing?* Alexis ran her eyes over the agreement, then handed it to her lawyer to review.

"Everything looks fine," the lawyer said. "Shall we sign?" He looked to Alexis, who offered a shrug, then turned her attention to Mason.

"How's Emory?"

Steven heard Mason clench his jaw. "She's fine, too," Steven replied, tossing a pen across the table to the lawyer.

"Is she enjoying the new house?"

Steven gripped Mason's arm and whispered to stay calm and

keep quiet. "What game are you playing here, Alexis?" Steven asked, then looked at her lawyer who helplessly shrugged his shoulders.

"I'm not the one playing." Alexis flipped her hair over her shoulder. "Mason's been playing house with his home-wrecking whore."

Mason jumped out of his seat. "You fucking bitch!"

"Now everybody just keep calm," the lawyer pled.

Steven stood up and placed his hand on Mason's shoulder, telling him to breathe and let him handle the situation. Mason ran his fingers through his hair and kicked a yellow legal pad on the floor into a box, as Alexis flashed a wicked smile at the brothers, clearly enjoying herself. Mason stood against a bookcase, glaring down at her. Her lawyer, too, looked at Alexis—in awe. Of all his peculiar clients, he'd never had one quite like her, intent on torturing her adversary. *Hell hath no fury like a woman scorned.*

Steven sat down. "By the way, the house in Charlotte is not negotiable."

"Relax, boys, I didn't say I wanted the house in Charlotte. Although after your little outburst, maybe I should rethink my position."

"Enough bullshit, Alexis," Steven said. "Sign the damn papers, and we can all leave. I think I need a tetanus shot after being in here."

The lawyer adjusted himself in his chair. Alexis picked up the pen and paused, holding it over the agreement. "I want a minute alone with Mason first." The brothers exchanged a glance, and Mason shook his head. She put the pen down. "After six years, Mason, you owe me a minute of your time."

"I owe you nothing," Mason snapped. "Not even what I'm paying you." Steven shot his brother a look, urging him to stop.

"And that's the problem," Alexis said. "I've always played second fiddle to Emory."

"That's not true," Mason said, but he knew Alexis was right. She was doing all this, making a big scene, because he was back with Emory. She'd initially challenged the prenup out of pure greed—upon learning his career wasn't over—but ratcheted up her wrath when he reunited with Emory. And he'd done nothing to keep his new relationship out of the public eye; indeed, it was all over the papers. *I should've listened to Mom and Steven.* Alexis was always the prettiest woman in the room—except when Emory was around—and he'd given her the ammunition she needed. He'd pushed Alexis over the edge, now regretting he hadn't done more to protect his assets and Emory.

"Can we speak alone?" Alexis asked for the last time.

"No."

"Fine. I'll say what I need to say in front of your brother."

Mason motioned for her to proceed, Steven taking a deep breath to brace himself for the impact of whatever was coming. He couldn't stop it. *They don't cover this in law school.*

"I spent six years in her shadow," Alexis said, a hint of sadness in her voice. "And when we broke up, you ran to her. It's always been about her. Even when we had sex, you thought of her."

Steven hid his face, mortified, trying not to form a visual image. The lawyer kept his eyes fixed on his messy table.

"You forget that you broke up with me, Alexis," Mason responded. "And our marriage, you know, never was based on love. I got a pretty face, and you got an NFL lifestyle. It was that simple."

"It wasn't that simple for me," she pled.

"It seemed to be."

"Well, it wasn't. I wanted some attention, too. And not just attention from fans or other players' wives. I would've liked some from *you*. But you were always just pining away for Emory, and I could always tell. You never even tried to hide it."

Mason threw up his hands. "Jesus Christ!"

"I got your name, but she had your heart." Alexis briefly diverted her eyes from his. "Did you ever stop for one second to think about how that made me feel?"

For the first time, Mason wondered if she'd actually entered their marriage with the hope of something more than a posh lifestyle. It didn't really seem like it, but perhaps she had loved him and wanted him to love her, but he didn't know how or was entirely incapable of loving any other woman besides Emory. But he knew that if Alexis truly had wanted love, her hopes for a loving marriage were dashed long ago, and she settled for financial security. And when that was threatened by his injury, she left—because he had nothing else to give. Then Mason reunited with Emory, bringing back all of Alexis' insecurities, and she was determined to make them both suffer for it. *Is that what really happened?* Mason felt a twinge of sympathy, his Catholic guilt churning inside.

Alexis whispered something to her lawyer and turned directly to Mason. "That's why you owe me, and that's why you'll pay."

With that, Mason's sympathy and guilt disappeared, and his eyes bored into hers. "Nice speech." He put his hands on the table, leaning over her. "Sign it!"

Alexis twirled her wedding ring. "I'm going to need to give this agreement some more thought."

"Unbelievable," Steven said.

"Alexis, we can go out and talk in my office, if you'd like," her lawyer said, standing up with his client.

"This is a fucking joke," Mason said. "I'm ready to get out of here." He walked towards the door, placing his hand on the knob. But the door flew open at him, striking him in the chest and pushing him back, nearly causing him to trip over a box on the floor. He regained his balance and saw what his brother, Alexis, and her lawyer had already seen—Kathleen standing in the doorway, polished in navy slacks with a crisp, white shirt and red peep toe pumps.

"Mom?" Steven asked, stunned.

Kathleen didn't answer. She walked into the small conference room and surveyed the clutter, criticizing it with her eyes. She kissed both of her sons.

"Mom, what are you doing here?" Mason asked.

Kathleen again didn't answer, but pushed Mason down into a chair. She looked at Alexis, still standing, herself confused by what was going on. "Take a seat, Alexis." She slowly lowered herself into her chair, then whispered nervously to her lawyer. Kathleen pulled a chair to the table and sat next to Steven. "Sorry, I'm late." She looked at her sons and shook her head slightly, indicating her displeasure.

"I'm Kathleen," she said to Alexis' lawyer. "Your client's mother-in-law."

"Nice to meet you," he said.

Steven leaned over and whispered to his mother. "Mom, I've got this handled."

Kathleen whispered back, "I was listening outside. It was a train wreck, Son." She patted Steven on the cheek.

Mason mouthed to his brother, "You got Mom involved?" Steven shook his head, baffled by her appearance.

Kathleen coldly stared down Alexis, feeling her blood pressure rise, knowing she had lost control of the room. During her marriage, Alexis considered Kathleen an ally, a strong-willed woman like her valuing financial stability. But now in the conference room, her mother-in-law projected a totally different vibe—one of dominance against a helpless, weak prey. Kathleen's presence had brought the negotiations to another level, cornering Alexis.

"Just when we were being honest with each other," she lashed out at Mason, "you have your fucking mother come rescue you."

"You watch your nasty little mouth, cunt," Kathleen replied, her words freezing everyone at the table, her boys looking at their mother, astounded.

"Excuse me?" Alexis said. "You have no right to talk to me that way!"

"Ms. Kathleen," the lawyer said nervously, "I'd ask that you please watch your language towards my client."

Kathleen smiled at him. "I don't usually talk that way. You can ask my boys or even Alexis. But I actually thought it was appropriate here. Your office is such a fucking shit hole. Can't believe you work here. And next to a gas station? My GPS couldn't even find it."

The lawyer fidgeted with his tie. He couldn't control his own client, and now her mother-in-law appeared just as crazy. His small contingency fee seemed hardly worth the trouble.

Kathleen turned her attention back to Alexis. "From what I hear, you have been running that mouth of yours for months, making demands and threatening my son." She pulled out a large envelope from her purse and set it on the table. "Making all kinds of false claims about him and Emory." She ran her fingers over the edges of the envelope. "You should be ashamed of yourself."

"I don't know what you're talking about," Alexis snapped back. "Before you barged in, Mason and I were finally getting to some truth, actually."

"Truth?" Kathleen laughed, fingering the envelope again, her eyes burning with an intense fire, as if possessed by some demonic force. "I'm all for the truth." Mason and Steven looked at each other, stunned and impressed, with no idea what their mother was up to. She was a force of nature who couldn't be controlled, but they'd never seen her quite like this.

"Well, let me give you some truth, Kathleen," Alexis said, leaning forward. "I know you think your little boy is perfect, but he's not. He was a lousy husband and…"

"Oh, be quiet! I will not sit in this nasty ass office and listen to your lies about my son," Kathleen interrupted, raising her voice. "I really will not. I know exactly who my son is." She picked up the envelope. "I'm more interested in the truth about you."

"Kathleen, you are losing it. I think your age is catching up with you."

"I may be old," Kathleen said, cocking her head back, "but that just means I've been a bitch longer than you have. And my age won't stop me from exposing your dirty little secrets."

Alexis shifted in her chair, ever so slightly, but still everyone noticed—a turning point. And Mason could sense it, a change in momentum, something he'd felt so many times before on a football field. His mother inexplicably had taken control of the negotiations and now had the upper hand. *Mother bear.*

"I'm still thinking about how to handle this," Kathleen said, stroking the envelope. "I might show you here, or we may just lay it out in the lawsuit we're filing in Charlotte. I haven't yet decided which way. But I'll be calling the shots from here on out."

The lawyer reached for the pen. "Maybe it's time we sign," he offered, feeling his fee slipping away, and placed the settlement agreement in front of his client. Alexis took the pen.

"Oh no, dear. Not that one," Kathleen said sweetly, then turned to Steven. "Where's the original settlement offer with the prenup?" Steven reached into his briefcase and handed the original agreement to his mother.

"What's going on?" the lawyer asked.

Kathleen slid the papers to Alexis. "My boy won't be giving you one cent more than you agreed to in the prenup."

Alexis laughed nervously. "What makes you think I'm going to sign that?"

"Because if you don't, I will spend the rest of my life exposing every secret you have to anyone who will listen. I will devote my entire life to it." *Mother bear had come to protect and destroy.*

"No one is going to listen to you."

Kathleen leaned back in her chair and pulled out her phone, scrolling her fingers down the screen. "Let me just look over my client list here. Oh, what about that pretty little anchor on the Channel 2 morning news show. I did her master bathroom. And then the police superintendent's wife—I placed the most lovely damask curtains in their dining room. Yes, and the Governor, too. He wanted the most terrible paisley sofa in his executive office. Had to talk him out of that. Took me three days."

Alexis swallowed hard, her lawyer whispering something in her ear, and she picked up the pen. She looked at Mason, conjuring up some tears, then signed her name to the original agreement. "I'll file the documents today," Steven quickly said, and Alexis rose to leave.

"Just one more thing, dear, before you run off," Kathleen said, rising to her feet and staring directly at Alexis. "If you ever again fuck with my son's career or his relationship with Emory in any way, I will bury you under the new wood floors I'm installing for a client in The Woodlands."

Steven lowered his head in embarrassment, while Mason couldn't believe his ears. *Tremendous threat. Maybe she's more like me than I thought.*

Alexis walked out defeated, her head down, her lawyer following behind.

When they were gone, Kathleen collapsed into her chair and slapped both her sons on their arms. "I just cannot believe what you were offering her. Why didn't you tell me?"

"I suppose it wasn't your business?" Mason offered gently.

"Everything is my business, Son. You should know that by now."

"Mom, how did you even find out we were here?" Steven asked.

"Olivia's big mouth."

Mason punched Steven in his shoulder. "You violated attorney-client privilege *again!*"

* * *

Emory and Olivia got a text from Kathleen summoning them and little Noah to her house. She gave no other information. Emory and Olivia didn't know why they were invited—they both wondered if they were in trouble—and also didn't know why Kathleen was even involved on a day supposedly focused on Mason and Alexis. But the women did as they were told: they stopped taking pictures of Noah and made their way to Kathleen's house.

Olivia barged inside, placing the baby carrier on the ground and picking up Noah. Emory entered slowly behind her. She hadn't been to the house in a long time, and it didn't hold the greatest of memories. Kathleen appeared out of the kitchen, welcoming them with a bright smile and leading them through the foyer into the living room. Emory looked around, much of it the same as she remembered. But one thing caught her eye—the picture she'd taken of Kathleen and Noah in the hospital set prominently on the wooden mantle over the fireplace.

Emory walked towards it, Kathleen approaching behind her. "Everyone who sees it wants to know who took it. They say you made me look better than any plastic surgeon could, but I'm not so sure about that."

Steven came in through the French doors off the deck. He kissed Olivia and stroked Noah's cheek. Emory looked back at the mantle, seeing Steven and Olivia's wedding photograph, and in a small frame, a picture of her and Mason from college. She picked it up and ran her finger across the glass. *So much has changed.* Kathleen placed her hand on Emory's shoulder, and they exchanged a tender look.

"I think it's time to upgrade to a wedding picture," Olivia said.

"Liv," Steven gasped, "Mason's been divorced about an hour."

"It all got done?" Emory asked.

"Yes," Kathleen said, a twinkle in her eye.

"Were you involved somehow?" Emory asked.

Mason appeared in the entrance to the living room. "As usual." He pulled Emory into a hug. "Mom dropped some threats, too. One was about wood floors—a real classic."

"Let's all go to the kitchen," Kathleen said. "I've got champagne chilling."

"Wait!" Mason said. "You never said what was in the envelope."

"What envelope?" Emory asked.

"It's in the kitchen," Kathleen said. "Go see for yourself."

Mason and Steven darted away like schoolboys searching for an afternoon snack. They found the envelope on the kitchen counter. Mason quickly grabbed it and tore open the seal, his brother looking over his shoulder. Mason poured out the contents, lining them up, then the brothers stared at them—newspaper clippings about Mason's career, a picture of Emory, and another of Noah surrounded by Olivia and Steven. *What the hell?*

"What does any of this have to do with Alexis?" Mason asked.

"Everything." Kathleen said, entering the kitchen with the rest of the family. "Everything I need to protect."

"You were bluffing?" Steven asked, with Olivia and Emory looking on, all confused.

"Emory's not the only good poker player," Kathleen quipped.

Mason ran his fingers through his hair. "But how did you know she would go for it?"

"Son, I've been in the game a long time. Bitches like us always have our secrets we can't have exposed."

CHAPTER TWENTY-FIVE

MASON HATED WAITING, wanting to do things when he wanted. But some things, he knew, were worth waiting for. *Sex.* Another thing was a shipment of boxes from Texas to Charlotte. It wasn't just any group of boxes, but a collection he'd kept in his former home. He could've made the shipment before his divorce was finalized, but the timing wouldn't have been right. It had to be perfect. It had to be when Alexis was out of the picture. The time had finally come.

He stood in the bedroom of his condo, surrounded by the boxes, hearing the front door open and close. *Shit, she's home early.* He quickly tried to gather his thoughts and placed a few more boxes around the room.

"Mason?" Emory tossed her bags down on the sofa and slipped off her shoes. "Hello?" She walked into the kitchen and opened the refrigerator, grabbing a water bottle.

Mason surveyed the room. It was the best he could do. He slipped out of the bedroom, closing the door softly behind him, Emory appearing in front of him.

"Hey, baby, everything OK?"

Mason nodded, gripping the handle behind him.

"What's going on? Why are you standing by the door?"

"No reason."

"Whatever." She slid out her ponytail holder and shook her head releasing her long hair. "I'm pooped out from photographing these two kids this morning. I need to go change."

She reached for the door handle, but Mason moved to block her. "Uh, you can't go in the bedroom."

"Why not?"

"Uh," he stammered, "there's a surprise for you in there."

Emory tried for the door again, giggling. "Well, let me see."

Mason stopped her again. Emory playfully pushed on his chest and felt his heart pounding through his shirt. "Mason, you're acting weird. What's going on?"

He drew a deep breath and took her hand, intertwining their fingers. He kissed the tip of her nose and forehead and slowly turned the handle, pushing open the door. The lights were off, but the curtains were open, filling the room with natural light. He led Emory inside, then dropped her hand and moved to the side, so she could see what he'd prepared—boxes of all shapes and sizes, wrapped in faded newspaper, scattered throughout the room.

"What is all this?"

"Gifts for you," he said nervously. "I've had them awhile."

Emory knelt on the floor near one pile, examining the wrapping. "I don't understand."

"The wrapping? Well, I used newspaper, so Alexis would think I was just packing up junk. I'm not a very good wrapper, either."

"What?" Emory asked, still confused. "When did you do all this?" She walked further into the room, running her fingertips over some other packages.

"Past six years or so."

She stopped in her tracks. "You got me gifts while you were *married?*"

"Yeah, I missed you at Christmas and on your birthday. And other times I would just see something I knew you'd love, so I'd buy it. It made me feel close to you."

A tear rolled down her cheek. "These are all for me?"

"Open one."

Emory walked around the room, trying to decide which to open first. She gently picked up a large box and looked at the date on the newspaper. It was from three years ago. She opened it, pulling out a floppy, pink sunhat. She put it on her head and made a silly pose, causing Mason to laugh. She read a note. *Was walking on the beach in Miami and saw this hat in a store window. The first night I saw you, your leotard was the same color.*

Emory turned towards him, still standing near the door. She removed the sunhat and bit her lip. They stood still, just staring at each other. Before Mason could register what was happening, Emory crashed into him, ripping at both of their clothes. They kissed and tugged at each other, their bodies colliding. Emory climbed onto him and tightened her legs around his waist. He pushed her up against the wall, as she kissed his lips hard, wrestling with his tongue. She gasped for breath, her nails digging into his back. Mason, fully erect, pulled back to look at her naked body, his blue eyes dark with passion. Emory bit her lip again. Mason thrust himself inside her in one smooth movement, and she let out a loud grunt, as she tightened around him. He moaned, relishing the warmth of her around him. He pushed her back against the wall, and she lifted her legs against his hips, as he held her, pounding into her, hard and deep. He'd waited months—years—for this moment. Emory felt herself building, as he dominated her.

"Come for me, baby," Mason said, as she tightened again.

After a few more thrusts, Emory did as he commanded, releasing six years of frustration and loss. Her body quivered and her legs weakened, but Mason didn't exit. Instead, he pulled her tighter to him, carrying her to the bed. He shoved a few boxes from the bed to the floor, then looked down at her, moving himself in and out of her slowly, savoring each thrust and turning his attention to her breasts, sucking and caressing them gently. He closed his eyes and moaned. Emory placed her hands around his back and held him deep inside her, urging him to go faster. Mason pumped short, hard thrusts, beckoning her to come again. She closed her eyes and screamed his name. "Em!" Mason shouted, finishing and collapsing on top of her. They rested on the bed for several minutes, still and silent, in an orgasmic coma.

Mason rolled over and propped himself up on his elbow. "I should've given you a sunhat months ago." He ran his finger across her blushed cheek and grabbed a little box from the nightstand. "Let's see what this one gets me."

Emory's eyes sparkled. It wasn't wrapped in newspaper like the others. She sat up and slowly opened it, removing the lid. She looked down and gasped at the diamond ring staring back at her. *My mother's ring.* Mason, naked, took a knee in front of her. Before he could open his mouth to speak, Emory shrieked and tackled him to the floor, planting kisses all over his face. When she finally stopped, he took the ring out of the box and pushed her hair out of her face.

"I've waited a long time to say these words. Emory Claire, will you marry me?"

"Yes!" she cried, smiling through her tears.

Mason slipped the ring on her finger and kissed away her tears. "I can't wait for you to be my wife."

Emory lowered her head onto his shoulder. "I love you."

Mason held her tightly, running his fingers across her bare flesh, with his eyes closed. "I've missed you so much." She felt the same as he remembered, every curve of her body.

Emory raised her head. "I had no idea all those years I was longing for you that you were doing the same."

Mason lowered his head onto hers. "I've been trying to make you understand that for months."

"I had no idea you still loved me."

"I never stopped. Look around the room."

"I don't need anything else," she said, flashing her ring, "but if you insist…"

Mason drooled over her naked body, as she stretched and arched on the floor for boxes, her ring sparkling with each move. She opened a box with a bottle of bubble bath Mason thought smelled like her, another with a CD of her favorite ballet, another with a black and white photography book he found at a vintage shop in New York City, and a small box with dangling diamond earrings from Beverly Hills. And there was so much more. There seemed no end to the boxes.

When the room was covered in torn newspaper, Emory straddled Mason on the floor and wrapped her legs around him. She kissed him slowly, rocking her hips towards him. She crossed her legs behind him, and he crossed his around her. She kissed his lips. Her hands in his hair, she felt him grow hard underneath her. She rocked herself slowly forward and slid him inside her. He moaned. She rocked her hips back and forth, sliding him in and out of her slowly. He grabbed hold of her, encouraging her—her slow, rocking motion driving him wild. She flexed her muscles, and seized control, pushing him down and mounting him. She grabbed his hands and sat atop him, riding up and down, slowly at first, her eyes never losing contact with his. Mason grunted, begging her not to stop. She thrust harder and harder, tightening around him each time, feeling him grow larger inside her, his muscles beginning to shake. She moved faster and harder and felt herself tensing. They came together, Emory collapsing on top of him, their bodies rising and falling together. Soon they were asleep, with Mason still inside her.

* * *

After spending the night, Emory couldn't wait to share the good news with Wesley. She returned to her apartment and ran up the stairs screaming for him. He met her at the door, and she held up her left hand.

"Oh my God! He proposed?" He took her hand in his, admiring the diamond.

"It's my mom's!"

Wesley grabbed her other hand, and the two friends jumped around in a circle like school children. Wesley pulled her into a tight hug, lifting her off the ground, then pulling her to the sofa. "Tell me everything!"

"The proposal is kinda X-rated," she said, blushing.

"Good. Tell me now."

Emory filled him on the gifts, the sex, and Mason's naked proposal, wanting Wesley to bask in every moment of joy, knowing he'd enjoy the sultry details.

"Girl, you need to come up with a PG version of that proposal. Your father wouldn't want to hear Mason banged you up against the wall, and then proposed naked with your mom's ring. I mean, I like hearing it—I like it a lot—but your father wouldn't."

Emory tapped her head with her finger, making a mental note. "Not a peep to anyone, ever."

Wesley laughed. "So have you talked about a date or any wedding plans? I can't wait to start planning."

"No, not yet. Of course, Mason may have the entire thing planned already."

"Maybe he hired Molly! Oh, by the way, would you be able to teach a few more classes?"

"Sure, what's up?"

"All the other classes are full. Since you got back with Mason, business is booming. Apparently everyone wants to take dance classes from the Panthers' quarterback's girlfriend."

"They may start that way," she said, "but they will stay because you're the best."

"I know." Wesley smiled but then turned serious. "Did you tell him about the baby?" He knew the answer from her face. "Oh, Emory, you've *got* to tell him."

"No, I don't." Emory sat straight up. "We both agreed to leave the past in the past. I even talked to a priest about it, sort of."

"You know I'll support you no matter what you decide."

"Good, because I've decided to be happy and move on. And I'll need you to help me plan and shop for my dress."

"How fun would it be for you, me, and Olivia to do that together?"

"Oh my goodness, I'm not sure the bridal world is ready for you two!" She paused. "But I wish I could do it with my mom."

"I know." He held up her left hand, so she could see her ring. "But your mom is with you." Emory nodded her head. "I know your dad will go with us, if you want."

"Don't be ridiculous," Emory said. "I'm not taking him dress shopping. I may actually have Kathleen come. If nothing else, she'll keep you and Olivia in line. She's really good with threats."

* * *

Mason was a Texas boy, used to deserts and droughts. Charlotte's rain showers, which seemingly came every April afternoon, caught him off guard. He couldn't get used to them. It was one thing to play football during a torrential rainstorm, but quite another to suddenly get soaked while walking from a parking lot into a grocery store. He preferred the burning sun. *At least I'm not in Seattle.* But the rainfall didn't damper his bliss with Emory. Rain meant Emory sometimes couldn't take photographs, freeing her up to spend time with him in bed and work on their home in Myers Park. So Mason found himself learning to love the rain.

In between work and play, they called their friends and family to share the happy news. Steven encouraged his brother to move fast and get hitched quickly, so he didn't have the chance to screw things up again. Kathleen loved Emory's offer to come dress shopping, and Olivia, too, couldn't wait to tag along, also hoping Noah soon would have a cousin. Emory texted her father a photo of her left hand, then laughed and cried on the phone with him, thanking him over and over again for her mother's ring. He assured her it was what her mother would've wanted, and he wasn't going to get in the way of that. There was no need to reserve judgment any longer.

* * *

Emory was busy at a photo session that was running long, so Mason, with no other plans, texted Wesley to meet for lunch at noon. He said he wanted to bounce around some wedding ideas. Wesley was shocked by the invite—and by the topic—but was excited Mason reached out. Wesley was willing to do anything to help Emory plan her wedding, and since Mason chose a hip downtown restaurant, it allowed him a rare opportunity to dress up. Plus, any chance he could get to escape the rigors of teaching children and to enjoy some adult company, he seized on it.

Wesley arrived promptly at noon. The reservation was under Mason's name, and the hostess led him to the table. Wesley ordered some water and looked around the room. It was a busy lunch hour, most tables full. The waitress brought the water and gave him with a menu. He told her Mason was late, and she left another menu at the table. She asked Wesley if he wanted to order an appetizer, and Wesley politely declined, preferring to wait for Mason. They obviously didn't have the same taste.

By quarter past noon, Mason still hadn't shown. Wesley thought about texting Mason but didn't want to pester, then worried whether something had happened—perhaps he was hurt at the Panthers facility, or got in a car accident, or was lost downtown. He then wondered whether Mason's unexpected invite was merely a joke but quickly dismissed the idea. Mason would never do that; it would upset Emory. Maybe he just forgot.

Wesley scanned the menu and took a sip of water before looking again at his watch. He looked up and saw the hostess walking towards his table with Tomás, dressed in a sleek black shirt and pants, Wesley's eyes popping out of his head. Tomás saw where the hostess was going, and his heart raced. The hostess pulled out a chair for Tomás, and he sat awkwardly, offering a shy smile to Wesley. He then fidgeted with his menu, as Wesley took a drink to cover his face.

The hostess summoned the waitress to bring another water. She told them the lunch specials and left them with a wine list, along with some final words. "Lunch is compliments of Mr. Mason. He said it was for second chances."

"What the fuck is going on?" Wesley asked.

"I don't know," Tomás said, clearly confused. "I got a message from Mason to meet him here at 12:15. He said he wanted a painting for his new house."

Wesley smirked. "He told me to meet at noon to talk about the wedding."

They shared a moment together, each man vulnerable, realizing Mason had duped them both. The waitress brought Tomás a water. "Why did Mason want to talk about your sister's wedding?"

"Not my *sister's*. Emory's!"

"Emory's?" Tomás gasped, fanning himself, his eyes welling up with tears. "Oh my God!"

Wesley hadn't shared Emory's good news with anyone he cared about until now. And he did still care for Tomás. Wesley knew he couldn't stay mad at Tomás forever. Wesley certainly liked telling him off at the coffee shop, but it didn't feel as good as snuggling with him during a movie marathon, a popcorn bowl between them. He missed Tomás, and Wesley was happy to see him again. And it warmed his heart to see the way he'd reacted—pure joy for his roommate. Still, Wesley tried to harness his emotions.

"Yep. Mason proposed about a week ago."

"I've obviously missed out on a lot." Tomás sighed and took a drink of water. "I've missed you, too."

Wesley winked at him. "Of course you have, you jerk."

Tomás could feel the ice thawing. "I've found myself watching action marathons at night—wondering if you were, too."

"That's pretty pathetic, though I probably was watching."

Wesley reached for his glass, and Tomás grabbed his hand gently. "Is there any hope for us?"

"Well, I don't know." Wesley freed his hand and took a drink. "Have you been banging a lot of guys in your art studio?"

"Of course not!" Tomás said, urging Wesley to lower his voice. "No one."

"Have you decided whether our relationship or your pride is more important?"

"Wesley, I obviously handled this all wrong. I said things I didn't mean. I screwed up. There's not a day I don't regret it." Tomás lowered his head and reached for his menu, but Wesley grabbed his hand, gently stroking his fingers. Tomás started to cry.

"I'll offer you a deal. You cook that shrimp dish for me each night for the next week, and you do whatever painting Mason wanted for free. If you do that, I'll promise you me—again."

"That's a small price to pay. Of course I'll do all that. I'll do whatever you want," Tomás said, wiping his face. "I love you."

"Damn right you do." Wesley took a sip of water. "Don't fuck it up this time."

"I won't." Tomás smiled, adding, "And I promise to treat strangers worse than you."

"Yes, that needs to be part of our deal, too." Wesley scanned the menu. "Now, should we run up a big bill on Mason?"

"Probably not."

Wesley looked up from his menu. "By the way, I love you, too."

CHAPTER TWENTY-SIX

EMORY AND MASON dedicated themselves over the next several weeks to passionate sex and home renovation. She took photos of clients here and there, and Mason spent an occasional night out with his new teammates, but by and large they spent their time together, looking to the future and creating new memories together. They discussed wedding plans, though she did most of the discussing, Mason nodding along to whatever she desired. Emory occasionally felt a twinge of guilt about the secret she still kept, but did what she could to suppress it. She wouldn't let it drag her down. After all, there was a wedding to plan.

Her first order of business was to choose a wedding dress, and Kathleen suggested a trip to Texas. A client of hers owned an exclusive bridal shop and guaranteed her future daughter-in-law would find the perfect dress, at a friendly price. Emory jumped at the idea: she'd get to see Olivia, and share the experience with family. Of course, Kathleen insisted Mason come along, too, though not to the bridal shop. She, like Emory, would never allow him to see the dress until the wedding. And Mason was fine with that: he didn't want to go dress shopping with three eager women, or the man coming along who himself couldn't wait to shop. Wesley could hardly control his excitement.

* * *

The foursome sat in a private room of the bridal boutique, Emory twirling her hair, wondering if such a large group was a good idea, concerned how all the strong personalities would mesh, if at all. "You three need to be on your best behavior."

"Of course," each promised, telling Emory she had nothing to worry about.

228

Emory wished she could just wear her mother's gown, but it was 1970's polyester. It was not an option. Her mother's ring would have to do. In the large shop, Emory found herself overwhelmed by all the dress options. It was easy to see a good dress highlighted in a magazine, but in a bridal shop, the choices were endless. She didn't know what style of dress she wanted and felt a good bit of pressure. As good as her relationship with Kathleen had become, the thought of trying on dresses in front of her wrecked her nerves. It also wasn't lost on Emory that Kathleen had footed the bill for the trip, perhaps a subtle—or not so subtle—way to exercise control over selecting the dress. If that was indeed the case, Emory would give Kathleen a pass; she meant well, and just couldn't help herself.

A young, attractive consultant entered the room. "Who's the bride?" She had a kind smile and smooth, mocha skin, with a pleasant face immediately putting Emory at ease.

"That would be me." Emory raised her hand, and Wesley patted her leg.

"Oh my, you are lovely. I'm Penelope. So, tell me about your wedding and fiancé." Penelope wanted to get an overall feel of the wedding and couldn't help but notice Emory had a body that would look good in any dress, both a blessing and a curse to a consultant.

"I'm finally marrying my college sweetheart. The wedding will be in Charlotte in the next couple of months. It will be very small and intimate." Emory gave a friendly glance to Kathleen, whom she knew wanted a large affair.

"Sounds lovely. So what style of dress are you looking for?"

Emory opened her mouth to speak, but Wesley answered instead. "Emory is a former ballet dancer, so I think she should be in something ballet inspired, perhaps tulle."

Emory looked at him and wrinkled her nose.

"Oh, yes," Olivia agreed. "Something big and poofy."

Emory turned to Olivia and dropped her jaw.

"I tend to agree," Kathleen interjected, and Emory swung her eyes to her. "I would love to see her in a ball gown with a cathedral length veil."

Emory cleared her throat and looked at Penelope. "You were asking me, right?" Penelope nodded, politely. "I was thinking something more form fitting, maybe a sheath. I'm not sure I can pull off a big ball gown."

"OK, how about this? I'll pull a bunch of different styles, and we'll go from there." Penelope smiled at Emory. "Price point?"

Emory hesitated to respond. When she'd discussed the wedding with her father, he told her to get whatever dress she wanted, and he'd pay for it. But Emory knew the dresses at this high-end shop were $3,000 at minimum and didn't want to strap him—on his meager high school football coach salary. Of course, she knew Mason would get whatever she wanted, but she didn't want that, worried it would offend her dad. *I'm only going to wear it for a few hours.*

"No limit today," Kathleen said.

"Kathleen, I…" Emory started, but Kathleen waved her off.

"Honey, you are marrying an NFL player," Olivia reminded her. "Live it up!"

Emory looked at Wesley for help, but he was busy fist-bumping Olivia.

"Penelope, make sure Emory doesn't see any price tags," Kathleen instructed. "I don't want her choosing a dress based on price, though I'm a friend of the owner, so I'm sure we are not paying list price anyway."

Penelope paused, having heard nothing about any price reduction, then nodded along to appease Kathleen, a woman who obviously got what she wanted. She then went off to pull some dresses.

"Emory, dear," Kathleen looked at her lovingly, "the dress is my wedding gift to you."

"But…"

"Now, now, don't worry, dear. I already talked to your dad."

"You have?" Emory asked, shocked.

"I asked if it would be OK if I bought your dress since I don't have a daughter of my own."

"Wait!" Olivia said. "You didn't offer that to my dad."

"I like her more than you, Olivia. At least I do *now*."

Olivia wasn't sure whether Kathleen was joking. She could never really tell and decided it was best not to ask. "John and I agreed I would buy the dress, and he'd cover the shoes and veil."

Emory hugged Kathleen tightly, thanking her profusely, and as they embraced, Kathleen mouthed to Olivia, "Just teasing you."

"Wait a minute," Wesley said to Kathleen. "You talked to John?"

"Yes, we've actually spoken a few times."

Emory still couldn't believe it. "A few times?"

"Wedding details," Kathleen said.

"Oh no?" Olivia teased, darting her eyes to Emory. "Daddy has some secrets!"

Wesley flashed a sinister grin. "Is John tapping that ass, Kathleen?" He exploded in laughter along with Olivia, both almost falling out of their chairs. "You better marry Mason soon," he continued, "before he becomes your brother!" Wesley fist-bumped Olivia again, and Emory slugged him hard in the shoulder.

Kathleen rolled her stone-cold eyes, then fixed them directly on Wesley. "You know, dear, I'm not opposed to a little homosexual hate crime. I'll do it right here in this shop."

Wesley came to attention, sitting up straight in his chair, looking around nervously. Like Olivia a moment earlier, he couldn't tell whether Kathleen was joking and didn't dare to ask.

Emory wasn't sure either. *Another crazy threat. Or was that one real?* Penelope returned with a handful of dresses and set them on a rack.

"I'm going to apologize now for anything else my friends might say," Emory said. "They are a rowdy bunch."

"No problem," Penelope said. "I hear it all."

"Well, good," Olivia said. "Can we get this show on the road? I pumped my breasts to be here, and in a few hours, I'm going to be making enough milk to feed a small village."

* * *

Mason sat behind home plate, holding his two-month-old nephew at his first ballgame. He was glad the women, and Wesley, were off dress shopping, and that he wasn't part of it. *I don't care about the dress anyway, just what is underneath. Thongs.* He took in the sounds and smells of the stadium. There was nothing better, he thought, than attending a sporting event with family and friends, unless of course he was on the field.

Mason held Noah up, so he could take in the moment as the Texas Rangers took the field at The Ballpark in Arlington, the crowd roaring. The Rangers' infield took their positions and tossed the ball around, as the pitcher began his warm-up tosses. Mason brought Noah back down on his lap and turned his head, looking behind him on each side, hoping his brother would hurry up and get back from the concession stand. "If you need to take a shit, Noah, you have to hold it until your daddy gets back, OK?"

Noah responded with a blank stare and some drool running down his chin. Then he began to cry, softly at first, then he amped it up, getting louder and louder, punctuating it with a high-pitch squeal. Mason scrambled for something to do, some way to make him stop. Helpless, he felt his face begin to sweat, as several nearby fans groused they'd had paid top dollar for good seats and didn't expect a crying baby. Mason apologized to those around him, adding the baby was not his, then nervously looked for his brother again.

Then Noah began to scream so loud Mason feared the umpire, dusting off home plate only twenty feet away, was going to throw them out of the stadium. He held Noah to his chest, as if protecting him from the umpire and fans, trying to quiet him before the first pitch. "Where the hell is your daddy? He's deserted us!"

Mason bounced his nephew slowly, but Noah only squirmed and screamed more, arching his back in apparent agony, as if Mason was torturing him by taking him to a baseball game. As the Rangers' pitcher took his final warm-up tosses, Mason saw the diaper bag on the ground and seized it quickly, fumbling around for a toy, pacifier, anything to calm Noah. Then he saw what he hoped was the Holy Grail. He grabbed hold of a bottle and stuck it in Noah's mouth. He gulped it down, like he'd been wandering the desert with nothing to drink. *Thank God!* Mason reclined back in his seat, the first batter stepping up to the plate.

Steven walked gingerly down the aisle carrying soda, popcorn, and hotdogs. "What did I miss?" Mason gave his brother an evil eye. "Looks like you're doing just fine." Steven unloaded the sodas into the cup holders.

"Only because of this baby whiskey."

"That's Olivia's breast milk."

"So I'm holding her tits?"

"Exactly." Steven held out his arms. "Give me my son."

"No way, man. Noah and I are just going to chill together. I worked hard to get to this point." Mason looked down at his nephew's heavy eyes, falling asleep with the bottle still on his lips. He slid the bottle away and handed it to Steven.

The lead-off man dug into the batter's box. Mason whispered to Noah about some options to start the top of an inning—whether to take pitches to draw a walk, or lay down a bunt and catch the infield napping. He rattled off some other ideas, as Noah was sound asleep.

Steven took a bite of his hotdog. "Looks like he's real interested in your wisdom there."

* * *

Emory tried Kathleen's choice first but could barely walk in it, a classic ball gown with a sweetheart neckline, weighing about half as much as Emory herself. Penelope led her out to the pedestal, to the waiting eyes of her crew. Emory stepped up carefully and looked at herself in the mirror.

"What do you think?" Penelope asked.

"It's beautiful," Emory said, not wanting to hurt anyone's feelings. *I could carry all my secrets under this dress.*

"It's a little too much dress," Olivia offered. Kathleen and Wesley both nodded in agreement.

Relieved, Emory nodded, too, then stepped off the pedestal, Penelope lifting the back of the dress to lighten the load.

Emory returned to the dressing room to try on Wesley's pick, a ballet-inspired, pale pink dress with a full tulle skirt and spaghetti straps. She looked at herself in the mirror, shrugging her shoulders, uninspired again, and walked out of the room.

Upon seeing her, Wesley brought his hands to his cheeks. "You look angelic, sweetie!"

Emory offered a polite smile and stepped onto the pedestal. "Maybe." She did a spin, eyeing the back of the dress. "I'm not sure I want to look like a ballerina at my wedding."

"I love the color," Olivia said. "It's so you."

"Pink?" Kathleen wrinkled her nose.

"I agree with you, Olivia," Wesley snarked. "She shouldn't be wearing white anyway."

"Wesley!" Emory cried. "In case you forgot, Mason's mother is here!"

"Kathleen, you wouldn't believe the noises I hear from her bedroom!" he added, Emory narrowing her eyes at him.

"Do tell," Olivia said.

"I can't make the noises right now," he said sadly. "I'd like to, but it would be disrespectful to our new friend Penelope."

Enjoying the banter, Penelope bit her tongue not to laugh.

"Yes, let's not be disrespectful to her," Emory said, "or me!" She stepped off the podium, her cheeks blushing.

As much fun as this was, Penelope needed to establish some direction for the appointment. "Let's try something a little less sweet and a little more sexy." She escorted Emory back to the dressing room.

Kathleen turned to Wesley. "You say you can hear Emory and Mason?"

He nodded. "Our rooms are next to each other."

"Then I guess they can hear you and Tomás, too," Kathleen said, Wesley turning bright red.

"Two men all sweaty and thrusting," Olivia said. "That's so gross. One man is quite enough." Wesley rolled his eyes. "But you want to know what else is gross? Steven and I have sex with my nursing bra on or else I leak everywhere!"

Kathleen threw her hands in the air. "OK, enough! You two are so bad. I don't want to hear anything else about the sexual habits of my boys."

* * *

The innings passed by, and Mason continued his instruction of the finer points of baseball. "Now, little dude," he said, Noah sleeping soundly in his arms, "everything I'm telling you is very important, but most important is this—football comes first in our family."

"It does indeed," Steven said, throwing popcorn in his mouth.

"And you also must remember," Mason continued, "that even though we are from Texas, we hate—and I mean, *hate*—the Cowboys. They passed on Uncle Mason in the draft."

"Big mistake," Steven said. "They've got that clown now."

* * *

Emory stuck her head out of the dressing room. "I'm not coming out in this one."

Olivia quickly got up from her seat. "Oh, yes, you are!" She walked towards Emory and pulled her out of the dressing room, Penelope following behind and watching more absurdity unfold. Olivia pushed Emory onto the pedestal, and Emory looked at herself in the mirror. She felt naked in the silk, backless dress, with a halter neckline, tightly hugging her curves.

Olivia whistled at her. "I'm sure that would be Mason's pick."

Kathleen frowned. "I don't think so."

"This looks more like a nighty than a wedding dress," Emory said, wrapping her arms around her chest to cover up.

Wesley walked around her on the pedestal. "Not sure you have enough up top to pull that one off."

Penelope grabbed plastic inserts. "We could always add a little boost."

"Nope." Emory stepped down, turning back towards the dressing room. "Next dress, please."

In the dressing room, Penelope could tell Emory was getting a bit discouraged. She pulled out an A-line silhouette with a bateau neckline, cap sleeves, and intricate beading.

Emory slipped it on, and looked in the mirror. It was floor length with a slight train, fitted perfectly to her lean frame. Her face brightened, her eyes filled with tears, immediately knowing it was the one. *I'm going to marry Mason in this dress!*

Penelope smiled widely and nodded in approval.

Emory took a deep breath to settle herself, still needing to run the gauntlet outside. She opened the door of the dressing room and cautiously walked out.

Olivia immediately started to cry. "It's perfect!"

Wesley agreed. "Oh yeah, baby girl. It's sexy and classy, like you."

Kathleen just stared, her hard eyes giving nothing away. Emory shuffled her feet and did a small turn, waiting for some reaction, not realizing until this moment how much she wanted a mother's approval. Penelope appeared with a cathedral length veil, and placed it on her, fluffing it out. But Kathleen still offered nothing. She stood up and inspected Emory and the dress, walking all the way around, eyeing her future daughter-in-law as if she were inspecting a car for some design defect.

She suddenly grabbed hold of Emory and hugged her tightly, both women crying. "This is it. My boy will love it!" Kathleen then exchanged a whisper with Penelope, causing her eyes to bulge, but quickly composed herself. "Now you run along, Ms. Penelope, and get me a good deal on it!"

CHAPTER TWENTY-SEVEN

A FEW SHORT days in Texas was just the escape Mason and Emory needed from the pressures of the NFL. But it brought with it the pressures of family and dress hunting, so getting back to Charlotte brought some relief. Fielding questions about the date of the wedding, and where the reception would be, and what kind of invitations, and colors they would have was exhausting. The only thing that Mason and Emory had decided was that the wedding would be on some date in the short window between training camp and the start of preseason, which left no time for a proper honeymoon. Mason knew where he wanted to spend their wedding night—in the suite with the pool table, and preferably with Emory in her red lace panties. A honeymoon would have to wait until after the season ended, though there'd been enough delays in their lives. It was part of the demands of NFL life, and Emory thankfully understood.

* * *

Emory grabbed a pool stick, while Mason racked the balls. They hadn't been back to Gus' Bar since the night their worlds collided. But on this night, it was pool, not ribs. Emory drew back the stick, and Mason watched her intently, leaning over the table, sliding the stick between her fingers wiggling her hips suggestively. She then slammed the cue ball into the triangle of solids and stripes, breaking them with great force, even pocketing a few balls. Mason raised his beer, impressed by her fast start, as she strutted around the table with a sexy grin.

She lined up to pocket a stripe. Right before she struck the cue ball, he asked, "So what do you want to talk about first—our wedding or house?" She swiped the side of the cue ball, bouncing it off a rail and into the corner pocket.

"Mason, damn you! Distracting me after my hot start."

"I don't know what you're talking about, Mrs. Mason."

"Emory Mason," she said to herself, trying her new name on for size. He eyed a solid and lined up for a shot. "Emory Claire Mason." She cocked her head to think it over.

Mason pocketed the solid and moved onto the next ball. "Don't even think about keeping your name."

"Relax, it's just strange for me to be Mrs. Mason when everyone calls you Mason."

"As long as we're clear," he said, lining up for another shot.

"Yeah, yeah, yeah." She waved him off. "I like the way Emory Mason sounds."

"Me too," he said, blistering a ball into the side pocket. "Remember the pool table in the hotel a few months ago?"

"Yeah," she said, slowly licking her lips.

He lined up for another shot. "Don't try to distract me, Emory Mason."

"You brought it up."

A few patrons came over with Panthers jerseys and hats, and Mason shook their hands and signed. They quickly left, sensing Mason was in a surprisingly difficult match against a diminutive woman. Mason took a sip of beer and laced his hands with chalk. "Now, house or wedding? I have news about both."

"What have you done now?"

"House or wedding?" He lined up for a solid in the corner pocket, but determined he needed the bridge. He reached for it against the wall, then lined it up on the table, carefully angling his pool stick, needing to bank the cue ball and somehow swerve it around a stripe to hit the solid. He pulled back his stick.

"House," Emory said, just before he released.

Mason whiffed on the shot, grazing the cue ball and scooting it only a few inches. "Emory Mason!"

"What did I do?" She removed the bridge and lined up her shot, quickly banging a stripe into the corner pocket. Before Mason could take a sip of his drink, she banged two more home.

Mason took a deep breath, sensing he was in big trouble. "OK, so you know that big room above the garage that we talked about making my workout space?"

"Yep." She added chalk to her stick and paced around the table, stalking her next ball.

"I talked to the contractor today and asked him to reconfigure it a little so that I can have my workout space, but there'd also be room for a dance studio for you."

"That is so thoughtful of you," she said, pecking him on the lips, but quickly turning her attention back to the table. She lined up her next stripe, pushing the stick gently to roll the cue ball slowly to cut the stripe, making a right angle perfectly into the side pocket.

Mason downed his beer. "I know sometimes you just need to dance, and I wanted you to have a place to do that."

"Perfect," she said, lining up another ball. "Now what about the wedding? You know I want something small and intimate."

On their Texas trip, Kathleen had suggested, as only she could, that Mason's career with the Panthers likely would benefit if they had a huge wedding in Charlotte. It would garner publicity and establish more ties for Mason in the community, all of which could help with a long term deal. Kathleen even offered to design the large wedding, which she admitted would help her business—both back in Texas and markets along the East Coast—since the press would cover every detail. Mason shut all of that down quickly, but in the back of Emory's mind, she wondered whether his mother somehow had convinced him otherwise.

Mason watched, as she struck the next stripe into the corner pocket. "I don't want a big production. We are getting married for us, not for our families, not the city of Charlotte, not the Panthers. Right?"

"Of course," Mason said.

She missed an easy shot in the corner. "Piss."

"Thanks for letting me play," he joked, walking around the table. "I just want to do this the right way, Em. To give you the wedding you want."

"The wedding is a few hours one day. It's not that important to me. The marriage is what is important to me."

The wedding, of course, was important to her. Indeed, she wanted the wedding to be at St. Peter's or some other Catholic church, but figured it wasn't possible since Mason had been married before. She was disappointed about that but didn't want to let on. *It would only make him feel bad.*

"Me too," he said, lining up a solid in the side pocket. "But what's also important is that we stand before God when we take our vows." He slammed the solid home. "So I'm having my marriage to Alexis annulled."

"Really?"

"Yeah. Steven is handling it. He's like my personal family law-yer now. He's pushing hard to get it done quickly." Mason eyed his next shot. "And apparently being the Panthers quarterback is helping move things along."

"This is so perfect. But I do need you to do something else for me?"

"Name it." Mason lined up the cue ball.

"Well, you know the way you proposed to me?" He nodded, smiling. "Well, I loved it, and it was perfect, but…"

"Spit it out, babe." He nailed a solid into the side pocket.

"Well, everyone keeps asking me how you proposed, and I don't really want to say we were naked, so we need to come up with a PG version, OK?"

"Whatever, guys don't talk about that stuff anyway." He banked a solid into the corner.

"OK, good. I told Wesley, but I don't really want to tell Olivia because then she would tell Steven and your mom, and then Olivia and your mom would blab to everyone."

"Makes sense," he said, lining up another shot. "Now stop all your blabbing. I'm kicking your ass."

Emory's phone rang, as Mason gripped the stick. "Now you're having people call to distract me?"

Emory smirked and took a few steps away to answer, Mason go-ing on with his shot.

"Hey, Wesley."

"Are you alone?" he asked cryptically.

"No. Why?"

"Step into another room for some privacy."

"I'm at Gus' Bar with Mason. Hang on." She looked at Mason and indicated she needed a moment, then walked nervously to a row of empty barstools. "OK, what's wrong?"

"A reporter just called. Wanted me to comment on your engagement."

"Just say no comment." A bartender offered her a drink, and she shooed him away. "What's the big deal?"

"It's not just that. The reporter knew things. He knew about your relationship with Mason in college and that you'd gotten back together. He said he had pictures of you wearing an engagement ring."

"So what? That's all pretty easy to find out."

"Yeah, but then he wanted to know about your dance career."

"So?"

"And your injury and hospitalization."

"Oh my God!" All the color left her face, and her heart raced, the room starting to spin. "How did he know about that?"

"I don't know."

She looked back at the pool table, ensuring Mason was still a safe distance away. "Did he know about the baby?"

"I don't think so, but I don't know how hard it would be for him to find out."

"Shit!" Emory dropped her head in her hands. *This bar apparently is the place for life-changing news.* She looked across the bar to the counter where Mason bumped into her months ago.

"He went on and on about how the public loves a good love story and how you and Mason fit the bill. College sweethearts torn apart and reunited years later. In the NFL, no less."

She looked at her engagement ring, shining through her fear. "I have to tell him." *He's never going to forgive me.*

"Yeah, you do. It's time. I'll be here if you need me."

Emory hung up the phone and turned nervously to Mason, now hitting her balls. The game was over. *It was indeed.* Her body tensed with worry, she didn't want to lose what she'd just found. She prayed to God, asking Him and her mother for strength and guidance. She walked cautiously towards the pool table, each step more difficult than the last. She reached him, her face pale and drawn. "We need to go."

"Why? You don't want a rematch?"

"Not now," she said firmly. "We need to go."

He put down his pool stick. "What's going on? Something happen on the phone?"

"I can't get into it here."

"Please tell me what's going on."

"Not here." Emory held back the urge to vomit. "We need to go."

"OK," he said, quickly returning his stick to the shelf. "Tell me in the car?"

* * *

They drove in silence. Mason prodded for information, but Emory refused—worried and in no mood to talk. She knew she'd eventually have to talk, but not in his car. Looking out the window, watching cars and lights race by, she needed quiet and space to expose herself. She'd hoped to put the past behind her—behind them—but that was no longer possible. She couldn't let him find out in the newspaper. *I flipped out over his contract!* Emory cursed inquisitive reporters, digging into her buried past.

They arrived back at the condo and walked towards his front door his arm around her, Mason feeling she was unsteady and weak. She walked inside and ran to the guest bathroom off the foyer and vomited. *What has her so scared?* Emory came out of the bathroom, as frail as he'd ever seen her. He wiped her mouth and patted her face with a towel, offering her a small sip of water. He walked her to the sofa in the living room and helped her sit down, placing the towel on the coffee table, keeping it close in case another round struck.

"What is going on, baby?"

Not that word. She hid her face in her hands.

"What is it?"

Emory looked up at him, scared, trembling, wiping a tear from her cheek. "There's something I need to tell you." She pulled her knees to her chest and rolled herself into a tight, little ball.

"Whatever it is, Em, we'll deal with it." He wrapped a blanket around her. "We'll be fine."

"Promise?"

"Promise."

She took a deep breath. "I need to tell you about my nightmare." With everything else going on, Mason hadn't given much thought to her bad dreams. He actually hadn't thought about them in weeks. But seeing the look on her face, he prepared himself for the worst. "A reporter called Wesley today, asking a lot of questions about our relationship."

"You and Wesley?"

"No. Me and you." She paused to gather herself. "Now and in college."

"I figured that might happen now that we're engaged." Mason rubbed her leg. "Reporters might start speculating that I left you for Alexis, which is not true. But these things usually blow over quickly."

Emory shook her head. "I'm not worried about that."

"Then what?"

"He was asking about medical records."

"Mine? So?"

"No, mine," she said.

"Yours?" Mason raised his brow. "Why was he asking about yours?"

Emory took a moment for a sip of water, then grabbed his hand. "Six years ago," she began, but then stopped, shaking her head. *Am I really going to do this, risk everything?* "When we broke up, I…"

"What is it?" Mason braced himself to be blindsided, this time by a petite ballerina.

"I…" She buried her head in her hands, then looked up through tears. "I was pregnant."

Mason laughed out loud. "What? No really, what's going on?"

But Emory wasn't laughing. She was serious and scared. He leaned back on the sofa, stunned, trying to wrap his mind around what he'd just heard, and slipped his hand from hers.

"I was twelve weeks pregnant," Emory said, her voice cracking, searching Mason's eyes for some reaction—anything—other than disbelief.

Mason ran his fingers through his hair. "Weren't you on the pill?" *This isn't happening.*

"Yes, and I learned it doesn't always work."

"Why didn't you tell me?"

"I didn't know that day—that day in the weight room." Emory reached for his hand, but he stood up, her eyes following him. "I found out a few days later."

"Why didn't you tell me then?"

"I tried!"

"What?" Mason cried, feeling his entire world crumbling around him. "You knew where to find me! Or call me!"

"You were with Alexis!"

"You could have told me you were pregnant! Jesus Christ, Em! You at least could've told me over the last few months!"

She put her head down. "I'm sorry. I'm so sorry. I tried to tell you, but something always got in the way—your arm, Alexis..."

"Give me a fucking break!" Mason paced around the living room, confused and angry.

This can't be happening.

"Where's my baby?"

Emory shook her head, unable to say, sobbing into her hands, too afraid to look at him. "Where's my baby?" But she still couldn't answer, the same question just bringing more tears and pain.

"What did you do, Em?" Mason barked, but she could only shake her head, her entire body trembling. "What the fuck did you do?" he screamed, a large vein bulging from his neck, his words echoing off the walls.

Emory looked up at him, defeated, her face drawn and frail. "I killed our baby," she whispered.

Mason stopped in his tracks and tightened his jaw, looking at her in disbelief. "You what?"

She said it again, even softer this time. "I killed our baby."

"You got a fucking abortion?"

Emory quickly shook her head, but Mason was too overcome to notice, kicking the coffee table across the room, flipping it upside down. Terrified, Emory shrieked and crouched into a ball on the sofa, bracing her head. "How the fuck could you do that?"

"I didn't," she wailed. "I loved our baby."

Her words took him aback, realizing he'd jumped to the wrong conclusion. Mason surveyed the wreckage around him, the coffee table and Emory curled up, and took some deep breaths to try to calm down. Emory took the chance to unwind herself. "What are you talking about?"

Emory wrapped the blanket tightly around herself. "I pushed too hard. You were with Alexis, and I just came apart. Wesley took care of me. The doctor told me to gain weight and not push myself too hard. So I gave up my spot in New York. You didn't even know that, did you?" Mason sat down. "But I didn't listen well enough. I couldn't listen. The only thing that made me feel better was dancing." Mason clenched his hands in front of his face and lowered his head onto them, looking away as she spoke, trying to come to terms with everything.

"Our college dance finale was coming up, and it was my last chance to dance on a big stage. I pushed myself too hard. You were off with Alexis and the draft." Emory glanced at Mason, still looking away. "I didn't want you to come back to me out of some obligation or pity. I thought you loved her. And I didn't want you to give up your dreams. I swear to God, I was going to tell you as soon as I had a plan for me and the baby." Emory took a deep breath, holding back tears. "But then I fell. I did a grand jeté across the stage. Something I've done a thousand times before, but this time when I landed, my ankle cracked, and I felt the tear." She grabbed her ankle and rubbed it. "I fell hard, Mason—really, really hard."

Emory peeked at him again, seeing he was trembling slightly. "Wesley carried me off the stage. And since he was the only one who knew about the baby, he took me to the hospital." She sniffled, crying hysterically, as her chest convulsed. "And there was no heartbeat! There was no heartbeat, Mason!" He closed his eyes. "Our baby was dead, Mason! I killed our baby because I had to dance that day. How fucking stupid! And I lost it after that. They had to sedate me. I don't remember much. Wesley says I just kept holding my belly, screaming at the doctors, begging for someone, anyone, to help me and our baby."

Emory took a few deep breaths to calm her breathing. "But all they did was suck our baby out of me. That's all they could do. And now I relive it over and over in my dreams." Mason turned his face and eyes to her, recalling her thrashing and screaming in bed. "I lost my dance career and our child in one second. I refused to eat or speak to anyone. I didn't tell my dad; I stopped talking to him. Wesley was the only one who could get me to do anything. I wanted to die. My last piece of you was gone, and it was my fault."

"I came to the hospital. You wouldn't see me."

"I didn't see the point in telling you after the baby died." Emory reached for his hand, but he pulled away. "Wesley begged me to tell to you, but I couldn't think what good it would do at that point. You'd moved on."

"Don't put it on me..."

"No, that's not what I meant. I..."

"That was my baby, too, Em, and you didn't bother to tell me for six years! I don't ever want to hear about me keeping secrets from you."

She lowered her head. "I know," she whispered. "It's horrible. There's no good excuse."

Emory reached for his arm, but he yanked it away, storming towards the front door. "I can't even look at you right now."

"Mason, please!" She rose from the sofa, stepping in front of him. "Please, don't leave! Please don't give up on us!"

He looked back, anger in his eyes. "Emory..." But he couldn't complete the thought, too upset and betrayed, not wanting to say something he'd regret. He continued towards the door, slamming it behind him.

Emory sank to the floor. *I'm back in the weight room, but this time without his baby.*

* * *

Mason wanted to escape but had nowhere to go. So he just wandered the downtown streets, passing the bright lights of bars and restaurants, theaters and museums. He looked through an antique shop window at a rocking carousel horse. It looked interesting, but he had no desire to go inside or anywhere at all. He just followed the sidewalk, putting one foot in front of the other, his load heavy, carrying all the baggage he thought they'd put behind them—only this time it was heavier, much heavier.

And no matter where he went, he couldn't escape his own mind. He'd made a baby—one he'd never seen or even known about—and never got a chance to see or hear the heartbeat. *My baby died.* He didn't blame Emory for killing the baby but was pissed she hadn't told him. He was entitled to know—and to know while his baby was alive, or certainly immediately thereafter. She had no right to withhold that from him. The fact that he was with Alexis, or entering to the NFL, was no excuse.

As he walked, Mason briefly wondered whether the baby was

his. He'd never ask; the question—even the idea—was insensitive and borderline evil, not to mention wrong. He trusted Emory had only been with him. *Of course the baby was mine. Unlike me, she didn't move on so quickly.* Nor would she ever cheat, he knew; she was loyal to a fault. *She's loyal to me to a fault.* His head throbbing and hanging down, Mason walked across a narrow street, and a taxi darted in front of him. He raised his hand, apologizing.

* * *

Next to the overturned coffee table, Emory cried for hours—for her baby and for her lies, for hurting Mason and for him to return. She wondered whether she should've told him at all, his screams still ringing in her ears. *Was it worth this?* She wondered whether the reporter would've ever found out about the baby, and whether she should've just taken her chances the story would never appear in the newspaper. That way, she could've just left the past behind—as Father Tony had suggested—and moved forward. But that was quite a risk to take, and the worry was too much. She tried to convince herself she'd done the right thing, the only possible thing. *Our baby is not a dirty little secret and deserves a daddy.* She wished she'd come to that conclusion sooner; perhaps then Mason would've reacted differently.

When she ran out of tears, she got up off the floor and turned over the table. The condo looked the same but was quiet and lonely. Her shirt soaked with tears, Emory flipped it over her head, and walked into the bathroom, turning the shower on and looking at herself in the mirror. Her eyes were red and swollen, and her hair, a tangled mess. She stepped into the shower, allowing the water to run over her. *Where is Mason? Where did he go?* She lathered her hair with shampoo and scrubbed her body, remembering the showers they'd taken the last few days, his hands running over her body. She shivered and turned up the hot water. Now she just wanted to be clean.

* * *

Mason walked a few more streets, with no purpose or direction, recalling how Emory looked in the hotel lobby on his first visit— how she felt, the smell of her hair, the purity and freshness about her, how she was different than other women. He also recalled her furious anger in the suite—and the red lace panties, too. The pieces were coming together in his mind—her rage, her desire to go slow, her nightmares, her concern about Olivia's pregnancy, her vomiting upon seeing him holding Noah. He thought back to the college weight room—she felt light-headed, sitting down on the exercise bench to gather herself. *Wow, she was pregnant then. Should I have known?*

Mason found himself at the Atrium Bar. It seemed as good as any place to be this night. He gave a polite wave to Clive and took a seat at the bar. "Whiskey. I don't want to see the bottom of my glass." Clive did as he was told, sensing something obviously was different about Mason—gone was the friendly, vibrant personality. Mason looked like a beaten man.

"You are like my best customer. Ain't that some shit!"

Mason was in no mood for Clive's insanity. "Just leave the bottle."

"You got it, bro." Mason slammed back his whiskey and poured himself another glass, Clive grinning widely, impressed.

"A man only drinks like this for two reasons: women or money."

Mason slammed the next whiskey.

"And I know you got money. I read about your contract in the paper." Clive poured the next glass. "So I'm betting it's that pretty little girlfriend of yours."

Mason didn't appreciate any man talking about Emory and narrowed his eyes. "You're very perceptive, Clive. Real fucking genius."

Clive slid a basket of pretzels in front of him to make peace, as Mason downed another. "Didn't think you NFL guys got so worked up about women? Thought that was just for us regular guys."

Mason shrugged, taking a pretzel from the basket. "Guess not."

Clive leaned forward. "You look like total shit," he whispered. "I know a guy who could hook you up with some real nice weed."

"What?" Mason recoiled, no interest in illegal drugs. He was as straight-laced as NFL players come—no arrests, tattoos, or steroids —and married and faithful to his wife, a woman he never even loved. Alcohol was the extent of his vices, and it was working fine at the moment.

Clive popped a toothpick in his mouth. "Make you forget all about the little lady."

"No, thanks, not my scene," Mason said, with a polite smile. "I'm not sure I want to forget anyway." Mason took a long slug from the bottle, then reached into his pocket for his phone. *Is she still at the condo? Should I call?* He was still angry, but a twinge of guilt was slowly taking its place.

*   *   *

After the shower, Emory needed a release. She was desperate to dance, but there was no room in the small condo and no music, either. She began to clean—mopping, dusting, and organizing every cabinet—not to placate Mason, but to pass the time and exhaust herself. She entered his bedroom and stood in silence, unable to bring herself to make the bed still messy from sex earlier in the day. She stared at the bed, then down at her ring finger, hoping Mason soon would come back. Cleaning had tired her, and she hoped for sleep, but she was too afraid—afraid of the nightmares awaiting her. *They would be bad tonight.* She got the vacuum from the hall closet.

*   *   *

Clive nodded his head to a table a few feet away. "Seems like you have some admirers." Mason looked over his shoulder at two scantily-clad young women, a brunette and a blonde. "That's some nice pussy eyeing you, bro."

"Not my scene either, but thanks again."

"Shit, man, you ruinin' the dream! I thought you NFL guys banged women left and right! And two at one time, no doubt!"

His head foggy, Mason mustered a small smile. He'd had some great sex with Emory over the past few weeks, but something about two women at once was quite intriguing. And they were all in a hotel already. "It doesn't exactly work that way. At least not for me."

"It could, bro. And I wouldn't tell nobody. Keep that shit tight— just between us." Clive nudged Mason's arm and stepped back. "Incoming!"

Mason turned and saw the two women approaching him, taking a seat on either side of him at the bar, their skirts barely covering their bottoms. Mason took another slug from the bottle and got up to leave, but a soft hand captured his arm.

"How about a drink?" the blonde asked.

"And maybe more?" the brunette added, batting her eyes.

Mason looked at Clive, sucking on his toothpick and gyrating his hips. *Is this a test? Is Clive the devil? How does he keep a job here?* He knew full well if he gave in, his engagement would be over, along with any future with Emory. He thought about his baby whose heartbeat he'd never heard. *I don't even know if it was a boy or a girl.* He couldn't do this to Emory again—he'd learned that lesson. Mason motioned for his tab. "Sorry, ladies, I'm on my way out."

"Ruinin' the dream," Clive whispered, as the two women shrugged and returned to their table. "What the fuck, man? Your girl must be *damn* good!"

"She is," Mason said, fumbling for some cash in his wallet, the many drinks catching up with him. "The best."

"Then what the hell you doin' here, bro? Go home and work that shit out! And then when you two are cool, you hit it from the front and the back!" Clive howled, thrusting his pelvis towards the bar and moving his hand like he was giving a little spank.

Mason chuckled, knowing he had to get out of the bar, and back to the condo before Clive got further out of control. "I'm going to take the bottle with me." He quickly stood up to leave, and the room began to spin.

"You are some fucked up, man." Clive motioned for the valet. "Let's take you round back to catch a cab."

Mason nodded. "Don't need to see my drunk ass in the paper."

* * *

The front door opened and slammed shut. Emory ran out of the bedroom to find Mason stumbling into the living room, a whiskey bottle firmly in hand, then seeking to lower himself onto the sofa. He paused to balance himself to ensure he didn't fall down. She'd never seen Mason so drunk, not even in college. Hovering over the sofa, he fumbled with his keys and dropped them on the floor. She walked towards them, picking them up, then extended her arm to help him sit.

"Look who it is," he slurred, pushing her arm away, "the mother of my dead child."

His words stung, but Emory didn't back off. "Mason, you're drunk. Let me help you."

But Mason was in no mood for help and decided not to sit, stumbling away from her into the kitchen. He began to randomly open up the cabinets, one after another, in a frenetic pace. "I need something else to drink." Mason tossed plastic glasses and paper plates to the floor in his mad search.

She tried to usher him out of the kitchen. "I think you've had enough."

"I'm mourning the death of my child," he said, dodging her. "Leave me alone. I have a right to have a few drinks."

"Enough of this!" Emory yanked him out of the kitchen, her strength surprising him, staggering to keep up. "We need to get you sobered up." She pulled him to her bathroom, turned on the shower, and pushed him in, fully dressed. Mason hollered, the cold water hitting his body, momentarily jolting him from his stupor. He adjusted the temperature and hung his head, letting the water do its work. When he came out, Emory helped him remove his wet clothes, then led him to the bed. "You need to sleep this off."

Mason quickly pulled her down on the bed, pinning her under his naked body, kissing her neck, as Emory struggled to roll him off. "Come on," he begged, "we can make another baby right now."

His dead weight not budging, Emory kneed him in the groin. "Nothing can replace our baby, asshole!"

Mason bent over in pain, allowing her to scoot away.

Emory watched him work through the pain, then stretch out on the bed, exhausted. She heard him snoring before she left the room.

CHAPTER TWENTY-EIGHT

WRAPPED IN MASON'S shirt, Emory sat alone by her bedroom window, staring through puffy eyes into the night sky, wondering what Mason was doing and how he was doing and if he'd ever forgive her. She looked down at her mother's ring. *What must Mom think of me?* She buried her nose in the shirt sleeve, taking in his scent, hoping for sleep tonight. She needed it. The past few nights, when she caught an hour here and there, her nightmares surprisingly had vanished, replaced by Mason's piercing, blue eyes filled with anger and tears, unnerving her, causing her heart to race.

Emory felt an arm slide around her shoulder. She looked up, sniffling, at Wesley beside her. "Has he called?"

"No, sweetie."

"Because he hates me, and I deserve it."

"He doesn't hate you." Wesley held her. "He just needs some time. You've had six years to deal with it. Give him some time."

"What if he just moves on like before?"

Wesley shook his head and patted her back. "I think he knows better now."

"I miss him. And with tomorrow..." She lowered her head.

"I know." He kissed the top of her head. "By the way, the article about your engagement came out." Emory looked up at him, worried her private life was now public. "It was all fluff. No mention of your injury—or anything else."

They heard a soft knock on her bedroom door, and Tomás peeked his head in the room, holding a tray of food. "Homemade potato soup with bacon and cheese." Wesley gave him an appreciative smile.

So did Emory. "It's good to have the chef back."

Tomás held up the bowl to her, seeing Emory's cheeks and arms thinner than he remembered. "Please eat something." Emory picked up the spoon and took a tiny sip and a few more, then moved to her bed.

Tomás left to clean the kitchen, and after a few minutes, Wesley came out, quietly closing her bedroom door. "She's finally sleeping. I haven't seen her like this since..." Wesley stopped himself.

"It's OK," Tomás said, indicating he didn't need to know.

As bad as the last few days had been, Wesley didn't know what to expect in the morning. Wesley assumed it would be rough—the anniversary of the miscarriage was rough every year—and likely even more so now. *Potato soup won't work tomorrow.*

* * *

Mason had holed up in his condo, blinds drawn. He didn't know whether it was day or night and didn't care. He'd let himself go, without shaving or showering in days, sitting alone in his den, gripping a glass of whiskey in one hand and their hotel room key in the other, surrounded by the stench of leftover takeout cartons and stale liquor. He'd drunk Emory off his mind many times over the past six years, but alcohol apparently had lost its magic. It couldn't change the past; it wasn't helping him forget. *Pregnant, fall, dead baby.* All they could've been, what they should've been, haunted him.

His phone rang constantly—his brother, mother, teammates, physical therapist, and coaches. He ignored every call, drinking more each time he saw it wasn't Emory. *Why won't she call? Why would she?* He closed his eyes, his anger transformed to guilt, as visions of Emory flooded his mind: her pink leotard, her voice, barbecue sauce, her naked body on top of him, the weight room.

Mason staggered into the kitchen for a snack. He grabbed a bag of chips and walked into the den, tripping over a pair of shoes along the way, his glass flying out of his hand, the chips crumpling onto the floor. He shrugged his shoulders. *Maybe that's my damn problem. I get in my own way.* Mason looked around at the shattered glass and crumbs, numb to it all, and decided it could stay. *My life's a fucking mess anyway.* He walked into his bedroom and took a seat on his bed, thinking about his decision to break up with Emory, and move on so quickly to Alexis. It got in the way of a happy future. It got in the way of Emory's health. It got in the way of learning he had a child and seeing the heartbeat. It got in the way of Emory's ability to make good decisions with her body. It got in the way of his child's life. As much as Emory blamed herself, he wondered whether he, too, caused his baby to die. *I left not just her, but our child. Just like my dad did to me.*

And Emory had suffered alone, while he was in bed with Alexis. He hadn't sufficiently paid for that mistake; indeed, he hadn't paid at all. He knew he typically was able to get by with a wink and a smile, or with the attentive help of his brother or mother, but this was different. It required more. It required him. It required Emory. His past had caught up with him, and he needed to pay. *I deserve to pay.* No one could bail him out. He needed her. *Why did I ever leave her?* Mason picked up the remote and blasted it through the television in his bedroom, glass and sparks exploding out of the screen.

* * *

It was barely sunrise when Wesley woke. He knew full well where Emory was—it was where she always was this day, regardless of the time. He decided to make coffee before he checked on her. He had time; she wouldn't be going anywhere for awhile. He turned on the coffee pot and watched the drip, drip, drip—one on top of another—and the resulting steam, all reminding him of Emory and the day. He'd hoped that over the years, the day would take on less significance—that time would somehow heal the wound. But it hadn't— not even close. Emory, rather, seemed to aggregate her pain, the current year's pain cumulating with the prior year's, all serving to burden her further. *Drip, drip.* Each passing year was another without her child: she had missed more time, and the pain grew worse. It never got easier, only harder, and the result was more and more pain, more angst, more steam inside—now for both her and Mason.

Wesley poured himself a cup, drank it quickly, and walked downstairs. He knew what to expect. He stared through the door of the studio, watching Emory at the barre, dressed all in black. It was her usual routine—locking herself away, starting with first position, dancing until her ankle was swollen, then collapsing. It was her therapy and penance, and Wesley hated seeing it year after year. He took a deep breath for patience and carefully opened the studio door, squeaking loudly.

"Get the fuck out!" Emory yelled.

"No." Wesley joined her at the barre. "You have to stop this. It wasn't your fault."

"You say the same shit every year. Leave me alone."

"I was there, remember?" Wesley slipped behind her and took her gently by the waist. "I heard all the doctors tell you."

She jerked away, and he caught her arm. "Let me go right now."

"No, stop this!" he pled. "I won't watch you do this again."

"Good, don't watch." Emory pulled her arm from his grasp. "I told you to get the fuck out."

Wesley turned his back to her and started to leave, but he then thought better of it. "Where do you think your baby is?" he asked, turning back around.

Emory glared at him, on the verge of erupting. "What kind of fucked up question is that?"

"A simple one," Wesley said calmly. "Where do you think your baby is?"

She knew Wesley could be a pest, but his simple question was beyond rude. She was grief-stricken, and this was all none of his business. But she decided to humor him, hopeful he then would leave, so she could resume her punishment. "In heaven."

"I think so, too." Wesley took a few small steps forward. "Do you think that those in heaven watch out for us? Want us to do well?"

Emory tapped her foot. He knew damn well this was her time— on her child's day—and he was intruding, his soft voice and multiple questions grating on her. "You know I do," she said sternly.

"You talk to your mother and baby, don't you?"

Emory looked away, trying to keep it together, her lip quivering and a tear falling. "Yes."

"Do you think your baby, just like your mom, wants what is best for you?" Another tear fell, then several more, as Emory nodded. "Do you think your baby wants to watch you do this to yourself?" Emory brought her hands to her face, covering an avalanche of tears. "Do you think your mother wants to watch you do this to yourself?" Wesley knew she knew the answer; she didn't have to say it. Her legs gave way, and she gripped the barre for support, Wesley rushing to support her. "You need to let go."

"I can't!" she cried.

"Letting go of the guilt and pain, doesn't mean you let the baby go." Emory clung tightly, digging her hands into his back. "Don't you want to be able to focus on the happy times when you were pregnant?" He pushed her hair back. "I know those few weeks were stressful, but remember how we played classical music to your belly and read the pregnancy books in bed."

Emory sniffled, then mustered a small laugh. "We had no idea what we were doing."

"And remember how I insisted you eat pickles?" Wesley asked, Emory laughing slightly again. "You loved that little baby. I saw it on your face when you first heard the heartbeat."

"But Mason should've been with me for all that, and..."

Wesley stopped her. "Don't." He looked into her eyes. "Be with Mason for *this* part. He has no idea today is the anniversary of his baby's death. Go share this day with him. You need the father of your child today, and he needs you."

Emory nodded and dried her eyes. Wesley had given her strength and a direction, but she needed Mason's forgiveness before she could forgive herself.

* * *

Emory stood outside of Mason's condo, key in hand. *Maybe I should have called first?* She said a quick prayer, unsure what she'd find when she opened the door. She doubted it was as clean as she'd left it. She turned the key and unlocked the door, stepping inside slowly and shutting the door quietly behind her. "Mason?" she called out nervously.

It was dark, and the pungent smell hit her immediately. She put down her purse and keys and called for him again. "Mason?" She stepped over empty food cartons and dirty clothes littering the floor. Just outside the kitchen, she heard a crunching sound under her feet. She took a few more steps and heard more crunching. She opened the blinds and saw a collection of empty liquor bottles and kneeled down to examine the glass and broken chips on the floor. *This is my fault.* She heard a little moan coming from the bedroom. "Mason?"

Emory pushed the door open and saw him on the bed, in his under-wear, an arm covering his face.

She flicked on the light and opened the blinds.

"Hey, stop that!" He threw a pillow in her direction.

Emory walked to the bathroom for a glass of water and aspirin. "Get up, drink this, take a shower, and put on a suit."

Mason didn't move but peeked under his arm, seeing Emory in a conservative navy dress and the coat he'd bought, her hair pulled back in a bun to show her pearl earrings. *Why all dressed up? What time is it? What day is it?*

"Mason, did you hear me? Get up!"

He covered his face and rolled over. "No!"

Emory climbed on the bed and with all her strength, pushed him out of it, Mason landing on the floor, hard.

"Damn, OK!" He staggered to his feet.

Emory picked up the glass and handed it to him. "Drink!" She then handed him the aspirin. "Now go take a shower." She gave him a slight push towards the bathroom. "We have somewhere we need to be."

"Where?" Mason pouted, squinting his eyes and running his hands through his hair. "I don't want to go anywhere."

"Get in the shower." Emory gave him a forceful push. "I'll pick out a suit for you."

Mason walked slowly towards the bathroom. *A suit?* He stood at the sink with his head down, groaning and holding his temples, as he looked into the mirror. He hadn't seen himself in days—bloodshot eyes, face covered in stubble.

"Hurry up!" Emory yelled, making the bed. She fluffed a pillow and looked towards the television—and the gaping hole in the screen, wires exposed, glass littering the floor. *Jesus.*

Mason decided against shaving. *Don't want to overextend my-self.* He did manage to get into the shower and wash his hair, the warmth of the shower refreshing him for a moment.

"Mason, hurry the hell up!"

He shut off the shower and dried himself, walking into the bed-room naked, still massaging his temples. "I'm going back to bed."

"No, you're not. Bed's made. Get dressed."

"I don't want to. I'm tired." He tried to go around her to the bed, but she stepped in front of him.

"Mason, have you been alone in here drinking for the past three days?"

It's been three days? "Yeah, so?"

She cast her eyes down. "Nothing."

"You thought I might be with another woman?"

"It crossed my mind." Emory swallowed hard. "I'm sorry you were alone."

Mason reached for her hand but stopped, seeing her engagement ring. "I wouldn't do that to you again, Em." *Damn you for tempting me, Clive, you crazy bastard!*

"I know." She gave him a small smile and handed him a suit. "Now get dressed."

"Why? My head is fucking killing me."

She cupped his face in her hands. "Because our baby died six years ago today. I think it's time we mourn that loss together."

* * *

They both agreed Emory should drive, Mason in no shape to do anything. His stomach was queasy, and his head hurt. It hurt to open his eyes, let alone look out the window at the rising sun. It hurt to talk, which was fine because he didn't know what to say anyway. And the turns were the worst, as if he was spinning into orbit. He decided just to keep his eyes closed for the most part, wallowing in guilt, blaming himself for the death of his child.

Emory didn't talk during the short drive. She could tell Mason was hurting and gave him his space. She thought about his condition —drunk and sloppy—and the condition of his condo. It scared her. She didn't have any magic words. She thought about her annual routine—how scary it was to torture and torment herself—and about Wesley's words in the studio, while well-meaning, were comforting for only a moment. She knew, in the end, she deserved the pain. In fact, she needed it to satisfy her own guilt.

She pulled into a parking space, and Mason lifted his head, look-ing up at St. Peter's. "We're going to church? It's not Sunday." *Should have extended myself to shave.*

"There's no better place today."

They walked inside and saw Father Tony greeting parishioners. "Thank you for speaking with me this morning," Emory said.

"Of course," Father Tony replied, patting her shoulder, then offering Mason a smile. "I like what you've done to your face." Mason rubbed his stubble, embarrassed. "Jesus himself had a beard." Father Tony then suggested Mason check out the Book of Jeremiah before leaving to prepare for mass.

Emory and Mason dipped their hands in holy water and made the sign of the cross. She walked in front of him, taking a seat in the last pew. The church was mostly empty, not uncommon for a weekday morning mass. Mason sat beside her, careful not to touch her.

Father Tony emerged, and the mass began, without any music or fanfare. It was a bare-bones service, with three Bible readings followed by a short homily which focused on the Book of Ephesians. *In whom we have redemption through His blood, the forgiveness of sins, according to the riches of His grace.* Such power comes from God in Heaven, Father Tony explained, and God's followers are commanded to share the power with each other.

Holding a tissue and dabbing her nose and eyes, Emory peered at the statue of Mary holding the infant Jesus, believing without question that her own mother was cradling her baby. *And Mason's baby.*

Mason peeked at her occasionally, fighting his every instinct to hold her.

After the homily, Emory and Mason bowed their heads, as Father Tony delivered the intentions of the mass, offering prayers for those serving in the military, for those affected by violence and racism, for the sick and suffering, and for lapsed Catholics to come home. He then offered one final prayer. "We pray for the peaceful repose of the soul of baby Mason, for whom this mass is being offered." *Amen.*

Mason's head sprung up, and he looked at Emory, tears in his eyes.

She grabbed him, fighting back her own tears, and held him in her arms. "I know, I know," she whispered, now crying herself. "I'm so sorry. I love you."

He buried his head in her neck, and she draped her arm around his head, the other around his waist, Mason clinging to her, his tears falling on the shoulder of her navy dress. *I finally brought Daddy to say goodbye.*

* * *

After mass, there still remained an uneasiness, a tension, between them. It was going to take more than an inspiring homily and a few tears to fix what was broken. Emory started her car, and hoping to drown out the silence, turned on the radio. "Summer of '69" came blaring through the speakers. *And now the times are changin', look at everything that's come and gone.* Emory's hand gripped her belly, having lost so much, worrying she may lose even more. *Sometimes when I play that old six-string, I think about you, wonder what went wrong.*

Mason glanced at her engagement ring, finding a different meaning in the lyrics now. He knew very well what went wrong and shut off the radio.

Emory drove to Freedom Park, their first date in Charlotte, a source of good memories and new beginnings, with everything now, and their future together, so uncertain. *I gave him a second chance. Will he give me one?* She didn't think she deserved one. She pulled into the park, and they started to walk towards a picnic table, Emory instinctively reaching for his hand, but seeing Mason had them in his pockets. They took a seat across from each other. "I figured this would be a better place to talk than your condo," she said, trying to lighten the mood. "I was afraid I might cut myself on the glass. I couldn't watch TV, either."

Mason offered a slight smile on his drawn face. "Probably a good idea. I'm going to hire someone to clean it up."

"Make sure it's somebody you trust, so they don't call the police," Emory teased, a hint of truth in her words.

Mason nodded, embarrassed, figuring the way he'd destroyed his condo and screamed at her days earlier, she probably was scared of him, recalling her curling up in a tight ball. *She deserves better.* He'd spent the past three days replaying his mistakes in his mind, and not just over those days, but over many years, an endless reel of regrets. They had consumed his mind and heart, leaving him in no mood for small talk. He had questions and wanted answers. "Boy or girl?"

His quick question stunned her, Emory drawing a sharp breath.

She hadn't expected him to be so direct, since he'd spent the past months avoiding serious subjects, only wanting to bask in the surreal glow of their relationship. "Girl."

Mason didn't offer any visible reaction. *I bet she would've looked just like Em.* "Was there a funeral?"

"No."

"Why not?"

"When you miscarry, there's nothing to bury." Emory wrapped her arms around herself, trying to protect what was no longer there. "Just tissue."

"Can you still have babies?"

Emory felt like she was in front of a firing squad the way Mason was shooting questions at her. She believed death was near—the moment he lashed out and delivered the blame she so richly deserved. "The doctor said there's no reason why not," she said. "Apparently miscarriages are pretty common."

"Did you consider abortion?"

"Never."

"Adoption?"

"No. I told you I gave up my dance career for her." Emory wiped her nose and patted her wet eyes. "I wanted her." *Death is closing in.*

I would've wanted her, too. Mason looked away, unable to watch her cry. "What reason did the doctor give?"

Now the guns were raised. "Inconclusive. They send the tissue off to a lab to try to give you a reason, but no reason."

"Not the fall?"

Emory shrugged, feeling her stomach knotting. "The doctor said he couldn't be sure what caused it."

"So, it might not have been the fall?" Mason responded quickly.

Emory shook her head, unsure, but she'd found her own certainty years ago. "Either way, it was my fault. Either I fell and killed our baby, or I took such bad care of myself that I killed her," she said, pausing to sniffle. "So if you're looking for a reason, for someone to blame, it's me."

She pulled at her clothes, waiting for Mason to accept her offer, but instead, he reached across the table, grazing his fingers over the contour of her hand, stroking her gently. "It's not your fault, Em," he said tenderly.

"It is," she replied, sobbing. "I danced too much, too hard. I didn't gain any weight like I was supposed to."

"Em…"

"No!" she cut him off. "I was so stupid."

"You're not stupid…"

"I was just so focused on having to raise a baby alone that I, uh, I…" She broke down, unable to finish the thought.

Mason lowered his head in shame. *Did she really think I wouldn't be around to help? I guess she did because I was already with Alexis.* "It's not your fault." Mason paused, then looked up into her eyes. "It's mine."

Emory knew Mason was prone to say outrageous things, but this was beyond absurd. *He's supposed to be yelling at me.*

"You weren't even there!" she cried.

"Exactly."

"But you didn't even know! That was my fault, too!"

"If I had just listened that day in the weight room…" Mason started, then stopped, searching for the right words in his despair. "If I hadn't been so selfish…"

"That just sounds crazy."

"I don't think so. I should have been there taking care of you."

"But I was her mother…"

Mason looked directly into her eyes. "And I was her father."

Emory's breath caught, his words making it all the more real.

"When I think of what I was doing, while you were carrying our child alone," he said, shaking his head, "it makes me sick."

Emory had never blamed Mason and wasn't about to let him continue to blame himself. She walked around the table, taking a seat beside him, and put her arm around him. "You are not the one responsible…"

"No, this is on me. I started it when I left you," he insisted, "and our baby girl paid with her life."

Emory lowered her head on his shoulder, her heart breaking for him. She knew exactly how he felt. *Does he really think our baby would be alive if he hadn't left me?* As he blamed himself, she could see how unreasonable and senseless the guilt was. She'd never seen it in herself before, but now she could—as clearly as Wesley could. "I can blame myself and you can blame yourself, but perhaps there is simply no one to blame. We both made mistakes, and for mine, I can't say I'm sorry enough."

"Me too," he said, crying. "I'm sorry I left you that day. I'm sorry you were alone. I'm sorry for everything."

Seeing his pain and regret as he poured out his heart, was hard for her to hear. "I doubt our baby would want us to keep hurting ourselves—or each other." She felt they'd both suffered enough, but she needed to hear something else, something she'd waited six years to hear. "But can you ever forgive me?" she asked, nervously twirling her hair. "For not protecting our baby?"

Mason draped his arms around her, running his hands through her hair, holding her close. "There's nothing to forgive." She refused to believe that, asking him the same question again, more fervently this time. But his response was the same. "There's nothing to forgive."

"And for not telling you?"

"Oh, that." *She's given me so many chances. I won't allow this to come between us.* He held her head in his hands, stroking her cheeks. "I already have."

Emory felt a weight lift inside her, six years of heaviness sitting on her heart, now gone, releasing the pain as Wesley had encouraged her to do. It was now time for something else, for joy—there had been enough pain. It was time to introduce Mason to his daughter— to have the joy they'd never shared before. Emory reached in her purse, digging through the clutter, and pulled out a black-and-white photo, its edges slightly curled and worn.

"I carry her with me all the time." Mason dropped his jaw in disbelief, carefully taking the ultrasound in his hands, never thinking he'd get the chance to see his child. "Look here," she said, pointing at the photo, "this is her head. So pretty. And here you can make out her arms and hands. So tiny. And there are her feet—can't really see the toes."

"She's beautiful." Mason gently ran his finger over the photo. "How old?"

"Twelve weeks here. That's the only photo I have," Emory said, watching him study his daughter, seeing her for the first time. "How about you carry her for awhile?"

Mason nodded, then tilted his head looking at the photo. "Looks like a little chicken nugget."

Emory grinned. "I like it. Let's call her that."

"My little nugget." He leaned his head onto hers, as they gazed at their daughter together.

"Are we OK?"

Mason tilted her head to look into her eyes. "More than that."

"Well, let's go back to the condo." She bit her lip. "I'll walk on glass to your bed."

CHAPTER TWENTY-NINE

If MASON WASN'T with Emory or on the field, he spent most of his time at their new house, very much still a work in progress, going over details of various projects with his contractor on an almost daily basis. One project of particular importance had just finished. Mason waited outside for Emory to come see it, though she thought she was coming over to discuss kitchen design with the contractor. She didn't care at all about kitchen design—she just wanted a refrigerator—but always pretended to be interested since Mason had spent so much time pouring over every last detail.

As the last of the crew pulled out, Emory pulled into the driveway. Mason waved and walked out to meet her. "Where's everyone going?" she asked. "I thought we had a meeting." Mason grinned mischievously and quickly took her hand, intertwining their fingers.

"What have you done now?"

"I made a few changes." He led her down the side of the house, along a cobblestone pathway to a crepe myrtle tree in the backyard. Under the shade of the tree stood a small cement statue, about two feet tall, of an angel holding a baby. Emory slowly knelt down before it, examining it, slowly running her fingers across the angel's wings. *My mother holding our baby.* She looked up at Mason with tears in her eyes.

"For nugget," he said. "I thought she should have a place in our new house." He pulled her up. "There's one more thing." He took her through the back of the house, together making their way to the unpainted staircase, side-stepping boxes and plumbing supplies along the way. Mason led her up the dusty stairs to a hallway, stopping outside a closed door. "Now I know we said we were going to redo the house together, but I did have one room finished."

"Really?" *Please not a man cave.*

265

"Yeah, I've been picking out some things here and there."

Emory looked at him in disbelief, trying to picture her muscular soon-to-be husband shopping for furniture, draperies, or anything. "It finally got finished today." He turned the knob on the door and slowly opened it, Emory having no idea what to expect.

She dropped his hand and stepped slowly inside, looking around in amazement, the natural light shining through the huge bay window filling the room, decorated in neutral creams and yellows, the floor a light-stained hardwood. An antique white crib stood against a side wall, laced with plush ivory baby bedding, flanked on each side with built-in bookcases lined with children's books and plush animals. An oversized chair and ottoman sat opposite the crib. A child-size table and chairs filled one corner of the room, while an old carousel rocking horse took up another.

Her mouth wide open, Emory moved gracefully across the room, touching the linens, picking up a stuffed animal, and looking through the huge window down at the crepe myrtle tree blooming a halo of pink flowers over the angel statue underneath. "This is the most beautiful room I've ever seen." She turned around to Mason, still standing by the door, his hands in his pockets, beaming with pride. "You picked all this out yourself?"

"Yeah." He took a step into the room. "I saw the carousel rocking horse a few weeks ago and couldn't resist. It kind of snowballed from there." Emory ran her hand along the railing of the crib, and on the wall above, she saw a framed Bible verse. *Before I formed you in the womb I knew you, and before you were born I consecrated you.* She looked back at Mason. "Jeremiah," he said. "A little tip from Father Tony."

She smiled, then turned her attention to a painting hanging next to the Bible verse, an abstract piece with soft green and yellow colors, the trace outline of ballet slippers and a football clearly visible. In the lower right hand corner, she saw the name of the artist. "Tomás did this?"

"He owed me a favor." *Second chances.* "I'll tell you later."

Emory was in love with the room—so breathtakingly beautiful, so meaningful, so perfect—though a part of her was unsure of Mason's expectations in creating a nursery. "Mason, the room is lovely, but..."

He interrupted her with a kiss. "Relax, babe. I'm not suggesting you get knocked up anytime soon, although that would be fine with me. I know you're scared."

He's right. I'm afraid.

"I want us to focus on the future. Nothing will ever replace nugget—that's why I got the statue. But we're going to have lots of babies, as many as you want, as soon as you're ready, and this room is a promise of that—of our future together." A tear fell down her cheek. "I won't miss a thing this time. I promise you that, too."

"This is all so wonderful!" She hugged him tightly, then turned to admire the room once again. "I love the painting! The Bible verse! The crib! I love everything!"

When she turned back to Mason, he was down on one knee, fully dressed this time, and she gasped, her hand covering her mouth. "You told me we needed a PG version, so here it is." He pulled out a three-carat, oval cut, pink diamond ring. "Em, will you marry me?"

"Yes, yes, yes!"

Mason took her right hand. "I actually had it fitted for this one, since I want you to keep wearing your mother's ring." He slipped it on, her face glowing, and she knelt beside him, Mason kissing the tip of her nose and forehead. "I think it's kind of shaped like a nugget."

EPILOGUE

2 1/2 Years Later

A CRISP NIGHT BREEZE blew through Mason's hair, as he stood, helmet in hand, on the sidelines of Bank of America Stadium, urging the Panthers defense to hold a tenuous three-point lead in the first-round playoff game, with just under two minutes remaining in the fourth quarter. He'd done what he could. It wasn't in his hands anymore.

Mason had started every game this season and last for the Panthers, including the final four games of his first season after the starting quarterback was injured. The coaches and management liked what they saw from him during those four games, all victories, and it helped Steven negotiate a five-year contract to allow Mason to finish his career in Charlotte.

After reaching mid-field, the offense took a time-out, needing only about fifteen more yards to try for a game-tying field goal to force overtime. But there was still time to drive the field and take the lead with a touchdown. Mason looked up at an end zone suite—everyone he loved was standing, nervously hoping, like he was, that the game clock would hit zero as quickly as possible.

He saw Emory holding their two-week-old baby, headphones covering the baby's ears. He'd urged Emory to stay home and avoid the crowds and craziness, but she wasn't about to miss his first play-off game as a starter. She didn't want their baby to miss it, either. So Mason arranged for suite tickets; at least there they'd be away from the real frenzy.

Next to her was Father Tony, wearing a Mason jersey over his priest collar, holding his rosary beads, praying for a miracle. Steven and a newly-pregnant Olivia stood right beside them; Noah, almost three, held his grandmother Kathleen's leg. The crowd roar during the time-out was deafening. It was well past little Noah's bed time, and a far cry from the quiet afternoon Rangers game he'd slept through years earlier. He now cheered for Uncle Mason and the Panthers. It was an experience for him like no other.

Emory's father longed to be down on the sidelines, coaching up the team, urging the defense to hold the lead. But all John could do from the confines of the suite was add to the crowd noise, and he did, with vigor. Wesley and Tomás, neither at all interested in football, watched the insanity of the crowd, all screaming and moving in unison, as heavy metal blared through the speakers. It was spectacular.

The offense took the field following the time-out, knowing the Panthers defense was tired. It had been a bruising, physical slugfest.

Mason looked up at the clock—one minute remained—and lowered his head. So much time left. *A minute can change a man's life. Gus' Bar.* He remembered the long-overdue vow he'd made just over two years ago, looking into Emory's eyes, wearing the most beautiful wedding dress. *I do.* He thought about words Emory had told him ten months earlier. *I'm pregnant.* And he never missed a doctor's appointment—not this time—never missing a chance to hold her hand and hear the unmistakable sound of their baby's heart. *Swoosh, swoosh.* Mason recalled being in bed in their Myers Park home, with his head and hand on Emory's belly. *Kick, kick.* They had decided not to find out the baby's sex, but Mason swore he had a kicker or punter on the way, while Emory insisted the baby was a Rockette.

With thirty seconds left, the offense moved to the twenty-five yard line and took their final time-out. They had to decide whether to play for a fairly easy field goal and overtime, or take a shot for a touchdown. The percentages favored running one play to position the ball on the proper hash, then spiking it and trotting out the field goal team. After all, they were on the road, in a hostile environment, and there was no need to take the unnecessary risk of throwing the ball downfield. Mason looked out on the field; he wouldn't play for a field goal in this situation. After all, he was never one to play for percentages. He played from his gut, relying on instinct. It's how he lived—for better or worse. *To hell with percentages, play for the win.*

Time stood still, the time-out seeming to last forever. Mason couldn't recall such an interminable wait since the final days of Emory's pregnancy. She'd insisted the birth be natural, relieving the pain from contractions through dance, sometimes hours at a time. *First position.* Mason frequently urged her to go to the hospital, but she held out as long as she could. By the time he drove her, she already was well into labor. But she didn't cry or scream once, accepting the process as a means to a beautiful end. And Mason thought he was a tough guy—he was nothing in comparison. After the many days of dancing, and only a few minutes of pushing, a healthy baby girl emerged—perfect toes, fingers, and nose. Chloe Annabelle, or Clo, as Daddy called her, had Emory's pale skin and blonde hair, but his daughter's blue eyes were unmistakably his.

The offense stayed on the field after the time-out. The quarterback plowed through the line for a few yards, positioning the ball on the right hash, then spiking the ball to stop the clock with five seconds remaining. The field goal kicker trotted out onto the field, as the stadium announcer whipped the crowd into a frenzy. Father Tony clutched his rosary more tightly. The kicker lined up and nodded that he was ready. The snap flew back and was fielded by the holder, spinning the ball to position the laces. He approached the ball and struck it cleanly. It sailed end over end through the uprights, as the clock hit zero. Tie game.

The crowd groaned, then turned silent. Mason shook his head in disbelief. He looked up at his family and friends in the suite. Emory, holding little Clo, blew him a kiss. *How blessed I am.* He put on his helmet, prepared to go back to work. Overtime. *I've already won.*

Acknowledgements

Many thanks to my husband for his tireless support and encouragement when so often the end seemed unreachable. Also thanks to my children for their patience and good listening when I told them not to read over my shoulder. Last but not least, a huge thanks to my big sister and childhood friend (you know who you are) for their helpful feedback and encouraging words.

Printed in Great Britain
by Amazon

48033797R00155